A DOCTRINE OF FEAR

Summer Haven II

Paul J.C. Edge

www.pauljcedge.co.uk

The Dark Ones

Edge Publications

A Doctrine of Fear - Paul JC Edge

Contents

- I. **PROLOGUE** 5
- II. **SKIN DEEP REVELATIONS** 7
    1. Dating with a Twist (JeT) 8
    2. The Signs 18
    3. I'm not Gregory's Girl (JeT) 32
    4. Getting Under My Skin 49
    5. A Rude Awakening 58
    6. A Conflagration with No Trace (JeT) 67
    7. Diversion or Misdirection 75
    8. Father Giuseppe's Protector 91
    9. Death or Glory… or another option? (JeT) 101
- III. **APOCALYPSE OR GENESIS?** 111
    1. I am Aleph and Tav 112
    2. The Enemy of my Enemy (JeT) 123
    3. The Healing of My Faith 137
    4. Demon Hunters (JeT) 148
    5. Return from Whence we Came 156
    6. As Normal as Life Gets 164
    7. An Incongruous Meeting (JeT) 172
    8. The Quest to Find My Brother (Paul) 178
    9. The Darkness Falls on Salina 193
    10. Light Must Follow Darkness 203
    11. From Russia… with Love 215
    12. Finding the Uomo Bianco 229
- IV. **DISCIPLES OF THE UNO OSCURO** 250
    1. The Unbelievable Unfolds 251
    2. Seeking Out Evil 270
    3. The Broken Temple 282

4.	BLACK HEART HUNTING 294
5.	THE SIEGE OF SUMMER HAVEN (HMS ASTUTE LOG) 309
6.	FOURTH OF THE SEVEN (PAUL) 316
7.	PLANNING THE IMPOSSIBLE (PAUL) 326
8.	PREPARING A STELLAR WELCOME.................................335
9.	THE YEAR OF THE WATER RABBIT (PAUL) 349
10.	A NEW SUN 360

V.   AFTERIMAGE – EPILOGUE 369

I. Prologue

"Is man merely a mistake of God's? Or God merely a mistake of man?"
Friedrich Nietzsche

This is a record of the events leading up to the so-called apocalypse of 2021, and the aftermath that followed. The narrative builds on my brother Paul's account of the construction and defence of Summer Haven in Scotland during the infection. Like my brother, I don't claim to be a creator of wondrous prose, but neither am I given to embellish the facts. This account represents my perception of the events to the best of my ability. A simple journal to honour those who gave their lives so we may survive. I have included sections from other accounts in order to explain the events in more detail. Paul and JeT's journal fragments are written in the first person, I have left their journals unedited.

I'm a simple family man, I don't hold great store with power, money, or religion; though I understand they have their place in our world, in the hands of man they can become tainted. My position remains true providing they are handled with good heart and mind and are not abused by individuals for their own gain. Above all, I hold love in the highest echelon of our human existence. Love binds people and encourages them to work together for common good. It brings comfort as we endure the disappointments, worries and sadly sometimes outright terror occurring in our lives. Love also augments our triumphs and achievements, making them sweeter. The diversity of people and their love for each other brings harmony and beauty to the world we live in.

It may seem strange to you that my formal name is Father Giuseppe, given my views on religion. I didn't start out in the world expecting to be a man of God. Although I have become a Catholic Christian, I don't hold any one of the faces of God above another. I strongly believe these faces are all part of a shared geometry which includes mother nature herself. God is present in everything and everyone. However, the events described herein haven't been shaped by the known faces of God, they were forged by living beings in our universe. Some of these beings are alien and appear to have god-like abilities and prescience, but God they are not.

The one characteristic which binds beings in the Universe is their ability to inflict evil upon each other. I've experienced wickedness first-hand, my scars run deep. Despite this, I haven't lost my ability to feel and share love. Love is the only means I know which will defeat evil once and for all. There is real malevolence out there, so my work is not complete in the Universe, and it will continue long after my death.

II. Skin Deep Revelations

"Religion. It's given people hope in a world torn apart by religion."
Jon Stewart

1. Dating with a Twist (JeT)

From the writings of Jennifer Travers

As I stood on the hot asphalt, my black lace up boots became partly immersed in a pool of arterial blood, the piercing sirens of police cars headed my way. The red and blue lights reflected off the buildings across the street, a vivid parody of the crime before me. I looked down at the mangled form of the hillbilly, lay next to the open door of his red Chevy pickup truck. The truck sported a "Good Ol' Boy" sticker along the windscreen. He was neither, a thirty something man who was quite evil in thought and deed. I glanced at the confused waitress, staring at me with a mix of horror and relief on her face. The blood trickled down her face where the miscreant had rammed her into the hood of his truck.

No one from 'Friendly Franks' felt brave enough to stand up to the toothless wonder and protect the waitress. I'd really fucked up this time, the cops were about to arrive, I was covered in blood and the onlookers had a perfect description of me. It wasn't looking good; my nerves were fried. I couldn't keep taking risks, something in my life needed to change.

My name is Jennifer Travers, or JeT to my friends. My account is a record of my life up to the events at Summer Haven; the remainder of the story has been well documented by the brothers. My account, or perhaps confession, is an attempt to put the record straight regarding the poor life choices I have made since leaving the army. Though the acts I committed were heinous I wouldn't change a thing, even though I have been forced to deceive those I care about the most. I have covered all of the facts, both good and bad, regardless of the shady light they cast me in. I dearly hope you will feel I have redeemed myself in more recent times.

In my years in the military, I had seen action in countries all over the world. In the special forces, I could be mobilised at the drop of a hat and be parachuted into a country with only a memorised briefing, a map and basic weaponry. There were very few females in the unit I was part of, I had to be able to hold my own with some big tough hombres.

When I was young, I realised I wanted a career in the Scottish Army. I spent the preceding years gaining black belts in three martial arts. I trained to handle karate and kendo weapons plus the limited range of firearms permitted to civilians in UK gun clubs. I joined the army able to look after myself, it was their job to mould me into an efficient killing machine; they succeeded. I'm not sure I came out of the army unscathed to be fair, there was something missing; I couldn't find where I had left it.

In my years in the army, I craved a road trip; especially taking Route 66 from the east coast all the way to the Los Angeles in the west. It was the first thing I did when I was finally decommissioned. I loaded a significant proportion of my last few years' savings onto my Amex pre-pay card and decided to enjoy it. I was 31, single and footloose. Life felt good. It all very quickly went to hell.

I had taken a flight from Edinburgh on an open ticket and landed at Chicago O'Hare mid-afternoon, though it felt like early evening to my body clock. The airport itself was enormous, I had never seen anything quite like it. I was more used to the tiny airport at Edinburgh, and the basic military airstrips I frequented. I walked almost a mile to passport control, where the Immigration Police really didn't seem to like the look of me. Even though I was athletically slim and dressed informally in Levi jeans and a Rammstein T-shirt, they seemed to spot 'military' from a mile away. It was probably my posture and efficiency of movement that gave me away. In the weeks to come, I learned to disguise my appearance to help me to blend in a little more. I simply smiled and explained to the frosty looking official that I was decommissioned and heading out for a vacation in his wonderful country. He seemed to ease a little, I was very relaxed and ready for some fun.

I headed into Chicago and bought a reasonably priced silver-grey open top Corvette Stingray from the car lot next to Franklin Park, just outside the city centre. I took the car to be checked over at Hot Randy's downtown and they upgraded the suspension and engine, it would help to make the long drive more fun. It took a couple of days to carry out the upgrades, I used the time to scope out the city.

When the car mods were complete, the bodyshell still looked stoic and a little scruffy from the outside, the paintwork was worn. On the inside, the seats and soft top had been refurbished and the mechanics were more than sound. She (all good things come in female) had a high-tech security system and new wide wheels and tyres.

I looked the car over, paid my dues and headed out onto the interstate in the beast. I had rented the Autobahn racetrack at Joliet for the morning to put the car through her paces and get a feel for how she performed under stress. The car drove great, it was fast, stable, and well-mannered in the corners. It was perfect for me; it was fun to drive but quite low key by muscle car standards. Potential car thieves probably wouldn't give it a second glance, she was easily underestimated, just like her owner. I drove her out onto interstate 55, with sparing use of the gas pedal. I swear I could see the fuel gauge actually move when I floored it. I travelled east along the wide highway, kicked back the seat, and played Alter Bridge on the retro CD player which had been installed by her former owner. I had found five other CDs in the glove box which I could live with and the others I trashed. I planned to drive the car for a few months and then sell it when it was time to leave. I knew I would lose money, but there you go. I could ship it to Scotland if I found it hard to part with.

I stopped for a late lunch at the Whistle Stop Café, a diner in Diamond Illinois. I ate fried chicken with salad and topped it off with a couple of delicious apple doughnuts. I avoided the fried green tomatoes, I had a vague recollection of one of my dad's old movies, where things didn't go too well. I didn't drive for long on the first day, I stopped for the night at the first motel I passed. I hadn't quite recovered from the jet lag; it had been a tiring few days.

I continued my journey at a steady pace and by the end of the week I had reached Tulsa. It was near enough to Oklahoma and it was a name I could remember, though I wasn't quite sure why. The hotel where I stayed was passible but the guy at the desk, Gregory, was an unpleasant lech. After I checked in, I took my room keys and ignored him. At this pace I would be in Los Angeles within a couple of weeks, I needed to slow down and start to experience the sights along the way. Too much driving and eating had started to wear thin, I decided to find somewhere to train for a few days. The weather had deteriorated so the pleasure of driving was diminished. It would clear in a few days, and I would continue west at my own pace.

On my second day in Tulsa, I bought a day pass at Sky Fitness in the city and started a gruelling workout. Following an hour of weights and stretches, I opted for a fifteen-mile run on the treadmill followed by kata and a swim. The exercise session took nearly four hours, so I needed to stop for a healthy carb input at one of the delis in town.

I returned to my hotel for a shower, only to find Gregory snooping in my room. He had rifled through my suitcase and found both my underwear and my Ka-Bar knife. The knife was a hunting blade, built from carbon steel. It was compact and not particularly intimidating in appearance but was deadly in the wrong hands. "Put that down and get the hell out of my room", I commanded. No one in their right mind would mess with an army colour sergeant, but I seriously doubted that Gregory was in his right mind.

Gregory smiled and slid the knife between his fingers suggestively. "What is a sassy gal like you doin' with a sharpmissy like this?" he hissed. "Get out of my room, or find out", I replied assertively. He decided the situation was going awry. It was unusual for a female to not back off when a man was holding a knife threateningly; his nervousness was precisely the effect I wanted. He put down the knife and left quietly. I chose not to change motels; it would be giving in to the cretin. I kept most of my belongings securely locked in the trunk of the Corvette for the rest of my stay. I hid the Ka-Bar knife in the top of my boot in its soft leather sheath.

A Doctrine of Fear - Paul JC Edge

I read magazines for the rest of the afternoon and strolled into Tulsa for dinner. I thought it would be good to see the lights and maybe take in a few drinks in a bar. I wore a mid-thigh length off the shoulder silver dress with heels, I never wore earrings in case I got into trouble, which often occurred after army outings. The last thing I wanted was an earring snatched off in a scuffle. It was good to dress up, it made me feel a little more feminine.

I headed into a bar called Valkyrie in East Brady Street. It had a striking open glass frontage, with mock Georgian toffee shop windows over the top. It looked inviting and there were enough customers to give it a bustling feel, without being oppressively busy. At the bar, I took a stool and ordered an Old Fashioned. It wasn't long before my flame attracted a small circle of flies, I found them mildly entertaining initially, but it didn't stay that way for long. Four men at the far end of the bar were laughing and appeared to be having a good time. They turned more serious when they sauntered over. "Come and have a drink with us, baby doll?" The more vocal of the four men was a blonde guy with a sharp blue suit. Clearly, they were out on a post-work drink. I declined politely, and they went their own way. Baby doll, really?

I spoke to a couple of local girls who found my Scottish accent mildly entertaining. They were nice enough girls, and we agreed to go for dinner after a couple more industrial strength cocktails. We took a table in back of the bar, where the lights were dim. The room was long and narrow with a lot of natural wood, and what looked like a bookcase full of bottles behind the bar. We chatted about the differences in our upbringings, and eventually the conversation came round to my stint in the army. I tried to avoid the subject, but they were very interested in my career. I had little else to talk about really, the army had been my life for fourteen years. I explained the unit I was in was similar to the US Rangers, and so I had seen the seedier side of life in places all over the world and I had chosen to drive route 66 as a complete break from it all. My basic honesty cemented our friendship; they were fascinated by my fortitude; it was so alien to them for a woman to want to become a soldier.

We agreed to dine at a restaurant called Amelia's around the corner. I fancied a burger, I had eaten healthily at lunchtime, and I needed some fat to soak up the cocktails. We linked arms and headed for the restaurant; the ladies were a little giddy, the drinks in Valkyrie didn't pull any punches. Out of the corner of my eye, I couldn't help but notice that blondie and two of his friends had followed us out.

We walked across the street, past Club Majestic and turned into the first side street. I spotted the Woody Guthrie centre; I couldn't help showing my ignorance to ask who he was. I received an answer I didn't fully understand, something to do with the 'dustbowl era'. Dustbowl was a Joe Bonamassa blues album, I remembered the lyrics referencing the horrific dust storms in the 30s. At Amelia's we were shown to a booth. We continued chatting as Connie ordered wine, the food came quickly and was delicious. We were nearly ready for a second bottle when blondie came over to our table for a second attempt at flirting. This time he was a little more drunk, and with that came with a side order of aggression.

The girls weren't impressed; we politely asked him to leave us alone. He didn't take rejection gracefully, but he left us when the staff objected to his excessive use of bad language. I'd seen his type before; he would stop at nothing to get what he wanted. I had a good idea he would be waiting for us when we eventually left Amelia's; some things in life were so boringly predictable.

I'd had a lovely night in the company of strangers. The girls were innocent to the darker ways of the world, and I didn't want to burst their bubble. Inauguration into life's seedier side would happen soon enough for them. They were young and deliciously idealistic, and it was a pleasure to share their outlook. I dearly hoped life would go well for them.

Towards the end of the night, Connie spotted blondie leaving the restaurant, and noticed he took a sly look back to our table as he left. "We need to be careful of him", she commented, "he's a bad 'un". "What do you mean? Do you know him?" I queried, "I know of him", she added, "he's trouble when he's been drinking". I waited, until she felt comfortable to expand.

Connie glanced at Amy, and continued, "Do you remember Cindy Dressler?" Amy nodded cautiously. "Well, she brushed him off last fall, he got drunk and raped her in Owen Park near the back of the Children's Museum. His name is Randolph Cutler, he thinks a lot of himself. Cindy's accusation wasn't proved, it was dark, and her evidence wasn't totally convincing. She knew it was Randy though. Myself, I would have lied; you can't let scum like that get away with crimes like that".

Connie and Amy had looked a little uncomfortable until the blond guy paid his check and departed, then the atmosphere returned to being relaxed. I had a bad feeling about Randy, and I seemed to be a magnet for dangerous situations. Live by the sword…

It was no surprise to me that Randolph was waiting outside when we left the restaurant. "Hi y'all. Hey, are you gonna come on a date with old Randy, ginger girl?" he asked pointedly. "Put that idea out of your head. Never in a million years, shit face", I articulated the last sentence clearly and slowly. It would teach him to call me ginger girl, my hair was auburn not damned ginger. I had enough of the ginger putdowns at school, it was like waving a red rag to a bull. He wasn't at all happy with my tough response, and he grabbed me roughly by the wrist, "You come along now, I'll show ya'll a good time".

The girls gasped as he brazenly grabbed me. They gasped again when I removed his hand by grabbing his pinkie and twisting it. Randy screamed, "You nearly broke my finger you bitch, I'm gonna learn you something you won't forget". He attempted to deliver a heavy slap across my face, which I easily blocked. I stepped inside his reach and kicked him in the crotch vigorously. He dropped down crying like the infant he was.

I walked Connie and Amy back to their bus stop. I suspected Connie would be on the phone to Cindy Dressler that evening. The girls were rather shaken up by the evening's events, but they were quite pleased Randy had received a taste of his own medicine. We exchanged phone numbers, promising to keep in touch but we never actually did. The girls boarded their bus safely, I took a cab back to my motel, avoiding revolting Gregory on reception by using the door from the parking lot.

A Doctrine of Fear - Paul JC Edge

My car was still parked directly outside the motel room, where I left it. When I opened the door to my room; I was immediately accosted by Gregory. He grabbed me by the throat and pushed a colt revolver in my face. I wasn't in the best mood; the evening was taking a significant turn for the worse.

2. The Signs

After my evening coffee, my wife Bridget read out a lame article from National Geographic, detailing an expedition into the darkest and little-known cavernous labyrinths beneath southern Iraq. The report droned on about the region of Iraq being historically significant under the rule of Mesopotamia and Sumer. My interest faded quickly, but Bridget loved this kind of stuff; she found it a little scary but informative. Bridget started to paraphrase the juicy part of the story to me. I listened out of respect for her, more than any specific interest.

"Dr Columbine found the burial site of the high priest to the fallen angel; the pivotal disciple of the oldest evil which eventually came to be personified as Satan in modern religion. He and his assistant, Foster, opened the coveted tomb together with a shared look of triumph. They had searched for the sarcophagus of the evil one for what seemed like a lifetime. Columbine dearly hoped that his find would substantiate his craving to become the greatest archaeologist who had ever graduated from Oxford. It would be a credit to the Natural Science Museum in London and would bring significant attention to Columbine as an academic. His theories had been mocked for years by so-called experts, and it was his chance to prove them wrong. Columbine could already visualise his face draped over the front cover of Time magazine. He and his team had risked their lives moving from location to location searching for clues. Iraq wasn't the safest place and experienced troubles in recent years. The team dug in secret south of An Najaf, with serious consequences if they were caught by the police without the right paperwork and permits. Columbine's field of work was shunned by Moslem clerics who closely advised the authorities. The consequences of the unapproved dig would be worse if they were apprehended by the zealots of predominant branches of the religions in the area. Columbine's team continued undeterred; their mission was too important.

Columbine had located the latest dig site with covert intelligence from an unknown source. The team had performed the initial excavations and had located the tomb portal in the precise location as was indicated by their secret informant.

The tomb portal opened with a soft whump. The team hurried to place pieces of wood beneath the large flat stone, so it wouldn't reseal itself. The stone exhibited familiar writings, which Columbine had managed to decipher at great cost, pulling favours from several experts in Jerusalem. The symbols were an ancient variant of the Sumerian language, and they spoke about the tomb of The Dark One. The phrase gave dire warnings and claimed the tomb was cursed. Columbine had previously heard such nonsense a hundred times and dismissed them with a wave of his hand. He believed such curses to be 'absolute bloody nonsense' and often voiced his opinion vigorously. He knew the curse was there to scare the ignorant masses from meddling. It had worked well over the ages, and it had scared his crew profoundly. However, the excavation crew needed money, for which they were prepared to risk the displeasure of long-lost demons.

Columbine's team levered the stone out from its housing, unveiling a dark staircase below. A strong musty smell radiated from the stairway, initially choking them. The excavation team covered their faces until the worst of the smell had dissipated and followed the staircase down into the earth. They followed the staircase until they were roughly two hundred metres below the surface. It was tempting to let fear control them, when they heard strange noises from down below. To an educated ear, the noises were rocks and ancient timbers expanding and moving as the temperature gradually increased in the tomb. The team's anxiety escalated to the point where they weren't at all comfortable continuing. It was rumoured, even amongst esteemed scientists, that ancient tombs contained long lost diseases waiting for fools to disturb them. On reaching the bottom of the staircase, the team found a stone sarcophagus with a rotten wooden chalice perched on top. Beneath the chalice was a fragment of ancient parchment. Columbine read the parchment using his flashlight as it was in Hebrew, he knew the language well.

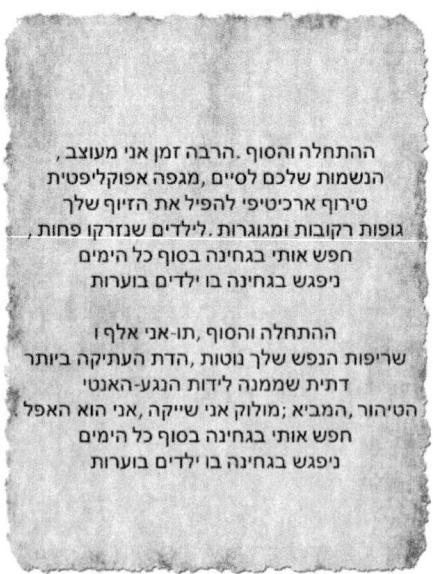

The message was a proclamation of the evil of the 'Dark One'. It authenticated Columbine's claims that the verse's subject later became known as Satan. Satan's aim was to bring about the end of days; to purge mankind from the world. The verse also referenced the burning of children by the Kings of Judah in the Valley of Gehenna and implied a threat to someone whose identity was unclear.

As he studied the manuscript, Columbine was staggered by a significant incongruence. The parchment appeared incredibly old, thousands of years BC, yet the Hebrew on the scroll was structured like it was modern Israeli Hebrew, rather than ancient biblical script. It made little sense to his renowned acumen. Columbine decided someone must have penetrated the tomb before him and placed the manuscript to tease him. He dismissed the thought again, it was impossible given the authenticity of the bindings and the untouched vaulted doorways. He saved his questions for later, stored the precious document in a vacuum envelope and placed it into his battered leather bag.

Columbine's team continued to open the sarcophagus. He translated the inscription on the headstone of the coffin, it warned of a demon imprisoned within the cask. He also noted the more predictable writings to frighten grave robbers 'desecrate this tomb and you will perish' and chuckled to himself, it was the usual nonsense. As the sepulchre stone slid to one side, a cold wind filled the tomb. The Doctor's team looked terrified but dared not run or they would face the wrath of Columbine and lose the money they'd sweated to earn. After all their effort, the tomb proved to be empty. The gang finally gave in to their fears and left via the long stairway leading to the relative safety of the night. Some shouted as they ran, their trepidation had the better of them. Columbine laughed at their ignorance, he ignored the warnings, as would most modern thinking archaeologists. He returned to England expecting praise and status but received none.

Within six months of opening the sepulchre, every man in the team, including the great doctor himself, died of unnatural causes". "How so?" I questioned, somewhat disinterested. "Forensic scientists concluded they were all killed using an oddly grooved dagger. Apparently, their blood was completely drained from their bodies whilst they were still alive. The forensic scientists found no evidence of blood clotting, and there were no traces of anti-coagulants. The scientists couldn't determine the method of exsanguination, it says here; though they speculated the grooved dagger was the only visible entry point".

"This is seriously messed up. It says the parchment is currently secreted in the archives at the Holy See awaiting analysis". I was unsure of the meaning of the Holy See. Bridget explained it was the jurisdiction of the Bishop of Rome; the Pope himself. "Wow!" I exclaimed less than enthusiastically; I really didn't know why she loved such nonsense. The article sounded more like a lame sensationalistic film script than an impartial scientific account. I guess the tales sold more magazines than the raw facts. 'Someone found an old empty tomb in Iraq' simply wouldn't make the headlines. I didn't give any of it a second thought.

The next day I woke from my slumber to a glorious sunny day. Bridget snored gently by my side, like a contented purring kitten. We rose, ate breakfast, and wandered into the garden to enjoy the sunshine. The smell of the flowers, the singing birds provided an aura of calm, it was a normal lovely summer's day.

A Doctrine of Fear - Paul JC Edge

I looked up to my son James' bedroom window, it was slightly ajar, but the curtains were closed. "What time do you think he'll be up today?" I asked Bridget with a sarcastic smile. "Oh probably 3pm, if he fancies an early start", she replied. His usual routine was to wake mid-afternoon, breakfast and start waging war on his gaming console. He was 21 years old, and he still did extraordinarily little, he treated us with abject disdain much of the time. Smiles and positive conversation were non-existent in James' world. He was struggling to find his place in life, and there was little we could do to help him. We were the last people on the planet he would listen to.

I unconsciously rubbed my arm; Bridget asked me if I was having a problem with it, "Perhaps you should get it checked out Joe", she suggested sensibly. Of course, I didn't bother. I was busy at work, and it wasn't causing me any trouble. I needed to be half dead before I visited our doctor, he was a pompous twat.

Just before 9am, I drove to the old people's home where I worked as a care assistant. I'd tired of the travel associated with life as a management consultant. I'd earned the big bucks and had chosen something a little more esoteric. I loved my job; I found great satisfaction in putting a smile on the faces of the 'young at heart' residents of the care home.

"Morning Joe, take off your hat, we can't see your halo". Funny, it was good to see that even Reg, who was in his eighties could still manage a little healthy sarcasm. I had wrapped up a rubber chicken for his birthday the week before, so he was keen to put me in my place.

A Doctrine of Fear - Paul JC Edge

My day was routine, I talked to the residents, tidied up and helped those who couldn't leave their rooms. I set the dinner table for the meals which were delivered at 11:10 prompt and cleaned up the aftermath. The afternoons were simply a re-run of the morning's activities. My job didn't pay well, but I always went home feeling positive.

As I collected my coat from the cloakroom, I almost bumped into Jeanette. "Watch out Joey", she laughed, "have you been drinking again?" "Yes, I've had three glasses of water and two mugs of tea, for my sins", I jovially replied. "Have you been writing notes on your arm?" she asked, "You'll get dermatitis".

I looked down, what I though was a small mole on my arm had enlarged. On closer inspection, a small phrase written in cursive script was becoming more prominent. It displayed 'Unus de septem'. "That's odd, perhaps James has been up his tricks again, he still acts like a baby sometimes. I'll wash it off when I get home, I'll probably have to scrub it, it looks like it's been written with an indelible sharpie!" The phrase seemed to be in Latin to my uneducated eye. I attempted to show it Bridget when I got home, only to find the writing was no longer present. It hadn't smudged, so I couldn't have rubbed it off by accident. Very clever James, I thought to myself.

It was Friday, the day when Bridget and I followed our usual evening routine of sitting down to a meal together with a bottle of wine. We enjoyed a bottle of 'Amarone della Valpolicella', my absolute favourite from northeastern Italy. It was moderately expensive; it had been given to me for my birthday a couple of weeks ago. James typically ate in his room, so it gave us time to relax and chat about the events of the day.

A Doctrine of Fear - Paul JC Edge

Bridget shared her juicy gossip from the newspaper, "The Times discusses how the Vatican has been moving to increase their liquid assets. They have sold a significant proportion of their shares in large corporations. The Vatican are also auctioning Caravaggio's 'The Entombment of Christ' and Leonardo da Vinci's unfinished 'St Jerome in the Wilderness' at an auction in Milan next week. They are hoping to raise tens of millions for the pair, it also states that they are considering the sale of more of their priceless treasures. What on earth could have happened to put the church in such a desperate state?" I considered Bridget's comments for a moment, "The church is becoming less popular, there are more people who declare their religious alignment as 'Jedi' on the census these days. What's the world coming to?"

Whilst Bridget enjoyed the wine, thumbing through her latest archaeology magazine, she noticed a new mark, "Let me look at your neck", she asked with a concerned frown. I leaned over, and she held my collar down so she could inspect it closely. "What have you written on your neck?" "What does it say?" I enquired. "Unus de septem", she replied. "Isn't that Latin?" I pondered aloud. "Let's see". She googled the words on her tablet. It translated to 'one of seven', which was odd. I had no siblings and had no possible significance. Bridget tried to take another look but found it had disappeared.

"Oh, it's bloody James again, he must have one of those invisible ink pens from the joke shop", I exclaimed with a laugh. "Rubbish, there are no pens like that, invisible ink appears when you raise its temperature, however, disappearing ink is a water-soluble acid-base indicator, the ink appears as soon as it's exposed to air. Unless James was writing on you a couple of minutes ago, it can't possibly be that", she explained. Bridget had obviously put her PhD in Chemistry to good use researching joke shop pranks. "So, what the heck is it then?" I asked. "Nothing I have heard of", she whispered to herself whilst clattering on her iPad. "And neither has Google, more to the point", she added.

A few weeks later, Bridget and I took our annual spring vacation to Agios Nikolaos in Crete. We had been looking forward to the holiday; the beautiful blue sea, the delicious food, and the infra-red overdose. We were up early for the taxi to Birmingham Ringway Airport. In the departure lounge, Bridget examined my arms and neck once more. She had developed a thing about it, the inexplicable fascinated her. I wasn't convinced; I still suspected James was behind it somehow.

The following day, we recuperated on our sunbeds after a fast ride around the bay on a jet ski. Bridget and I were soaking up the rays when it happened again. The words 'Unus de septem' appeared on my left forearm for around twenty seconds and then disappeared. Unless James had followed us to Crete, it put pay to my theories of his practical joke. Later at dinner, the writings appeared again on my left elbow. Luckily, no one other than Bridget spotted them, they might draw unwanted attention, I didn't want to be labelled a freak.

As we sat on a church wall overlooking the sunset in Mirabello Bay, I took the opportunity to snap a few selfies with my phone. When Bridget looked at the photos, she saw the writings again. From that point, Bridget had specifically checked for the writings and spotted them immediately. The usual phrase, together with 'Vox clamantis in deserto' emerged, both scripts disappeared at the same time. Bridget managed to take a photo of the writings just in time, before they disappeared. A few moments later, the phrase 'Multi enim sunt vocati, pauci vero electi' appeared on my left underarm spontaneously.

A young teenage boy, eating a fig as he passed, spotted the writing, and became alarmed. He disappeared into a nearby church. After a few minutes, the boy reappeared with a Greek orthodox priest, wearing his heavy black cassock and hat in the heat. The priest was old, his beard was bushy and grey, but his eyes were as sharp as needles. He smiled warmly as he approached us.

The priest spoke in broken English, but the boy helped to translate. He explained that the boy had seen writing appear on my arms and was deeply concerned for me. Bridget showed the priest the pictures on her phone. He translated the phrases as 'A voice crying in the wilderness' and then 'Many are called but few are chosen'. He explained they were Latin phrases from the Holy Catholic Bible. "My Grandfather says you need to see a Catholic priest as soon as possible. He hasn't seen such markings before, but he has read about them. They are stigmata transcribed on your flesh by God. He says you are most blessed, and it was a wonderful gift for him to meet you". The old priest pulled a crucifixus from his robe and looped it around my neck. He laid his hands on the top of my head and uttered a short phrase in Greek, which I interpreted as a blessing. He then kissed me on both cheeks, which as an Englishman, I found a little uncomfortable. "The cross will save you from the Dark One, go in peace my son", were his final words.

A Doctrine of Fear - Paul JC Edge

I wasn't a Christian, but I valued the priest's gift. It was a kindness and in some ways a comfort, I wear it to this very day in the old man's honour. Bridget was surprised the Greek orthodox priest could read Latin, Catholic priests had worshipped in Greek long before the bible was translated to Latin, more than a millennium ago. When the churches agreed to separate, there was no obvious need to read Latin in a Greek church. Bridget argued the priest must have been a student of Romance languages such as Italian, French, Spanish, Portuguese and Romanian. It was much easier to cross over between such languages if you first spoke their origin, Latin. Her breadth of knowledge was beyond me; however, she had studied the more classic subjects at university.

In the evening, we ate and drank far too much, Bridget became greatly amused by the fact that I persisted in wearing the cruciform, she couldn't reconcile it. "You are an atheist, why on earth would you wear a religious icon?" I retorted, "I'm not an atheist, you know I'm agnostic". "Okay, why would an agnostic wear a cross?" "Well, I don't disbelieve; I simply don't believe. I don't know", I replied honestly. "So why wear the crucifix then?" "It's not a crucifix", I commented jokingly aiming to match to her pedantry, "A crucifix has the corpus of Christ crucified. It's just a cross, a crucifixus. I wear it because it was a gift from a priest, and because it makes me feel comfortable, it may be connected to the writings, perhaps it wards off evil". I winked as I became more melodramatic. Bridget continued to push; she was having fun making me feel awkward. "A lump of metal on some old string makes you feel more comfortable?" "Well, yes. I can't explain it, but have you noticed the number of writings has reduced since I started wearing it?" "Tosh", she laughed, "There's writing on the back of your shoulder, right now as you are speaking". "What does it say?" I asked. "Dickhead!" she chortled.

From that point I resolved to wear the cruciform, not just because half of me believed the rationale, but simply to annoy the argumentative bitch (said endearingly). There were no more strange events on our holiday, we returned home refreshed and ready to resume the monotony of work. The writings calmed down for a while, but they had a habit of reappearing at the most embarrassing times. They were abnormal and would always shock bystanders. My usual excuse of James' magic pen was wearing thin. I started to cover up my arms and torso, avoiding short sleeved and open necked shirts to stop the difficult questions. It became unpleasant in the warm summer; even linen shirts were too hot. I couldn't allow myself to become the talk of the town; Whittington was a small place, and word would soon spread.

Bridget and I were rowing on Ellesmere Lake on a cool autumnal evening, when we decided I should seek advice from a member of the clergy as the old priest had recommended. The words were in Latin after all, Bridget and I were both curious and needed to understand how and why the writings appeared.

The following Sunday, Bridget and I joined mass at Our Lady and The Welsh Martyrs in Overton. I understood truly little of mass or its structure to be honest. I struggled to find the hymns in the hymn book, and the regulars appeared unwelcoming. It was an awkward experience for us both. After the service, the rector chatted, he was very friendly but had little time for us, he was keen to talk to the entire congregation. We quickly asked if we could discuss a christening with him and we made an appointment for the following Tuesday.

Was it really bad to lie to a priest? We didn't think so, we would be honest when we met him. The truth was I didn't want to advertise my condition to everyone at church, it was freaky. Before I knew it, I would see my face in the newspapers, and my condition would be broadcasted to the world. I wondered how many had claimed to have stigmata who weren't compulsive liars or charlatans? Not many I suspect.

As we drove home from Church, Bridget was adamant, "I don't want to go to church again. I really didn't enjoy it. I didn't understand anything, and the congregation actually shunned us like we were lepers". "That isn't true Bridget, the congregation were just shy. I bet if we went regularly for a couple of months, they would be friendly and more welcoming". "It's really not a good showcase for attracting people into the Church though, is it? Remember the Jewish wedding we went to for Kelvin and Tara, the Rabbi was so inclusive. I felt welcomed, he explained absolutely everything in a cheerful and fun way". Bridget made a fair point, but then wasn't it just a case of different folks, different strokes? I added, "They probably thought, here they come the new guys. They must want their kid christening or a wedding and then we will never see them again. We played right into their hands, didn't we?" Bridget wasn't convinced.

As we drove home through the lovely countryside, we stopped for an ice cream at a shop in Oswestry, it was just the Sunday thing to do. We felt energised that we had actually taken our first steps, and with luck we would soon learn the meaning of the phenomenon. The events which followed were something else entirely.

3. I'm not Gregory's Girl (JeT)

From the writings of Jennifer Travers

There was truly little I could do, Gregory's gun was roughly pushed in my face, he was clearly having some kind of psychotic episode. His eyes were distant, and he was sweating. "Not so sassy now are ya", Gregory whispered in my ear before he licked the side of my face. "You will pay for that", I pointed out calmly. "I don' have to pay, not for a sleazy bitch like yo", he whined as he cuffed my hands behind my back.

He put his gun on the TV cabinet and slapped me across the face hard. I turned and punched him harder. I had bunched my muscles as he applied the cuffs and dislocated my thumb and tugged my hand free. His nose cartilage snapped, and blood streamed down his face. He looked at me with utter shock, mouthing the words, "How?" He suddenly realised the revolver was sat within my reach. I popped my dislocated thumb back into its socket with a snap. Gregory's mistake was to assume I would make a mad rush for the gun. I didn't need a gun to dispose of the nasty little shit. I treated him to a roundhouse kick to the solar plexus for starters, which winded him badly, he fell to the floor whining like he was about to die. For the main course he was served a snapping front kick to the jaw, which whipped his head back like a puppet. He fell to his knees, as I offered him dessert of an open-handed strike to the bridge of his already damaged nose. I had performed my escapology trick a few times, but my thumb socket was starting to pay the price.

I held the Ka-Bar knife in the soft part of Gregory's throat, he looked at me with scared enwidened eyes. I took the keys from his back pocket and unlocked the handcuffs which dangled from my right wrist. My left hand was still sore from the dislocation, but I ignored it, it was a minor discomfort. I cuffed him to the radiator tightly. "Ow! Tha hurts bitch!" He continued to shout abuse and threats, so I gave him another blow to the abdomen for his trouble. Then I ripped a strip from the pillowcase and gagged him. Tucking his pistol into the back of my jeans, I opted to explore his seedy quarters behind reception, whilst I decided his fate. It was a simple curiosity; he was horrible, I needed to know more about the secrets he kept, it would guide me as to how I would deal with him.

The carpet was sticky and there was a strong smell of Gregory's own brand of body odour coming from the inside. I listened carefully, but there was no one else around. His bedroom was filthy, the bedding hadn't been changed for months despite the fact that the laundry room was virtually next door. There were clean clothes in his wardrobe, they were on wire hangers, wrapped in cellophane fresh from the laundry. A pile of degrading magazines was stuffed into his wardrobe drawer; I didn't care to touch them, they looked contaminated. The bathroom revealed little of note, other than he clearly used floral sprays to cover up his stench. Washing and a simple personal hygiene routine might have proven more effective for him, but there you go.

In his bedside drawer I found an unusual carved box with a hidden sliding latch. It looked Indian or possibly Indonesian in origin and eastern deities were carved into the intricate design. I had seen similar rubbish in the mall or TK Maxx sometimes, but perhaps he had actually travelled, who knows. Inside the box were an eclectic collection of small items: children's toys, small cheap trinkets, a lock of hair and... I dropped the box on the floor as I found a bloodied human fingernail and a rank piece of flesh, carefully wrapped in linen, it could only be a blackened decomposing child's finger. A small matchbox contained painted fingernails which must have been collected from infants.

I examined the room more thoroughly and found a hidden compartment in the dresser, I was on a roll. In the compartment was a steel locked box, which I broke open with the thicker part of my knife blade. It contained photos of child torture; the images of the children had clearly been taken by Gregory's own hand.

The man was a monster, he needed some retribution. A few years in a mental hospital before receiving a clean bill of health didn't cut it. I cleaned my fingerprints from the box and left the evidence in the open for the police to see. I returned to my room, but Gregory had gone. He had managed to separate the radiator pipe joint and free the handcuffs, rusty water freely flowed onto the floor. The photos had triggered something dark inside me, I went on the hunt for Gregory but slowly like a monster in a nightmare. He hadn't got far; he was in the maintenance room trying to cut through the handcuffs with a hacksaw; he balked when he saw me. I looked him in the eye as I stabbed him in his carotid artery; blood spurted as I withdrew the blade. The anger in me reached a crescendo, I stabbed him over and over again. Blood spattered all over, including on my lovely silver dress.

In the euphoria, I lost my self-control, which was regrettable. I relished bringing justice to this horrible creature. I sat down and tried to calm myself, I had made a terrible mess, the room was filled with my DNA. All it took was one person to see, and I would be in serious trouble. It was pure luck there was no one around.

I cleaned my knife in bleach, which I had snagged from the supplies in the maintenance room. I then bagged my clothes along with things potentially containing traces of my DNA. I changed into a spare cleaner's uniform and started to clean the room. I was fortunate, it was after midnight on an off-peak night, and the motel was mostly empty. After cleaning up, I deposited Gregory's corpse in his bedroom. I ripped the pages containing my name from the visitors' book and the bookings diary. It was easy to locate the CCTV disk drive, hidden behind the AC vent in reception; I took that too.

My next tasks were to pack my room and clean it up. I disposed of the vacuum bag in my trash sack ready for burning. Although the bed had only been slept in once, it was incriminating, so I took the bedding and bagged it with my cleaning clothes. I showered and squirted a large quantity of bleach down the drain.

I started a fire in one of the dumpsters in the back yard, to burn the evidence. I hoped my cleaning efforts had been sufficient. It was 4:30am; I jumped in the Corvette and headed off down the highway, hoping to have covered a few miles before the fire was spotted. I was an hour into my journey when I realised, I paid for my room with my credit card. With a little luck, Gregory's body wouldn't be discovered until the next day. I could claim I had left earlier and had seen nothing. When I pulled over at a motel just beyond Oklahoma, to catch up on my sleep, I checked the news sites, to my relief nothing had hit the news so far.

It was the following morning, when the first news stories were broadcast, the press made a huge deal about apprehending a serial killer who had been preying on children. The reports focused on identifying Gregory's victims, the detectives were less interested in the perpetrator. The reporters might simply assume Gregory's killer was the father of one of his victims and not dig too deeply. It was a horrible week, constantly looking over my shoulder and freezing whenever I saw a cop car, which was all too often. Tulsa's police diligence quietened after a couple of weeks. The press lost interest sooner, as you might imagine, they were always in search of their next story. I decided to lay low in Oklahoma City, for the time being. It was another week before I dared to continue my trip.

The weather had become humid, summer was fast approaching. I headed to the highway and spent a few days slowly cruising the endless roads, through the wind farms of Weatherford and Elk City, on route to Amarillo.

Elk City was a small town with a strong and thriving petroleum industry. I drove past the small business airport and roughly scoped out the place. The large brass longhorn sculpture summed up the place, it was cowboy country for sure. A nice clean town, which focussed your mind on oil and cattle through its range of stores and monuments. It reminded me of a TV set for Dallas, an old TV show, with its pastel-coloured buildings and well-manicured gardens. I parked at the Flamingo Inn Motel and took a room for a single night. I paid cash to reduce the risk of being traced. I withdrew cash in small denominations from wherever I could before moving on, to minimise the use of my card for a while.

A Doctrine of Fear - Paul JC Edge

I had stowed Gregory's revolver in the glove compartment of the Corvette, but I was uneasy leaving it there. It was evidence, even though the weapon hadn't been discharged. It would be just my luck if there was a license for it in the grotty apartment. I needed to dispose of it safely. I briefly toured the sights, but I opted not to visit the Route 66 museum; I wasn't really interested in street signs and photos.

After a day of exercise, I felt I needed a substantial meal. I chose a BBQ restaurant for dinner which looked like it wouldn't disappoint. At the table, I found I was becoming more aware of my surroundings than I normally would when off duty. As an illustrious people watcher, I noticed fading bruises on my waitress' wrists where someone had probably grabbed her roughly a few days before. A lady, who walked in holding her husbands' arm, looked less than happy. Her fat companion strutted nonchalantly in his cowboy hat like he owned the town.

I continued to eat my pulled pork sandwich as he talked continuously. If the man's companion had dared to open her mouth, he would put her down thoughtlessly. I also noted the cook flinched, when a tall thin man with an oversized moustache entered the restaurant. The room presented a whole mix of stories, many of them seemed less than pleasant.

Acting on a whim, I decided to follow the bruised waitress home, when Billy Sims BBQ closed at 08:30pm. It was light and warm, as she steadily drove her small Honda through the side streets. I kept my distance trying to remain inconspicuous in my Corvette, which was a challenge in itself. When the waitress pulled into a driveway, the satellite navigation showed I had parked in West 6th Street; her house was a white wooden

A Doctrine of Fear - Paul JC Edge

framed bungalow needing TLC. She parked next to a beat-up gold Oldsmobile; the owner was presumably her partner, who must have been relatively successful at some point in the past. The neighbourhood looked well-kept and decent, very few were cruising the street. The waitress' home was inexpensive but nice enough. The absence of toys gave me the impression there were no children in residence. I decided to stop being so nosey, after all the bruises could have been caused by a hundred different possibilities. I passed it off as me being oversensitive, and decided it was none of my damned business anyway.

I returned to the Flamingo Inn and took a short walk. I popped into the bar for a beer before turning in early. I browsed the newspapers, to be sure events in Tulsa had settled down; it appeared that they had. No one really cared about old Gregory biting it, but townsfolk were very animated about the children he had taken from the world. The coverage of the poor families included the father of a young boy who had died at the tender age of nine, he told reporters he would like to meet the perpetrator in a dark alley. Nobody expected the killer to be a woman.

The next morning, I impetuously opted to stay in Elk City another day. I visited the Farm and Ranch Museum and the Parker Drilling Rig. The museum was reasonably developmental, if a little boring. I wasn't sure I needed to know about crops and oil in such detail, but there you go. You never know the knowledge you will need in the future; it could just save your life. I headed back to Billy Sims BBQ for dinner, I had really enjoyed the pulled pork, so I uninspiringly chose the same meal, but with the ranch salad instead of fries. I arrived early and sat at the back of the place, people watching was quickly becoming my mode of operation. As I tucked into my salad, an angry looking man abruptly entered the restaurant through the front door. With his greased back salt and pepper hair I aged him in his early fifties, although he could have had a hard life.

The bruised waitress from the previous evening became agitated when the man entered, her body language was a dead giveaway. She unconsciously rubbed her bruised wrist when she saw him and frowned, a subtle mini movement, but a clear telegraph to me. The man was clearly angry and spoke in a raised voice for a while before leaving. The waitress apologised to the manager who looked at her with warmth and empathy, "You deserve better", was all he said. As the waitress refreshed my beer, I looked at her more closely, concealer covered up a sizeable bruise on the left side of her face. Her wrist looked worse too, implying the injuries were a regular occurrence. As I left the restaurant, I brushed past her and gently lifted her wallet from her inside pocket. I needed an excuse to pay her a visit.

I was waiting down the street when the waitress arrived home in her Honda. The Oldsmobile was parked in the same spot as the previous night. There were no passers-by or activity in the gardens nearby, no nosy neighbours peeking through their window blinds. The place was like a morgue, and it was only 20:45 for god's sake. I was interfering in people's lives again and I honestly couldn't explain why. I had a crazy notion that the world needed fixing, and it was my job to mend it. In retrospect, I realised it was a reaction to the bad things I had seen in the army, the terrible injustices I had witnessed and often been a part of. I felt an overwhelming drive to put things right, whenever I could. It could be PTSD or something of that nature, but I didn't take the time to investigate.

I needed to be careful, after the Gregory incident. I took steps to ensure there were no witnesses, my car was inconspicuously parked, it wouldn't stand out to a passer-by or on a CCTV recording. I popped a baseball cap on and tucked my hair inside to ensure my face was obscured as I crept up the driveway. The back gate hung from its hinges allowing me to slide through without touching it, the back porch gave me good cover as I padded gently up to the kitchen window.

The waitress' husband, the greaseball, yelled at her. Suddenly, pop! Without warning he punched her in the stomach, as he clung onto her wrist viciously. She squealed at first, her voice turned to a soft whimper as he continued berating her. Clearly it was how he managed to hurt her without creating too many outward signs. I strode directly round to the front door and rang the bell, whilst seething quietly inside.

With the sound of the bell, the shouting stopped abruptly, urgent shuffling came from kitchen. The waitress opened the door cautiously. She wiped her face and steeled herself, she was clearly following instructions to answer the door. I sensed the greaseball was close by, out of sight, listening carefully. I smiled warmly and handed the waitress' wallet over. "Hi, I'm JeT, you served me at the restaurant earlier this evening. You must have dropped your wallet as you got in your car, it was lying on the tarmac in the car park when I passed. I found your address on your driver's license; I hope I haven't come over at an inconvenient time?" I nodded towards the kitchen. Relief filled the woman's face as she accepted her wallet. "Thank you so much honey, I wondered where I had dropped the darn thing. I don't know what I'd do without it, what a gift from God you are. Could I offer you some lemonade? Its fresh and cold". Her face and body language were subliminally pleading with me to accept. I agreed and followed her into the house. "Missy, you have a strange accent, where are you from? And what is 'tarmac'?" she asked. "Scotland and asphalt", I replied tersely. "Wow, that's a long way from these parts. It looks beautiful from the pictures on the TV. I love those nature travelogues", she continued.

The greaseball waited in the kitchen, clearly expecting an explanation as to why there was an intruder in his domain. His face was dark and angry, he hesitated when he saw me. He clearly wasn't expecting a visitor, especially when he was in full flow. Suddenly becoming artificially friendly and charming, he reminded me of a sleazy car salesman. "Who is your friend Claudette? You didn't mention we were expecting a house guest". I blanked the creep and turned to Claudette, I asked her in a gentle but forthright tone, "Why do you put up with this bastard hitting you? Every day you come into the restaurant with more bruises. You should call the police and file a report, they will sort him out for you".

The creep bristled; his attention was focussed on his wife menacingly. She stammered looking at her wrist, "I don't know what you're talking about, I shut the door on my arm. How dare you come in here and...". She was cut short as the greaseball stepped between us, "Get the fuck out of my house, bitch! Don't you come into my place making no false accusations; you lying little slut". He attempted to backhand me across the face, but I stepped in and hit the base of his nose with the palm of my right hand. The creep's head jolted back, his face consumed by a look of surprise as he fell backwards to the floor, stiff like a plank of wood.

"Lord above, what did you do?" whispered Claudette. "Where did you learn to do that?" Her question disarmed me, especially when she continued, "I wish I could've done that ten years ago!" "I was in the army, you learn to look after yourself", I commented. Claudette kicked her husband between the legs, hard. "The dirty creep; that felt good. I've been living with this shit for a good long time", she added. "Well don't put up with it for one second longer", I offered. The hairs on the back of my neck raised when I realised the man was out too cold. I reached down and touched his neck. "Shit", I whispered as I took a sidelong look at Claudette and nodded in the negative. "Oh God, is he okay?" she queried. "He's dead", I replied slowly.

My mission to fix the world was going down the creek without a paddle. I waited for screams and accusations from Claudette, but none came. I filled the tense silence with words, "The harder cartilage behind the soft part of his nose must have penetrated his hypothalamus. It can be sharp when it snaps. He died instantly, I'm so sorry, it was an accident. I meant to knock him down, but not this". "Don't you go on bein' sorry girl", she added, "this fat hog made my life a damn misery. What do we do now?" "We have three choices Claudette", I observed. "One, you call the cops, I might get twenty for manslaughter if the judge is kind. Two, you call the cops and tell them an intruder has attacked your husband. Three we clean up the place, bury the body somewhere quiet, and don't call the cops".

A Doctrine of Fear - Paul JC Edge

"I could report him missin'", thought Claudette out loud. I started to verbalise my thoughts too, "But then you could end up a suspect, and that simply isn't fair. Cops always suspect the spouse first in these cases. Either way you would be faced with a load of bother. Best to let them believe you are the victim, tell them you were attacked and robbed by an intruder; you could make up the burglar's description, but you will need to stick to your story. Show them your bruises, you will need to be on your guard, though, they will be looking for small inconsistencies in your story. You could empty your wallets and the places where you keep spare cash. Stash your money in a safe place before you report the crime. Say nothing was stolen, you don't want jewellery and rings to resurface later, they would give you away in a heartbeat". The middle-aged woman thought for a while. She looked down at her dead husband and choked, it was a hell of a shock for her. "Do you have any friends or family locally who could support you?" I asked. "No family now; just a few friends down in Oklahoma", she replied gently. "We'll clean up, then call the cops, and stay with your friends for a few days?" She agreed, so we set to work arranging the scene of the alleged crime.

We cleaned the hall and kitchen of prints and evidence where I had been. I closed the front door, Claudette locked it from the inside, I then smashed it open with my boot, breaking the lock. We took the money from both wallets; Claudette hid the cash in the bedroom under a loose floorboard. I discarded the empty wallets on the front garden randomly, using Claudette's kitchen gloves. We agreed I would drive away, then she would start screaming and run into the front garden to prompt a neighbour to call the cops. I thought we had covered everything, but in retrospect it was impossible unless you had worn a Tyvek coverall for the proceedings. We hugged, as I left, she mouthed thank you to me. I was surprised she had accepted her partner's death so calmly. It proved to me her life had been hell, and the unforeseen events were worthwhile in a twisted kind of way.

I sat on the bed in my room contemplating the crazy events of the day. Why did I always walk headlong straight into trouble? I felt I positively looked for it. I admit I relished the opportunity to bring a little karma into the lives of bad people. On my supposed vacation to forget the army, I had continued my own private war. The horrific events I had experienced in the army had penetrated my outer shell more than I had realised. Also, the abuse my mother had suffered at the hands of my father, and the fact I couldn't help her, weighed heavily on my soul. Both my parents had died in the crash. I didn't get the chance to say sorry or make things right.

It was time to move on, the next day I headed out on the highway. When I went to reception to settle the bill, I wore my cap and paid in cash, avoiding the scrutiny of security cameras. I dropped the soft top on my car and found another of my acquired CDs, it was an oldie, 'The Best of the Ramones'. I hadn't heard it before, but soon found I was singing along. It was infectious and more than a little rebellious. The previous owner had good taste in music, but why leave the CDs? Probably because no one wanted CDs these days.

I drove through Shamrock and into Amarillo. The long straight roads made a boring drive, but the scenery was dramatic with its large, rugged hills. Amarillo was anything but featureless; this was Texas, and it was a larger city than many I had previously visited on my road trip.

A Doctrine of Fear - Paul JC Edge

I took a room at 'America's Best Value Inn' near to the airport. A lot of people were coming and going, allowing me to remain relatively incognito. The hotel had no security cameras, the sticky carpet made me wonder if I had sold myself short. The room was functional, adequate for my immediate needs. I opened my laptop and studied the news sites. Nothing of note. Claudette didn't even get a mention, Elk City was too far off the beaten track for the larger papers.

After an early dinner, I chose to take a long walk through the city to get to know my bearings. I had already located a good gym, which I would visit in the morning. I preferred to simply wander; I liked to get lost to explore a new town. It was a good way to see unusual sights, experience the culture and get a real feel for a place. I wandered into a neighbourhood called San Jacinto; it was a poor area, my nose told me it might be trouble. I turned and headed back towards the centre of Amarillo; I wanted to avoid any more turmoil. I was too late; I had been seen. A car pulled over to my left, the guys in it were a mix of Hispanic, African, and Caucasian origins, they had one thing in common: trouble. They were unpleasant people for sure. "Get in the car honey!", the Hispanic guy in the front called after me. The guys in the back started cat calling lewd sexual suggestions. They became more aggressive when I completely blanked them and walked off calmly at a brisk pace.

"I like a good corn-fed gal like you. Git in the car! I'm fixin to have a good time with ya'll", shouted the Caucasian. I kept walking. "Git in the car, or ill cut ya", he hollered. The situation was becoming a little more dangerous now. I kept walking regardless. They pulled up a few metres past me and started to get out of the car. This was a big mistake. As the Spanish looking guy opened the door, I kicked it hard, the door's steel frame hit him in the face. The back door opened and the other two spilled out onto the street. The driver remained in his seat, I suspect he expected me to be bundled into the car and they would make a quick escape. The pair from the back of the car spread out and pulled knives, the guy closest to me hesitated. I drew the Ka-Bar from my right boot, and before they could react, I threw it.

The knife hit the closest guy to the left of the breastbone, he went down, probably with a collapsed lung. I feinted with a punch to draw the knife arm of the other guy and kicked him hard in the lower ribs, there was a sickening crack. He fell onto his buttocks screaming. I took my knife from the first guy, who was lying prostrate; suddenly arterial blood surged from his wound. It didn't look good, onlookers gathered. The remainder of the gang limped to the car and sped off, leaving the unconscious body of their friend in the street like trash. The guy with the smashed ribs had managed to get in the car but was still screaming, I suspected he'd be in discomfort for some time, pain killers wouldn't help too much.

I pushed my way through the small gathering and headed off down the street at a run. I randomly turned into several alleyways to make sure I wasn't followed. I ditched the Ka-Bar down a drain and checked myself over, there were just a couple of minor abrasions. I had been really careless allowing myself to be seen. The adrenaline rush was amazing, however, as it faded, I became more concerned. The violence in my life was escalating and becoming almost a daily event. I was travelling headlong down a dark path, if it continued, I would end up in a casket at my own funeral.

I returned to my room, packed, and quickly left. I explained to the guy on the reception desk that my mother had become seriously ill, and I needed to fly home to Scotland. I drove directly to Albuquerque, parked in a secure car park, so my car wouldn't be too visible and checked into a cheap hotel in a less than salubrious area. I wasn't sure of my specific location, I thought I would be safer if I didn't know my location, like an ostrich hiding its head in the sand. It was madness. The news reports terrified me, the story made the front page, the articles detailed how a young auburn-haired female had beaten and killed a low life in downtown Amarillo. The reports included a rough photo of me, taken on a smartphone. One web site showed a blurry recording of the fight. It was an unmitigated disaster. I needed to plan quickly, I found a 24-hour pharmacy and bought scissors, hair dye and sunglasses.

I didn't sleep a wink. At 8am I left the hotel a mousy brown-haired woman with a ponytail. The sunglasses and Dodgers baseball cap did a good job of hiding my features. I headed to the car park and took the Corvette to the nearest rough looking body shop in the area. I managed to get the car painted there and then, it cost $500. I didn't need a professional job and no questions were asked. I deliberately drove through puddles and dirt, so the paint didn't look too new.

The guy at the garage was helpful, for an extra few hundred he recommended another place where I could change the plates and get the vehicle records tweaked. It cost quite a lot, but it was minor compared to the two alternative identities and passports I bought. The city had a dark underbelly, that was for sure, I was in New Mexico, and anything was permissible. My mitigations proved to be a smart move, but they weren't enough, not by a long shot.

4. Getting Under My Skin

We walked through the lych gate up to the rectory door. I pulled the rope, a huge brass bell tolled; it seemed oddly significant, like a premonition of meeting our death. Bridget looked at me uncomfortably. A lovely, warm octogenarian woman opened the door, "Are you Joe and Bridget Fairbourne?" she enquired in a friendly tone and smiled warmly. We affirmed and walked into the hallway. It was an old-style house, with period furniture, some of which were probably valuable antiques. "I'm Myriam", she volunteered, "I help out around here a bit, you know".

She showed us into the office, the rector sat at a large oak desk with brass trim. It was a lovely piece. "Hello, I'm Father Ravenscroft. I believe you are here concerning a Christening. Please take a seat, we will discuss how the process works", he smiled. "I am afraid you'll have to attend church for a few months before...". "I'm so sorry Father, please could I interrupt you for a moment. I'm afraid I wasn't completely truthful with you concerning the purpose of our visit, I didn't want anyone to overhear the real reason you see". "Oh, my goodness", he mumbled, "this is most irregular".

"It would be much easier to show you rather than try to explain, it is such a surreal condition", I offered as I started to take off my shirt. "Oh, it's really not appropriate", he started to mutter as Myriam entered the room and looked rather embarrassed. The father stopped midsentence as he saw the writings on my torso. They were appearing more frequently; the phrases seemed to come and go. There was no part of my torso, arms, or shoulders without a couple of phrases at any point in time. The increase in writings may have been caused by my close proximity to the church, unless the condition was simply worsening. "I'm really worried about the writings Father; a priest in Greece called them 'stigmata' and advised me to seek a Catholic priest with haste. The priest sat back in his chair, he put his hand on the top of his head and paused, deep in thought.

"This isn't actually stigmata, Joseph", the priest clarified. "It is dermatographic urticaria, or Skin Writing. I haven't experienced anything like this before. It is quite remarkable how the phrases come and go from your skin. Stigmata is when you feel pain or see wounds or marks resembling the five wounds received by Jesus at the crucifixion. No, this isn't stigmata at all, it is something really quite different. "Let me see the phrases, what do they say?" "They change from time to time but are usually a selection from the following". I passed him a list phrases we had seen, plus the Google translations:

- "Unus de septem" One of seven
- "Vox clamantis in deserto" A voice crying in the wilderness
- "Ut sementem feceris ita metes" As you sow so shall you reap
- "Multi enim sunt vocati, pauci vero electi" Many are called but few are chosen
- "Stipendium peccati mors est" The wages of sin is death

"Fascinating", he exclaimed clearly in awe. "The first isn't a known Christian phrase, it's quite unusual, however, the remainder are all common phrases from the Bible. It's most strange that the script appears to be in a recent Anglicana font". "How modern?", queried Bridget, piqued by her curiosity. "Oh, it's almost Middle Ages", he replied with a smile. Father Ravenscroft clearly read Latin fluently, our translations must have appeared patronising to him. He stood looking at us with a furrowed brow, "Please excuse me for a moment? I have an urgent phone call I need to make. I will be back in two shakes of a lamb's tail", he smiled and left the room. "He looked interested in the markings, I have to say", exclaimed Bridget, "he couldn't get on the phone fast enough. The reporters will be here in ten, just as soon as he's negotiated the fee". "Don't be so damned cynical", I responded a little too heatedly; I sat back and tried to relax a little. "Sorry, but I think he's genuinely interested and is probably seeking advice from his peers. It's not a regular thing, is it? He's a local priest, there will be greater expertise in the wider church". "You would think", she added sarcastically.

Father Ravenscroft returned to the room after around twenty-five minutes. We had twiddled our thumbs, checked emails, and then simply sat there bored. We couldn't understand the delay. Father Ravenscroft's face was gravely serious, Myriam followed with a tray of tea and biscuits, which were most welcome. He began, "I don't quite know how to say this, but I'm afraid I've been asked to detain you". "I beg your pardon", challenged Bridget rising from her seat. "No, sorry. Please let me explain myself a little better. Don't worry, we would simply like someone more senior from the church to meet with you to help explain the writings. They've decided it's most important, so they've already set out to meet with you here in person. It'll take them roughly two and a half hours to get here. I've spoken to the Bishop of our Diocese who immediately referred you to the Cardinal, the Archbishop of Westminster. It's the Archbishop who is travelling here post haste. This is quite exceptional and exciting; I haven't had the honour of meeting him in person". "The archbishop is coming here, just to see me?" I queried more in awe than wonder. "But why on Earth would he want to do that, just because of the marks?" The father explained that the Pope had given specific and confidential orders to a small number of highly trusted church seniors to look out for anyone exhibiting your specific phenomenon. "It must a really important matter to gain the attention of the Holy Father", Bridget observed cautiously.

Bridget manoeuvred her handbag awkwardly, she then stood and started to put on her coat. "That's fine, Father. We'll pop back in a couple of hours. We will grab some lunch and head back here at 1pm?" "Oh no, this won't do at all", replied the priest, "You see, your lives are in grave danger. You mustn't leave here, not under any circumstances". The Father explained that the archbishop was meeting an armed contingent of the Swiss Guard, who were flying here from northern Europe by helicopter. "What is it all about, why would we be in any danger?" I asked carefully. "You are in mortal danger, the Holy Father will explain, I am in the dark the same as you. It's not just yourself who is in danger, but also those closest to you. Let me know the names and precise locations of everyone in your family including your closest friends". "The archbishop will explain?" requested Bridget. "No. the Holy Father, the Pope himself. We are currently making arrangements for you to meet him".

I sensed Bridget was becoming seriously worried, she had turned unusually quiet. Gone was Bridget's bravado and sarcasm, she sat like a little girl outside a doctor's waiting room. I was sure the father's reaction was a mistake; it was beyond my ability to assimilate. I felt weak, like the floor had opened up beneath me, I was in emotional freefall. Bridget felt sick and ran for the bathroom. "My son, James, is at home", I exclaimed.

"Give me his address and all of those close to you. We'll look after them for you. The Swiss Guard are extremely efficient, it's so unusual for them to leave the Holy See like this", soothed the father gently.

I jotted down a full list of those we cared about. James, my parents, my in-laws plus Bridget's sister, Cornelia. I didn't have everyone's information, but when Bridget returned, she added the remaining details using her smartphone. Father entered the data into an officious looking website, he explained he wouldn't send the information via email, due to the risk of emails being easily intercepted. It was possible even the archbishop was under surveillance so the undesirables could trace my whereabouts and identity. "This is crazy, what on earth is this all about? It's only a few words on my arm", I argued. But the father just shook his head and told me he had no idea. He hadn't seen such a situation in his fifty years of serving the church.

We sat quietly, nervously at first. We occasionally got up to pace around the room, the atmosphere was intense. The study was at the front of the house, so we had a good view of the street. Our natural paranoia had been given a hard jolt, so we reacted to the slightest movement. We immediately noticed a black Ford which pulled into the street, the two occupants were dressed in black, their faces were covered. "Looks like the cavalry's arrived", I commented sarcastically. As the figures emerged from the car, I noticed they didn't look like regular soldiers. They were shadowed by hoodies covering most of their heads. They didn't appear to be armed until they picked up a pair of wicked daggers from the car's passenger footwell.

A Doctrine of Fear - Paul JC Edge

Alarm bells screamed in my head, I bustled Bridget and the priest quickly upstairs. I pushed them into the bathroom and made them lock the door. I looked around the first-floor rooms but found nothing to defend myself. I had seen martial arts experts on the TV defending themselves with knitting needles and a rolled-up copy of Hello, but that wasn't me. I needed a shotgun, or at least an axe. No such luck.

I slipped quietly downstairs, staying low to avoid being seen. I entered the garage from the internal door and grabbed a pair of claw hammers from the workbench, it was the best of a bad lot. I padded back to the hallway as the garage door was forced open, it was a simple door and the catches at the sides were easily forced with a screwdriver.

I climbed the stairs on all fours, to reduce the chance of them creaking, concentrating my weight on the outer parts of the steps. I'm not a light chap to be fair, but I managed to get up to the landing reasonably quietly. I hid behind the door of the second bedroom and peeked through the crack. Only one of the hooded figures had entered the house, perhaps the other was keeping watch. Utterly terrified, my heart was beating so loudly, I was sure the intruders could hear it.

A dark blur slid past the doorway; my state of panic triggered adrenaline to overload my body with energy. I lurched out of the room and hit the dark figure solidly in the side of his head with the hammer. Not being a violent person by nature, I would normally hesitate, but the words of the father had really wound me up into a frenzy. It was fight or flight, and flight was clearly not an option.

A Doctrine of Fear - Paul JC Edge

The blow was more devastating than I had intended, the figure flew backwards into the master bedroom and hit the floor unconscious, perhaps even dead. I slammed the door, only to find the second figure directly behind me, his dagger descending towards my heart in a downward arc. The man's face was twisted into a demonic scowl, deriving twisted pleasure from the assault. His arm stopped mid blow and froze.

Myriam, who had hidden in a back bedroom, had witnessed the action, stabbed the man between his shoulder blades with a sharp pair of needlework scissors. The small craft scissors should only have caused minor damage, but the figure suddenly burst into blinding flames, the sparks flew up to the ceiling.

Within seconds the figure was reduced to ashes on the floor, setting the rug aflame. Luckily, the flames were easily extinguished with a few swift stamps from my foot, which was odd considering the intensity of the fire. I opened the door to the master bedroom, a few molten ashes remained, and the beautiful oak wooden floor was charred. The first figure seemed to have met its end in the same way as the second.

In my complete state of shock, I didn't think to thank Myriam. I heard more car doors slamming and feet approaching the house, half a dozen soldiers entered the driveway, one yelled, "Get down". Gunfire erupted from a second black vehicle parked across the street; the soldiers ducked behind their bullet proof car doors. I joined the others in the bathroom, my legs shaking. Bridget tried to comfort me by placing her hand on my arm, but she looked more frightened than I.

A Doctrine of Fear - Paul JC Edge

The Swiss Guard entered the house through the garage. I repeatedly heard the word 'clear' shouted each time they secured a room. They moved upstairs and repeated the operation leaving the bathroom until last. After a soldier announced the 'all clear', two more soldiers entered the bathroom cautiously. "We are secure now, but we don't have much time. The assassins seem to be aware of your location; we need to move you immediately".

Father Ravenscroft and Myriam remained in the house under armed guard, but Bridget and I were bundled into the back of a green Range Rover. We left at speed, fumbling with the seat belts as the car veered from side to side. Within minutes we arrived at Sleap, a small aerodrome near the Shropshire town of Wem. Bridget was bundled into a nearby helicopter which was already preparing for take-off. I was moved to a Subaru waiting with its engine running. "I'm going with my wife", I announced assertively, my demands were ignored by the soldiers. I tried to move, but a firm hand grabbed my arm. "Not today, son, you'll meet your wife again soon enough. She's in the absolute best hands, I promise you. Let's not put her in any more danger than we must", the soldier explained tersely.

Bridget screamed in panic, but her voice was drowned out by the helicopter's engine, the rotor started to spin as the chopper rose up in the air. The Impreza screeched off the runway onto the narrow B roads of Shropshire. I was unable to see my surroundings, the night was closing in. The car's acceleration pushed me back in my seat.

We covered a lot of ground on long winding roads. The car twisted and turned violently; careering around narrow lanes and ignoring the risk of potential oncoming vehicles. The driver didn't even turn on his lights even when the road illumination became very poor, he donned a pair of odd-looking goggles which glowed pale green, and he continued at pace. After roughly three hours, we stopped for a short respite, I was given a hot drink from a flask and allowed a toilet break. We then continued on our way.

5. A Rude Awakening

James woke around lunchtime; he sat in bed stuffing dry cereal into his mouth from the box with one hand whilst playing a multi-player melee on his console. His room was darkened to improve his gaming experience; his noise cancelling headphones completely blanked him off from the outside. His dulled senses meant he failed to perceive anything around him in the real world. James was completely subsumed in a game with several friends, connected into a single hive via the internet.

When the gunfire abated in the game, he suddenly became aware of something in his room. A figure stood in the darkness in the back corner. James threw off his headphones and jumped out of bed, placing the bed between himself and the intruder. He wore only a pair of blue Diesel briefs. "What the fuck?"

From the darkness, a voice with an incredibly soft French accent murmured, "I wondered when you would become aware of the dangerous world which surrounds you". The light snapped on, as James' eyes adjusted, a young woman blocked the doorway. She was about five feet eight, but solidly built and didn't look like someone you wanted to mess with. She wore khaki camouflage battle dress and held a pistol in her hand. Although the pistol wasn't pointing directly at James, he recognised it as the Sig Sauer 9mm he had often used in his games. "The World can be risky if you insist on living your life in a state of sensory deprivation. You don't know who might sneak into your room. You need to dress and make it fast!" James started to object, but when the pistol was raised and pointed in his face he soon cooperated.

He dressed in joggers and a hoodie, the girl commented, "Your trousers will fall and trip you in a struggle, the hoodie will impair your peripheral vision, and your Air Max's will fall apart. We'll have to kit you out with more suitable clothing at the base". "At the base? Where are you taking me? What is this about? I haven't done anything; it wasn't my fault. It was only cannabis, I promise!" he exclaimed. It was pointless, the woman wasn't listening to his babble, her attention was on the door and the window. It was quite a disturbing situation for the young lad, he had experienced extraordinarily little in the world outside his console.

Once outside, the girl became more intense, she spat, "Shut up and get in the fucking car!" James complied without argument. It was probably the first time he hadn't challenged an adult in three years. He hadn't seen a real gun before; he would have preferred not to have seen one on this occasion either. The girl hustled the car through the bends not bothering to slow for road junctions, they arrived at RAF Shawbury in a little over fifteen minutes.

The woman showed a pass at the barrier and the car proceeded to the main building without delay, she was clearly expected. "Get out", she commanded. The female soldier led James by the elbow into the building and left him outside an office with two armed guards. When the door opened; a grey-haired, moustached officer looked at him with intense eyes set in a deeply wrinkled face. He smiled "Come on in, son, and take a seat. I've been expecting you".

The officer waved James to sit and offered him a strong coffee. The caffeine was welcome, though it failed to stop his hands shaking. "I am Brigadier John Crockett, welcome to RAF Shawbury. I guess you're wondering why we have kidnapped you, let me explain. We are on an RAF base, so I'm only a guest here. Luckily, the commanding officer is a cooperative soul, he's been extremely helpful in allowing me set up camp for a couple of days. I see you've met Wachtmeister Jane Grendell". He winked as he leaned forward, "That's Sergeant to you and me. I'm sure you got to see her sensitive side", he added with a grin.

"Jane is a sergeant in the Swiss Guard, I have to say she's rather formidable. She was trained by the SAS and doesn't appreciate her new assignment; she probably considers the role to be babysitting duty. The irony is the Swiss Guard are the main bodyguards for his Holiness the Pope, so our job is mainly babysitting". He smirked to himself. "The Swiss Guard have never resourced such a highly trained arm, clearly something interesting is going on, but I'm not privy to any of it.

"I can see you have applied to the British Army on three occasions, requesting to join the SAS amongst other roles. Obviously, you can't be recruited by them directly, you need to prove yourself first". "Yes", explained James, "but I wasn't accepted by the army because of my tympanic membrane perforation". "True, that is quite correct, in a battlefield you could become the weakest link for your team, you would put them at risk. Imagine spending three days under cover in a swamp, and you contract a middle ear infection. You would be a liability to your squad". "I guess", James started to wonder where the brigadier's spiel was going and why on earth had he been dragged out of his house.

Crockett went on to explain how James' family had been unintentionally involved in a sensitive 'situation' and their lives were in danger. His family had been moved somewhere safe to ride it out. "What situation?" queried James worriedly. "It's above my pay grade, I'm afraid. It's gravely serious, but don't worry your family are being well looked after by the Swiss Guard". "Why would the Swiss Guard need to protect them?" asked James, "If they're the personal army who protect the Pope, how does it affect Mum and Dad, they aren't religious?" "The Pope has requested we take all of you into protection. I have no clue why the Holy Father would do such a thing, but we are cooperating with the church quid pro quo. Many serving officers are Catholic including myself and we consider it a great honour to assist the Holy Father".

Crockett's response flagged up more questions than answers, but it was clear they weren't going to be answered today. James needed to be protected but the main aim was to keep him away from his family, protecting the individuals who could be used for leverage. Rather than locking James in a room in the Vatican where he could cause trouble, the Swiss Guard had chosen to enrol James into their ranks with immediate effect, he would be inducted and personally trained by Sergeant Grendell. "Normally recruits to the guards must be Catholic men with Swiss citizenship and have completed basic training with the Swiss Armed Forces. The recruits must also have completed a professional degree or high school diploma, all of which you do not possess. The Vatican is currently arranging for a Swiss joint citizenship for you, you will need to learn and accept the basics of Catholicism, although you cannot be forced to believe, you must be aware. You also need to be mindful that the training with Jane will be intense and will surpass the drills you would be subjected to in army boot camp. It will push you to the limit, and beyond".

James naively felt enthused by the thought of army training. "To be honest, I've always wanted to join the army, as you can see from my file. I'm fit, I go to the gym three times a week and I box, so I'm sure I will smash the training. But why me? Why the Swiss Guard? Why the Catholic church? I'm an Atheist". "Honestly, I don't know. It's the single most unusual request I've ever made of anyone". "So, if it's a request, then I have a choice?" "That's a negative", he responded with a brief understanding smile.

James was escorted to the quartermasters and issued with basic military clothing and boots. As it was an RAF base, the uniform wasn't the normal camouflage battlefield type clothing, but they made him feel good. Jane smiled and looked into James' eyes coldly, "So you will 'smash' my training, will you?" she uttered and snorted derisively. They boarded an RAF Hercules with the propellers turning, it was in the air before James could fully strap into the rough seating. He held onto the webbing and took a breath wondering what the hell he'd got himself into this time.

James asked nervously, "Where are we headed, Sarge?" Jane looked him in the eye and offered, "Swiss Alps. You any good at climbing? You better be, we don't use safety ropes". James' heart sank, it was much easier being in a virtual army when he could sit in bed and use a PlayStation controller. He started to feel a little trepidation at the thought of the training.

A Doctrine of Fear - Paul JC Edge

On landing at the Swiss Army base, he was handed the correct military issue clothing, a loaded Sig Sauer P220 firearm, a heavy waterproof jacket and climbing gear. A large rucksack containing a small tent, food rations, water bottles plus other items he didn't recognise was included with the kit. Jane had picked up additional weaponry, she demonstrated each item as she loaded them into the 4x4 and explained the basics of their operation. It included a SIG SG 550 rifle, a Heckler & Koch MP7 submachine gun and two rapiers. James became more disturbed by the swords; the situation was looking deadly serious.

"When does the training start?" asked James. "It already has", Jane responded curtly, "name the weapons we loaded in the 4x4 and explain how to prime them and turn off the safety". James stammered for a while but then started to remember the basics. He was well founded with the names of the weapons though hadn't seen them in the flesh before. Loading a gun was a button press on the console in his world, it was fascinating to do it for real. He remembered the procedure quickly, holding a gun in his hand felt so cool.

Sergeant Grendell explained they were going into the Alps, where the physical training would be second to none. James would learn weapons and survival skills, but they would be camped a long way from prying eyes. "How long are we going for?" "Three months. It'll seem like a couple of years to you soldier, but I assure you for me it will feel like a fucking lifetime", Jane scowled.

"Now button up we've got a long walk to the cabin, and its cold up there". They loaded up the gear. It was heavy, the rucksacks were fifty kilograms plus, then there were the duffels containing the ropes, guns and climbing gear. James was shattered after half a mile, but Jane ascended effortlessly. Jane's superior fitness made James angry and spurred him to push himself, Jane was building quite a lead. James arrived at the cabin feeling half dead, the only response he got from Jane was, "You smashed it!" and another heavily sarcastic laugh. James already wanted to quit, but he decided to give it one more day. He didn't realise at the time, the only way to quit was to eat a bullet, the Swiss Guard wouldn't compromise his father's protection detail. Jane wondered how long he would last before she needed to make the point, now that would be entertaining!

In the morning Jane and James went climbing. It was treacherous and they used no safety ropes. At one point, James slipped and was close to falling down a crevasse. Jane just laughed and grabbed his jacket by the neck, choking him as she pulled him back onto the rock face. He faced his death on an hourly basis; sufficiently for his anger to overcome him. He felt useless but forced himself to continue. He wasn't going to beaten by a girl, but sadly for him he consistently was. In the afternoon James' hands shook too much to focus on the target practice, but he found the activity more fun. James started to shoot closer to the gold centre of the target as time progressed. "You're supposed to hit the ring in the centre, not the mountain the target is fastened to, hammerhead".

Jane was relentless, but determination overcame James' anger as time went on. Jane used alternative psychology to motivate him; she knew exactly how to press his buttons. She understood because she'd experienced a similar baptism of fire herself during her training, she wasn't so different from this arrogant young man in those days.

After a month, the routine became easier, some climbing activities actually became enjoyable for James. In the evenings, James flopped, completely exhausted, but then Jane's evening training sessions started. He was expected to dismantle and clean a gun and rebuild it blindfolded whilst Jane timed him, scolding him with the words "Too slow!" One night she hogtied him tightly and told him to escape, he failed, it was impossible. Jane left him for an hour to think about his failure, before showing him her tricks. She demonstrated keeping his fists side by side and tensing his wrist muscles whilst being tied would give him some slack in the ropes when he relaxed, which he could then use to his advantage. James was unnerved by Jane's demonstration of dislocating her thumb in order to slip his hands through a knotted rope. Climbing was hard the next day, James' thumb was sore, but luckily, he often used his middle fingers for grasping the rocks.

When the three months training was nearing its end, Jane informed James coldly that he was adequate, which to him felt like one hell of an accolade. The long runs with full packs, the climbing, the hand-to-hand combat lessons took a hell of a toll on his body. His last test was a surprise, early the next morning. Jane woke James at 3am, bound and gagged him and took him on a three-hour drive in the trunk of the truck. She then released him with no map or compass and instructed him to return to the cabin by nightfall. He had learnt well. He knew basic directions and the lay of the land. He used the moss growing on the trees to determine North and the Sun's position to calculate the time, he headed off in the direction of the cabin.

After a gruelling six-hour march, James realised he had travelled in the wrong direction. It was difficult to ascertain the route Jane had driven him in the first place, even though he had listened for tell-tale sounds and gradients. All the gullies looked similar; the main bearing he calculated from the highest peak was in fact the wrong mountain. It was one minute to midnight when he arrived at the cabin. "You're late soldier! Time for some real-world urban warfare training, have you ever ridden a superbike?"

6. A Conflagration with No Trace (JeT)

From the writings of Jennifer Travers

Freshly sprayed in matt black, the Corvette looked mean and in better condition than before, despite collecting it before the paint had properly hardened. The New Mexico number plates were bright yellow and didn't match too well, but what the hell. I had changed my name to Monica Santini, and I spoke with a slight hint of a Spanish accent. I bought new clothes, favouring a light floral dress to cope with the summer humidity. The old me needed to disappear for a while, I returned the car to the secure car park I had been using and found a new hotel. I went to ground for a few days.

The news sites took an unexpected turn, they reported the FBI were investigating Claudette's attacker. It could only mean one thing; the investigators had pieced together two or more cases and had escalated the crimes into a cross-state investigation. I had been careful, how on Earth could they have come to such a conclusion? I was going to have to take it easy for longer than I expected.

I stayed in the hotel as much as I could bear. I ate out in the local cafés and the darker corners of the nearby bars. After four days I started to become stir crazy. The FBI weren't giving much away to the reporters, so it was hard to figure out how they had threaded the evidence together. The only possibility was that traffic cams had picked up my car, or they had found DNA or links in the forensic evidence. The local cops wouldn't notify the FBI unless they had found something significant, they hated to have their cases usurped. I needed to get out. I also felt a strong need for action, as disturbing as it may sound to whosoever is reading this.

I headed out into the darker parts of the city, where I felt safer, I found it easier to fade into the background. I popped into Max's for a meat loaf lunch. I was virtually unrecognisable; I thought it was worth taking a small risk. I needed exercise, so I took an afternoon session in a seedy looking gym. I drew no attention to myself; the place was full of meatheads who were more interested in themselves and their heavily muscled reflection. I then showered and went for a long walk, venturing into the mainstream of the town. I felt more confident my new appearance was safe. I popped into a small store for sun cream, a little colour would help me to adopt my new persona. I took in the Rio Grande and the Biological Park and then cut into the city via Central Avenue.

At Broadway Boulevard, I found myself next to St Francis Xavier Roman Catholic Church as dusk slowly closed in. The yellow rendered building was quite disappointing, I guess I am more accustomed to the ancient grand churches in Scotland. As it became darker, I figured I should head back to my lodgings post haste. En route, I noticed movement in my peripheral vision, there were two outlines in the tree covered area between the church buildings.

The figures were partly in the shadows, one held the other by the throat and shook him violently. It was just typical; I had avoided the more dangerous areas trying to keep myself out of trouble and yet here it found me once again. I carefully hopped over the iron railings using the cover of trees to approach quietly. My dress snagged on the railings, but luckily didn't make a noise. I knew there was a reason I tended to wear jeans. I came within earshot of the figures without taking too many risks. The man being accosted was a priest, raising my hackles more than a little. I'm not a practicing Catholic, but I've taken confession from time to time. Although my family claimed to be devout, especially my father; bloody hypocrite that he was.

The priest pleaded with the man to leave 'the children' alone. The attacker spoke quickly and menacingly to the priest. "Let me be clear, priest. I won't kill the children in your precious choir, I will slowly torture them, leaving the entrails as decorations for your foul shrine. I will eat their flesh in front of you and staple your eyelids to your face and force you to watch". The priest broke down as the man continued mercilessly, "If anyone in your damned state reports a man bearing the marks, then you must report it directly to me. If I find you have failed me, I will bring all of hell to visit your community, Father". He spat his last word, 'Father' at the poor priest in a derogatory and demeaning way. The attacker reinforced the message as he released the priest with a violent shake, "Skin writings", he left the phrase hanging in the air.

The assailant was startled for a second as he turned to see me standing in front of him. He quickly recovered and pulled a long strangely grooved dagger from beneath his jacket. I drew my pocketknife, I opened and threw it at him in a smooth motion. The man was fast, he deflected the knife with the dagger and smiled menacingly. The chances of my blade striking flesh were low, but it was an excellent distraction, most of the time.

The man lunged at me with the dagger at great speed. I was startled by his aggression and fell backwards onto my spine, with my knees bent into my abdomen. It was a dangerous move; one I saved as a last defence. I had avoided the blade by a fraction, I needed to take it as closely as possible to set up my counterattack effectively. I kicked my assailant's kneecaps as hard as I could from my supine position with devastating effectiveness. He fell backwards with a bloodcurdling scream, the dagger clattered to the stone floor. I leapt to my feet retrieving his dagger, I thrust it through his sternum in a fast continuous motion. The man burst into flames in a spontaneous combustion; it was the damnedest thing I had ever seen.

The fire burned white hot but gave off extraordinarily little heat. When the flames receded, only the hilt of the dagger remained, the blade was molten. Within a minute the body and all evidence vanished, other than a few pieces of melted metal.

Darkness returned to the alley between the buildings. I glanced at the priest, who looked at me with relief and astonishment. "May the Holy Spirit save us", he whispered. "What was he?", I demanded. The diminutive man took a moment to recover and looked into my eyes carefully. "That, my dear girl was a demon. A spawn of Satan. Praise God you arrived when you did. Let's go inside where it is safer, it's hallowed ground, there may be more of them". I followed him into the Church and sat on the nave steps as he bolted the main doors. The priest disappeared into the vestry for a moment and returned with two chalices of red wine. "Don't worry, this isn't the blood of Christ. It's just wine; cheap wine to be fair. Please accept my apologies, I'm Father Gordon, I am the parishioner here at St Francis Xavier". He smiled gently and passed me the cup, which I drank deeply. He sipped at his and looked at me kindly with a hint of inquisitiveness.

A Doctrine of Fear - Paul JC Edge

"What did the creature want with you?" I asked bluntly but not too aggressively. "They're looking for someone. A person who plays an important part in our forthcoming struggles. You see, we are facing the long-predicted battle between good and evil. It is imminent, the Holy Father has seen the signs. The armies of evil wish to take a major piece from the chess board, so to speak. The Holy Father himself is waiting for his champion to appear. He will lead God's army at Armageddon", he replied earnestly. "Arma-fucking-geddon? Sorry Father. Do you mean we are talking about the end of all things?" I questioned, more than a little shocked by such an obscure concept. The priest was unfazed by my bad language. "Yes, my dear, I do. The Holy Father believes the time is close and we all need to be on our guard. It isn't just a story; it's very real".

The priest sat down and reached out to hold my hand. "So how did a pretty young creature like you, learn to fight like that?" he enquired. "I was in the army for over a decade", I replied gently. "Not just the regular army I'm guessing, I was assigned to a unit in my younger days, but they didn't fight the way you did", he smiled, "you just sent a demon back to hell. Not many veterans could've achieved such a feat. You showed real skill".

The father's words made no sense and were disturbing, I started to wonder if he had lost his mind. However, there remained the question of the burning man, though there must be a rational explanation. The Father pondered for a moment, "I feel I owe you a debt, is there anything I can do for you, would you care to partake in confessional perhaps?" I looked at the priest like I'd been stung. "I can't Father, I'm so sorry", my words came out falteringly. "Now why not, young lady? The Lord is here for us all. He gives benediction and forgiveness for all our sins".

A Doctrine of Fear - Paul JC Edge

"Because I'm afraid I have committed acts he may not forgive", I whispered through my tears. I rose and ran from the Church. The priest followed me part of the way begging me to stay, "Please wait". I unlocked the large door and bolted through it before he could complete his sentence. I ran back to the hotel and locked myself in the seedy room. Armageddon? Demons? What on Earth was the priest talking about? The poor man was clearly insane". I lay down in preparation for another night of troubled sleep. The events of the day had shaken me; I hoped tomorrow would bring a better day. I couldn't forget the image of the figure bursting into white hot flames. It was impossible, wasn't it? It must have been a trick, an illusion he used to make his escape.

The following morning, I hit the road without hesitation after a quick $1.99 buffet breakfast. I wanted to get far away from this terrible place. Obviously, there was no evidence of any wrongdoing this time, but I had to get away to protect my sanity. Either way, the FBI might be on my tail, and it was better not to take any chances. Albuquerque was an enormous metropolis with a gigantic population, it was a concrete jungle but with some lovely green spaces.

I headed out to a quieter place where I could see my pursuers coming, whoever they may be. I travelled further south towards the Mexican border, figuring I could escape into Mexico if I needed to get away from the authorities. Failing that, I would follow the border towards Austin in Texas. My route skirted a desert, it was terribly hot. In an attempt to make the journey more comfortable, I closed the soft top and switched on the air conditioning. I needed cover from the hot sun and the infra-red which poured down onto my sunburned face.

A Doctrine of Fear - Paul JC Edge

After 60 miles of fairly straight roads, I arrived at the small town of 'Truth or Consequences'. The name seemed kind of appropriate to me. Strangely, T or C was named after a radio show in the 50s. I drove in on the dusty I-25, past the Elephant Butte Dam and reservoir. Such an unusual name, but comical in dumb kind of way. I took a room in Motel 6, my room was in a line, from across the road the views across the reservoir were both desolate and beautiful. I left my bags in the car, and I strolled towards the nearest eatery, it was too hot to bear, so I headed back to the room, which gave me little respite from the heat. I decided to wait until evening before I ventured outside again. I ran a cold bath and soaked away the hours.

As the sun set, the hills became a red and ominous backdrop to the town. I walked to the La Cochina restaurant and ordered enchiladas and drank a few bottles of cold Corona with a fresh lime wedged in the neck. I sat at the back of the restaurant, watching the front door, it had developed into my habitual position. A couple of Hispanic customers looked worse for wear, sitting at the bar drinking tequila like it was on a continuous drip.

After an hour and a few more beers, a man entered the place on foot. I hadn't seen him drive into the car park, he was dressed in khaki shorts, a rather too flowery Hawaiian shirt, and dark Ray-Bans. The man's bright red short, curly hair and neatly trimmed beard looked a little too regulation. He winked at the middle-aged waitress and proceeded to walk directly towards my table. He called to the waitress in a mild but classy Scottish accent, "Same for me please". I could tell from his bearing he was military. My hand immediately hovered over the revolver in my bag. He smiled holding his hands up showing he was

A Doctrine of Fear - Paul JC Edge

peaceful and indicating he wasn't armed; he took the seat opposite without consulting me.

What were the chances of me sitting in restaurant in New Mexico, and meeting a Scotsman for Christ's sake? I knew one thing for sure, nothing in this world happened by sheer random chance. The man knew exactly who I was, he had been hunting me.

7. Diversion or Misdirection

I had no clue where I was staying, I was forced to remain indoors at all times. We moved from place to place every couple of days. I was disoriented, I didn't know what was happening or even where we were going. I struggled to sleep, I worried. It was tough, I was in danger, but I didn't know why or how I could resolve my situation. The stigmata, as I incorrectly called them, appeared more often and constantly changed on my body. I felt like a freak. The soldiers were friendly but knew little more than me, they were merely following orders. They dressed in civvies, but still looked like soldiers. Whenever we moved location, I was required to wear long sleeves to cover up the markings.

I lost track of time; I didn't know what day it was nor how long it had been since I last saw Bridget and James. One evening, I sat in the back seat of a large Nissan with blacked out windows when the soldiers (I didn't know their names) became agitated. We were stopped at traffic lights, a temporary diversion sign in the road ahead had raised their suspicions. A black car suddenly broadsided the junction and blocked our way. Another black car appeared to our rear, moving quickly. How had they found us? I couldn't venture a guess. Our car was trapped, it seemed like a terrible dream.

As the soldiers jumped out of the car and opened fire, I felt a strange tingling sensation, the skin writings were guiding me to be brave. Men exited the black cars, four behind us and four in front. They moved at an alarming speed. When the two figures from the car behind were shot by my bodyguards, their bodies burst into flame, the sparks flew into the sky as they vanished.

A Doctrine of Fear - Paul JC Edge

Our driver opened fire and took down a man in front of the car, who proceeded to combust. The driver took a hit and fell lifelessly. The assassins closed the gap and moved in with alacrity, even though three more of the squad had died and combusted at the hands of the Swiss Guard. The three men apprehended the remaining soldier. They dragged him from the car roughly, cutting his throat almost effortlessly. The assassins turned to me simultaneously, I saw a brief smile flicker across their faces.

I sat, locked in the back of the car, powerless to do anything. The squad's leader hit the side window with the hilt of his dagger, the glass smashed into a myriad of small cubes on the seat beside me. He reached in to open the car door and gestured to me to get out. I had no choice, I started to exit the vehicle carefully; I was frightened but determined to make a break for it if possible, though I felt I had little chance of eluding my attackers.

I became aware of a buzzing sound in the sky above me; it was a regular four propeller drone flying in over the fields. The drone careered towards the car, alongside the three dark figures, who looked at it curiously. It emitted a thin sounding electronic voice, which ordered me to get down. I didn't need to be told twice; I sank into the footwell of the car as the drone exploded. Ball bearings flew in all directions, the glass in the car imploded. The three dark figures burst into flames as they were ripped apart by the ordnance. The ball bearings peppered the car's exterior, several had hit me with reduced energy as they smashed through the seat in front of me. My right arm was bleeding, a ball bearing had passed through the fleshy part of it, it hurt like hell. I made my escape quickly and ran headlong into the night. I was dazed, I didn't know where to go. I just ran as fast as my legs could carry me. As my lungs started to burn, a car approached me at speed. I was about to turn into a driveway to avoid it, when a voice shouted, "Joe, get in, we're here to help you!"

In hindsight, I probably took a significant risk, but the guys in the car weren't dressed in black like the Dark Ones, so I committed myself. I got into the car, we immediately headed down the street at pace. We drove around the countryside in what appeared to be random directions, with another aspiring rally driver in the front seat. A couple of villages seemed familiar as we passed through, we seemed to be following the east coast, somewhere in the proximity of Suffolk.

We arrived at a private airstrip; I still had no clue of our location. I didn't recognise the name on the gates, it was hard to read at speed. We boarded a ridiculously small airplane with twin propellers and a jet engine, it lifted into the sky without delay. The plane flew low and fast, it headed east over the sea. One soldier, who wore stripes below his shoulder, sat down next to me. For the first time in ages, I was with someone who was prepared to discuss my situation. He had grey cropped hair and an ultra-short ghost of a beard. He looked like he had been around the track a few laps. "Well, his holiness the Supreme Pontiff is very keen to meet you, my friend".

Sergeant Brancsan went on to explain, the Pope had been awaiting a sign for some time, large networks of priests were providing vigilance on his behalf. I blurted out my foremost thoughts, "Do you know what this is about?" He explained he didn't understand the motives of his Holiness, but he could help to explain the 'Dark Ones'. The skin writings with specific biblical phrases were the sign the Church had been waiting for.

"The Dark Ones have been hiding in the shadows since before the time of the crusades. They were founded as an Anti-Templar movement in pursuit of evil. They claimed to be part of 'the oldest religion' and aligned themselves to Satan. Dormant for centuries until they were recently re-activated". "So why do they burst into flames when they die?" It was the phenomenon I'd been most disturbed by, it defied explanation. "Some say they're lesser demons, called back to hell when they have failed their master.

"Failure is not tolerated by the Dark One himself, it's believed they suffer terrible torment in hell. However, others say they're merely men with explosive vests and their leader is venting his anger at their ineffectiveness. I can't comment, it sounded a bit hocus pocus to me, until I actually saw it happen". "Me too", I replied.

It appeared odd the leader was the 'Dark One' and his followers were called 'Dark Ones'. It all seemed rather confusing to me. Brancsan continued, "When his holiness became aware of the Dark Ones' objective to destroy mankind, he inaugurated a new division of the Swiss Guard to defend against the evil we faced. That's why we're here. We aren't regular Swiss Guard and we're certainly not all Swiss. We're special forces, handpicked from garrisons all over the world, pulled together for a single purpose". His team's specific remit was distinct from the main body of the guard. They weren't assigned to protect the Pope himself, but to protect me, assuming I was the 'one' who the Pope had seen in his visions sent by God. "My favourite rumour is that the Dark One feeds only on human blood, which is the reason his followers collect it".

Curiosity got the better of Brancsan, he asked to see my skin markings. He was really surprised by the words which appeared and disappeared randomly on my arm. It was unlike anything either of us had ever seen. "It's like something from the fucking Exorcist", he muttered under his breath. I had serious doubts, I honestly believed it was all a big mistake, and the Pope's attention had led me to be targeted by the 'Dark Ones'. Hopefully, all would be resolved in the next few hours when we landed in Rome.

The aircraft landed at Ciampino International Airport; it was to the south of the city. Five black Mercedes G-Class 4x4s arrived at the door of the plane, their blacked-out windows were probably armoured. Everyone on board the plane disembarked, other than Brancson and I. They walked directly to their assigned cars and sped off. I was left at the back of the plane, crouched with Brancsan feeling dumbfounded.

After a moment, I realised it was a textbook diversion tactic. We quickly dressed in airport ground staff uniforms, which had been left in the plane's toilet. We collected pre-arranged bags and boxes to appear busy, pretending to stack the boxes as we left the runway. We moved through the rear of the airport into the staff car park. Brancsan located a Vespa, he quickly mounted it and passed me a spare helmet.

Brancson started the motor using a key, which he found in the ignition. The small engine buzzed like its namesake, the humble wasp. I jumped onto the pillion seat, and we set off. Brancsan weaved in and out of the traffic on the main ring road, narrowly missing car bumpers, kerbs, and other cyclists. It was a crazy ride; I was stressed out of my mind. We headed north on the Grange Raccordo Anulare ring road and exited onto Autostrada which took us close to the Vatican. Brancsan then took a complex web of side streets to ensure no one was following and headed into Vatican City through a smaller, less used entrance. I recognised St Peters Basilica from the pictures I had seen. We headed into a stunning building which Brancsan regarded as the Apostolic Palace.

Brancsan parked the scooter, and we dismounted. "Still in one piece?" he queried cynically. A man stood at the front door, dressed in formal regalia. Brancsan humbly introduced him as Monsignor Roberto, the right hand of his Holiness the Pope. It was an overwhelming experience for me, I felt way out of my depth. I was compliant, smiling inanely like a village idiot. I didn't know the places or buildings they talked about. My religious knowledge was negligible, as was my understanding of their customs, plus I couldn't speak Italian. How should I greet such important people? Should I bow? Luckily, they were aware of my dilemma and were very patient. They treated me like I was the important one, it was most irregular.

The Monsignor took us into a side room where my family and friends were waiting. It was such a relief, Bridget fell into my arms and kissed me, "Thank God you're safe". Quite honestly, for once in my life, I'd say her statement was quite correct. "I would be dead now if it weren't for God's helpers, they've protected me through some nasty situations, and many lost their lives doing it. It hasn't been fun, and I still have no idea what this is all about". It suddenly occurred to me James wasn't there, "Where's James?" "He's joined the Swiss Guard; can you believe it? He's in training with them, he's doing well, he emails the Vatican from time to time to let me know he is alive and coping", Bridget explained. "Sorry, James is in the army?" I asked in a daze. I was dumbfounded, he hadn't achieved anything recently, other than sit on his bed. "What motivated him to join?" I asked, then I answered my own question, "the church arranged it didn't they?" Bridget confirmed, she added he had found his calling and was enjoying himself. The truth was in fact that the calling had found him and didn't take no for an answer.

We had limited time for refreshments before an audience with his Holiness. I acknowledged as many of my friends and family as possible in the available time, most interactions were apologies and feeble attempts to explain the situation was a big mistake. Bridget and I had so much to catch up on, but these were worrying times, so the answers from his Holiness took priority over listening to each other's experiences. We needed the Church to realise they'd chosen the wrong man!

Armed guards were present in the room for our protection, I hoped the Holy City itself was secure. I suspected the high level of protection could be due to an unpredictable group coming in close proximity to the Pope. They were managing the risk both ways. It was not a ceremonial occasion, none of the guards carried formal halberds or swords, they were armed with submachine guns.

Bridget explained that our close family and friends had been gathered in a secret location in Northern France, before they were transported to the Vatican by a variety of means. It was an immense logistical exercise with an inordinate expense. Bridget was concerned about our family at first, but they all felt safe here in Vatican City, the overwhelming imperative was to understand and make sense of this madness.

The guards stood to full attention as his Holiness, the Pope, approached. Pope Matthew John I entered the room, our friends and relatives were shocked. It was to their utter amazement that he would consider granting an audience with us. Many of my family were Catholic, so to them it was the biggest day of their lives, a great honour to be allowed into the palace, never mind meeting the Pope. Pope Matthew needed no introductions; he addressed the group directly. He empathised and understood our confusion. We didn't understand why we had been abruptly transported to Italy, without a thought for our jobs or lives. It was force majeure, his holiness had no choice but to act quickly, in order to protect us. He explained my condition had set off a chain of events for which the church had been preparing for quite some time.

Many of my family were unaware of the skin writings I had experienced. His holiness explained my condition was a sign of hard times to come, armageddon, the 'end of all days' as predicted in the First Testament of the Bible. The church was aware of fanatics who wanted to kill me, they would mercilessly use those close to me to blackmail a surrender or worse. To avoid such horror, the church had taken steps to ensure everyone was safe, the fanatics wouldn't enter consecrated ground at any price. I wondered how my family would react to being ripped from their everyday lives, but the threat of mortal danger seemed to quieten most of them. Attendance of mass was requested as a minimum, to keep up appearances in the Vatican and avoid suspicion. There were eyes everywhere, even in the Holy City itself.

A Doctrine of Fear - Paul JC Edge

The Pope's address caused concern amongst the group. My old friend, Barclay, decided to speak up, "I need to be back at work, I can't stay here. I'll be fired. I demand to be taken home right now". The Monsignor looked at him sadly, "If you were to leave, you would be kidnapped within the hour. They would torture you and send pieces of your body to force Joe to surrender. Joe cares about you, so he would seek to protect you. Joe is vulnerable if you put yourself at risk. However, if you wish to leave, go now. My men will provide you with transport home, though don't expect to arrive there safely. It will probably be your last day on this world". Barclay balked and backed off. "We'll talk to your employers and take the necessary actions to help. The Vatican is not without influence, please trust me". He added, "It will be some time before you will see Joe again, it's far too dangerous to keep him here". Before leaving, the Holy Father recited a short prayer, "May God bless you, I will pray for you. Joe will be moved first thing in the morning".

Bridget was mortified, we would be separated again for who knows how long. My family spent the evening sharing their hopes for my safety. I must admit my feelings were of trepidation, if not stark terror. At 10pm I was called for a private audience with his holiness. I was ushered into a small office; it was rather less grand than the hall in which I'd mingled with my family. The Monsignor was sat in the corner, talking quietly to his holiness as I entered. "Welcome Joseph, please come in; we've much to discuss. Firstly, could I trouble you to show me the writings, I'm fascinated". I hoped this would be the moment of truth, when he realised I wasn't the person he was looking for. He would be disappointed, but we would be allowed to go home.

A Doctrine of Fear - Paul JC Edge

I removed my shirt; the writings were rapidly metamorphosing over my upper body. "Yes, they are precisely as I've foreseen, they are a strange phenomenon, but rest assured it's nothing to be afraid of. It's the hand of God sending a message to us. My dreams have been giving portents for several years, predicting such a sign. God instructed me to ensure you are well protected. You are the one who is destined to lead us through the next few years safely. We need to understand the messages in your skin writings. I must say, it's strange I didn't expect Latin, occurrences of this nature are reputedly written in Hebrew or Aramaic. My other concern is the phrase here". He pointed to a phrase near my left elbow. "It says 'One of seven', it isn't part of the scriptures. You need to contemplate the messages, they may help you in the future, they here for a reason.

"Indulge me for a moment more, I find it most unusual that a reputed non-believer wears the cruciform of our Lord. Has an event in your life lead you to wear it?" I'd forgotten about the cross; it had become part of me these days. I explained it was a gift from a Greek priest, and it gave me comfort when I was worried about the writings and their significance. I guess I had watched too many horror films with Bridget, where characters who experienced stigmata were hunted by devil worshippers. To be honest the Pope's words hadn't reassured me, I wasn't sure his Lord existed.

"God has provided a sign that Armageddon is imminent, which isn't something of the Lord's making, it's the work of the fallen angel, Satan. Our Lord needs us to work together to survive. Many will die, which causes me the greatest sadness. I suspect I will be one of them, but I know I'll be in good hands. Your role is unclear, but I know you have a part to play in saving those who remain. You must save the people from the followers of Satan and lead them to a new promised land". I didn't feel I was a great leader; he had implied my role would be akin to Moses.

"I'm sorry if this is a disrespectful question, but I need to ask it for my own sanity. Are you certain I'm the right man? Are you sure God actually spoke to you?" "Don't be sorry, it is a perfectly reasonable question from a logical enquiring mind. I've spent a great deal of time deliberating it myself, I needed to ringfence significant resources to protect you. My commitment has brought our church close to financial ruin. I consulted my peers across the major religions, but I was reassured by the fact they experienced similar visions. I know in my heart that my course of action is correct, and I have every confidence". "Who is trying to kill me?" I pressed again. Pope Matthew looked at me patiently and responded, "Ultimately Satan works hard to prevent the undoing of his apocalypse, he feels your presence would cause a clear and significant threat to his plans. Satan is himself a fallen angel. He's interfered on Earth for an exceedingly long time; he plots, perverts and persuades in his quest for destruction and despair".

"The stories of Satan aren't limited to Christianity; he is also mentioned in other religions such as Islam and Judaism. The legends of Satan date back to 4,000 BC, to heretics and cults. The ancient region of Mesopotamia was the home of a multitude of cultures: the Sumerians, the Akkadians, the Assyrians, the Babylonians, and the Chaldeans reference the devil in one form or another. Even the ancient Greeks celebrated Pan, who exhibited his familiar horns and cloven hooves. Satan has been a universal figure who opposes religions, an adversary of all that is good.

"Ancient writings detail the worship of Satan as the oldest religion, but I believe Satan was cast out of Heaven by God himself, and God is the one we worship. God is universal, sitting above the politics and petty squabbles of the world. There is only one true God. God is Good". "Amen", whispered the monsignor.

"Other leaders who received visions and messages from our Lord, chose to invest in their faith, rather than making practical arrangements". I considered the pope's words for a moment, I wondered, "Was it simply luck I chose a Catholic church to investigate my condition?" "There was no luck, the events were always meant to happen, Joe. Your skin writings were specific to the Catholic faith, they were in Latin. You were destined to come to our church for help". "Perhaps God anticipated the church was well prepared, and chose your faith for this reason", I added, more sarcastically than I'd intended. My cynicism was not lost on the Holy Father, who patiently elected to ignore it.

The monsignor enquired about the 'Dark Ones', the satanic followers I'd encountered recently. I described the spontaneous combustion of their bodies, the hot ashes, their physical prowess and speed; also, their ability to locate me.

The Holy Father returned to his previous question, "You believe you're not a Christian my son, I find it most surprising you're the 'chosen one'. I find it even harder to understand why you wear the cross of our Lord". I expanded on my feelings about religion, and my perception of an afterlife. I realised my explanation exhibited determinism but I couldn't rationalise it to a specific branch of theology. I believed some things were meant to be and the universe had a plan for us all. "The Greek Orthodox minister must have heard rumours about our search for you, so he gave you the cross and asked you to seek counsel from the church. Firstly, we've established you are spiritual. Secondly, you are open to religion, but you've chosen your own path towards the light, whereas Christians follow a known well-trodden path. It takes bravery, my son, to walk a less used path alone". "I'm not on my own", I replied, "I have my family and friends, I have Bridget and James".

Pope Matthew reverted back to discussing the Dark Ones, "They were the followers of Satan's most noted disciple, and self-appointed leader, Barak. The cult was inactive, but since their reactivation by Barak, they have aggressively sought the prophesised leader exhibiting skin markings. The Dark Ones are driving the apocalypse; their aim being to wipe out humanity".

The Holy Father adopted a mercurial expression, "How do you explain the fact that Dark Ones erupt into flames?" "I've no idea; it's impossible. As I see it, it's as if they're wearing jackets covered in an exotic accelerant to amplify the flames, like magnesium. However, accelerant would burn for longer and alight surrounding objects. It would merely char the body, not reduce it to ash. Scientifically it's impossible, surely? It takes hours to burn a cadaver in a crematorium". "Our thoughts exactly", added his holiness. The monsignor joined the discussion, "I have commissioned scientific studies to examine the ash, but they have failed to reach a conclusion. We can only assume the flames are supernatural in nature". I agreed, when you exclude all possible explanations, it leaves only the impossible.

"If you accept the flames as supernatural, you are drawn logically to believe it must be the work of Satan", stated the Holy Father. Again, it was hard to disagree with his well-considered logic. "Which brings me to my point. If you admit Satan exists, then surely you must accept God does too?" The logic opened a huge question for me, but one I couldn't answer immediately. "Give it some consideration, my son", he added gently.

The Pope was an incredibly gifted man, he'd accepted my heresy and understood my thinking, but built an argument for Christianity in a way I could grasp. "If you believe in God, then any religion is a clear trusted path towards him. Why not choose Catholicism and join us?" He was right, I couldn't refuse his indefatigable logic. "As a man, or a leader, the church can provide little to ensure your safety. However, as a member of the Catholic priesthood, I can use all my resources to protect you. I can even provide diplomatic immunity as an emissary of the Vatican. My ability to protect you as a priest would be significant".

"I will help however I can, in these difficult times", I assured the Holy Father, "If it means being ordained, then so be it. But if I do, it won't be in a half-hearted fashion, I need help to self-orient quickly". The Pope smiled understandingly. My mind turned to the multitude of communities worldwide, "What about everyone else, how can we help them?" "It's not clear to me yet", replied the Pope, "I have been made aware that you are important. There are several others who've have experienced visions. Not all of them are religious or civil leaders, merely ordinary folk who have witnessed divine intervention first-hand. They're attempting to create safe havens to ride out the storm, they're secretly building small fortresses away from prying eyes". "It can't be easy to keep the fortresses secret. They will need serious construction and weaponry unavailable to any Tom, Dick, or Harry. It must be like climbing uphill with their legs tied", I observed. "I know, my son, the Swiss Guard are assisting, using the camouflage of intermediaries. We've ensured the havens have sufficient equipment to survive and be shielded from undesirables, whose attention they will inevitably draw. My network has worked hard to cover their actions. We've also inserted a handful of key people into the teams to keep a watchful eye and assist where they can. Our biggest issue at the moment, is the haven in Scotland where the team are requesting exotic weaponry for their defence. It's helpful the Vatican is an independent country; we can justify our own covert defence budget".

The Pope broke many of the long-established rules, he felt justified, due to gaining approval from the highest authority imaginable. I don't know how he achieved it, but he ordained me as a priest in a private ceremony, it was held the same day at the basilica of St Pauls. Seven cardinals were in attendance plus the monsignor, who later explained the church had accepted the Pope's decision to break protocol, once they had witnessed how God had marked me.

To be ordained, a priest normally undergoes six years of seminary training to become a minister. I was tasked with intensive study, to find my vocation and the ways of the church; but that I could handle. My ordained name was Father Giuseppe, it was the Italian form of my Christian name. I wondered how Bridget would react to my news. "You won't see me again for some time", the Pope remarked. "You need to keep moving, for your safety. I believe we will face Armageddon in April 2021, my visions showed that only a small number of locations will survive the onslaught. I will ensure you re-join your family in one of the safe havens. Your vows will protect and provide cover from those who seek you. Good people will support you but be careful who you trust. Remember, you will always be safe from the demons on consecrated ground. May God be with you".

I kissed the Pope's ring and he left wearing a concerned smile. If his visions proved true, it would be a long time before I was reunited with my family, and then there was the small matter of the End of Days and my readiness to lead an army.

8. Father Giuseppe's Protector

I can't begin to articulate my family's reaction when I entered the room accompanied by Monsignor Roberto. When Bridget spotted the dog collar beneath my light cotton jumper, her jaw dropped to her chest. She didn't utter a word but continued to stare at me in utter disbelief. The room fell into complete silence, and I felt an overwhelming need to fill the void with words. Stumbling amateurishly through a rambling explanation of why I had been ordained, I introduced my new persona, Father Giuseppe, but made it clear I preferred the informality of Father Joe. I unloaded my heart-breaking news that we may not meet again for nearly two years. Bridget and my parents were understandably inconsolable. Bridget had seen first-hand the threat of the Dark Ones, so she understood the menace they posed, but it was no less painful to let go.

Jane and James were invited into the guard's common room. They both wore dress swords, complementing a bold striped dress uniform, it was adorned by silver morion helmets with brightly coloured ostrich feathers. The red plume on top of Jane's armour and the gold cord across her chest signified her rank as Sergeant. It was most unusual for a female to be a member of the Swiss Guard; her clothing was clearly tailored for a man. "I feel like a right twat", whispered James. "Shut your bloody mouth, or I'll ram my fist in it", whispered Jane angrily, "we are on guard duty now". After a brief meeting with the Monsignor, Jane and James met the Pope, who underlined the importance of their mission. They must not fail, even if it was at the expense of their own lives.

After the meeting, Jane and James changed into their service uniform with their black berets and awaited a detailed briefing from their commanding officer, Captain Hauptmann Jean Blum. They stood to attention and saluted as he entered the room, "At ease" he ordered. They were to be allocated a dangerous two-year protection assignment. The captain explained the details of the mission, available safe houses, modes of transportation and the limited intel on the enemy. They were assigned to Father Giuseppe Fairbourne, which made James double take. "That's correct, it's your paternal father, Gardist Fairbourne. You must be aware of the skin writing he's been blessed with?" James was forced to answer in the negative. How could his dad be the person the Pope had discussed earlier; it made no sense to him.

"Listen James, we've trained you specifically for this mission. We need someone close to put Father Guiseppe at his ease but retaining the ability to defend him at all times. There are no shifts on this job, you must be ready for action, even during your rest. You mustn't allow him to lay down his life to protect you". Following a sharp nudge from Jane, James responded, "Understood Sir".

Monsignor Roberto motioned to me; he explained that my detail had arrived to take me into their protection. A tough looking young female soldier strode through the door confidently, followed by a younger very fit looking man with a serious expression on his face. "Oh my God, it's James!" shouted Bridget at the top of her voice. The Monsignor intervened gently, "Please don't blaspheme in the house of the Lord". She apologised as we both hugged James, "It's so good you're here, I didn't know if or when I'd see you again". Bridget took a step back, "Let me have a look, you're so fit and strong; I can't believe it's really you. What's happened to my little boy, you used to be so...chubby". James' superior officer, who I later found out was named Jane, worked hard to suppress a chuckle. Bridget looked at James and me, pleading with us to come back safely. We promised to do everything in our power to stay alive.

When the time came to leave the room, everyone cried, even James had a slight wetness in his eyes which he tried hard to disguise. Bridget struggled to let go of me when the time came to leave. "It's just not possible; you a priest", she cried at last. Then finally she added, "Oh my goodness, I'm married to a priest, the girls at work won't believe it", she pondered, "I might not see them again either".

The church found Bridget a lab technician job in a local English school, it was the best possible role on offer as she couldn't speak Italian. Jobs were found for my family and friends and private Italian tuition was arranged for the children. They were confined to a tight defensible radius, close to Vatican City, and monitored at all times. My family were as safe as they could be, which gave me scant comfort.

A dark Mercedes with blacked out windows conveyed Jane, James, and I through the city to a nearby garage, where we were equipped for our travels. We were roaming western Europe, as far as I could tell from the scant information from my protection team. I was handed a lightweight armoured Kevlar jacket and trousers, plus a motorcycle helmet. The latter concerned me greatly, I had never ridden a bike. Jane and James were issued clumsy looking smartphones called

ComLinks, which turned out to be encrypted battlefield comms devices, a full computer with maps. The device couldn't be tracked or intercepted, it provided access to assistance anywhere in western Europe within a couple of hours.

Locations of equipment stores were marked on the map, as were Catholic churches, rectories and sympathetic contacts. Our location was to be confidential; it meant no phone calls to loved ones. We donned the clothing, we were then allocated Sig Sauer pistols, which I refused. "I really don't want to carry a weapon, thank you. Let alone a concealed one", I refuted adamantly. The Monsignor proved most persuasive, "What would you do if James was under attack? Would you help him, or would you prefer to watch him die?" I stopped for a second, then strapped on the shoulder holster and shrugged into my jacket. It had been tailored so the weapon fitted snugly under my arm and was invisible to a casual observer. "We won't always be on motorcycles; we've arranged several transport options. We need to change our routines regularly, so we're not easily identified", added Jane.

The mechanic gave us the fifty-cent tour. "These motorcycles are a customised variant of the Ducati Multistrada, they are a tall comfortable bike, you can travel long distances on them. At the touch of a button, you can firm up the suspension and deliver the full 150 brake horsepower of the Testastretta engine. We've tuned up the sport mode and added nitrous oxide injection, so be careful when you open it up for the first time, they're quicker than even the fastest sports cars. With the larger fuel tank we've fitted, their range can be 250 miles at reasonable speed, but they drink fuel when the engines are pushed. You'll need to wear quick release rucksacks for your limited belongings, as the rear panniers have been repurposed with defensive weaponry.

"The left pannier is a simple grenade drop, whereas the right tosses an anti-personnel grenade into the air. It's fairly standard, except it's wrapped in a ball bearing jacket and calibrated to take out the occupants of a pursuing car. It will detonate a metre above ground, so be careful where you let these babies loose, they will kill nearby civilians and you too if you don't accelerate hard to get clear.

"Along the centre of the bike is the barrel of a semi-automatic carbine, ensure the front wheel is straight before you deploy, or the bike will disintegrate, and you might get caught in the ricochet. Careful of the bike's recoil when you fire the weapon, practice using it before you need it". "This isn't just simple transport; it's a lethal weapon. Treat it with respect and try to hand it back in one piece".

I was riding pillion with Jane, we mounted the bikes and prepared to leave. Monsignor reminded us we could claim diplomatic immunity if we were caught in a difficult position with the small arsenal we were carrying. He wished us the best of luck and godspeed. Then we were away, moving quickly into the busy strada's of the city.

The bike proved terrifying at first, the acceleration was extreme even in basic touring mode, it took all my strength to hang on. Jane shouted through the Bluetooth radio a few times; I was not leaning into the corners properly. I soon got used to it, we were going so fast it was hard not to give into fear. I wondered how James had learned to ride a motorcycle so quickly, but he was no slouch, he shadowed Jane every step of the way. I found out months later, he didn't even have a valid motorbike license.

We weaved in and out of cars, merging into roundabouts at breakneck speed but we always managed to avoid getting hit. We cleared Rome in minutes, despite the terrible congestion. I didn't know where we were heading, I didn't recognise many places. After four hours, Jane finally stopped for snacks, a brief comfort break and then we continued. We eventually arrived in Pontremoli, a small village in Tuscany and checked into a small family run hotel next to the river called 'Il Glicine e la Lanterna'. It was comfortable and served robust hearty home cooked food. I ate and went straight to bed, I was exhausted, both physically and mentally.

The next morning, we made an early start, it was a rerun of the previous day. By evening, we arrived at a small hotel in St Etienne between the rivers Loire and Rhone in central France. At the end of the third day, we'd reached a tiny village called La Petite-Pierre, near the German border of France, northwest of Strasbourg. The old village was on top of a large outcrop of rock in the middle of a huge forest, with pine trees as far as the eye could see. The village was enclosed by a castellated wall, it was breath-taking. We stopped at the 'Hotel Des Vosges' just on the outskirts. Our hotel had strong Germanic influences and reminded me of pictures of houses I'd seen in the Alps. Jane advised we would stay here for a couple of weeks if it proved safe.

The village was awfully quiet, which was typical in springtime, apparently. The hotel owners were devout Catholics and were immensely helpful. They felt it was quite an honour for a priest to stay, although they were curious of my purpose, especially with us arriving on motorcycles. Their interest helped explain why I couldn't stay in a place for too long; too many questions drew the wrong attention.

Two weeks passed very quickly, though I desperately missed Bridget, although it was wonderful to be with James again. He'd matured into a man I could hold sensible conversation with. La Petite-Pierre was a wonderful place, we spent many hours walking in the woods, jogging and drinking coffee in the old town. Jane and James were under strict orders to abstain from alcohol, but they took turns in indulging in a single glass of wine now and again, partly due to my insistence.

My fitness started to improve with my new lifestyle, but I felt Jane and James held back a little, so I wouldn't feel discouraged. They often took turns in scouting the path ahead, which usually meant running at double speed. Jane spent many hours teaching me to shoot a pistol, choosing a remote location in the woods, so no one would hear. My stance and basic shooting technique improved quickly. As the targets moved further away and Jane's expectations of my accuracy raised, it became considerably more difficult. "It's much harder to hit a moving target, or one that's shooting back", Jane explained one evening. "You should avoid members of the public where possible. Our standing orders are to not put civilians at risk unless we're on protection duty for the Pope, however, our directive has been extended to include you. I've no idea why the Vatican would consider you to be so important". "Me neither", I replied humbly.

We spent every evening sitting in cafés or restaurants in La Petite-Pierre, it was such a lovely place. I consumed a little wine and lots of coffee. It soothed my frayed nerves; the air was clean and packed a punch with its high oxygen concentration. The small, cobbled street in the old town was a joy, its diminutive buildings and the lovely church at the point of the ridge. It was distant from the hubbub of society, which brought me some comfort too.

James clearly enjoyed his new role, I suspected he had a slight crush on Jane too, but he hid it very well. Although she was quite plain, her self-assured persona and well-toned physique more than compensated. I don't usually find over-confidence appealing, but then physical attraction is one of life's little mysteries. Jane made me feel safe when she was by my side, especially if the Dark Ones were out there hunting me. In my free time, I tried to learn the basic rituals of my new religion, it wasn't easy for a self-confessed heretic. The sum total of my possessions were: my clothing, my pistol, my Bible, and a book of basic priest know how. I assumed it was akin to a dummy's guide, for example I had no idea how to perform confessional duties, anyone taking it with me would assume I was a charlatan. I was a priest in name only.

Our stay concluded and we hit the road again with a vengeance, another five hops and three weeks of short stays. We travelled across the west coast of France in an almost haphazard way, in order to throw potential hunters off our scent. I enjoyed the lazier motorcycle journeys, although my ageing knees started to hurt without regular breaks to stretch. Jane generally kept below speed limits to avoid scrutiny. We arrived at a small village called Châtelaillon, just a few miles south of La Rochelle, a seaport on the Bay of Biscay.

La Rochelle was a coastal community known as the white city (La Ville Blanche); luminous limestone facades glowed in the bright sunlight. Châtelaillon's shops and restaurants clustered around a central main road, giving it a quaint, typically French feel. We stayed at the Hotel Majestic on the Boulevard de la Republique, it was basic but acceptable.

We spent a few days strolling on the beach and frequented the waterside cafés. It was a quiet place, becoming more familiar with the locals helped us identify new faces. On the fourth day, I noticed the writings on my arm had changed. The message was obvious, for the first time the writing appeared in English: 'Leave now! They have found you'. James and Jane were shocked when I stood up suddenly and announced we must depart. Any explanation would sound illogical, but I knew the warning was real and we had no time to spare. We ran to the hotel, left cash for our stay at the front desk and collected the bikes. Luckily, we'd been disciplined and packed our belongings in our rucksacks each morning. We jumped on the Ducati's and drove south down the main road at speed. The loud roar of the motorcycles turned heads, as Jane and James gunned the engines down the quiet street.

As we travelled, a black Citroen performed a handbrake turn blocking our path, three Dark Ones leapt from the car, sprinting towards us, with knives drawn. James screamed, "Turn back". James and Jane turned the bikes and accelerated the way we came. Another black Citroen swung round to block our way. Simultaneously, James and Jane fired the integral machine guns. The raucous tone of the Ducati exhausts drowned out the load bark of the weapons. The bikes shuddered; the black car was riddled with bullets as its occupants flamed. Jane shouted, "Move it!" Jane dodged the flames as the other car careered after us, weaving past the burning vehicle. The Ducati's shot out of town like lightning, I held on for dear life. Our pursuer wasn't driving a conventional family vehicle, they almost kept with us as we accelerated. Jane shouted, "Fire in the hole", then launched a grenade from the bike's rear pannier. Simultaneously the bikes gunned their engines and accelerated hard. I watched the grenade's progress over my left shoulder, it was lobbed into the air and exploded at windscreen level. The pursuing car was obliterated with the high energy ball bearings, its occupants flamed. The shop windows at either side of the car shattered and alarms began to sound, I couldn't see any obvious civilian casualties.

We left the area at pace to avoid further pursuit, or in case the local police scrambled quickly. I have no idea how the onlookers would explain the events. The next day's press reported a terrorist attack, the motive for the explosion was unclear and no organisations claimed responsibility. We rode south for six consecutive hours, only stopping for fuel and toilet breaks, I felt sick. We pressed on as if a demon was on our tail and perhaps it was.

9. Death or Glory... or another option? (JeT)

From the writings of Jennifer Travers

Captain Brian McDonald sat opposite me appraisingly. I felt it was presumptuous to join my table without the courtesy of asking, he seemed intrigued to find a fellow Scot in the back and beyond. His smile seemed genuine, but I wasn't born yesterday. McDonald wasn't specific about his battalion or his rank when we discussed our time in the army. He became more than a little evasive when I questioned the details, speaking volumes to me, he was secretive. We established that we both served in the Royal Regiment of Scotland around nine years ago, I must admit I think I vaguely remembered him. We drank a few beers, talked about old times in the regiment and people we knew. It was pleasant to be in the company of someone who understood me, my paranoia eased as time passed.

We talked into the early hours; the time passed so quickly. I'd enjoyed the evening all in all, though I felt I couldn't completely drop my guard. I admit I fancied him a little and he seemed to feel the same way, but what would I know? I'm not the sensitive type and I'm not great with feelings. I expected him to invite me back to his room, but he smiled, shook my hand and left; I felt a little disappointed if I'm honest.

I totally missed the minor detail that he had called me JeT, the realisation I hadn't disclosed my nickname came later and I'm ashamed to say I gave in to a moment of panic. I roughly cropped my hair with my new knife and clipped it down to a brutal stubble. I used the last pack of hair dye, blonde, which I had bought in case I needed to change identity in a hurry. I added a fake nose ring, and I was transformed into my new persona, Melissa Goldwyn. I knew I would need to ditch my car at some point, it had most likely been tracked. I snapped my phone's SIM card, replaced it with a new pay-as-you-go and dumped the broken pieces in the trash. I picked up a brown faux leather miniskirt and a Levi denim top from the all-night store in town to complete my new look.

I opted for an 11-hour drive to Austin, Texas, I would then sell the car and find another mode of transport. I hoped the drive would be safe, given it was late. I stopped at in El Paso at 2am for coffee and carbs. The car purred gently as I drove into the dark night, I knew I would be gutted to let my dream car go. Everywhere was pitch black, except where illuminated by the beam of my headlights, there was no road lighting, no houses, no signs, nothing but stars to light my way.

After an hour, roughly fifty miles out of El Paso, I took the Texas Mountain Trail towards Austin at Van Horn. As I left the town, I became aware of the shadow of a car travelling behind me, it had no visible running lights. It was difficult to spot, I simply felt its presence. The car was closing on me. I gunned the powerful V12 engine and left it behind. After half an hour I relaxed but soon felt the car's presence again.

When I passed through towns, streetlights illuminated my route, and the car backed off in the distance. I felt a little paranoid, I had a legitimate concern, the FBI could be tailing me. The mysterious Brian was also in the frame, he had triggered my flight instinct after all. I decided not to draw too much attention to myself, holding a steady 50mph through a place called Kent.

A Doctrine of Fear - Paul JC Edge

As I left the township, my pursuer approached at speed and rammed my tail end. I accelerated quicky, but the car kept pace with me. It was astonishing, given the performance modifications made to my Stingray. I reached to the glove box, grabbed my revolver and placed it on my lap. Clearly the car was not the cops, they had a more nefarious purpose.

The car rammed me again, but this time at a much higher velocity. I was following the snakelike mountain road at 100mph, the terrain was becoming dangerous. I could easily end up as a fireball rolling down into the valley. The road narrowed, so I slowed into a sweeping left bend as much as I dared, I then accelerated hard without warning. My upgraded suspension paid dividends; it placed a decent gap between the cars. I took a sweeping right bend at breakneck speed, pushing my car to the max. As I came out of the bend, I affected a handbrake turn, stopping the car broadside across the road. I quickly exited the passenger side as the pursuing car careered around the bend. It had no chance, the car t-boned my car violently. Their airbags deployed, the cars were both wrecked, three men staggered out of the pursuing car, shaken. In testament to them, they recovered quickly and were ready for action in seconds.

I lay prostrate behind a pile of rocks, gun in hand waiting to ambush the men. I shot the leader, he burst into flame. The flames were so bright on the dark lonely mountainside, it lit up the whole area for a couple of minutes. More damned demons! It became a battle of who would regain their night vision first. I backed away to the side on all fours, making it difficult for the two remaining demons to locate me. It would be just my luck if the blinding light hadn't affected their vision, who knows what they were capable of. I rose, my sight returned to observe a single figure approaching. It had sheathed its dagger and was pulling a firearm from its shoulder holster. I opened fire too hastily and missed. As I turned to check my flank, the third figure sprinted towards me, dagger in hand. I blocked its extended blade arm at the elbow and threw the demon into the hard rock behind me, using an Aikido hip throw. It hit the rock face hard, headfirst and dropped, stunned. My problem was that in order to throw the demon, I had to drop my revolver. Meanwhile the first figure pointed a weapon in my face. "Checkmate", it uttered in a serpentine voice.

I demoted the threat of the demon beside me, he was semi-conscious; I focussed my attention on the one pointing a weapon. I slowly side stepped away from the fallen demon, to reduce the risk of being attacked without warning. "We have been looking for you, bitch", the one pointing the pistol uttered slowly, emphasising each word. "We are going to bleed you and rip you apart. You don't get to dispatch our brothers, and live to tell the tale", it hissed, smiling gleefully. My peripheral night vision sensed movement close to the bend in the road. A firearm barked and the figure before me burst into blinding flame. I quickly turned to the demon beside me, knife in hand, only to find it had driven its own blade through its chest and had also flamed.

I stood frozen in a state of shock as Brian approached me. "They like to do that. They don't care to be caught, their master forbids it", he explained. "Who is their master?" I enquired. "Satan's emissary on Earth, the Dark One", he replied carefully. I noticed he looked over his shoulder to check the road as he spoke. It almost looked like he expected him to appear when his name was uttered. "Quick, follow me. My car is just around the corner. Let's get the hell out of here". We agreed to push the damaged cars off the edge of the cliff, after I had retrieved my things. We tried to make it look like an accident as best we could.

"Who the hell *are* you?" I demanded, staring intensely at Brian as he headed towards Austin. "Captain Brian McDonald of the Swiss Guard", he replied with a smile, "nice to meet you, for the second time". He passed me his creds to prove he was telling the truth; they looked legitimate. "Swiss Guard? Aren't they the guys who perform protection duty for the Pope? What are you doing here, and why are you following me?" "It's a long story, let's get something to eat. Trust me, I mean you no harm. I have a proposal for you. Nice hair by the way", he winked at me and smiled. "I'm not marrying you", I replied sarcastically, but then softened my demeanour a little.

"I figured you were on my side from the assist. Thank you, by the way. I was in trouble there, I allowed them to outflank me, I must be getting tired", I observed sincerely. He countered assertively, "Hold on a damn minute, you weren't fighting middle eastern terrorists, they are demons, they are fast and deadly. You were lucky to escape with your life. You must have been shocked when the first one flamed, it would take away your night vision. You fought well; you have great reactions to recover so well". I shook my head, "I've seen one of those bastards before", I explained. "I know, it's why I followed you. I knew they'd seek you, once you had taken one of them out. They exact revenge with relish, it's a code of honour. There was one on my tail too, but he hasn't shown himself yet. I'm hoping

A Doctrine of Fear - Paul JC Edge

I've lost him, but you can't be too sure. They don't let anyone who can ID them live; their mission is too dark and secretive". "What's your interest in them?" I queried. "I hunt them", he replied. "What, on your own?" I queried somewhat mystified. "That's why I wanted to talk to you, I need help. My partner was killed a few weeks ago and I'm flying solo", he stated carefully.

We drove 200 miles towards San Antonio, through the night into early morning. Brian played the Ramones on his phone as we drove, to keep us alert. "Rockaway Beach" blared out as we hurtled down the winding roads. How did he know I liked the song? This guy knew too much for my liking. When we arrived in San Antonio we headed to the nearest motel. Brian suggested we shared a room, for security purposes; he requested twin beds, as a true gentleman would. He was forced to pay for two nights as our arrival was mid-morning, he handed over the cash without argument.

We were both dog-tired and ready to collapse. We took a couple of bottles of water from the vending machine in the hall and retired to our room. We checked the room briefly and then lay on our separate beds without undressing. I loosened my boot laces, kicked them off and tucked my knife under the pillow. My mind was spinning but exhaustion took over, I was soon sound asleep. Brian had rigged up a movement sensor beneath the door to provide a few seconds warning of intruders, luckily there were none during the night. Brian and I both slept a solid ten hours and woke around 7pm. Brian extended our booking for an additional night. "Let's go grab brunch, I guess I have some explaining to do". "Why not", I replied a little more tartly than I intended.

A Doctrine of Fear - Paul JC Edge

Brian ordered an all-day breakfast for us both with fries and a bottomless coffee. I dug into the food relentlessly, barely stopping to breathe. We finished by ordering pecan pie and a refill of coffee. Brian sat back, looked out of the window for a moment, and began his much-needed explanation. I let him finish before I posed any questions, allowing him to keep his flow. I wanted to know everything.

Brian explained, "The Pope has made preparations for the arrival of God's champion, and the demons hunting him. The champion exhibits biblical writings on his skin, the churches are awaiting his arrival". "The priest who was attacked by the demon in Albuquerque was searching for the chosen one", I added. "The 'Dark Ones' are seeking God's messenger so they can eliminate him", Brian continued. "They've been sent to all corners of the world in significant numbers to infiltrate our governments, our religions and our industry. We believe they plan to bring about the end of the world, the problem is, we don't know how. It could be nuclear war or disease. Although I might rule out nuclear war as its too visible and we have good controls of the isotopes, there's poor insight into international research laboratories. I would bet my house on the pathogen route".

Brian's story was corroborated by the account from the priest in Albuquerque, but his story was much more disturbing. He continued, "The Holy Father has pulled in all his favours to build an army, he's spent much of the Vatican's financial reserves to recruit soldiers and put measures in place to prepare for the protection of the chosen one when he is found. He's secretly leveraged the help of friends and senior leaders who support the Catholic church globally. I'm part of a special unit of the

Swiss Guard whose sole purpose is to combat the Dark Ones. I'm hunting demons alongside cells in other countries. We are a tight network of operatives spread thinly, but we are outgunned. We're investigating the intended genocide and aim to stop it before it happens". "So, you're a goddamned vampire hunter then?" I chuckled; "How can you be expected to find and kill these creatures, when the US cell comprises of only you? They are hunting you as you pursue them presumably?" I pondered. "With great difficulty", he replied, "our organisation takes all the help we can muster".

My curiosity finally overcome me, "How did you find me?" Brian smiled, "It wasn't easy with all your disguises and name changes. I was activated when you saved the priest, my organisation instructed me to find you, due to the sensitivity of recent events. If the public knew of the Dark Ones and their plans, it would lead to widespread panic. At Albuquerque, Father Gordon planted a tracking device in your bag, which I used to find your precise location once I was in sufficient proximity. It was your car that gave you away, we followed your registration plate using ANPR at traffic lights, intersections or via cameras on government vehicles. The CIA have helped us, as you can see". "But how did you link the car to me?" I pursued. "You are ex Special Forces, the second you entered the US you were tracked, but only with a light touch. We knew you'd bought the car when you registered it, and we noted you'd modified it. When the priest tagged you, we linked your movements to the car. When you changed the plates, we reassociated the vehicle in the same way".

Suddenly, I became worried by the sheer effort and investment expended simply to locate me, I needed to know why. Brian sat up straight in his seat as the pie arrived, it looked delicious. I found I couldn't eat a bite; I was unusually tense. I drank more coffee as he continued. "I guess you're wondering why we've gone to all this trouble?" I nodded affirmatively.

"Let's look at your recent activities for a moment. You've spent the last two months wandering round the USA, selecting people carefully and killing them with tell-tale emotional cooling off periods in-between. Even though you have been saving people, the FBI have still been forced to classify you as a serial killer". I gasped; hearing it put so plainly wasn't something I welcomed.

"You've also killed seven people in the UK and two in Europe before you took your joy ride down Route 66. Then there are those you eliminated before you joined the armed forces. You took this holiday to create some space between you and Interpol I suspect. Don't worry, I've pieced my dossier together with the FBI's assistance, but they're not progressing your case at this stage. My superiors coerced them to leave the investigation to me". I replied, somewhat flustered, "I'm not a serial killer, I never…". I halted mid-sentence as Brian held up his hand to stop my train of thought, "The key difference between you and Ted Bundy, is that you select and kill extremely dangerous, evil sociopaths. The FBI profilers were extremely interested in you, as there are so few female serial killers. I, however, see a double negative here". I stammered "What?" Brian continued, "The enemy of my enemy is my friend". He must have seen the bewildered expression on my face, and continued his explanation, "It's possible that a killer of killers is doing good, not evil. Given the number of Dark Ones I've eliminated in the last year, I hope I will be judged in the same light.

"We are the same, you and I, we only hurt people who hurt others. My problem originated when you encountered the Dark Ones; I either had to silence you or recruit you. Observing your skills first-hand and having witnessed your exemplary army record, I vastly prefer the latter. Would you consider joining us in our fight against the Dark One?" I stopped to think about my options, but Brian didn't give me much time, another thought was uppermost in his mind, "I've a nagging question, if you don't mind". "And that is?" I replied, still feeling like I was heading into dangerous waters. "Was it you who eliminated the O'Shaughnessy family in your last year of high school in Glasgow?"

III. Apocalypse or Genesis?

"I came to the conclusion long ago that all religions were true and that also that all had some error in them, and while I hold by my own religion, I should hold other religions as dear as Hinduism. So we can only pray, if we were Hindus, not that a Christian should become a Hindu; but our innermost prayer should be that a Hindu should become a better Hindu, a Muslim a better Muslim, and a Christian a better Christian."
Mahatma Gandhi

1. I am Aleph and Tav

Bridget coped well, considering the enormous shock she had been subjected to. She was a pragmatist, and was keen to get on with things, activity distracted her. She enjoyed her allocated job, in the science lab at a local Catholic school, especially the interaction with the students and teachers. Many were keen to practice their English with her and proved tolerant of her poor Italian. Her language skills had improved a little, but it would take years of immersion into the culture to gain an adequate level of mastery. She found little time for worry during the busy days, but at night she feared for her boys. She hadn't seen James for months; he had reappeared briefly and left. It filled her with pride to see his transformation.

On bad days, Bridget became anxious about James and me, she didn't like the sound of the evil pursuing us. How could anyone survive in the face of such terror? It was hard to be unfazed when she'd previously lived such a happy ordinary life, only to be shown a darker and monstrous side of the world we didn't know existed. Her thoughts were filled with supernatural fears, she sought to understand more to help her deal with the overwhelming dread. After numerous sleepless nights, she decided to be proactive, the only way to manage her fear was through knowledge.

Bridget's first objective was to determine where she could acquire knowledge about the Dark Ones. It wasn't the kind of subject you could simply research in a library; the internet was littered with obtuse junk and nonsense. She struggled to find answers until she realised the church retained exorcists with real hands-on experience. Who better to understand evil than those actively combatting it? She felt the Dark Ones couldn't be included in passing conversation, she decided to be circumspect when she approached the priests. They wouldn't offer such knowledge lightly; she used an open question to introduce the subject and let the conversation unfold. Bridget approached one of the younger, friendlier looking priests to gently probe him on the matter. The priest explained that the church wouldn't expose him to such evil until he became more experienced. He suggested she should talk to Father Enzo, who was wiser and had gained hands-on knowledge of such subjects.

The young priest ushered Bridget to a quiet corner of the church gardens, near to the museums. She could see the beauty of the squared Roman lines framing the Sistine Chapel. An older cleric sat on a stone bench; he wore a small cap keeping white fluffy hair under a modicum of control. His bushy beard and little round glasses were a cliché, but he wore his cassock informally, giving him a slightly laid-back demeanour. He looked up as the younger priest approached and grinned.

The older cleric must have vaguely recognised Bridget as he elected to speak in English. "Things are looking up my friend, you are introducing me to a beautiful lady. The last time we spoke you brought me your terrible homemade pasta full of floury lumps". He smiled warmly as the young priest and Bridget sat beside him. "Father Enzo, this is Bridget. She's Father Giuseppe's wife". Enzo's ears pricked up a little; Father Giuseppe was big news around the gossip mill. "His wife you say. So not only was a non-believer ordained by the Pope in five minutes, without any knowledge of the scripture, but he's also allowed a wife? I need to speak to the Holy Father; I find the situation quite unbearable. It is a cruel penance even to look upon her pretty face, please guide her away from me".

Bridget became a little upset; how could this man be so damnably rude. Father Enzo suddenly beamed with delight, "I'm joking with you Bridget, I'm sorry I didn't mean to upset you. Please take no notice of my childish humour, it's all I have these days. We all understand Father Giuseppe's position, he's in our hearts and many of us wish to lighten his load. His journey with our Lord has only just begun, whereas mine has nearly run its course". The younger priest grinned, "Yes, he always likes to bring me down a peg or two, he must be sitting on a thistle". "A thistle he says!" blustered Enzo and laughed rather too loudly.

"Now, how can I help you, young lady?" Father Enzo asked sincerely, his eyes brimming with curiosity. Bridget explained she needed some help understanding the threat to her husband. She wanted to comprehend everything from the appearance of skin markings, to being swept away to Rome; it was all so confusing for her. Then there was the matter of the 'Dark Ones'. "Hush! Don't invoke those words in the open, you don't know the terrors you will bring upon us", he whispered carefully. "You seek more knowledge about our current threat, I understand that much. We cannot talk about such things here, there are ears everywhere. I'll collect a few things from my study and meet you shortly". Father Enzo rose and scuttled into one of the museums, returning a few minutes later with a couple of folders and a well-thumbed bible. The young priest nodded and made his way back. "Thank you for your kindness and help Father. Sorry, I didn't catch your name", asked Bridget genially. "It was a great pleasure Bridget", he replied, "My name is Father Alfredo... like the sauce", he winked and was gone.

Father Enzo took Bridget into the rear of the Sistine Chapel; they occupied an old study which was used for quiet discussions or for times when priests needed tranquillity. "I feel safer here, it is Holy ground, long blessed", whispered the priest. Father Enzo explained, "In latter years, I have become the Vatican's leading expert on matters Satanic and numerous forms of the human worship of evil. I am one of the few remaining exorcists in the church". He began to explain the Vatican's knowledge of the 'Dark One' and his followers.

"It's quite a strange case", he began after a long pause to organise his thoughts. "Legends of Satan have been around for millennia, from the Greek legends of Pan through to the Gods of a myriad of religions in old Mesopotamia. For example, the Sumerians understood the concept of an evil god long before modern religions existed, they go way back to 5300-1940 BC. All religions have a concept of Satan, whether you are Moslem, Jewish or Christian". "So is the one they call the Dark One actually another name for Satan?" queried Bridget. "It's not clear, but please let me continue with the basics, before we go into more detail".

"It was probably only a few decades ago when the Dark Ones resurfaced. Their organisation is relatively recent, compared to the ancient legends and writings we have been discussing. There is no historical or anecdotal evidence they existed in their current form prior to this century. They've been inactive until quite recently, when the premonitions of Armageddon started to appear. I need to be pedantic with my definitions here, Armageddon is the battle for the end of the world. There's a clear implication of good and evil armies in combat. Many of my brothers talk about an Apocalypse, but this isn't correct. I don't believe Armageddon will result in the end of the world, based on the prophecies. The Dark One indicates the world will be purged of man, to allow 'the Elders' to return to Earth. It's not clear who these Elders are, they aren't mentioned in any religion I am aware of".

Bridget sat quietly, listening. "The church hasn't recovered much of the Dark One's doctrine, it's kept secret. However, I have limited information", he smiled naughtily. He showed Bridget an ancient parchment he kept in a vacuum sealed pouch. He laid it gently on the table. It was a fragment of a larger manuscript. "This was found in an ancient tomb in Iraq by an anthropologist and scientist named Columbine". Bridget's ears pricked up.

A Doctrine of Fear - Paul JC Edge

Enzo handed Bridget a page with pencil annotation:

Long I have crafted, the beginning and the end
Apocalyptic plague, your souls to rend
Archetypal madness will lead ?you? to my forge
Discarded children, graveless, rotten and gorged
Seek me in Gehenna at the end of days
We'll meet in Gehenna where children blaze

I am Aleph and Tav, the beginning and the end
The oldest religion, your soul's fires tend
The Anti-Religion from which births the scourge
I am the Dark One, Moloch; I am Shaytan; The Purge

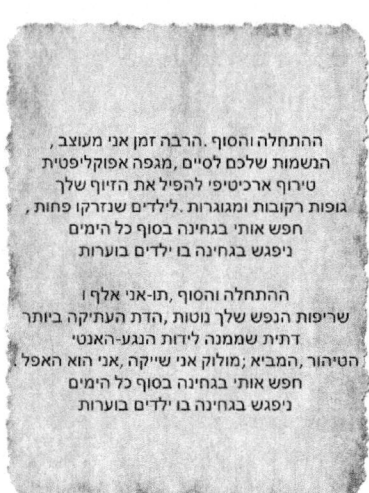

"I enlisted a couple of colleagues to translate the Hebrew manuscript into a dozen languages, but English is by far the most interesting. You see, this fragment is quite a mix of messages which seem unrelated, it's all rather confusing. The script threatens the end of days. It cites Aleph and Tav, the first and last letters in the Hebrew alphabet. Normally a script of this kind wouldn't need to enumerate the significance of beginning and end to a Hebrew reader. It mentions the 'oldest religion' implying Satanism in its ancient forms, but it doesn't include a specific branch. It mixes up doctrine across religions, as an example, the Moslem word in the Qur'an for Satan is Shaytan or Shaitan".

"The text also mentions Moloch, a Canaanite deity, who in the Bible is associated with the death of children. This relates to the concept of Gehenna, a valley where the kings of Judah sacrificed their children by burning them. Gehenna is commonly regarded as the abode of the damned in the afterlife. The valley, now called Hinnom in modern Israel, was regarded as accursed and is left untouched to this day.

The document is a mix up of different doctrines. The most unusual aspect is the Hebrew used is a more modern form than would have been used when the scroll was allegedly written. It's closer to the language used in modern Israel. The classic differences were quite obvious to someone who had studied the ancient writings, Columbine spotted the inconsistencies immediately. The grammar, phonology and vocabulary between ancient and modern Hebrew are subtly different. For example, a sentence always began with a verb in the ancient texts whereas in modern Hebrew, a sentence starts with a subject followed by a verb and the object".

Bridget pondered for a moment. "So why is the document script written in modern Hebrew when clearly, it's ancient? Surely, it should be written in the old hand. It makes no sense. It's like a translation, but the physical document seems to pre-date the text written on it, it doesn't add up. It must be a fake, surely". "Yes indeed", responded Father Enzo with a warm smile, "you're really a quick learner". He continued his line of thought, "In addition, why does the rhyme in the verse appear in the English translation but not in the Hebrew version?" Father Enzo gave Bridget time to think, like all good influencers he encouraged Bridget to draw her own conclusions. "Because it was written in English in the first place and was then translated into Hebrew". Bridget continued, "This isn't ancient text at all; it's been fabricated and translated into Hebrew to get the attention of the Vatican. It's written to create fear and despair in the church". "Brava", praised the Father, "Something the devil has sought since the beginning of time".

Enzo reviewed his thoughts, "We need to establish why someone would go to all this trouble. The fabrication itself is amazing, but the content is, well, a little amateurish. We can surmise it's related to the Holy Father's visions of Armageddon. It was probably a threat to desist preparations, which of course the Pope ignored".

Enzo explained he felt the document was trying to build on Satanic works of ancient cultures, such as the infamous Red and Black scrolls. It was then translated into Hebrew, yet the age of the parchment was authentic. The Vatican had carbon dated the parchment roughly to time of Christ. It was a most confusing conundrum. "When Columbine found the document, he suspected the tomb had been penetrated but he couldn't find any evidence", commented Bridget. "You have been doing your homework", remarked Father Enzo clearly impressed. "Where is Gehenna, the place where the Dark One claims to be waiting?" Bridget wondered aloud. "The Valley of Hinnom, it is south of the city walls of Jerusalem", he explained.

Enzo returned to the matter in hand, "Over the years, there have been several messages delivered to the Holy Father via various nefarious means. This one was on a similar parchment which came from a museum curator in Jordan", he explained as he handed Bridget another pouch. "This parchment is also in Hebrew, I'm not sure if it's addressing the Pope. Roughly translated it says 'I make an unholy vow: I will find you white one. I will locate your seven and destroy them. I will feast on the souls of all who aided you. There'll be no mercy for you or yours'. Very melodramatic, isn't it?"

We also received a parchment from a leading anthropologist at London's Museum of Natural History, which contained the simple phrase, repeated ad nauseum: 'Earth will be ours once again. I am legion'. The messages are not addressing the Pope or our church, so we can't see why anyone would send them. Perhaps the author foresaw that you and Joe would play a role in the defence of mankind and aimed to make you despair". "Well, that worked quite well then", replied Bridget sarcastically, "what on Earth does he want with us?" "A story yet to unfold", Enzo replied vaguely.

Bridget indicated the word 'Seven' on the parchment. "Joe's stigmata stated 'One of Seven'. It's the only phrase which didn't originate in the Bible". Enzo replied "It's most curious, it again leads us to the idea that the occurrences are linked. Also, the reference to the 'white one' in the manuscript is unusual, it doesn't seem refer to the Holy Father. However, the Pope talked about God appearing to him as a white figure. It implies the church is being used as a messenger. As I said, extraordinarily little of the text in the parchments makes sense. We're missing a key piece of the puzzle, and we need to find it quickly. We know the Dark One is planning to start Armageddon and he's doing it in the name of Satan. Your husband seems to be an important piece in the chess game, to the point where the Holy Father is fast approaching bankruptcy of the church to protect him. There are many more questions than answers, I'm afraid".

"So, who or what are the Dark Ones? They attacked before the Swiss Guard took us to a safe house. It was sheer luck we prevailed", Bridget persisted. Enzo looked troubled, "There's no luck at play in this game, I suspect. The role of the Dark Ones is also confusing. The animal part of my brain believes they're demons sent by Satan, but the logical half of my brain thinks they're the brainwashed servants of a cult, who are planning a terrorist attack to destroy the human race. The role of the Dark Ones seems malign, we must take the threat seriously". Bridget continued to feel confused, "So why do they burst into flame when they're hurt? There's nothing on Earth which can render a corpse to ash in a split second". "Also, how can a demon be killed by an ordinary bullet, a tool of man?" added the Father. Bridget continued, "Joe said the Holy Father foresaw the end of days when they spoke. Is it really possible?" Enzo replied carefully, "Anything's possible, many claim to speak to the Lord. We've all doubted the authenticity of the 'white one' in the Holy Father's dreams, but I know the Pope is not the type to have flights of fancy. He's a pragmatist, he would deeply contemplate a vision before acting upon it.

"Looking holistically, the manuscript is the work of someone trying to appear evil in order to rule a cult through fear and ignorance", summarised Bridget. "I couldn't have put it better myself", replied the Father, "I can only conclude this document was written by the hand of man, not a by fallen angel". They sat contemplating for a while, but few insights were added to the discussion. "But why would he do this?" whispered Bridget to the vaulted ceiling. Father Enzo insisted on reciting a short prayer to ward off evil following their discussion. Bridget was happy to stay involved, despite her views; these were dark times. Bridget thanked Father Enzo for his help warmly. It had helped her to understand, but the picture was by no means clear. They continued to meet again from time to time and became firm friends. There was little movement in their shared understanding; true insight would only come with experience which was upstream in the rapids of their turbulent lives.

2. The Enemy of my Enemy (JeT)

From the writings of Jennifer Travers

I started at the beginning, "The O'Shaughnessy's were a particularly dangerous Irish family who lived close to my home in Easterhouse, a less desirable suburb of Glasgow. My mum and dad were forced to stay there for a while during my last year of school, when my father lost his job, and we were left virtually penniless. Seamus O'Shaughnessy was extremely violent, but Ma was by far the most terrible and hateful of the clan. The family were mostly into drug peddling, extortion, and robbery; but were always happy to hurt people, just for entertainment.

"My Mother and I had the misfortune of bumping into Ma in the Outpatients at Glasgow Royal Infirmary. Her family had been bullying and stealing from my parents for six months. Outside the hospital, Ma punched mum in the face, demanding the contents of her purse to pay for her taxi fare home. The hospital staff didn't utter a single word, but it was the last straw for me. The O'Shaughnessy's had led many of our family and friends to poverty or put them in hospital and I simply couldn't take any more. They were a bad family who needed sorting out, even the police seemed to avoid them, but they had probably threatened their families too. I was young and weak, what could I possibly do?"

Brian asked the question once more in a patient tone, "That's all very interesting, but did you kill them?" The question hung in the air for a few minutes as I pondered. The simple fact Brian had linked me to the O'Shaughnessy's left me in a difficult position. I felt like I was stood on top of a cliff looking down, about to leap to my death. Brian already knew enough to have me locked away for a lifetime, so I decided that honesty was the best policy. I wasn't prepared to hurt Brian, he'd done nothing wrong. The atrocities committed by the family were no surprise to him. It felt like a confessional as I explained how I 'd taken down the Easterhouse Mafia, all on my own, at the tender age of sixteen.

"I watched the O'Shaughnessy's under cover for a few weeks using my dad's old binoculars. I observed from the littered scrubland bordering their semi-detached post-war prefabricated house. I decided to take down the brothers at 11pm on their usual round to the off license for whisky and cigs. The routine was predictable, Seamus waited in the car with the window half down smoking, as Conor went into the shop. On average, one in three nights Conor disappeared behind the shop to take a piss. I decided that Conor's comfort break would be the trigger for my plans.

"I nonchalantly walked behind the off license, away from the prying eyes of his brother; Conor smiled as I looked down at his member with mock surprise. He would never expect a young girl to attack him. He was confident, he was, after all, the only monster on his patch. I hit him hard on his left kneecap with a cling film wrapped claw hammer as he looked down to brazenly finish his pee. He didn't see it coming, he clearly had other plans for me. Conor screamed in pain, moving around in an agitated manner. I pushed him into the wall to steady him as I injected one of my pre-prepared syringes of Mr Muscle drain cleaner into his neck. The viscous fluid had been diluted with bleach to make it flow through the needle smoothly. My toxic concoction would finish him quickly, I was certain of that.

A Doctrine of Fear - Paul JC Edge

"My attentions then turned to his brother, Seamus. I picked up my Costa coffee cup from beside the off-license wall and walked over to him. He looked vaguely concerned by the short-lived scream, but not so much that he'd bothered to exit the car. Cries of pain were normal to their evil family; they were in the business of hurting people. I walked towards the car pretending to take a drink from the cup, whilst casually removing the lid. When I reached the driver's side of the car, I pointed to the off license with a guarded look of concern. Seamus angrily rolled down the window, so I could speak to him.

"My coffee cup was full to the brim with lighter fuel. I threw the contents into Seamus' face and quickly ignited it with a stick lighter. The heat was more intense than I expected, the car went up quickly with a whoosh. I injected drain cleaner into Seamus' neck with my second syringe, using an oven glove, he writhed in a rhapsody of pain. I threw both syringes, the cling film from the hammer and the glove into the inferno and left. I couldn't take any chances with such gangsters; they were the worst kind of scum and would seek revenge relentlessly. There was no hiding from them, they were merciless and brutal. It would take hours for the cops to identify the charred vehicle and its occupants.

"During the attack, I burned my wrist quite nastily, but I didn't feel any pain at the time due to the adrenaline surge. I still have the scar, though I partly hid it with a tattoo". I held up my hand for Brian to see, as I continued. "I walked round to their house, which was several blocks away, and waited until I was sure the occupants were all asleep. I could see the glow from the car fire in the sky and I heard the fire engines and police arrive and leave. I was safe enough; I couldn't be seen in the cover of the scrubland. The noise wasn't enough to rouse the family. To be honest, in hindsight I took a terrible risk, someone walking past the car could alert the O'Shaughnessy's and ruin my plan. One by one the house lights went off, by 1am the house was quiet. At 3am I gathered my equipment. It was the magic hour when the SAS preferred to mount an attack to confuse their enemy, according to Bear Grills' biography. I was already committed to continue following the attack on the brothers, I needed to complete my mission, or my entire family would be in grave danger.

"I donned a fresh pair of latex gloves and threw poisoned meat over the fence into the O'Shaughnessy's barbed wire compound and waited patiently. The dogs growled and jostled each other as they fought for the best share of meat. Within ten minutes, after whimpering and vomiting, all was quiet. I really didn't like hurting the dogs, but they were trained killers and part of the family in my mind. I used a jemmy to remove a few of the slats from the fence and large wire cutters to take a section from the wire fencing behind it. I don't know why my dad kept tools in the garage, he rarely soiled his hands with construction work. The tools proved most useful, but it was hard work; I wasn't so strong in those days. The wire cutter's long handles gave me leverage and I eventually snipped through the fencing.

"My preparations had taken more than a week; I used my skateboard to move the heavy propane cylinder to the hedgerows near the house. I disguised the cylinder to look like a damaged empty bottle, using old paint. I also scuffed it with emery cloth and a chisel. I had syphoned kerosene from my father's garage heater for months and stored it in coke bottles under the shed. It was easier for me to put the empty 3-gallon drum in the hedge and fill it a couple of bottles at a time. The weight of the gas cylinder pushed me to my limits, I was exhausted.

"I used the last of my strength to push the heavy cylinder and the three gallons of kerosene through the gap in the fence and then entered the compound carefully. I was terrified I had made too much noise. I hefted the kerosene up onto the porch lintel and secured it, pushing the pipe through the letterbox and allowing it to bleed slowly using gravity. I fed the propane gas pipe through as well and fully opened the regulator valve, leaving it for a few minutes to empty its deadly contents into the house. I squirted more kerosene around the door and inserted a soaked cloth halfway through the aperture. I left a trail of lighter fuel back to the hole in the fence so I could light it from a safe distance. Everything incriminating, including my latex gloves, were left next to the door covered in kerosene, so they would be incinerated in the blaze.

"I climbed through the fence and lit the place up using my stick lighter. The whole house exploded into flame. I ran home fast, carrying my dad's jemmy and wire cutters under my jacket, my heart felt like it would explode out of my chest. I left nothing traceable behind. The house burned ferociously until the fire brigade attended and extinguished the fire, there were no survivors. The emergency services had a busy night, I could see the glare in the sky from my bedroom window. Dad and mum were fast asleep after their usual weed and cheap vodka binge, so I had no worries about them waking. They would be certain I was in the house all night, if I needed an alibi.

"At breakfast, mum and dad told me the story with relish, they had heard on the radio someone had sorted out that evil family at last, and how they felt they deserved it. Apparently, we didn't need to fear them anymore.

"The police hung around for a few days, they assumed the violence was gang related and didn't pursue the matter further. There was extensive news coverage, a few of the interviewed neighbours actually had the gall to claim the O'Shaughnessy's were a good, Catholic family. Ma and three of the clan were killed in the house that night and good riddance. The fire was so ferocious, it also damaged neighbouring properties.

"Sadly, an eight-month-old boy was also killed, I deeply regret that, I'd no idea he was in the house. I've lost many nights sleep battling with my guilt over the child; he was the innocent victim of my actions. On the positive side, the neighbourhood became much safer for a few years until the next family of gangsters moved in on the territory. We moved back to the Highlands the following year and I started my army training as soon as I finished school". "Jesus" breathed Brian gently, "and you were just sweet sixteen. Remind me never to upset you".

Brian looked into my eyes and smiled, the offloading of my actions that night was somewhat therapeutic, it helped me. I must say, I found it a little odd that Brian was still smiling though; it was a heart-breaking story. "Wow. Okay. I completely understand the horrors of the O'Shaughnessy family. Seamus murdered my younger brother in a row about a measly few hundred pounds he didn't owe him. He beat him to death with a piece of three by two timber. I'm more than happy you put him in the ground, I simply wish I'd had the courage to do it myself. My family was also forced to move to Easterhouse at roughly the same time, but we didn't return to the Highlands afterwards. You showed guts and ingenuity at such a young age, the consequences of any failure in your plan don't bear thinking about".

Brian quickly got to the point, "I only realised a few weeks ago it might be you who took them down, I put two and two together after tracking your movements. I sincerely thank you for your actions that night. It partly sparked me into dreaming up the idea of recruiting you into the Guard, we really need tough soldiers like you. Tough, ingenious vets who have a strong moral compass but aren't afraid to act, regardless of the word of the law".

"You can't possibly recruit me into the Swiss Guard, I'm a woman", I pointed out. I admit the thought of becoming a member of a tactical unit sounded appealing, rather than doing time in prison or facing an impending execution. I felt in real danger, and Brian's plan might help me fend off my demons (in both senses). He took his explanation a little further, "It's a special arm of the Guard, it has none of the usual constraints. There are already women in our unit, they're all very capable, believe me. You'd be in great company, what do you say, Sergeant Travers?" I thought about Brian's offer as I finally tucked into my cold pecan pie. I really had no choice and at least I'd get a chance to take the war to another evil gang. I took great pleasure in slaughtering wicked people, so it was the perfect role for me.

I got down to business without delay, why waste time? "Ok I'm in, but I'll need weaponry PDQ if these things are after us. I'd prefer a couple of Ka-Bar knives with boot sheaths, a pair of

A Doctrine of Fear - Paul JC Edge

Heckler and Koch 9mm compact tactical autos with modified handgrips if you really want me to function at my best". "They're in the trunk waiting for you, I've studied your MO remember", Brian beamed a rather infectious smile.

"I'd advise you to learn to use these babies". Brian placed a star shaped piece of metal on the table. "A serious puncture will set the demons aflame; these are quiet and very deadly, invaluable when you're in public areas". I picked up the wicked looking ninja star, it was incredibly sharp and had good balance. "I haven't seen a shuriken for a long time and certainly not one this well made", I observed, "I've no skill with these suckers". The captain dropped a belt clip on the table which held six of the stars in a magazine. "Press this button to eject one into the palm of your hand but keep your fingers to the sides of the caddy, or you'll lose them", he explained. "Wow. That's really cool, good suggestion about the practice. I could also do with two caddies, I'm ambidextrous as you will already know", I stated plainly. "Of course, no time like the present for training", he added rising to his feet. I found they were much easier to throw accurately than a knife, I took to them like a duck out of water. The risky part was keeping my fingers when I handled the magazine.

We spent four days on an intense training programme, mainly in the woods. Brian was very fit and able, but he was clearly not special forces trained, he lacked a certain finesse. In the end it became less clear who was training who, but we both valued the experience. Brian's strategic skills were astounding, he considered all angles at great speed. In one of our breaks, he expanded on his theory that the demons were planning to build a pathogen. He explained he'd managed to track several senior figures in major pharmaceutical companies who were highly likely to be followers of the 'Dark One'. Some were corrupt and had been influenced, but others were selected and coerced or even brainwashed by the cult. His plan to engage pharmaceutical leaders lacked certainty, how could we be assured our targets were actually demons before we engaged them.

"Why don't we stab them and see if they burst into flames?" I suggested wryly. Brian pondered, "You know what, it could work. If we gave them a small puncture wound with a bradawl, they should flame. We could test it on a known cult member; if it works, we then target each of the suspects", he winked wickedly. I added, "We won't know until we try it". Brian's superiors gave the plan the thumbs up. That evening, we took Brian's black Crown Vic on a long haul to Philadelphia to meet his handler face to face. It was a gruelling thirty-hour drive, we took turns driving to stay sharp. We needed to be prepared for anything on these long, lonely highways.

We checked into the Delaware Doubletree hotel on route 202. We ate at the Lone Star steak house across the road, crunching our way across the peanut shell littered floor, before returning to the hotel. Early the next morning, Brian left to continue the journey to his meeting solo, I sat tight for 48 hours. Brian explained I should stay in the vicinity of the hotel, but there was the Concorde Mall next door where I could pick up a change of clothes and get my hair trimmed. Clearly, he felt my punky look was inappropriate for a newly recruited Swiss Guard, my close crop was a poor cut.

I hadn't received formal paperwork about my new role; I suspected I never would. My work was 'unofficial', as Brian so tactfully put it. I spent an uneventful day shopping, I retired early. The next day, I challenged myself to an extensive 6-hour workout in the mediocre hotel gym. Workouts were becoming problematic as they had been fragmented recently. The gym was small and rather ripe, but it did the job.

On the second evening, I took a taxi to Friendly Franks, a nearby diner reputed for the best prime rib steak in the area. I was full to the brim when I left the diner, I'd eaten too much. The girl on checkout finished her shift as I paid for my meal, so I followed her out, at the front door I changed my mind and decided to use the toilet.

In the car park, I was shocked to see a man pinning the waitress down by her hair and forcing her to have sex on the bonnet of his pickup in full view of the diner. The man moved his grip to her throat to stifle her scream, turning her a worrying shade of purple. I shouted to the guy to let go, he reluctantly turned to face me as he hitched up his trousers. The man smiled creepily as he looked me up and down. The attacker was dressed like a hillbilly and seemed out of place in Delaware. He shouted filthy abuse at me as he lunged forward with a knife.

I swayed to the left as he thrust his knife at me. I calmy informed him, "That's not a friendly way to greet a girl", as I took his arm at the wrist and hit his elbow joint with the palm of my hand. The hillbilly screamed, "You broke my fuckin' arm, you shit". His words were cut short as I headbutted him on the bridge of his nose. He staggered backwards and pulled a small snub nose revolver from his jacket pocket. He raised it to shoot me, in full view of the restaurant. Some folks just didn't care or worry about the consequences of their actions. I closed the distance between us in a heartbeat and punched him in the throat, I pulled the Ka-Bar knife from my boot using my left hand. I stabbed him in the neck severing his carotid artery, it was fast becoming my signature move.

As I stood on the hot asphalt, my black lace up boots became partly immersed in a pool of arterial blood, the piercing sirens of police cars headed my way. The red and blue lights reflected off the buildings across the street, a vivid parody of the crime before me. I looked down at the mangled form of the hillbilly, lay next to the open door of his red Chevy pickup truck. The truck sported a "Good Ol' Boy" sticker along the windscreen. He was neither, a thirty something man who was quite evil in thought and deed. I glanced at the confused waitress, staring at me with a mix of horror and relief on her face. The blood trickled down her face where the miscreant had rammed her into the hood of his truck.

No one from 'Friendly Franks' felt brave enough to stand up to the toothless wonder and protect the waitress. I'd really fucked up this time, the cops were about to arrive, I was covered in blood and the onlookers had a perfect description of me. It wasn't looking good; my nerves were fried. I couldn't keep taking risks, something in my life needed to change. I mouthed 'you haven't seen me' to the waitress as I ran towards the highway. A familiar black sedan careered into the car park, tyres squealing. Now that was excellent timing, Brian had been keeping an eye on me again. Thank goodness I had forgotten to ditch the tracker he'd hidden in my jacket.

"Get in the car", yelled Brian angrily. I yanked open the door and dropped into the passenger seat, smearing the blood from my shoes onto the upholstery. "Shit", he exclaimed, "what the hell are you doing! That'll stain the car. Can't I leave for a second without you killing someone?" I attempted to reply but he cut me off. "I'm trying to give you a second chance here and you've just spat in my face. We're supposed to be lying low and inconspicuous, and you bring the state police on top of us. This is plain stupid!" I shouted back, "The bastard was raping the poor woman on his truck bonnet, and the diners just sat back to enjoy the show. I couldn't let it happen!" Brian replied, more gently. "You've got to understand, this is especially important. Yes, you saved her. Yes, it was a noble act. I may have done the same thing, but not when I'm on a delicate mission. You saved one woman; I'm trying to save everyone on the planet. I have to know you're with me and it won't happen ever again".

I sighed and took a moment to calm myself before I replied. "So, I should just walk away and let a girl get hurt?" Brian replied almost reluctantly, "We must, we'll have no chance if we don't keep our focus. Remember the demons, the ones who are trying to kill everyone. We need to stop them, and we need to stay out of a police cell to be able do that. Anyway, it's called a hood". "What?" I retorted. "We're in the US. it's not a bonnet, here it's called a hood". I looked at him feeling confused but saw the twinkle in his eye. I couldn't hold my laughter, the more I tried the more difficult it became. Brian stopped the car whilst we controlled ourselves. How could he make a joke in the middle of giving me a roasting? As God is my witness, I loved this man. I knew I always would.

We drove silently for 40 minutes, which gave me time to think. Our first stop was the King of Prussia Mall for essentials, I bought a mousy brown curly wig and a pair of small round glasses with clear lenses. I changed into some slacks and a Gant sweatshirt.

Brian was pleased, he thought I looked completely different. "Those boots will give you away one day", he grinned. "They're like new, now I've wiped all the blood onto your carpet", I said attempting gentle levity. I had to be a little careful, the atmosphere was delicate.

We headed to Whitehouse Station in Hunterdon, County New Jersey, home of the pharmaceutical giant Merck's headquarters. We proceeded down highway 22 and drove past the slip road which led to reception. After scoping the place out, we turned around at the next interchange and headed back towards Bridgewater. We turned right onto the 202 stopping at the Sunset Motel, near Branchburg Park. Brian checked into a twin room and parked the car outside.

The intel dossier documented that Mark Von Pimm, the Chief Operating Officer at Merck, owned a substantial house in the vicinity and frequented the nearby park with his collie most evenings. Sources indicated that he was in the office this week, so our chances of encountering him were high. Brian felt I was best suited for the assignment; he thought I was less likely to be seen as an attacker to the casual eye. The irony was delicious. He handed me a small object similar to a bradawl; a carbon steel handgrip with a very sharp titanium nail jutting out. Brian explained the obvious, "Hold the handle in your fist allowing the nail or spike to protrude between your third and fourth fingers. When you are ready, deliver a semi contact punch, and the nail will do sufficient damage to cause the combustion".

I turned the weapon over in my hand. "Are you sure this'll do the job? It's hardly going to administer a killing wound, is it?" "That's precisely the point, if Mark isn't a Dark One then it'll give him a sharp pain but not inflict too much damage. You can apologise and walk away". "But is it enough to make a demon combust?" I replied. "I'm not really sure, let's see. We are on untrodden ground here". "What if Mark is actually a demon and I hurt him but not enough?" I queried. "Then we'll have a fight on our hands, I guess", he offered with a smile. I thought to myself, I'll have the fight, you'll be sat here in the car drinking coffee.

On the first evening, Mark was a no show. We'd studied his picture, driven past his home, and finalised our research. "He'll be watching the Great British Bake Off, I suspect", laughed Brian. "No, if he's a demon, he won't have access to UK TV. He'll be watching Gilligan's Island reruns on HBC", I countered. We laughed until I unconsciously put my hand on Brian's arm as we giggled. We looked at each other seriously for a moment, before I knew it, we were kissing. I forgot where I was for a moment, we soon suppressed our feelings, we had a serious mission to execute.

3. The Healing of My Faith

We headed over the Pyrenees and into northern Spain, the views were splendid, although some of the hairpin bends were extreme. We stopped in a tiny village called Formigal and checked into a small hotel. Over dinner, Jane posed the obvious question I'd been awaiting with some trepidation, "So Joe, how did you know the Dark Ones were coming?" I explained to the best of my ability, given my lack of understanding of the skin writings. Jane rationally concluded that God had spoken to me through the writings. I hadn't really thought of the writings in that way, I had a strong feeling there must be a more logical explanation.

James looked increasingly troubled. He was keen to work out how the Dark Ones had located us in the first place. We'd been really careful to cover our tracks, so we couldn't build a credible theory. We avoided using credit cards, everything was paid for in cash; we hadn't made telephone calls, and we hadn't accessed the web. It made no sense unless someone had fitted a tracker in our clothing or on our bikes. The latter would be more disturbing, it would indicate an inside job. We'd stayed at La Petite-Pierre for fourteen nights and had no issues. I guess it took time for the Dark Ones to mobilise.

The following day, we searched all of our possessions thoroughly, including removing the armour from our leathers. We stripped the bikes as far as we could, only to find the GPS SIM card had already been removed. We checked the insoles and heels of our boots for suspicious cuts or remoulding. There was nothing, no trackers, no evidence of tampering. What else could the Dark Ones use to locate us? I had a sudden thought,

"Let me see the cash", I requested urgently. Jane passed me the bills in the plastic wallet from her money belt. I thumbed through the notes, the first thing I noticed was they were all brand-new unmarked bills. "There's nothing to identify them, unless they have an ultraviolet or radioactive marker". Then James spotted the most obvious connection, "But they're brand new, they have consecutive numbers".

James was quite right; my son was proving to be intelligent and resourceful. When I thumbed through the notes, they did have consecutive numbers within each denomination. We struggled to understand how they could be tracked. Shops don't scan bank notes when they are placed in the till. Notes could only be tracked at the bank when they were paid in, but the serial numbers would need to be flagged across all bank networks. It required enormous manpower to check serial numbers in every bank in Europe, unless the Dark Ones had infiltrated electronic currency counters to track all notes deposited. It would need a sophisticated computer network to capture the data. Also, they must have prior knowledge of the bank notes we were given by the Vatican.

The following morning, we moved to a nearby village and took accommodation. I stayed in the room, whilst Jane and James took shifts watching our previous hotel from a nearby hillside. In the previous hotel, we had paid for our room with cash, so we could establish if currency was the trigger alerting the Dark Ones of our location. It was midmorning when the hotel owner took a trip into town to deposit his petty cash. Within an hour, the Dark Ones arrived. They spent time in the hotel and moved around the shops and other buildings in town. They figured we were no longer present, they split up and left using the two most obvious routes out of town. We'd hid our bikes, so there were no obvious signs we'd chosen to stay nearby; it would be an illogical assumption. They'd hopefully assume we'd travel a significant distance before stopping, based on our previous behaviour.

We agreed not to stay in any location for more than two nights in future. We also exchanged a significant portion of our Euros for British Pounds Sterling at the next bank. The new currency would be in our hands before the serial numbers were spotted, by which time we'd be well out of town. The mixed notes would be impossible to track. Jane was concerned our bikes may have been identified and it would be advisable to move them on, so she tagged the switch on our ComLink device. We headed for a safe house in Madrid, where we could leave the bikes and acquire a different mode of transport. Before we hit town, we fitted suppressors to our pistols in case there was any trouble. Gunfire would attract the worst kind of attention in a city.

Madrid proved to be a terrible idea on several fronts, it was a large city. Such places have lots of eyes, we felt especially conspicuous, we probably drew more attention to ourselves by acting abnormally. We arrived on the day of the US presidential visit. There was bunting and posters, crowds lined the streets to watch the presidential procession. The traffic became chaotic, even our bikes struggled to weave around the long tapestries of cars. We parked them just off the Paseo Del Prado, Jane arranged the collection of the bikes, using the ComLink. We left our helmets locked to the bikes but retained our Bluetooth earpieces. We waited for the coordinates of the new transport in a side street café, eating tapas. We were hot in our leathers; we needed to shed our skins quickly.

As Jane drank her coffee, she identified a suspicious figure across the road. His black hoodie obscured his face; it was such a warm day; it made him conspicuous. He wore shades, but we felt certain he was staring straight at us, his head tilted slightly to one side. Something about him gave me the creeps. He spoke into headphones which disappeared into his neckline.

Jane jumped to her feet and dragged me out of my chair, much to the surprise of the other diners. She headed down an alley at speed, we stayed close behind. As the black figure entered the alley, Jane drew her Sig and fired a single shot. The man burst into bright flames; the blaze was searing to the eye even in the bright daylight. The noise from the pistol was loud even with the silencer. It drew the attention of the crowds, many were hanging around, hoping to catch a glimpse of the dignitaries.

A second figure entered the alleyway, dashing from an intersecting passageway. As we ran, Jane's voice bellowed in my headset as we neared a number of industrial dustbins, "James, take cover behind the trash cans, we'll keep their attention". James ducked behind the bins as instructed; I was short of breath but managed to continue. I heard another shot, James appeared beside us breathing more heavily. The crowds in the streets panicked, they started to move around in an unpredictable way, some ventured onto the road itself. Cars halted suddenly, drivers shouted and sounded their horns chaotically. Then, the howl of police sirens approached at speed.

A Doctrine of Fear - Paul JC Edge

As the convoy of police cars passed, we dropped to a walk in an attempt to blend in. The crowd's confusion was good cover, they moved in different directions with haste. In hindsight, we'd been lucky. Jane took us to the nearest tram station; we boarded a single hop to the next station. The tram was packed, we almost had to fight to board it, as the crowd desperately tried to leave town amid the turmoil. The ComLink informed us that the Swiss Guard were waiting with a pickup truck at a nearby gas station. The truck incorporated some unusual modifications on its flatbed.

As James drove to a safer location, Jane studied the user manual which had been left on the passenger seat. She reached into the glove compartment and pulled out a triangular remote control. "There's a full set of tacticals onboard and an array of blast drones", she exclaimed enthusiastically. "Wow", retorted James, "No expense spared for this trip. I haven't seen blast drones deployed before; I hear they're devastating". I became interested in the concept of blast drones but during the explanation I realised I'd already seen one when I was first attacked by the Dark Ones in England. The explosion and shrapnel from the drone had taken out the enemy, it almost took me out too. I rubbed my scar unconsciously, where one of the ball bearings had hit me after penetrating my car door.

Over dinner, we discussed the varying tactics of our enemy once again. I was still confused by their preference to attack with blades, they seemed to have little chance against modern weaponry. Jane explained it was a common view in the guard that it was a matter of honour. They used ceremonial daggers as they were part of a sect which coveted the blood of their enemy. Like the Zulu, a bloodied knife was a priceless artifact to them, it brought great respect. Given sufficient time and cover, they'd fully exsanguinate their victim, storing the blood in aluminium flasks. The Guard had recovered a dagger recently, they found it had unusual markings, even the Vatican's linguists couldn't interpret the language.

The Dark One's daggers featured a curved, serrated blade with twin grooves to the hilt, the recesses channelled blood into a chamber in the handle where a tube could be attached. The effectiveness of the Dark One's attacks usually depended on surprise, cunning cat and mouse chases didn't play to their strengths. This was precisely why we kept moving and travelled light. I wondered aloud, "Why don't we make use of hallowed ground, we could just sit tight in a church?" Jane thought for a moment, "That's true but they would have us cornered. It would give them time to plan, they could drive us out quite easily using fire. The Dark Ones fall back on modern weaponry when their old combat methods lead to a tactical disadvantage. It's naive to assume they would always attack with daggers". We needed to keep moving, it was a no brainer.

It was extremely exhausting, continually moving from place to place. I struggled, not being able to let Bridget know I was safe; I would have given anything to hear her voice again. I managed to exercise regularly; we ate well whenever we stopped. We practiced combat weaponry and tactics in quieter locations away from prying eyes. The practice became more difficult as I progressed. I was no soldier, but I could handle a gun and defend myself in a pinch if needed. I slept well but, on several nights my dreams would swim in and out of focus, they mainly repeated the warning that a great war was inevitable.

Travel was more comfortable in the pickup; it had four luxurious seats which we could sleep in if needed. Jane wasn't as keen on our new mode of transport; she thought the truck wouldn't be fast enough on the bends and would be problematic in the cities. However, she did see an upside, in the truck we could go off-road if necessity drove us to it. We saw little trouble for a couple of months, as we improved at avoiding the Dark One's tracking methods. Subtle changes to our appearance from time to time helped us remain anonymous, but it was hard to change the two males and one female dynamic. Jane experimented by dressing in more masculine outfits, but it made little difference to her look. Her hair was short and needed to wear utility clothing for combat. Hats worked well though, they made a significant change to our look, and they could be ditched quickly when needed. Jane opted to wear a large colourful braided straw hat, even in the car. Coupled with her oversized sunglasses, it made quite a transformation to her appearance. She looked rather glamourous until she got out of the car, her stance and body language were soldier-like. Some things you couldn't change.

After the quiet spell, we experienced trouble in El Palo, a small village near to the coast in Malaga. We dined in the fisherman's quarter; we were enjoying barbequed salted prawns and salad. As I raised my drink, a dark figure appeared on the promenade in the distance. The figure peered inland, so we assumed he hadn't seen us. Whilst we observed, another darkly dressed man entered the restaurant by the rear staff entrance. Our attentions were drawn by the man in the street, so he almost went unnoticed. We were alerted to his presence by derogatory comments from the staff, complaining about his use of the wrong entrance. But the warning came too late, the figure burst from the back of the restaurant at terrifying speed.

Jane kicked her chair backwards, drawing her Sig smoothly. James rose directly into the path of the assassin, his arms flung outward to block the attack. The Dark One's blade flashed; James was stabbed in the abdomen, pushed aside and the figure stormed towards me unrelenting.

Jane's Sig barked, the figure flamed, its knife had almost touched my chest. The dagger fell into my lap; it was so sharp that as it brushed my leg, it severed the fabric of my trousers. I quickly moved aside; the dagger dropped to the floor. I swept it under my jacket before it could be seen. Jane pivoted, her Sig barked again, a bright flame took my eye only twenty metres away. The spectres were fast. A huge commotion started in the restaurant, caused by the shots but also confusion triggered by the instantaneous combustion of the demons.

A cacophony of screams and shouts reverberated around us. I grabbed hold of James, tucking my shoulder under his arm pit; he was bleeding badly. He attempted to apply pressure to his wound as I helped him to the truck, it was parked in an adjacent side street at the rear of the restaurant. He was pale and was fading in and out of consciousness. Once in the truck, Jane sped off without hesitation, to avoid the scrutiny of the police. James was weakening fast. I placed his head in my lap in the back of the car, my hands pressing his seeping wound ineffectively. "What can I do, he's dying?" I pleaded.

Jane replied, "You need to get his bleeding under control. It's spurting, it'll be a severed artery". Jane passed a med kit over her shoulder to me. I followed her instructions as she barked them, as if she was reciting a list from memory. "A tourniquet is no use on a chest wound you idiot! You need to act fast, or the bleed will lead to volume shock. He won't last long if that happens. Cut away his clothing and wipe away the excess blood whilst maintaining pressure on the cut. Feel for build-up of blood in other areas near the wound". I couldn't find any additional sources of bleeding, so Jane continued her instructions. "Ok, grab a haemostatic dressing from the kit, open the pack with your teeth. Wipe the wound again until you can see the source of the bleed. Apply the dressing firmly but sustain the pressure with your other hand. Pack the dressing into the wound and continue pressure". I did precisely as she instructed and waited for three or four minutes. "If it's stabilising, overpack the wound and put a pressure bandage over it. The haemostatic bandage has a clotting agent and should help stop the bleed".

I screamed, "It's not working, we need to get him to a hospital". "No can do", shouted Jane, "they'll find us in a heartbeat. It goes against my orders". "Fucking orders, are you insane? Can't we drop him at the hospital and leave him?" I queried frantically. "No. The Dark Ones will take him and torture him mercilessly to blackmail us. They'll send you parts of his body in jiffy bags, you'll be forced to give yourself up in order to save him. It's how they roll, they're deadly and evil, the spawn of Satan".

I was losing James fast and there was nothing I could do, tears welled in my eyes, blurring my vision. I was desperate, what would a priest do in this situation? Giving James the last rites wasn't an option, and I didn't know how to. I needed to save him; I needed to focus. The crimson blood oozed between my fingers, I did the only thing I could think of, I prayed, I was desperate.

I pleaded to save my son. He had tried to save me at the expense of his own life. I rambled in a state of panic, explaining that James wasn't a Catholic, and I was an extremely poor one. I begged for help but in my heart, I carried no hope for my poor lad. In a brief spell of consciousness, I could see my face reflecting in his eyes. Jane was forced to stop the truck; the light was blinding; it hindered her ability to see the road ahead. My corneas glowed, almost effervescing. Fierce sunlight streamed in through the truck windows, the air tingled as if was crackling with electricity. "What the fuck are you...?"

The light quickly dissipated; I could see James again; I couldn't believe my eyes. James' colour was returning, he looked into my face and smiled. We were transfixed in a state of shock and awe. James' wound had closed, and the bleeding had stopped. He sat up, he was weak, but his eyes had cleared. "What in the name of God did you do?" I had no answer to his question, it kind of answered itself. We had borne witness to something extraordinary and elemental; the shock made us question reality. "I prayed for you Son. I was lost, there was nothing else I could do". "Well, your call was answered, God has blessed you", added Jane with tears in her eyes. James sat up and within an hour he had visibly improved. He didn't seem to need the field dressing I had applied, so he removed it, it exposed scar tissue beneath. The packing had been pushed clear of the wound from within.

Jane significantly changed after the incident in the car. Gone was her disrespectful arrogance, gone were her feelings of being coerced into an assignment she didn't care for. Suddenly, she realised the importance of her task; she was seeing her destiny unfold. We found somewhere to stay; I didn't know where. The three of us needed to sit down, eat, and have a stiff drink, this time both Jane and James joined me. It had been the worst of days, but in some ways the best too.

Saving James had provided a clear focus and understanding of my place. My faith had become unquestionable, and I began to study more intensely. Given my new focus, I was surprised how quickly the long services and prayers were memorised.

4. Demon Hunters (JeT)

From the writings of Jennifer Travers

Brian and I continued our scrutiny of the suspects and their habits, those we believed were attempting to manufacture a pathogen to commit genocide. On the second night of surveillance, we used hidden infrared cameras to monitor the park where the COO of Merck reputedly walked his dog. We spotted the target entering through the west gate with his collie. He was a tall, slim man with a grey goatee beard and wire rimmed glasses. He looked far too innocuous to be a Dark One. Having said that, appearances can be deceptive.

"Show time", murmured Brian in my earpiece. I exited the foliage, walking up the main track to cross paths with the target circling the park. I reached inside my jacket and took the safeties off both my firearms; I couldn't be too careful. As I approached, I took the bradawl-like device into my gloved fist, it was near invisible.

I took a deep breath as the mark approached. He closed in; I made a show of admiring his dog. I reached down and stroked the collie's head and talked to it in exaggerated baby talk. I rose and 'accidentally' bumped into my target. My shoulder struck his chest, and I punctured him in in the softer tissue of his latissimus dorsi muscle, just below the left armpit. He shouted, "Ow! What the fuck, you goddamned stupid bitch". I quickly tucked the bradawl in my pocket and apologised in character, "I'm so sorry, my ring must have caught you. I'm such a klutz, I really am. Are you ok? I'm so sorry. I was just admiring your lovely dog, and...". My show of utter confusion seemed to work, he said it was ok, but left as quickly as his legs could carry him. Strike one.

Following the assault, we found ourselves in a difficult position. It was impossible to know if the device was effective. Either the test had failed, or the target wasn't a Dark One. "If he was a demon, he certainly wouldn't have been so polite. I must have really hurt him". Brian agreed. We decided to test our second suspect, in for a cent, in for a dollar.

I tackled our second victim at Garwood Lanes bowling hall, where the target frequented on Tuesday nights. Again, we experienced no flames, our hypothesis wasn't looking sound. We wondered if the pathogen concept was still a runner, we decided to give the theory one final attempt, then cut our losses.

We planned to accost our third and final suspect, the R&D Special Projects director of Merck, at Kings Food Markets. John usually shopped there with his wife on a Thursday evening. I had a good feeling about this one, on paper he looked the most likely of the three, he could gain access to the technologies needed to execute a genocide. He was sufficiently senior to initiate blue sky research remits on 'medicines' without further authorisation. It was unusual for a captain of industry to roll his sleeves up and help with household chores, I quite respected him for that at least.

According to our intel, John and his wife routinely started their weekly shop at 7:15 pm, then they visited 'Yi En' for a Chinese meal afterwards. When in town, they'd followed this pattern for the last three months, regular as clockwork. However, tonight John was late.

A Doctrine of Fear - Paul JC Edge

Brian and I sat in the Crown Vic at the edge of the car park as cracks started to appear in our fortitude. "Give it another fifteen", suggested Brian patiently. Luckily, John and his wife arrived at the fourteenth minute looking flustered. "That's nothing, wait till I punch a hole in him", I said, smiling evilly. "Take care, JeT, you don't know what he's capable of. Don't let his prissy wife persuade you he's harmless, it might all be for show", advised Brian carefully. Brian's bright red hair glistened in the neon lights, "Be ready and keep the engine running". I proceeded across the car park, following the couple into the store. The shop was enormous, it was easy to intercept them in a quiet aisle. I strolled behind them, basket in my right hand, the bradawl concealed in my left. As I neared, the target glanced round to check my approach, he was clearly alert and observant. I made a show of indecision, comparing random groceries, he turned back to his wife unconcerned.

I lunged at my target, making a small puncture wound below his armpit, as with my previous victims. I began my apology but left it unfinished as his body burst into furious white flames. The victim's wife was initially stunned, but soon recovered. She pulled a small revolver from her oversized shoulder bag. I launched a shuriken from my right hand, it hit her in the throat. I had little time to plan my attack, a knee jerk reaction. She erupted into flames, falling next to the ashes of her husband. The ninja star was white hot and misshapen.

I walked briskly to the tills but not in too much of a hurry to attract undue attention. I could hear sounds of alarm from the isles, a babble of confusion where the victims had fallen. The guy at the checkout queried me, "What the hell was the bright flame, is there a fire?" "Didn't see nothin", I drawled, "I saw some guy lightin' a ceegar, told him good, ain't no sense smokin' in a store". My dialect didn't sound east coast, but it was the best I could do at short notice. I paid for my shopping and grabbed the brown paper bag, exiting without delay. I dumped the shopping in the trash can and approached the car. Brian looked more than a little excited. "It's two for the price of one in there", I announced with a dark grin.

Brian drove onto the highway; we headed out of town. "Where are we going?" I asked. He replied solemnly, "Washington, we have been assigned another mission". Over the next couple of months, we carried out another seven clandestine assassinations, five of them being successful.

On a long drive back to Philadelphia from Milwaukee; Brian pulled over to take a private call from the sidewalk. The conversation must have been important, he rarely excluded me. He re-joined me afterwards, "Just got a call from HQ, they've located the man they've been looking for, the one with the skin markings. Everything's going ape shit, the game has changed; we've been reassigned". "Reassigned where? To what? We were just starting to make progress", I exclaimed. "Apparently, the guy they've been waiting for is in the UK. The guys in his protection detail are taking him to a safe house, then they'll keep him on the move, so the Dark Ones can't easily target him. He has a good crew, the best. My superiors anticipate that the demons will focus their energy on finding and eliminating the chosen one.

"Seven safe havens have been built by ordinary folk on the hush hush, our mission is to protect the most important one. The havens are intended to help weather out the Dark One's storm, the Pope is calling it the battle for the end of the world.

"The Pope perceives that the leader of one of the larger havens, Paul Collin, represents a direct threat to the Dark One. We will form Paul's protection detail. Except...". "Except what", I demanded. Brian continued undeterred, "Except, our orders are to create a pretence that we are ignorant of his mission. We mustn't draw attention to ourselves, we should protect him from a distance. It will make the assignment much more difficult. The good news is we're shipping out to England, he and his family live in Cheshire".

Brian exited the I95 and headed directly to Philly airport, we took the red eye to Manchester. A pasty-faced man with overly short trousers collected Brian's car keys at the entrance to departures. "Inconspicuous", was the only word which left Brian's mouth, more than sarcastically. The trunk was full of weapons and luggage we couldn't take with us.

I suddenly realised my passport was counterfeit. My real documentation was in the glovebox of my car, halfway down a cliff in Texas. The fake might pass a casual inspection but definitely not a formal one. Brian must have anticipated my dilemma; he smiled and passed me a brand-new document. When I checked, it was a full UK passport, including a recent photo. It included a new name to match my new look. Brian had asked for a photo for my file a week or so ago, but I hadn't anticipated a new passport. He was well organised, and clearly knew more than he was letting on.

We slept the eight hours on the overnighter to Manchester, following a dire meal and three brandies. I woke as we descended, feeling groggy. We arrived at 7:15am to a grey, cold spring day; it was quite a departure from the hot, humid days we'd recently experienced in the US. We passed through passport control without difficulty. A local fixer handed Brian a set of keys as we entered the arrivals hall.

It felt chilly as we left the airport's main concourse. Brian located a Ford hatch in the car park and drove into the morning with the heater on. The car wasn't standard specification, I knew from the engine tone. "I need warmer clothes", I pointed out, "It's parky here, can we find a shop?" "Are you sure you're from Scotland?" Brian laughed. "Ok, ok, I'm on it. I need to make an equipment stop first; I'm meeting a colleague nearby. But then we'll head up to the Trafford Centre for clothes. Brian parked illegally in a bus stop and alighted for a few minutes. The equipment was stowed in our boot as we parked, by a well-dressed Jewish gentleman. The holdall moved from his vehicle to ours in seconds, as we sat in the car, not a single word was uttered.

The shops at the centre were quite good, but the trip was cut short by an urgent phone call. "We've had a possible sighting of the enemy", explained Brian. "Our guys have been monitoring a pair of suspects who recently entered the Holmes Chapel area, it's highly probable they're a threat". We briskly exited and returned to the car. We threw our purchases in the back and headed to Paul Collin's hometown. "How do you know their location? How do you track the Dark Ones?" I queried. "We have deployed cameras on the routes in and out of town, they link to the computer network in London. They analyse every vehicle entering the area, they put a watch on suspicious vehicles. To be fair, there are thousands of suspects so we can only report possibilities. It's not a scientific process; it just runs the statistics".

A Doctrine of Fear - Paul JC Edge

Brian drove to Paul's office in Congleton, I spotted his car in the adjacent car park. We watched from a vantage point in a nearby road, waiting for a sighting. At 5:30pm Paul left the office and drove towards home; we followed, keeping a safe distance. The weather turned unpleasant; the hard rain hampered our visibility.

I became concerned when I observed an obstacle in the gloom further down the road. My suspicions were confirmed when the two occupants of the car in front drew weapons. We assumed they were the suspected Dark Ones. The cars behind us had faded into the distance, which seemed questionable, it looked like a set up. We couldn't delay, we needed to prevent Paul's vehicle from stopping. Brian accelerated hard and side swiped the rear end of the car in front. The suspect's car T-boned; our car rammed into its offside with significant force.

Brian and I exited the vehicle and opened fire immediately, the two occupants jumped out of their car and targeted us. A brief exchange of ordnance followed and both Dark Ones flamed. When Brian and I pushed their car into a farm track, I realised Brian had been clipped. I helped him to our car, my shoulder supporting his arm. Luckily, it was only a flesh wound.

Paul must have been driving in a bloody dreamworld, he had managed to crash his car into the obstacle, which turned out to be an illegally parked car. Clearly, the Dark Ones had left the car in advance to set up the ambush. We cleared up quickly, so the authorities wouldn't find evidence of gunfire immediately, picking up casings and smashing the glass with bullet holes. Luckily, our car was still drivable, but in its current state it could draw attention from the police.

Parking a few streets from Paul's home, we continued our vigilance on the area using optics. It was hard to appear inconspicuous in a residential area, but luckily there was unused industrial land to the rear of his property, which we used for cover. I fixed a field dressing on Brian's wound; I promised to stitch it properly later.

A repair vehicle for Paul's car attended and towed it away. The fixer had already dropped a replacement vehicle for us, but it was a standard car. We took shifts watching the house, the situation was starting to heat up. Brian and requested another vehicle, separate cars would be less conspicuous and provide more flexibility. The second car arrived within a few hours. After a few days, Paul began to meet with men in various locations. We took shifts following him to ensure his safety as best we could. I dearly wished we could punch some sense into the man, he was taking all sorts of risks and was completely oblivious to the dangers surrounding him.

A few weeks later, he ventured into Manchester using the train. He met six men at the Midland hotel, a motley crew with no eye for security. We obtained positive confirmation that the men were the individuals Paul had been meeting over the last few weeks, with a single exception. The wildcard was an aging guy who looked clearly capable, probably ex-military. "That one is Sipall, he's ex Marines and he did a spell in the SAS according to his records", explained Brian, looking through the files on his iPad. "Well, at least there's someone savvy to look after Paul. It looks like they're great friends, hopefully he will keep him close", I concurred.

5. Return from Whence we Came

Over the following year, we moved continuously throughout Spain, France, and Portugal. Every couple of days we were somewhere new. In general, we successfully evaded trouble. However, in Porto we walked directly into the maelstrom, our bad luck seemed to catch up with us all at once. We must have been spotted in a bank exchanging money retrieved from a safe house. The familiar man-woman-priest combination could be easily recognised if we were in the wrong place at the wrong time. A number of black figures loomed in the shadows across the street, as we left the bank. They calmly hung back in doorways, alleys, and corners so they would not draw attention from the public around them. Although they kept out of sight, the Dark Ones ensured we saw them, it was clear intimidation.

James and Jane immediately opened fire at the figures, and I followed suit. Shoppers and passers-by screamed and ran in all directions as the gunfire erupted. The dark figures that were hit burst into flames. I jumped into the truck as one of them smashed the side window with the hilt of his dagger. I fired my Sig automatic in its face, the figure flamed. I hadn't killed anything before, it made me feel dirty and I became anxious.

The blinding flames shook me back to reality. The demon wasn't actually a human being, I now knew it was a manifestation of the purest evil. The police arrived on the scene quickly, presumably with reinforcements close behind. Luckily, we were just ahead of the curve, moving before roadblocks were put in place. I didn't want to end up in a police cell arguing for diplomatic immunity as our enemies gathered around us.

Jane drove out of the city on the A1, the main artery, over the river Douro road bridge. Something had changed in the way the enemy were deployed, their attack didn't follow the usual pattern. Three black saloons streaked after us, James spotted a helicopter, airborne and heading our way. Close behind the enemy vehicles were the blue and red lights of numerous police interceptors. James and I discharged our firearms, aiming for the drivers of the pursuing blacked out vehicles. A Dark One leaned out of the leading car sighting a machine gun. James grabbed a remote control from the glove box and frantically pressed buttons, "Leave the chopper to me", he shouted.

A drone launched into the air from the cargo bed at the rear of our vehicle, it took a couple of seconds to stabilise after being exposed to the velocity of the car. The drone careered along the road towards the helicopter, accelerating past our vehicle. James kept the drone low, weaving between cars, so the helicopter pilot didn't see it until it was too late. The helicopter's machine gun opened fire on the drone as it shot up into the air and exploded. The shrapnel smashed the glass of the helicopter's cockpit killing the occupants, the chopper erupted into a fireball.

Half of its rotor was ripped away, the helicopter spiralled down towards the road. Thick black smoke billowed from its vents, making visibility poor. When the helicopter hit the tarmac, it exploded into a million pieces. A tail section hit our bonnet; it jarred the truck but luckily passed overhead. The front of the truck was damaged considerably, but the vehicle remained drivable. Jane continued to make huge demands on the truck's traction.

Jane violently swerved the vehicle around the chopper, missing it by a hair. Three saloons approached rapidly; one nudged the rear of the truck causing it to spin. Jane managed to counteract the skid and kept going. The car on our flank collided with the chopper and was wrecked, the one behind hit a stinger that James had dropped using the truck's remote control. The tyres were ripped to shreds when they hit the stinger's array of sharp spikes.

The final Dark Ones' pursuit car accelerated towards us; James quickly deployed another drone. It didn't exit the back of the truck cleanly, due to Jane violent manoeuvres, it hit the floor and smashed. James detonated the drone as per the Swiss Guard's instructions, so it wouldn't be found intact. All civilian vehicles had been blocked by the helicopter wreck, so the road became clear behind us. The last of the chopper's shrapnel hit the last pursuing car, unfortunately the damage wasn't catastrophic. The passenger opened fire with a machine gun, it wasn't looking good for us.

Jane swerved, many bullets sprayed wide due to the car's sudden movement, several hit the back window and tailgate. The bulletproof glass was scarred badly. James leaned out of his window and returned fire immediately, their car wasn't armoured, and the bullets hit their mark. The driver immediately flamed; the car veered into the central crash barrier. The passenger flamed in the wreckage.

Jane shouted, "I can see more cars joining the road in the distance, where the hell are they all coming from? Press the

SOS button on the ComLink device, there's too many for us to handle. There's also a small army of cops approaching". How had they mobilised so many vehicles so quickly? It just didn't seem possible.

The ComLink displayed a waypoint in the city and issued new directions. Jane left the highway and took a roundabout at such speed she almost collided with another car. She headed back on the opposite side of the highway. Four black cars raced around the burning helicopter, using the hard shoulder. The passengers stared at us but there was little they could do; they were on the other side of the crash barrier. Any remaining Dark Ones in the City would now be informed and readying for our arrival. Our situation was becoming critical; another car swap wouldn't help; it was highly likely we would face a roadblock before long. I dearly hoped our destination was this side of the city limits.

Our luck held; the Dark Ones must have deployed all their operatives in the vicinity to the original chase. We didn't perceive any further threat immediately. More police cars, ambulances and fire trucks appeared on the city outskirts, we kept our heads and speed down and hoped they would focus on the wreckages of our pursuers. Jane headed to the port, we dumped the truck in the main car park and moved away from it, in case it was spotted. Jane flagged the vehicle for immediate pickup by the Swiss Guard using the ComLink, to avoid exposing the presence of the weaponry on board to the authorities.

I followed Jane towards the waypoint, which was a small, navy frigate. As we neared the ship, two black cars screeched towards us at significant speed. A large machine gun on the frigate opened up; the staccato of the big gun was ear shattering. The black vehicles were reduced to trash in seconds. Our shadows glistened on the tarmac in front of us, as the Dark Ones burst into flame. The frigate was prepped and ready to go, as we boarded the gangplank the ship was unmoored, it departed post haste. I don't think anyone saw us board the vessel, so we were good for now. It wouldn't be long before the port authorities called the police and the coastguard intercepted us. We headed out into the Atlantic at full speed.

Twenty sailors crewed the ship, they seemed remarkably informal for a navy frigate. The captain addressed us semi-formally, "Welcome on-board the Phoenix, Father Giuseppe. I'm Captain Philip Checkson, call me Phil". He then turned to Jane and James, "You must be Father Joe's Swiss Guards?" Jane replied, "Affirmative, thanks for the assist, Captain". Phil introduced his first mate, José. After mispronouncing José's name a few times as 'Hosé', he advised me gently that the first letter in his name was pronounced J as he was Portuguese.

The crew turned out to be navy veterans from several countries. "Looks like we've become mercenaries", they laughed. They claimed to be part of the Vatican Navy, which I had never heard of. I suspected the concept of a Vatican Navy may have been a private joke, but it was lost on me. The name Phoenix wasn't lost on me though, a creature which turned into flames when it died. Given the attack from the Dark Ones, I'm not sure I found it funny; my sense of humour was failing me rapidly.

On his tour of the vessel, Phil proudly informed us that the ship was an advanced prototype, based on the new Type 26 frigate under development by the British Navy. It had been fitted with a few special modifications, the largest of the changes was the Rolls Royce nuclear reactor powering the ship, it provided significantly improved thrust. I can't remember its top speed, but it sounded rapid for a sea going vessel. Phil threw a lot of stats at me in a short burst, he was obviously enthused by the diminutive warship. I thought only the really large vessels were nuclear powered, such as submarines and aircraft carriers. The Phoenix could sail for several years without refuelling, it had two large machine guns, a cannon, and a rocket array amongst other features. In addition, it carried advanced countermeasures, in case it was attacked by missiles. A small helicopter, located at the rear of the vessel, was provided for emergency use. It was no wonder the Vatican were struggling financially; they had gone to great lengths to protect me. I must admit, I felt safer once on board.

Jane relaxed visibly once we'd exited the port and had left the mainland well behind us. It was a sign that things were good for now. Out at sea, it would be much harder to locate us, wouldn't it?

We showered quickly, changed, and ate in the rather well-appointed galley. Jane insisted we continued to wear our firearms, so we brazenly wore shoulder rigs over our shirts. I must've looked quite a sight with a gun and a dog collar, I noted a few doubles takes from the less senior crew members. I always felt good near the sea, Bridget claimed we'd evolved from sea creatures, and it welcomed us home when we were near; as God only knows, I missed her desperately.

We remained at sea for several months, occasionally stopping for a swim, which was wonderful. I learnt to fish, in the quieter hours of the afternoons. I hooked my first live one, a large tuna which nearly pulled me into the sea. Jane joked that the tuna was probably sent by the Dark One and it would burst into flames when I stunned it.

Our time at sea was pleasant enough, after so much road travel, the predictability of each day felt good. We didn't need to re-fuel, so avoided being seen near ports. I guess it was near impossible for anyone to locate us. I had been assured by Phil that the stores onboard were extensive and could last for months. We sailed constantly for weeks; when we finally docked for supplies, I hid below deck. The crew disguised themselves as British Navy when they disembarked. The ship docked for a couple of days to avoid suspicion; we were forbidden to go on deck during daylight. One day was ridiculously hot, we could only take cold showers to keep us cool. We played cards mostly, whatever the game, Jane tended to win.

It was the Summer of 2020 before our feet touched land once more. From a distance, our destination, Isola Salina, looked very green with two high volcanic mountains and a smooth coastline. Salina was an Aeolian Island due North of Sicily. It was beautiful and a great pleasure to finally leave the ship. Some time passed before the ocean's roll left my legs, and the land felt solid once more.

I was painfully aware that the date of the apocalypse, earmarked by the Holy Father, was rapidly approaching. My mind began to wander to my loved ones and their whereabouts; then, out of the blue, Bridget appeared by the waterside. It had been nearly two years since I last set eyes on her, we embraced hungrily. "Mum!" James ran over to give her a huge hug. Later, we joined Jane in a small café, we had lots to discuss. Phil informed us that we would plan to ride out whatever was to come, here at Isola Salina Haven.

6. As Normal as Life Gets

My team were allocated residences at the Sanctuary of the Madonna del Terzito, situated in Valdichiesa in the centre of Salina. Valdichiesa was located between the island's twin volcanoes, with the townships of Malfa to the north and Leni to the south. The sanctuary was consecrated ground, I was assured the area was quite safe at night. It tended to attract religious visitors and pilgrims at various times of year, but visitors had been temporarily suspended due to the corona virus pandemic. We were swabbed and had our temperatures checked on arrival, but we all tested negative, luckily.

Twin towers flanked the square frontage, they dominated an incredibly old building. Inside the rooms felt a little cool, but on hotter days it was a blessing. As the months moved into winter, I suspected the rooms could become cold, but then there were large fireplaces, and a well-stocked wood store was located at the rear of the building.

The island itself was volcanic, the five volcanoes had been inert for a long time. However, in more recent months, the main two craters had shown minor activity, making the air a little sulphurous. The experts believed an eruption was improbable in the next five to ten years. The wealth of minerals in the soil, due in part to the dissipation of minerals from the volcanic ash, made the island rich in a large variety of crops. More than 400 species of plant grew on the island: the grapes, olives and capers were first rate. The mountains were covered in ferns, poplars, chestnut trees, caper bushes and prickly pears. Additionally, orchards, olive groves and vineyards had been cultivated. The golden 'Malvasia' white wine was lovely, I would sit for hours with a glass of wine in the company of my family. It was so pleasant to be back amongst the people I loved, I had missed them terribly.

The island's population was in excess of two thousand people. The community deserved good care and support, which meant I really needed to learn my craft quickly. After three months, I still felt I'd barely scraped the surface of the rituals I needed to practice. I learned the key ceremonies and rites: Mass, Baptism, Confirmation, Marriage, Anointing of the Sick and Last Rites. I found confessions challenging; my understanding of philosophy and theology was weak at best. I leaned on Father Enzo for support, he was a wise old owl who was more than happy to be my mentor. I found it easy to make friends with Enzo, he and Bridget already had such a warm, light-hearted bond, gelled by their irreverent sense of humour.

The islanders had fared well with the COVID-19 epidemic, the borders to Isola Salina were completely closed, other than for supplies. We were lucky to secure priority vaccinations prior to commercial release, our fairy godfather must have arranged it for us.

On Christmas Eve 2020, we were delighted to witness an extensive display of shooting stars. My thoughts became troubled as I remembered the words of the Holy Father, meteorites were the first sign of the end of days. He predicted the beginnings of Armageddon barely a few months later. If he was right, all hell would be unleashed in April. Humankind would turn evil; we would face a plague like nothing we'd ever seen, followed by a great war. How could I protect the islanders from something so terrible?

A Doctrine of Fear - Paul JC Edge

Salina was one of the seven safe havens that the Monsignor had spoken about, but I knew nothing of the others. What of the church? Why had the Holy Father not joined us here with his Cardinals? I called the Monsignor to raise my concerns with him, he didn't have all of the answers, but he promised to discuss them with the Holy Father and come back to me. I must admit he didn't seem overly concerned. Now that's true faith!

My brain raced; how could we protect everyone? What could I do to help secure the island? The answer I received from Father Enzo and Father Alfredo was wholly unsatisfactory. Their remarkably simple Christian response was to have faith in God; he would provide. Many people on the planet would soon test their faith, and most of them would die if the Holy Father's dreams came to pass. I dearly hoped the Pope was wrong. I expected that we would laugh about the apocalypse as a ludicrous, false premonition at some point in the future.

Why had we chosen to avoid engaging the Dark Ones directly? They represented the threat; how could so many remain invisible to us? Enzo explained it was difficult to target a secret society; if their members were known, then ergo it wouldn't be secret. My other concern was we hadn't yet captured a Dark One, when wounded they spontaneously incinerated, our understanding of them was minimal.

Once the plague was unleashed, the best option for our protection would be to prevent refugees from drifting to the island. Our small contingent of Swiss Guard were a boon, but not sufficient to protect our towns and villages. I encouraged the Guard and our local police force to form an informal militia, to help safeguard the community. The Swiss Guard also managed to arrange more firearms and munitions in preparation for the fateful day. Travel to the mainland for supplies would be discouraged, food was plentiful on the island, we needed for very little.

I was lucky, my close family members were already in the haven. It wasn't the case for the guard's families. In the Spring, I urged them to invite their loved ones to the island. We organised a small festival to encourage families to visit the island, but travel was expensive so very few were able.

When the day of the predicted apocalypse came, Bridget, James and I sat in the Sanctuary with Enzo, Alfredo and Jane. We were glued to small TV, awaiting the inevitable news. At 23:00, small meteorites pummelled the breadth of the Earth. The news reported that all major land masses were impacted but the damage was minimal. By 23:30, it emerged that the meteorites carried some kind of plague which transformed those infected into ravaging beasts, precisely as predicted by the pontiff. Massive toadstools sprouted from the heads of the dead, dispersing infected spores everywhere. No-one stood a chance. Deeply concerned for the Holy Father, I telephoned the Vatican, but all the lines were dead.

By midnight, all TV channels and radio stations had stopped live transmissions across the globe, we were completely cut off. Internet access continued for several days. A few blogs reported for a while, they became increasingly urgent and fearful. One blogger reported how an infected man attacked others like a wild beast. He fed on his prey, but he was shot by the police. A mushroom grew from his neck and rapidly exploded, filling the air with spores. Everyone in the vicinity suddenly began to behave like wild animals too, attacking each other. There were no more entries...

A Doctrine of Fear - Paul JC Edge

Within a few hours, much of the world's population was dead, including the church leaders and the Pope himself. I shed a few tears for the fate of the world and its people, I prayed for the Holy Father and his priests. It was a desperate fate, even for those who survived. The islanders were terrified, priests and town hall officials tried to calm the situation as best they could. We could only pray for the souls of the victims and ensure our islanders were safe.

By chance, no meteorites struck Salina. The Guard cut off the ports to prevent incursions, I instructed them to use lethal force if necessary. I must admit, a priest giving them orders was rather a shock to us both. I resorted to openly wearing my sidearm, which shocked some older folk in the congregation, as it had on the Phoenix initially. I joined Fathers Enzo, Alfredo, and Alessandro, we agreed to spend more time in the community providing spiritual and emotional help to the islanders. Luckily, there was no evidence of the plague on the island, putting our minds at rest for the time being. It further confirmed the Pope's prediction that we would be safe here, which was positive news we could share.

On our rounds we found people walking the streets in various states of bewilderment, some exhibited outright panic. Others desperately sought news of their kin. The priests and I quickly suppressed the unrest, the townsfolk trusted our words and calmed over time. We emphasised the importance of vigilance and teamwork. I nominated the Sanctuary as the headquarters for the haven. Our small island police garrison was cut off from the mainland, so they agreed to formalise their arrangement with the Swiss Guard, calling themselves simply 'The Guard'.

A Doctrine of Fear - Paul JC Edge

Jane and James insisted on remaining in their roles as my personal bodyguards.

A police sergeant called Caron emerged as the leader of The Guard, which certainly received Jane's support. The Guard set up a lookout point on the largest volcano, Fossa Delle Felci, it provided visibility of the whole island. Receiving early warning of possible ingress was critical to survival.

We had no communication from the wider world for several weeks, until Phil made contact on his ship's long wave radio. He spoke about a haven in Valletta, not far from us. When contact was fully established, Valetta informed us they were in communication with Summer Haven, a larger commune in Scotland, I remembered the Pope mentioning the latter during my time with him.

Father Alfredo and I drove to the port at Malfa to meet with Phil and José aboard the Phoenix. The Monsignor had instructed them to stay alert and ready for attack at all times. José put us in contact with the haven in Scotland, it was wonderful to know we weren't the only survivors. Kulbir, from Summer Haven, confirmed they were safe and well. I conversed with their leader, Paul Collin, who had everything under control and had been well prepared. He confirmed the other havens were Valletta, Formentera in the Balearics, Zakynthos in Greece, Samsø island near Denmark and Mont St Michel in northern France. It was good to speak, and we arranged to stay in regular contact.

A week later, we received news that Valletta had fallen; a handful of survivors had managed to escape via the sea. They were heading to Scotland, which seemed ludicrous. They were only a few miles from us, why would they choose to travel so far? We would've welcomed them, provided they agreed to be quarantined for a few weeks.

The following Sunday, I led the entire mass for the whole island, under the guiding eye of Father Alessandro: The Introductory Rites, the Liturgy of the Word, the Liturgy of the Eucharist, and the Concluding Rites. We prayed for the fallen and requested God's help and support in our troubled times. We also prayed for the other surviving havens to give them strength to ward off evil, and for the lost souls at Valetta.

The following day we experienced our first incursion, a single visitor from Lipari Island, our nearest neighbour. The figure appeared to be infected as it floated on an inflatable Li-Lo and ran aground on the beach at Lingua. It was possible that many had attempted the crossing, but only one had traversed the currents, finding itself on our island by complete chance. The creature landed on the beach and attacked the islanders. It assaulted two local fishermen, killing one and subsequently feeding on his cadaver. How vile and degrading our race had become in the face of this evil!

The Guard arrived whilst the creature was feeding. The villagers sensibly locked themselves in their houses and plugged the cracks in the doors and windows, they had been well informed of the dangers and the evil spores the creatures transmitted. The survivor of the attack became similarly enraged; The Guards correctly presumed he was infected. He turned feral and joined the feeding frenzy, the creatures fought amongst themselves for the best share of the spoils.

A Doctrine of Fear - Paul JC Edge

The Guard opened fire; the infected fishermen was killed. Two flowers emerged rapidly from his fallen body. It was like watching a mushroom grow in a time lapse film. However, after a few minutes, according to the report, the growths faltered, and they failed to bear spores. Clearly something in the environment had hampered the infection. The Guard doused the cadavers in kerosene and burnt them. The church fellowship helped placate the families of those who were lost to the senseless violence.

The following Sunday, I held a combined service for those who died, although we couldn't commit their charred remains to the ground, due to the risk of reinfection. Caron sent the burnt remains out to sea in a small boat, which we set alight to prevent risk of further infection. It was reminiscent of a Viking funeral, but it seemed strangely appropriate; the relatives and mourners understood the dangers of burying the bodies in our soil.

We made contact with Summer Haven on a weekly basis. We heard about their battles and challenges, but also their learnings concerning the plague. We quickly realised it was no coincidence our island was safe from infection, as the pathogen was fungal it was averse to the sulphurous fumes emitted from our volcano. God had provided for us. Little did we know that a year later, trouble would re-appear on our shores in the form of the insidious followers of the Dark One.

7. An Incongruous Meeting (JeT)

From the writings of Jennifer Travers

Brian and I set up surveillance of Paul and his team meeting at the Midland Hotel. Their plans were embryonic but were developing at a decent pace as far as we could tell. There were no significant threats, all was quiet. Brian maintained reconnaissance on the rear staff doors and fire exits, I sat in the square close to Manchester Central Library, monitoring the main entrance. Stakeouts were tedious, I got high on my colossal caffeine intake from a nearby Café Nero whilst I pretended to watch the trams.

At 5pm, Paul's team exited the hotel and went their separate ways. We followed Paul to Piccadilly Station, but we never made it. A member of Paul's team, Sipall, got the jump on us from behind a boarded-up shop front. A brief scuffle ended in him holding a fishing knife to Brian's throat. "Who the fuck are you, and why are you following us? Speak quickly or I'll take you out permanently". I couldn't counter to the guy without injuring Brian, so I stood down and appeared relaxed. "We're Swiss Guard, I'm going to slowly reach into Brian's pocket to show you his creds". I slid my hand into his pocket, without losing eye contact with Sipall. When he saw Brian's creds, Sipall released him, he folded the knife blade and pocketed it.

"What the fuck are Swiss Guard doing in Manchester, there's no Papal visit that I'm aware of? Also, where are your creds lady?" Spall demanded. His face lost none of its distrust, he was hard to read. I started, "I've no creds because I'm newly recruited and this is unofficial business". "No shit", replied Sipall, "they don't take women in the Swiss Guard, they don't worry about offending the feminists, however, I suspect it would have been a serious lack of judgement in your case".

I ignored the backhanded compliment, Brian pulled himself together. "We're not regular Swiss Guard", I continued. "No shit", responded Sipall again. I resumed unabashed, "We've been assigned to protect Paul, we're his unofficial bodyguards". Brian took in a deep breath, "What the hell are you doing JeT? That's privileged information. You just compromised our mission you bloody fool". Sipall grinned, "Let me get this straight. The fucking Pope has assigned a black ops lady and some kind of secret service dude to watch over a Project Manager from Cheshire. You must think I came here on a booze cruise. I have no problem with you guys looking after Paul, believe me, but you'd better get to the truth quickly or I'm gonna make your job extremely difficult".

We agreed to grab a coffee and take the discussion somewhere more private; we had lost Paul anyway. I declined another caffeine shot and ordered mineral water instead. "You shouldn't let an old guy get the drop on you like that", chided Sipall mockingly, with a twinkle in his eye. "You wouldn't have got the drop on me", I contested. "I go by the name Spall. I got the drop because I observed you have one critical weakness", he replied sincerely. I suppressed an intake of breath and looked him in the eye questioningly. "Him", Spall pointed his thumb at Brian and smirked. "I suspect I'd have got my ass kicked if I'd tried to grab you", he offered generously. "I'm not sure about that", I replied magnanimously. "What on earth makes you think I'm Black Ops?" I asked. Spall looked at me and smiled, "I was in the SAS for a spell, as I'm sure you know. SAS guys are tough and trained to function in near death conditions. They are fit as hell and just keep going whatever they face. Special forces tend to walk in a certain way, they carry their bodies lightly to be energy efficient. I can spot them a mile off. Black Ops dudes have the same blood, but they carry it with a certain...", he hesitated for a moment, "a certain grace. Female operatives are as rare as hen's teeth and can be an asset, they blend in and appear innocuous, whereas men often cannot".

Suddenly, the penny dropped, "That's why you recruited me, isn't it? So, I could sneak up to our...". I halted suddenly as Brian gave me the look. I had overstepped the mark again. He decided to take over the dialogue before I made any more slips. "Ok Spall, the truth is I really need your help. Keep what I'm about to impart confidential until the day you die". Brian paused; Spall responded with curt nod. To Brian and Spall, a nod was a binding contract. "I'm Brian, this is JeT. The Pope has received notice that Armageddon is coming. We're part of a new arm of the Swiss Guard, commissioned to protect the leaders guiding humanity through the forthcoming war".

"What the fuck?" Spall expressed, with a measure of incredulity, "are you having a laugh?" "I really am not, allow me to explain", added Brian. He elaborated on the Pope's visions and Paul's special purpose to protect the human race from the predicted events. "Our presence needs to remain a secret from Paul as it may influence the outcome. Paul's actions need to be taken without external interference or coercion. We're assigned to protect Paul from darker influences, those who wish to eliminate him". Spall sat back, "Paul has visions too, he's spinning a web of lies to cover them up. His friends wouldn't help, if they knew the truth. He's planning to build a bunker in

Scotland; he's bought an island in the Highlands. Our meeting today planned our next steps. A few of us will be visiting the island in a week or so".

Spall continued, "Look, even Paul will see you coming a mile away. The island's really remote, your mission is likely to fail unless you're on the inside. Paul needs local knowledge, a guide. We're also going to need soldiers to defend the place. Why not pretend you're regular soldiers? Help out a little at first, befriend Paul, then become part of the team. You can protect him more effectively from our side of the fence".

"Where in the Highlands are we talking about, precisely?" queried Brian. Spall looked at him carefully, took a deep breath and continued, "Summer Islands, near Ullapool". "Holy shit", replied Brian, "I was born in Dundonnell. I know the area like the back of my hand. The waterways, the inlets, the towns". "Some things are just meant to be", I whispered thunderstruck, remembering my mother's oft spoken words.

Brian passed his firearm to Spall under the table, "You might need this my friend", he then handed him a couple of extra clips. Spall pocketed them quickly. "H and K, do you always use those? I find they can jam if you don't keep the mechanism pristine. I prefer the Sig personally, but then it will do the job nicely, thank you". Spall appeared thoughtful for a moment, seizing a potential opportunity he asked, "Can your organisation source weaponry? I need some fairly exotic stuff?" "I would expect so, but we'll need to work through intermediaries, the Vatican is trying to keep it's distance from such matters, I'm sure you will understand", replied Brian.

On the day of Paul's scouting trip to the island, we were already waiting for his team in Ullapool. I'd driven up two days before, it was an awful drive. The only thing that kept me sane was Brian's choice of music, the Ramones was becoming our go-to playlist when we needed a lift, we both favoured sing along punky rock.

Spall kept watch in Cheshire but planned to arrive in Scotland the following day. Brian and I bunked at a B&B in Dundonnell, which made Brian feel a little sentimental. I used it as an opportunity to wind him up, "Nostalgia ain't what it used to be, Brian".

His parents still lived in Glasgow, but he still knew a few of the locals. We rented a mid-sized motorboat so we could scope out the island. The weather wasn't good for venturing out to sea, but Brian had done a spell in the Marines, it was no issue for him. Rough seas would be an unpleasant experience for the team on their first day in Ullapool, the land lubbers would suffer terrible seasickness. We observed as Paul arrived with two of his team. Before mobilising, they ate at the Seafood Shack, talk about swanning around. We were relying on these guys to avert the end of the world, God help me!

Over the next few months, the work on Paul's project started in earnest. We were involved in a few minor skirmishes, but the Dark Ones couldn't trace us easily, it was too remote. We were forced to lean on some of the more vocal townsfolk as the project continued, especially when the building became more obvious. Sometimes it involved negotiation at the barrel of a gun, as the construction and shipping were conspicuous. Brian stayed in Scotland permanently as the project progressed, it became my job to protect Paul when he returned to Cheshire. Mine was an easy assignment, as it turned out.

Brian and I got on well with Paul from the outset, he was a regular guy but very warm and engaging. He looked after his friends; we began to understand why he was so important to the powers that be. I still remember the very first time we met face to face, Paul approached us as we sat on the boat in Ullapool harbour, he was investigating transport to the Summer Islands. He booked a trip for the following morning at 8am sharp. As Paul was leaving, he hesitated and strolled back, smiling warmly. "Sorry mate, what was your name, I didn't catch it?" he asked. Brian smiled, "Och aye, my name is Rusty, Captain Rusty and this here is my wee girlfriend, the lovely Sheena". WTF?

8. The Quest to Find My Brother (Paul)

From the journal of Paul Collin

Having experienced what appeared to be very real dreams signposting the end of the world, I set out to build a safe haven in the Summer Isles in the Scottish Highlands with a few trusted friends. Before the apocalypse, we persuaded our families and friends to join us in a celebration at the haven, our ulterior motive was to make them safe in the confines of the facility during the infection.

After a couple of years of living in solitude, our team ventured out to the most northern parts of Scotland, where we learned how to combat the Shroom. Shroom were ordinary people that had been infected by a terrible airborne fungus, which turned the host into a rabid killer.

I discovered I had an identical twin, Francisco, who joined me in Scotland after the fall of Valletta haven. Although neither of us had prior knowledge of each other, we were unified as soon as we met. To our mutual surprise we found we were both immune to the fungal pathogen and survived fighting in close quarters with the Shroom.

We managed to find a way to clear the north of Scotland from the menace of the infected and returned to a natural life living on the bountiful lands. Together we executed a Dark One on the shores of the Scottish mainland, a forbidding figure who was planning our demise. Its death was both terrifying and spectacular, as soon as the sniper's bullet hit its target, the night was scorched with white fire. The hot ashes from the intense combustion floated up into the night sky.

A Doctrine of Fear - Paul JC Edge

Soon after, Franc and I were plagued with dreams again, they instructed us to find our brother and gave stark warnings about the duplicitous and dangerous nature of the 'Dark Ones'. The visions indicated that we needed to work together to find our brother and ultimately meet with the white figure from our dreams. We were baffled by the thought of another brother; the concept was bizarre. I had assumed the white spectre in our dreams was supernatural, however it emerged that he was physically present on our world, a living breathing person. Franc and I discussed the white figure with Spall.

Spall was uncomfortable with our plans to leave the haven in pursuit of a man from a dream. He felt our loyalties lay with the haven's community; they needed us. My wife, Kate, was deeply concerned, she felt I was travelling to my death. In her words, "You are meddling with dangers we don't understand". Neither Kate nor Spall bought the concept of our immunity to the infection, they considered us lucky. Regardless of our resistance, there were dangerous rabid beasts out there waiting for us.

Franc and I sat in Summer Haven's atrium, sipping expresso and mulling things over. "The way I look at it", I tried to explain, "the white figure saved us from the infection. Without his help, none of us would be alive today. We owe him everything. How can we ignore his request? Perhaps he needs our help this time". I attempted to articulate my feelings more precisely, "I have trusted the white figure so far and he has proven worthy. We simply have to go; we have no choice".

Spall thought deeply, "Well, I'm going with you", he added. "You can't Spall, we need someone here to keep an eye on the place, you've led all the military defences and expeditions.

The community need you here". "Rusty, Wrench and Sheena are more than capable", he took a deep breath. "Look, your vision saved us. You feel a sense of duty to the white being, I get that, I feel a sense of duty too. I need to protect you and keep you safe". "I'll have Franc with me", I replied. "Yes, two men against a billion rabid Shroom and the other dark creatures or whatever the hell they are. I really don't think so! Anyway, my mind's made up, I'm coming along, end of debate, no negotiations". He stood and looked resolutely into my eyes. There was no way we would change his mind; I looked at his grumpy time worn face and smiled. I hugged him warmly, I loved him like a brother, he responded reluctantly at first, then he sighed and hugged me back.

The haven community leaders mulled over my plans, they didn't want me to go, but reluctantly accepted my point. Simes, the civil leader of the community and my conscience, stepped forward and shook my hand, "We have a debt, we must honour it". Later, we packed a few things and made arrangements for our quest. Franc planned to head out towards the Mediterranean on the Eagle, the sailboat that Franc had appropriated in Valletta. We hoped more clarity would come to us along the way.

As Spall, Franc and I prepared to sail out of the haven, we were stopped by our friend Steve. Steve was an engineer, a master of all things mechanical and electrical. He was someone we relied on and valued technically, but his interpersonal skills were less than perfect. "Thanks for coming to wish us well Steve, I really appreciate it". "It's not that, but yes I do wish you well, of course I do", he said awkwardly. "We've received a message from Mont St Michel's leader, Sacha, who has shared the dream too. His vision has directed him to the Mediterranean, he is embarking on a quest to locate the entity who's been aiding us. When he found out you were going, he wondered if he could travel with you. He feels the journey would be too dangerous alone, so I agreed that you could give him a lift, I hope that's ok?" Steve looked flustered for a moment and added, "But yes, good luck and…whatever". He left, he obviously had too many things on the go. He stopped for a moment, turned once more and tried again, "Keep safe guys, we need you back here. Don't do anything stupid".

We joined Gio and Rene on the yacht, they were completing their final checks. They were Franc's friends from Valletta, skilled sailors who could pilot the boat through heavy seas. We were five men against the raging world. As we left port, I raised my hand to the commune, in return I received looks of deep concern accompanied by tentative, nervous smiles. At least they were honest, many presumed they wouldn't see us again. My heart was breaking to see Ciara and Matt in tears at the quayside, they were probably afraid to say goodbye in case it tempted the hand of fate. I'm sure Spall felt the same. Drake, our master builder, shouted at the top of his voice, "Come back to us alive! Don't take any fool chances. I'll pray for fair wind and calm seas". And so, we left our safe haven in search of a nebulous truth, upheld by the beleaguered prayers of an atheist.

It was a freezing cold day in April; the rough sea made the passage to northern France unpleasant. I vomited more times than I care to mention, my face was perpetually green. To my relief, the journey took less than three days in the strong winds. Gio teased Franc with a sly smile, "Remember it was you doing the vomiting not so long-ago". Rene couldn't resist an opportunity for banter with Gio. "Don't listen to the Italian stallion, he isn't so used to the big seas as he pretends, he is all chat, chat, chat. His testicoli are like peanuts when it comes to the challenge of the real ocean!" We laughed unstoppably until one of the sails came untied and we scrambled quickly to catch and re-tie the line to the cleat. Spall looked out from the prow, stoic and unflappable, he'd been a marine so rough seas were nothing to him, though even he kept his eyes on the horizon. We weighed anchor at Mont St Michel in the late afternoon gloom, roughly half a kilometre out from the silty inlet adjoining the island. No one appeared to notice our arrival.

We'd hoped for more of a cordial reception, it was almost as if we weren't expected. Eventually a small rowing boat bobbed across the waterway to join us. Sacha climbed the small ladder at the aft of the yacht, nimbly jumping on to the deck. He dropped his bag onto the bench seat and waved the rowing boat off. The boat was difficult to see, the oarsman turned around and headed back to the island silently, without engaging us in any way. "He was a friendly chap", I said smiling. "Oh, bear him no mind, he's a Philistine", replied Sacha coolly.

We'd spoken to Sacha from time to time on the radio. As you would expect, his voice sounded different in real life. Radio clips the extremes of the frequencies and lends a voice a thinner tone. We introduced ourselves and resumed our journey heading through the straits of Gibraltar. Sacha was a short man; he was slim and athletic looking with a small slender moustache. He wore a dark hoodie under his coat and kept the hood up. Noting my scrutiny, her said, "Froid, oui?... Sorry cold, isn't it?"

We rode the waves of the Atlantic Ocean quickly with minimal pleasantries. Sacha was charming, but his conversation was mostly superficial. It wasn't worth becoming too familiar too quickly, it was going to be a long journey. I thought we would have plenty of time to get to know each other, we could take our time.

As the journey progressed, I felt it was time to better understand our new colleague. "What brings you on this pleasurable cruise, Sacha?" "Like yourself, I've had dreams summoning me to Zakinthos to meet the, how you say it... the homme blanc". Sacha's comment instantly raised our attention, it was an immediate inconsistency. In his usual suspicious way, Steve must have sewed the Zakinthos seed as a test, in their original radio discussion. "Zakinthos? Are you sure? We're heading for Isola Salina to meet Father Giuseppe and hopefully our brother". Sacha's surprise took us off balance, but Spall brought the conversation back on track, "A nice trip then, from Sicily and on to Greece". Our mission when we arrived at Salina was unclear, but Sacha's intentions were anybody's guess, it was likely he had a totally different mission.

The voyage from northern France down to Gibraltar was less onerous, once through the straits, the sea was much calmer and warmer. We shed our outer jackets and chanced the odd swim. Rene began fishing again, we soon had plenty of protein for our table.

We hoped the infection would be less problematic on the mainland with the passage of time. The long hours of boredom on the trip were accompanied with friendly banter and lots of laughing. Laughter was the cure for every ailment. Sacha was quite aloof and avoided the humour, so the crew avoided targeting him with their abuse. I attempted to engage him in conversation a few times with little success. Our chats didn't go beyond superficial pleasantries, I eventually gave up trying. It was hard to understand the reasons behind his travel or his end goal. Despite his lack of engagement, he always completed his share of the chores and took his turn sailing the vessel. Although inexperienced, he was keen to play his part.

Later in the day, Gio hooked a large swordfish which was extraordinarily strong; it took him a long time to tire it. Gio let the fish pull the weight of the boat then gave it more line and gently pulled it in again repeatedly. "Look you can see it on the top of the wave. It's a big one", Gio beamed with excitement, "it'll feed us for a week". Rene quickly put him down as usual, "It's been dead for at least a month, look at the green on its gills". "Rubbish, you Algerian slug eater. It's a fine fish; you're so used to catching tiddlers!" Sacha looked concerned that a fight was about to start, but instead Gio and Rene laughed like brothers. Rene offered, "Come on, let me help you bring it in". Spall grinned but his eyes remained on the horizon.

Franc had been quiet for a few days, making me feel concerned. It was always a bad sign; he tended to brood on the horrors of his past when faced with time on his hands. "How are you doing, bro", I asked him gently. "I'm fine. I'm just not sure what to expect when we arrive at Salina. For most of my life I have faced death and loss, so I always anticipate the worst, at least until I met you. In the last few days, I've started to wonder if I could begin to enjoy life again". "It's called hope", I offered gently, "I always get a good feeling when we are together, we'll make a difference somehow. It's just a feeling, but so far, the dreams have steered us on an accurate bearing".

"The dreams are messages sent to you by the white guy. Don't you ever feel you're being manipulated, used like a pawn in a great chess game?" he queried sincerely. I responded patiently, "If I am being influenced, then the outcomes so far have been benevolent for us. We need to trust the messages until they prove unworthy". Franc was still concerned, "But what if we are being used, someone could be building our trust before destroying us?" I assured him, "We need to be vigilant, we're here for each other, we must trust each other when the time comes". Franc persisted, "True, but how do we know we are actually going to meet our brother?" I pondered it for a moment, it was a fair question, "At first, I was unsure you were my brother, but now I am certain. We must have faith in the white one, but more trust in those we love. It's all we have". Franc seemed more comfortable after our chat; he'd had such a terrible life I could understand him anticipating doom around every corner. But I trusted him, if he was nervous, then I should be too. Something was niggling him, but I don't think he truly understood what it was.

Spall woke me gently during the night, "Your watch, mate". I moved to the aft and took the wheel. The Eagle was easily skimming through the rolling waves of the Mediterranean. "There's something off", whispered Spall. I was unsure where he was going with this. "Haven't you noticed we're in a warm climate, we're all in T shirts, but Sacha hasn't taken down his hood once nor joined us for a swim?" "Well, I guess he's feeling a little cold", I replied. "Sacha has lived in northern France all his life, so he should be used to the cold. Not only that, but I'm also unsure he understands our mission. He says he's had the dreams, but he doesn't seem to understand the nature of our objective. It's like he's listened into our conversations, but he hasn't actually experienced the dreams with the white guy. It's only a hunch, but we need to be careful his cold bloodedness isn't because he's a reptile". We agreed to keep our guard up and take extra care, Spall was quite right there was something odd about Sacha, but then we didn't know him well enough. I thought he may open up to us, when we became more familiar, some folks take more time to build trust, especially if they've been through hell.

We didn't have a long-range radio on the boat, so it wasn't possible to contact the havens to communicate our concerns. We were long past Mont St Michel, and it was too far to Sicily to make contact with the havens quickly. I suggested to Spall that we changed course. The winds had dropped, and progress was slow for the time being. We headed towards to the Balearic Islands where we could contact Formentera Haven to confirm everything was ok. Spall passed the word about changing course to everyone except Sacha. The next day, Sacha spotted our change of course during his shift as pilot. Spall tried to make some bullshit excuse for Sacha not taking his turn, but Sacha was adamant. He knew something was up, he could sense our mood change. The atmosphere became fragile, as we neared Formentera tensions built up. We would be in radio range by the morning, hopefully we could confirm Sacha's identity, to relieve the unease.

A Doctrine of Fear - Paul JC Edge

That night I couldn't sleep, too many thoughts filled my mind. The gentle roll of the waves felt like Mother Nature rocking me to sleep, but it took a while. I woke to a strange sound in my cabin, the soft shuffle of stockinged feet and delicate breathing. It was odd. I couldn't see into the corners of my room despite the moonlight streaming through the porthole. Given my conversation with Spall, I felt my alarm bells ringing. As I reached for my nightlight, a figure approached at speed, I was pinned to the bed beneath the thick quilt. The moonlight reflected on the evil twin grooved dagger as it slashed through the air towards my throat. Time slowed as my adrenaline kicked in, then a bright light blinded me. My assailant suddenly burst into the fierce flames. Through the inferno the tip of a blade emerged and quickly withdrew.

"Get out of bed, it's on fire!" shouted Franc. I twisted violently; the burning corpse hit the floor, I thrust the bedclothes over the body to put out the flames. It became so hot, I had to get clear, the bedding was already aflame. Luckily, there was sufficient insulation in the quilt to protect me momentarily to aid my escape. Gio ran into the room with a bucket of water and threw it onto the burning figure, it had no effect whatsoever. Sacha continued to burn for a few seconds until his body turned to ash, sparks floated around in the cabin. We started to cough as the smoke thickened. We needed to get clear of the cabin. The others arrived with buckets of water and CO_2; the flames were soon extinguished, but the cabin was ruined.

"Are you ok?" asked Spall. My adrenaline rush had suppressed my senses, I hadn't noticed. I looked a mess; my hair had caught fire, but it had extinguished in the struggle, my arms and neck suffered minor burns. Spall grabbed the med kit and applied Alocane cream to the injury. "You were lucky", grumbled Spall, "lucky your brother always sleeps with that bloody sword beside him. Good job Franc, my god you got here fast". "I'm always waiting, trouble is always around the next bend. I had my suspicions about Sacha", Franc replied mercurially.

A few hours later, over breakfast, we discussed the events of the night. Franc became animated, "Did you see how he burst into flames as I skewered him? My sword only pierced the bastard's body for a fraction of a second and the blade became so hot I could barely hold it by the hilt. It was white hot, like it'd been in a forge, if I hadn't withdrawn it quickly it would have melted". I noticed Franc had stopped referring to Sacha by name. "What sort of creature was it?" Spall reminded us that we'd shot someone or something from the Crow's Nest a few weeks before who had also consumed by white flame. At the time, we'd referred to the creature as a Dark One.

"Was Sacha a man or a demon?" queried Gio. "He seemed like a man to me, he was relatively normal", I responded. "He was an oddball at the very least", objected Spall. Franc continued with his original line of thought, "Nothing could burn that hot but contain most of the heat within. It should've burned you to a crisp, it makes no sense. The heat hadn't fully penetrated all the quilt's insulation layers before you threw him off". Rene added, "It can take five to seven hours to burn a body. A human body can't be reduced to ash in seconds. It's crazy!" Gio couldn't resist a golden opportunity, even when the mood was serious, "Yes, five to seven hours to burn an average human body, obviously it would take at least ten hours to burn a big fat piccione like you". We laughed, but the atmosphere soon cooled. "It was demonic", asserted Gio. "It was a Dark One. We know they're hunting us, but we don't know why", responded Franc.

Rene managed to raise Formentera on the radio, they were recovering from a skirmish with the Shroom, so seemed a little off hand. However, they agreed to put in a call to Mont St Michel as soon as they could, to ascertain their status. We decided to maintain our position within range until we received confirmation from Mont St Michel. We dropped the sails and took a swim. A normally pleasant experience was stained by the adrenaline still coursing through our veins, but the exercise proved therapeutic. We returned to the yacht feeling more at ease.

The call came in from Formentera, Rene routed it to the loudspeaker, "MSM is in disarray. Their leader, Sacha, who has been missing for three days, was found floating in with the morning tide. Sacha had been stabbed in the heart; his blood exsanguinated. The team at MSM are in a state of shock following the senseless murder and are mourning him. He was a great leader who saved the inhabitants lives many times over". MSM claimed to have no knowledge of the radio message or our intention to visit. They would have prepared a welcome if they had known. Rene retold our story of the previous night. These were dark times indeed.

Without delay, we set sail for Sicily against a backdrop of beautiful blue skies with a few wispy white clouds. It was roughly 650 nautical miles to the island; the moderate wind meant we were only able to travel at around 7-8 knots. Our journey would take three days at a minimum, if we sailed through the night.

A Doctrine of Fear - Paul JC Edge

Without warning the boat lurched violently, a loud explosion from down below made the yacht falter. It could only have been a bomb, there were no reefs this far out to sea. The IED may have been in Sacha's bag, it clearly contained more than a few clothes. The situation soon became hopeless, the vessel was filling with water, it would only be a few minutes before it scuppered. Gio screamed, "Abandon ship!" We lowered the small inflatable motorboat into the water and climbed in. Spall noticed Rene was missing and returned to the cabin, finding him floating face down in the water. Rene's arms flailed in the flow forcing its way into the hull. Spall ran up to the helm and disappeared. Franc yelled, "Come on! It's going down fast; you need to get your ass over here!" The hull was two thirds submerged when Spall reappeared, the yacht suddenly reeled starboard; Spall fell into the water. I wasn't too worried, Spall was a great swimmer, but he only needed to snag his clothing, and he would go down with the yacht.

Spall climbed onto the stern and lithely stepped across into our dinghy. He passed Franc his katana. "You took a risk going back for my sword. Thank you!" exclaimed Franc. Spall replied in his usual deadpan, "De nada". The reality of the situation hit Gio like a tidal wave, "Rene! Where is Rene?" Spall explained, "He's gone mate, he was in the cabin when the IED exploded, he had no chance". Gio cried uncontrollably, "We need to save him! Let me go back". Franc wrapped his large arms around Gio and held him tight. "Let me go! Let me fucking go! Let me…". Franc loosened his grip but kept Gio in a bear hug as he sobbed. "I'm so sorry, I couldn't help him", comforted Spall, "he was a good man and a good friend". These words became his epitaph; it was all we could say as the yacht went down; it vanished down into the darkness of the ocean. "God bless you my friend", whispered Gio through his tears.

We headed to the marina in the north of Formentera, where we were met by a lukewarm welcoming committee. The team behaved as we would in the same situation, they needed to protect their island from infection. We were tired and rather unhappy, probably less than tolerant. Remaining at a safe distance from the harbour wall, we introduced ourselves and explained our recent misfortune. The Formentera team clarified their island was under quarantine and we weren't able to join them, as much as they would enjoy fresh company. We understood but requested a vessel to sail to Salina plus sufficient supplies for our three-day journey. I also expressed our need for any ammo they could spare. They generously selected a boat from the marina, there were more harboured vessels than they needed. They loaded supplies and a sailor piloted the boat out to us. He used our small motorboat for his return trip; it was a more than fair exchange. We kept a safe distance to reduce the risk of infection, remaining at the stern of the boat until we made the switch.

Their leader, Generale Enrico, hailed us from the harbour wall. He was interested in our trip to Salina and why we were risking so much to reach it. I explained about my dreams, he understood immediately. Although he hadn't experienced that particular dream, he was aware of the visions and so was curious, I promised to keep him informed. He agreed to update Summer Haven with our status, it would also help alleviate Kate's trepidations.

The pilot from Formentera returned to the marina whilst Franc chatted with Enrico in Spanish. Their conversation was cut short when one of his team shouted, "El Tigre!" The ensuing commotion made Franc visibly stiffen, he forced himself to relax, smiled genially and waved. A cheer went up from the crowd gathered at the quayside. I was certain Franc didn't revel in the attention; I knew he hated the nickname. "They are excited to see you Franc, you give them hope. They can see you still fighting after all you've been through and aspire to be like you. They're glad to have you on their side", I suggested gently. Franc replied thoughtfully, "I get it, Paul. I just don't like all the fuss to be honest, that's all. I don't feel like much of a hero". "You can't say that to me, you've saved my life on two occasions, one of which was only last night", I added, hoping he could see the love and gratitude in my eyes.

"This is a big rotten fishing boat, they've given us a cucciolo", moaned Gio as we headed out to sea. We all gave him a little slack; he'd had a bad day. Gio opened the sails, and the boat picked up speed. The wind was strong enough not to need the engine; we would save the fuel until we required it. It took nearly five days to reach Malfa on the northern coast of Isola Salina, the salt-lake island. We didn't arrive to a warm welcome there either.

9. The Darkness Falls on Salina

It was the end of a balmy, early summer evening. Bridget and I were finishing the day in a street café people watching, with a cool bottle of golden Malvasia wine, accompanied by some salty olives, and deliciously sweet figs. I wasn't wearing my cassock; I typically dressed informally for a priest: jeans, a linen shirt plus my firearm on my belt. I'd long since lost my embarrassment about the moving letters on my arms, but onlookers were often fascinated by them. They revered me rather more than I was comfortable with. I was an ordinary man in extraordinary times, the islanders seemed comfortable to follow my lead, I needed to show their trust wasn't misplaced. Father Enzo often reminded me; a Pope was often selected for his humility and beauty of spirit. This meant the one elected was often least expecting the papacy.

Without warning, Bridget dropped her wine glass. I reached down to help pick up the larger pieces of glass. "No!" she exclaimed, "Don't! Just leave the bloody glass Joe, look at your arms!" Unfamiliar phrases appeared on my flesh. A middle-aged red-haired woman sat behind me saw the writings and gasped. The words 'Tenebrae Factae venturus est' covered my arm.

We ran to the sanctuary and gathered the team to show them the warning, 'The Darkness is coming'. From experience, I presumed the writings were to alert us of imminent attack. They typically gave us direct warnings only in the direst situations. We quickly mobilised the priests and the Guard, preparing for the worst. They helped secure the elderly and those less capable of defending themselves safely into their homes and barricaded the doors. It'd been a long time since we'd been under threat, but we were ready. We never dropped our defences in these difficult times.

The guards at the island's three main ports reported multiple contacts on the radar. We instructed armed personnel to gather at the waterside and prepare our defence. Father Enzo insisted I stayed in the Sanctuary with Bridget, James, and Jane. We heard gunfire and then explosions from all sides of the island. Sparse details of the attack were reported via the radio, seven boats had approached the island, they steered into our ports on half throttle with no one aboard and exploded as they ran aground. Even within the thick stone walls of the Sanctuary, the sound reverberated. Jane urgently whispered, "We're like sitting ducks in here, we need to get out, it's a death trap!"

I commented, "The boats are empty, so it surely this means there isn't an issue?" Jane looked concerned, "The boats didn't pilot themselves. They were a planned distraction; the explosions were intended to draw our attention whilst the intruders' ingress the island in an alternative location". Jane's logic was indefatigable. She and James each picked up an H&K submachine gun and passed a pistol to Bridget. "I don't want that bloody thing!" she argued. "You will if someone tries to stab your bloody husband", asserted Jane. Her brutal but effective logic had worked on me in the past. Bridget picked up the pistol, a small revolver with no safety catch. "Just point and fire, very simple", instructed Jane, "but don't ever point it at anyone you don't mean to kill".

Jane estimated that, given the size of boats used, there were probably twenty to thirty assailants abroad. "They'll be dressed in black so won't be easily seen at night, it's most likely they'll hide during the day, but don't count on it". "Where are we going?" I asked in a state of near panic. "Somewhere with good visibility so we can see them coming". James returned from his room with four pairs of night vision goggles and Kevlar vests. We jumped in a Jeep that Jane had appropriated the day before and headed up towards the summit of Monte Porri volcano. The volcano was reasonably inactive, but tufts had been observed in 2005, it was as safe as these craters get. Enzo had informed me that a crater never erupted twice, an emission was more likely elsewhere, a very comforting thought.

We drove part way up the volcano, Jane abandoned the vehicle when the road became too steep. It was dark, we donned the infra-red night vision goggles, they lit up the surroundings in an eerie green. It was a hard climb, ascending the volcano at Jane's aggressive pace. James had no bother keeping up, but Bridget and I struggled. We kept ourselves in shape, but we hadn't completed army training and were almost hyperventilating. As we neared the top, James and Jane gathered large pieces of black basalt rock and used them to supplement an elementary circle that the Guard had pre-constructed near the highest point of the volcano with the crater behind us. Bridget and I joined in; before long the black wall reached waist height. The black volcanic rock was extremely heavy and dense, so was great protection from ordnance. However, if we were attacked with more sophisticated weaponry, it would prove ineffective.

It was likely the Dark Ones would attack stealthily from the shadows using daggers, so we needed to be vigilant. On foot, it would be hard for them to charge at speed, whilst ascending a very steep slag heap. The hill would constantly give way under foot, moving around would expend lots of energy and slow them down; it would also make noise. Jane had clearly been planning defence scenarios for some time. In the worst case, she explained, our assailants would ascend at the rear of the volcano, following the rim of the crater, and attack us from our flank.

Radio messages reported no activity. Jane called for increased vigilance and explained more about our enemy to the members of the Guard. Most islanders saw the Dark Ones as demons and were fearful of them. I had tried to explain that Dark Ones were not demons. They were simply men and women who could be stopped; we needed to face them head on. But uncertainty remained, the evil warriors used their mythology to breed fear in their victims, it weakened them.

We passed a couple of hours on tenterhooks before the trouble started. It must have taken some time for the Dark Ones to enter the island unseen from the water using the least populated places to gain maximum cover, they then had needed to dry out and regroup.

Jane radioed the Guard to concentrate their forces on defending the Sanctuary, the most likely place of attack. She also asked the priests to leave the building, Father Enzo politely refused. Enzo and a handful of monks had bolted the doors and armed themselves in preparation for trouble. Well good for them. It is said that God looks after those who look after themselves.

All hell broke loose at the Sanctuary, we could hear a barrage of gunfire. In less than an hour, we began to see figures moving up the path, ascending the volcano. The dark figures stopped to examine our jeep and continued their climb almost without breaking stride. I'd not used night vision goggles before; the cooling engine of our vehicle appeared in yellow whilst I could clearly see figures pursuing us in red. The climb was vigorous, their colour turned scarlet with their exertion. Jane and James opened fire; bright flames erupted on the hillside. We lifted our goggles until the fires burnt out and the burning embers floated away, the extreme heat and light rendered our night vision useless. We had counted fourteen Dark Ones approaching the jeep, eleven remained but they were no longer visible with or without the goggles. They had used the dense basalt rock of the volcano as cover. They now knew we were watching their approach, and we were armed.

Jane informed us that a squad were crawling directly towards us, staying low. As we'd opened fire, they were more likely to reciprocate with firearms. I could only see them occasionally, but they were closing in hastily. James indicated that a small number of Dark Ones were attempting to circle behind us. He slid out of the protective rock circle and moved silently around to the north side of the crater. He lay quietly, observing. Bridget and I felt useless, our pistols were drawn but we could only use them in close quarters, so we were unable to help. Jane opened fire, her gun barking rapidly, three figures exploded into balls of flame on the hillside. Then, the Dark Ones opened fire; they shot blindly in the direction of Jane's muzzle flashes. Her wise decision to move a couple of metres to the left after opening fire had probably saved her life. The gunfire stopped and the waiting game continued.

James opened fire in our direction, Jane screamed, "What the fuck?" but then quickly identified his reasoning. Two figures had climbed up the hillside in our blind spot. One flamed, rendering our infra-red goggles useless again for a few seconds. In the time it took for us to raise our goggles, the other assailant leapt over the wall, its dagger shining in the firelight. Jane leapt from a crouched position, pivoted and kicked the figure in the jawbone with her heel. A loud sickening crack signified she had hit her target, the Dark One dropped its dagger and staggered sideways under the full impact of the kick. Jane turned her rifle and shot it full in the face. The figure flamed as James ran back to the protective circle raising his weapon.

The remaining five Dark Ones saw their opportunity and charged up the hill. The moving mass of shale beneath their feet slowed them but despite this, they maintained an impressive pace. They ran in opposing patterns to make them harder to pinpoint. Guns barked and bright flames reflected from the sky. Every time a figure flamed; we lost vision for a couple of seconds. The last Dark Ones approached from our flank, the leader leapt over the wall, James shot it in the chest mid-flight, as the remaining three figures joined the fray.

I froze holding the gun in front of me, Bridget fired in a state of panic, aiming vaguely at a figure approaching us and almost blew the Dark One's head off. Before the cadaver hit the floor, it flamed. Jane smashed an assassin on the bridge of its nose with the butt of her rifle viciously, jolting its neck, it immediately combusted. The last assailant charged, screaming at the top of its voice. Jane kicked the flaming figure into the attacker as it leaped towards me with dagger raised. The burning corpse hit knocked it off course, it hit the wall on its knees. The Dark One instantly regained its footing and twisted as it raised its knife to strike. The stress of the situation overwhelmed me, I overreacted; I emptied the whole magazine of my pistol in its chest in blind panic. "Calm down, you got him", yelled Jane. It was strange because this one didn't explode into flames like the others, it simply dropped to its knees and fell forwards. Jane lifted its head by the hair, it was just a man. His face was bloody, and part of his jaw had been blown away. He was no demon. "This one's dressed differently to the others, I think he might have been their leader", observed James. "Yes, he wasn't so keen to become a human furnace, was he?" added Jane. "What's the strange ring around his head?" I queried. Jane chose not to touch it. A pair of curved metallic bands emerged from behind his ears and entered his skull at the temples. James tugged at the band, but it wouldn't come free.

The brutality of the battle left Bridget and I shaking, the attack was borne from the purest hatred. "Keep down, there might be more", commanded Jane. "We need to go to the Sanctuary, people have died there tonight, I can feel it, they need our help", I mumbled. Jane considered the request; she knew her priority was to protect me, but reluctantly agreed. We jogged and half slid down the slaggy hill to the Jeep, only to find the tyres had been slashed. Someone was keen to prevent our escape, no surprise there. Despite the damage, Jane advised us to strap ourselves into the vehicle.

Jane drove the jeep down the hill without the luxury of tyres. The poor traction made meant the vehicle swerved from side to side randomly as we descended, making terrible grinding noises. We traversed the majority of the volcano's slag quickly, nearing the bottom we hit a wall. The jeep's airbags detonated, filling the cabin full of dust. We were all shaken, but ok. Our night vision goggles didn't help on the rough basalt paths, the ground was dense and emitted very little heat. We walked to a nearby olive plantation, Jane soon located an older vehicle that she was able to hotwire. Having started the engine, she rammed her foot in the steering wheel spokes to snap the lock.

We arrived at the Sanctuary to find much of the community in disarray, many were sobbing, it had been a bloodbath there. The dead and injured had been carried into the square at the front of the building. Four of the deceased were priests; they were my friends. I was forced to hold myself together for the sake of the living, so I focussed my attention on triaging the injured.

Father Enzo had received a terrible slashing contusion across his neck. A parishioner desperately attempted to compress the wound with a towel, aiming to hold back the river of blood seeping from his neck. "I'm done, my friend, it was a privilege knowing you", he gasped, his voice croaky. "Will you perform the…", he stopped to regather his composure, "Last Rites for me?" His face was deathly pale; but his expression turned to shock when I refused him this last dignity. "I won't let you go, you're far too precious to me, to all of us". "Please", he begged. I removed the towel and staunched the blood flow with my bare hands. I prayed for his salvation, "Don't let dear Enzo die like this!"

The darkness of the night was suddenly broken, as the entire plaza was swathed in light. The whiteness grew in intensity, onlookers gasped, I could see Enzo as if it was daylight. He began to shake, the colour returned to his face and his bleeding was staunched. The terrible wound closed beneath my fingertips; a faint scar remained in its place. Gently Enzo placed his hands on mine and leaned into me. "I'd heard about this, but I didn't believe it, sorry I had such little faith", he gasped. The crowd looked on bewildered, confused by what they'd witnessed.

Bridget grasped James' arm, "What the hell has just happened? What did your dad just do?" James held her hand tenderly, "Dad saved my life in the same way. I took a terrible abdominal wound in Spain, and he fixed it. Dad believes that God performs his work using his hands". Bridget cried, but her face wasn't sad, they were tears of happiness for Enzo.

I helped the remaining casualties, most of their cuts had been stitched by Sister Maria, some exhibited minor bruising. Brother Phillippe, a visiting French Benedictine monk, suffered a terrible gunshot wound to his stomach, whilst trying to reason with a Dark One, an impossible but noble act. I put my hand on Sister's shoulders as she treated him, she made room whilst continuing to compress the wound firmly. I gently released her grip and placed my hands directly on the wound then prayed. Once again, bright light filled the square. Brother Jean, Phillippe's travelling companion, cried as the injured man sat up. Jean hugged me, but quickly moved to his injured colleague, gently taking him into his arms.

Five others needed my help that day, the Lord was willing to aid us. The square filled with our community as the islanders heard the news, they joined the crowd with an overpowering need for fellowship. They looked on in awe and wonder. I scanned their faces, I felt the crowd would benefit from the unity of prayer. They'd witnessed great wonders and needed to feel close to the Lord. I held out my hands and uttered the first words, Father Alfredo joined me. I paused for a moment and smiled at him warmly, I was glad he was alive and well.

Alfredo wore his long robe with the hood up, which was unusual on such a warm night. His hands were grasped together inside his robe; when the folds separated it revealed his right hand gripping a long wicked blade.

Alfredo calmly announced, "I've been waiting for this moment for a very long time, Guiseppe". His face darkened into a menacing grimace as he lifted his arm to strike me, but his arm didn't move, remaining upright. The expression of hatred left his face, and he became calm. His head slid down towards his chest and his body burst into flame. I stood frozen to the spot, bewildered. Alfredo had been decapitated by another man from behind. As the blinding flame cleared, a mirror image of me appeared through the conflagration. For a split second, my confusion engulfed me, but I realised the figure was another man, he merely looked like me. He had three claw-like scars across his cheek. "Well met my brother", the figure uttered to me, with a hint of a Spanish accent.

10. Light Must Follow Darkness

"That fucking rattlesnake", spat Bridget, "He was playing me all the time". "He was playing us all, Bridget. I loved that young man", added Father Enzo patiently, with a sad smile.

I conducted a service for those we'd lost in the main square. The congregation slowly filtered back to their homes, they discussed the harrowing events of the night, but also the wonder of the healing. They carried a little hope with them, we had all witnessed divine intervention. As word spread, the seriously injured were brought to the Sanctuary for help. I was exhausted, hardly able to stand afterwards.

The death toll had been too high, we had lost over a hundred islanders. The Dark Ones had avoided the location of key strategic points where the Guard were stationed, they'd been well informed by the traitor, Father Alfredo. They were well briefed on our tactics, our strengths and weaknesses, but we had overcome the attack, they'd underestimated our resolve; next time they would be better prepared.

Bridget and I strolled from the Sanctuary to a café in the village of Leni. Paul and Franc joined us with James and Jane. Bridget sat at our usual table, gone were the days of service, we helped ourselves. I downed two glasses of wine rather quickly and expressed my gratitude to Franc for saving my life. It felt unusual to be sitting with two men who were my double. I was a few years older than Paul and Franc, but we were so alike it was eerie. A man named Spall arrived, and Paul introduced him to us.

Paul felt the need to clarify, "I had no idea I had a brother, let alone an identical twin, until I met Franc. The white figure set us on a quest to find our third brother, which we found disturbing". "How did you actually know we were brothers, and I would be here?"

Paul explained, "The white figure in our dreams alerted us to the existence of another brother and dispatched us to locate you". I replied, "The Pope mentioned seeing God in his dreams as a white figure. He was warned of the crisis and made preparations. It sounds like the Lord been speaking to you too". "The white figure has supported and helped me all my life. It wasn't just the apocalypse that brought the visions to me", explained Franc. Spall listened with a neutral expression, awaiting some kind of revelation patiently. I clarified I hadn't experienced dreams with the white figure, my messages were received in the form of stigmata-like writings, which were equally unusual. "Our Lord and saviour is leading us on a path to our salvation, we can rely on him in this crisis", I pointed out. "Many of the seven haven leaders have experienced the dreams", noted Paul.

Paul appeared thoughtful for a moment and changed the subject to a matter concerning him. "Sorry to bring up a sensitive subject, but Alfredo's decapitated head worries me, there are very few Dark Ones' artefacts for us to examine". "Another Dark One didn't self-combust at the volcano", added Jane. "What disturbs you, Paul, other than the obvious fact that you have Alfredo's head in your bag?" I asked curiously. "I found some kind of fine silky fabric under the hood of Alfredo's robe", observed Paul. He then removed a piece of bloody fabric from the bag. Paul further examined the thin metallic membrane; it was gruesome, causing Bridget to turn away in disgust. Paul very carefully cut a tiny section from the cloth of the hood and placed it on the table. He then struck the cloth with the handle of his hunting knife, as the fabric absorbed the energy of the blow, it burst into white flame. The intensity of the flames shocked us. The cloth extinguished almost immediately. Fortunately, the table remained intact, although the heat was immense it radiated upwards, we moved to avoid getting burned. "The flame is hotter than a blowtorch, yet the heat only emanates from one side of the cloth. The conflagration activates when someone strikes a significant blow". Spall interjected, "This proves that the Dark Ones aren't demons, they're just men, as we said. Men who are mortal and can be killed in the same way as we can". "Please, no more talk of killing tonight, I can't bear any more", I requested. "Sorry", muttered Spall understandingly.

We asked James to take the remaining fabric to Enzo's friend, Umberto, so he could examine it in more detail. He was a prominent physicist who lived in the village of Pollara. He'd leased analytical equipment from the University in Rome for his studies. Hopefully, he would be able to use the equipment to assess the nature of the cloth.

Afterwards, I strolled leadenly with Bridget to our room in the Sanctuary and collapsed into a deep sleep without undressing. Bridget tugged off my shoes and covered me with a blanket. We were still waging war, but with whom and why?

Father Enzo organised lodgings above the café for Franc, Paul, and their companions. Spall remained in the cafe with Jane and Gio, they needed one for the road. Jane was happy to leave me in the capable hands of the Guard for one night. Gio realised that Isola Salina was an oasis and had ridden the wave with little change. Perhaps things weren't so bad, he raised his glass and proposed a toast to his fallen friend. "To Rene" they echoed.

I suffered with night terrors, dreams of dark figures attacking with sharp daggers. Islanders in flames, screaming. Burning inverted cruciform spanned the horizon, I woke in a cold sweat. I rose quietly, trying not to wake Bridget and took a cool invigorating shower. It was a new day, perhaps it would be better than the last. After breakfast, everyone gathered in the empty café, where my new friends were staying. James updated us on Umberto's thoughts concerning the fabric.

When James arrived at Umberto's, he found him in a catatonic state, brought on by copious amounts of brandy. Umberto managed to regain full faculty when James explained the situation, and the evening's attacks. He made excuses that he didn't have the equipment for the analysis to hand, but he would have the results within a week. He briefly inspected the fabric with an atomic microscope, he believed it was an intricate mesh of tiny, microscopic devices. There was little more he could add at this stage.

The radio dialogue with Summer Haven continued, they were keen to ascertain if their team were faring well. We warned the havens of the impending threat of the Dark Ones. It was odd that the other havens hadn't attracted much interest from the Dark Ones so far. Rusty and Sheena at Summer Haven were deeply concerned their leaders would be forced to confront them without their support. I had a strange feeling they already knew about this cult, but they weren't giving anything away.

A Doctrine of Fear - Paul JC Edge

We made contact with Captain McCreedy, the commanding officer of a navy nuclear submarine, Paul had previously made his acquaintance; he seemed decent enough. He was heading to Russia via the Gulf of Finland, having received a confusing radio transmission from St Petersburg. McCreedy intended to investigate the message and check for survivors. His vessel had been travelling to Samsø Haven with a food delivery and had diverted when they received the SOS.

Jane, James, and I took a little time to get to know the team from Summer Haven properly, last night's introduction had been a little rushed. We sat with Paul and Franc and exchanged tales. Our stories were a little fragmented, it was impossible to see the threads binding them. Paul and Franc had both experienced dreams of a white figure asking them to join me in the search for the white one. Personally, I believed the white figure was our Lord, though I failed to convince Paul and Franc. I sensed God was always around us and we simply couldn't go on a trip to meet him in person, it made no sense. The concept of finding him was a metaphor; God was suggesting they opened their hearts to Christianity. They didn't understand the subtle ways of the Lord. I suspected they would in time, they had good hearts and souls.

I changed the subject, the atmosphere was becoming uncomfortable, "Please don't interpret my thoughts as a lack of gratitude for your help last night Paul, but how did you access the Island so easily? Our Guard was patrolling the main ports and villages, with orders to intercept all ingress to the island with lethal force, and because of the Dark Ones, they would most likely shoot first and ask questions later".

Paul summarised their arrival, "We followed the four launches piloted by the Dark Ones but couldn't keep pace in our old fishing boat. Gio tailed the last of the Dark Ones' motorboats into the port at Malfa from a safe distance. On reaching the port, the Dark Ones dived from their boats. The boats were rigged to ram the port and explode as a distraction, allowing the Dark Ones to sneak onto the island at various points, using scuba gear.

"During the confusion, our small fishing boat arrived undetected. Spall, Franc, and I were able to sneak on to the beach and quietly move into town. We had previously encountered the Dark Ones on our journey here, one of them joined our yacht posing as Mont St Michel's leader, Sacha. He attacked us and destroyed our vessel; we picked up this old tub from Formentera Haven on the way. We walked into Malfa using the cover of the buildings, most people were safely barricaded inside. We ran across a solitary Guard member who seemed to be afraid and was trying to summon his courage. Spall approached him unthreateningly and encouraged him to rejoin his comrades. As he did, he probed him for directions to Father Giuseppe, he was told to head to the Sanctuary in Valdichiesa along the main road.

"By the time we reached the Sanctuary, it was in disarray. A team of Dark Ones had penetrated the building, the priests had put up a fight. Father Alfredo was supposedly leading the effort, but he disappeared when the trouble started. When Franc and Spall entered the sanctuary, seven intruders remained. Guns barked and the dark figures were dispatched quickly, initially they were only armed with daggers. Several priests had been tortured, including Father Enzo, but I don't think they divulged your whereabouts.

The Dark Ones managed to find your location in the end, presumably due to the treachery of Alfredo. Gio and I kept watch on the outside of the church, we witnessed the firefight on the volcano; the gunfire was too far away for us to offer meaningful assistance".

"We've been incredibly lucky", I ventured. "How do you know?" asked Jane, "There could be another team on their way right now". Paul responded, "From your report, there were fourteen attackers on the hill and seven died at the Sanctuary, plus seven at various points of ingress". Jane added, "Four groups of seven, the Dark Ones prefer to operate in teams of seven for a strike force. We need to identify if any others were killed, to be certain". "You won't find the bodies, so we need to rely on witnesses. I counted the Dark Ones on the volcano, so let's exclude them as they are confirmed kills". "I'm on it", asserted James. Using the radio to quiz the Guard teams, he ascertained twenty-eight Dark Ones were killed. "We always come back to combinations of the mystical number seven", commented James to no one in particular.

"Is the Type 26 frigate in the main port fully operational? I didn't think they'd been released into operational service yet", queried Spall. I explained the Pope had commissioned it as a special one off, its sole purpose was to keep me safe. Spall was flabbergasted the Vatican owned a ship at all. I still couldn't understand why I was so special to warrant such a humungous spend. Spall suggested we deployed the frigate to the north side of the island. North was the bearing from which the Dark Ones' launches approached. The frigate's sensor arrays, and long-range radar would detect any vessels inbound from miles away. It could also intercept potential threats before they got close to the island. It was sound logic; the vessel was launched immediately as the crew remained on permanent standby.

I questioned how the Dark Ones had managed to enter the sanctity of our home, "My understanding was the Dark Ones couldn't enter hallowed ground. How did they penetrate the Sanctuary?" Father Enzo had been sitting at the back of the café drinking a strong expresso, he appeared to be unaffected by the torment inflicted upon him only a few hours before. He was an old man, but he was still wiry and strong. Enzo joined the group to vocalise his thoughts, "Last night's attack was unexpected, Alfredo must have systematically desecrated our Sanctuary. I found the chapel's crucifix and many precious holy icons defiled". "An inside job by that rattlesnake, Alfredo", concurred Bridget as if she were spitting the snake's venom from her mouth.

"How did the Dark Ones survive the infection?" enquired Gio to the group in general. "If they are just men, then they should have been infected along with everyone else, surely". No-one could venture a response to his question, other than inferring they also prepared a haven. James became curious, "Why attack with daggers? They are able to use conventional weapons; we were assaulted with guns in Porto and also on the hill. It makes no sense; they know we have guns". "I guess they were reliant on the element of surprise, they prefer to use daggers for some reason", observed Paul. "If they worship Satan, the use of daggers may have ceremonial significance", added Jane. "Perhaps it's a matter of honour", mused Spall, "if they comprehend the concept of chivalry".

"In our dreams, the white figure asked us to join you in finding him", reiterated Paul. "Yes, it's a curiosity", I responded. "Why would God request such a thing? I've pondered your question, and it makes little sense to me. My only conclusion is, he is asking you to have faith, as I have already said". "How do you know God is talking to us?" challenged Franc once again, "could it be another person or being? I'm not blaspheming or disrespecting you, I just wondered if there were multiple hands at play here. Is there anything in the bible where God intervenes in matters of man in such a way?" I confirmed God's direct intervention was an Old Testament concept, but many cultures still believe it to be the case. Paul chipped in, "Where is the white figure? Why don't we go and find him, once and for all?" The problem was we had no clue where he could be found.

A few eventless days passed, we discussed the plan to look for the white figure and where we might start. Firstly, we needed transport, and the frigate was the best option. My brothers and I would be accompanied by the crew plus Jane, James, and Spall. Gio and Bridget would stay on the island to help provide support and leadership.

Our plan didn't go down well with the wider community, they didn't like to see their priest leaving them in such difficult circumstances. The Dark Ones were hunting me, if we left aboard the frigate, Salina would be unlikely to need its protection.

Umberto delivered his assessment of the Dark Ones hood in the main hall of the sanctuary. It was critical to understand the threat posed by them, and the fabric may be a critical piece of the puzzle. I closed the doors, I didn't want the results becoming general knowledge, at least until I understood them myself. Umberto began with caveats, "I don't have the right equipment or expertise to give you detailed analysis, but this is the best I have". "The best you have is more than good enough for us", I reassured gently. "Don't make it too complex, I beg you. We're not scientists". Bridget coughed from the back, "Ok, most of us aren't", I added wryly.

"Essentially, the fabric is way beyond any technology I have ever seen. I don't think its properties are conceivable in even the most radical research institutes", he began tentatively. "First of all, I noticed the fabric emits harmless levels of radioactivity. To be honest, the signature is of the order of radium used to create radioluminescence in a traditional watch. The cloth consists of a weave of microscopic devices, linked together in a chain. I would normally classify them as nano devices, but they are much smaller, the term pico devices may be more appropriate. The pico devices are impossible to dissect and examine without the use of specialised equipment, but the microscopic X Ray and ultrasound scans showed they have similarities to a nuclear reactor". "Hold on, are you saying the fabric comprises of thousands of reactors woven together?" Paul queried. "I am indeed".

The room fell silent, Umberto had acquired a hundred percent of our combined attention. "When you provide the fabric with energy, such as a bullet piercing the cloth, it triggers one or more devices, which sets off a chain reaction across the network. Triggering it only requires a small input of energy, a hard blow with a hammer or a stab with a sharp implement would suffice". I used an example to confirm his assertion, "An elderly lady set one off with a sharp pair of needlework scissors when I was attacked in England". "I'd have liked to have seen that", said Spall grinning maliciously, "the old girl must have chutzpah".

Umberto continued, "In the fabric, the energy expended in the chain reaction is vectored in a single direction. It's a fair assumption that the energy from the vest is directed inwards, therefore the heat escaping outward is negligible, probably through apertures such as the cuffs. It's thermal monodirectional properties are quite remarkable, given that the temperature inside the garment is similar to the surface of a small sun. I ran an experiment with a thermocouple on either side of the fabric, when I activated the cloth. The temperature on the cool side registered a deviation of only 23°C. I wasn't able to register a temperature reading on the hot side. The thermocouple and its stand became white-hot molten steel which burnt through the bench, at least until I extinguished it with CO_2".

The fabric's characteristics explained our vanishing enemy, but also the commonly held perception they were demonic in nature. "The heat shielding must be phenomenal, a Dark One ignited on my chest in the boat. There was only a thick quilt between me and the flames. I escaped with a few mild burns on my arms and face. The quilt was incinerated when I threw it off", explained Paul. "It must have been a heavy fireproof quilt with plenty of insulation", observed Umberto.

"My conclusion is this material presents quite a conundrum; its manufacture is implausible given current science. Whoever made the fabric has used technology beyond my experience". Umberto's results were highly informative, they showed the expertise we were up against. Whilst being helpful, the briefing left us with more questions than answers.

We were left shell shocked. How could the Dark Ones deploy such advanced technology? It made no sense. It was clear they weren't supernatural; they were simply well equipped. We were yet to understand their motives. "We come back to the old question then", cited Spall, "Given their advanced technology, why would they attack with blades?"

11.   From Russia... with Love

Extract from the HMS Astute ship's log:
Commanding officer: Captain B. K. McCreedy
CLASSIFIED
Dates and coordinates redacted

Date: Day 00604
Coordinates: XXXXXX   Course: ENE   Sea: Choppy   Wind: High   Temp: 6°C
Remarks: Current position: North Sea to the east of Aberdeen; completing our mission to transport goods to Denmark, whilst liberating survivors from oil rigs in the area. Crew on the rigs found dead, there was insufficient food and potable water available. First Officer Caterham and I decided to abandon the mission, it's no longer viable. Plotted our revised course to return to Denmark with supplies. Received a weak radio signal from Leningrad area. The region is not a known haven and merits investigation. Course re-planned for Gulf of Finland. Travel underwater full speed ahead, XX knots.

Date: Day 00643
Coordinates: XXXXXXX   Course: NE   Sea: Mod   Wind: Gale   Temp: 0°C
Remarks: We entered the Gulf of Finland. Made good progress, nothing of note. Winds: gale force (Beaufort level 8) on the surface so proceeding underwater for maximum speed.

Date: Day 00665
Coordinates: XXXXXXX   Course: E   Sea: Mod   Wind: Mod   Temp: 1°C
Remarks: Approaching Kotlin Island, Russia. Travelling on the surface, winds dropped, so we can reconnoitre. Passed the Fort

Grand Duke Constantine on port side and entered Neva Bay. No activity seen. The radio transmissions clearly received, identified as standard Morse SOS. Attempting to triangulate the source.

Date: Day 00666
Coordinates: XXXXXXXX   Course: -   Sea: Calm   Wind: Low   Temp: 2°C
Remarks: The source of the signal is Novgorod, a city roughly 200km inland and 600km from Moscow. Attempted communication via duplex radio and simple Morse Code but not received a reply. Planning an expedition to the source, making port in Leningrad, plenty of empty bays. Shroom activity minimal. Plan to take local vehicles to execute the expedition inland, with a task force of six, led by myself. First Officer Caterham remains in command. Aiming to leave at first light.

A Doctrine of Fear - Paul JC Edge

From the personal journal of Captain B. K. McCreedy
CLASSIFIED
Dates and coordinates redacted

Date: Day 00667

A search and rescue team of 6 has now been scrambled: Myself, Thompson, Howard, Callaghan, D'Astri and Kravlov. It's a multidisciplinary team to allow us to affect any emergency as may be required:

Callaghan – Engineering
Kravlov – Communications, has fair local language skills
Thompson and Howard – Marines
D'Astri - General deck hand but has mechanic skills to assist with hot wiring vehicles

06:00 Departed the docks via the main entrance, D'Astri acquired two vehicles from the port's parking area. It took him around three minutes per car, this information won't be added to my captains log for obvious reasons, though I guess no one will care now. We proceeded through Tosno to the main M10 highway. The road signs were not easy to follow, but Kravlov did a fairly good job. No Shroom activity evident in the area. Many vehicles littered the roads. We managed to push most of the vehicles causing blockages out of the way, but we were forced to backtrack on three occasions. In general, progress was acceptable, considering the state of play.

08:37 Followed the main road into Novgorod city, no visible Shroom activity. The SOS signal was triangulated by Kravlov to a point in the Valdai Hills near to the Valdaysky National Park. Followed the M10 to a hillside which looked unusual to the trained eye. The natural geography had been tampered with; the large chain link fence was a dead giveaway. We located the bunker vents; they had been deliberately hidden by a small copse of relatively new trees. It's a beautiful part of the world, no time for sightseeing. The bunker was the obvious source of the signal. Recon for main bunker entrance.

09:42 On closer examination, we found a cold war era nuclear bunker and vent system within the compound. Plan to approach the facility with care.

10:12 Callaghan took down the gates with an angle grinder. Drove vehicles into the compound. D'Astri checked for traps and mines on foot, we proceeded slowly. Unusual for such a Neanderthal heavy construction to be built in such a beautiful area. No-one would expect to find a bunker here, which is kind of the point, I guess.

11:32 Located the entrance to main bunker. The door is 10m standard blast door, jammed shut by two large articulated lorry tractor units. They've been rammed into the door at an oblique angle in order to stress the runners and prevent the door from opening. If it's a standard fit out, then the door would be circa 1m thick reinforced steel plate. Cutting through was not an option, it would take months. CCTV doesn't appear to be operational; the retinas were seen to be unfocussed. Thompson and Kravlov started looking for an emergency exit, low probability of success. Why build a nuke proof bunker and then put a weak back door into it?

12:55 After lunch, Callaghan attacked the doors with an enormous adjustable spanner in frustration. The spanner made an unholy clang which set our teeth on edge. It was a stupid thing to do, it would alert living beings (or Shroom) to our presence. I was about to reprimand him, but we got a response from the other side of the door. There was a standard SOS sequence followed by a rhythmic pattern which was clearly code.

13:31 SNAFU. We have established dialogue in Russian Morse Code with a team trapped in the bunker. Russian Morse code approximates standard Morse using the Latin alphabet, for which Kravlov has basic understanding and can translate for us (mostly). Roughly 200 people have been trapped in the bunker for the last six months. They locked down on A-Day in an attempt to escape the infection. They reported a plentiful supply of air, water, and rations, but morale is low. In frustration, the assassins (very probably Dark Ones as were encountered at Salina) blocked them in the bunker, effectively burying them alive. The assailants had attempted to poison the air filtration vents to eliminate those trapped. It was a cruel and wicked move but was obviously unsuccessful. The trapped had been sending international standard SOS since the day they were entombed. They had little hope of a reply, they presumed the infection had killed everyone. The assassins have sabotaged the base's aerial tower explaining the weak signal transmission. We have a lot of upset people down here, need to see what we can do PDQ.

17:12 Finally got the trucks untangled from the main bunker door, some good work from Callaghan and Howard in getting the trucks running again. The main door has opened a crack, 15cm high, allowing us talk to the occupants, which is giving them hope. The runners on the doors were irreparably damaged when they were rammed by the trucks. Callaghan jerry rigged grappling hooks to pass under the door and has used the tractor units to pull the door back onto its runners, though the huge guides buckled. He has fitted three lorry jacks under the blast door to bolster the tired motor array. Let's hope Callaghan's magic does the trick.

21:00 The doors have opened roughly 40cm, incredibly happy but bewildered people are emerging from the bunker. There were big smiles, hugs and tears all round. 212 people (mix of soldiers and civilians, both M and F) emerged all told. Kravlov attempted to translate, though some of the rescued speak a decent level of English, which helped immensely. They were all very keen to understand the status of the infection. I have clarified the activity of the infection is quite low these days, which was a big relief to them (and us all). Once they were all out, we stopped for food and rest. The Russians kindly supplemented our travelling rations with the bunker's stores. I'm not sure I wanted them to re-enter the god forsaken place at any price, if anyone farts loud enough the bloody door will drop again.

23:07 After a few vodkas and some food, the survivor's stories emerged. The Russians had advance warning of the infection due to an incident near Kostroma a few months prior to A-Day. They were forced to use a tactical nuke to destroy the Shrooms, it also took out the remaining civilian survivors. The death of innocent citizens would cause significant political embarrassment, so the Russian government kept the event under wraps. President Putin was not informed of the severity of the infection initially, to provide plausible deniability. But as the situation worsened, his permission was needed to deploy the nuke to contain the issue.

When the main meteorites struck, the Russian government didn't anticipate the high mortality rate, given the countermeasures they had planned. Military units were awarded emergency powers to contain infected areas. Military aircraft were placed on standby to set fire to infected regions using kerosene, incendiary missiles, and napalm. The measures to contain the infection failed.

The military allocated six nuclear bunkers to manage the risk of losing key members of government. Government leaders and high ranking military officers were housed in the bunkers, with the plan to reinstate the government after the epidemic.

In the last year, the bunkers have been systematically attacked by the assassins. The Russians don't know who the black figures are, or their motives. Of the six bunkers, two survived the attacks, the Valdaysky bunker and a bunker close to Moscow. These bunkers were more modern, they were equipped with advanced air filtering systems which detected the toxins injected into the vents and purged them. When the toxin failed, the attackers barricaded the door instead.

Date: Day 00668
06:15 Early breakfast and set to work to widen the opening of the bunker door.

12:12 The bunker door has been opened halfway. Equipment and vehicles are being mobilised from the interior garage. They have been well maintained by the team here, despite their plight. Civilians have begun to move everything to Novgorod Kremlin, their new HQ, with a small armed escort led by a man called Gradtov. They refuse to make the bunker their home at any price and will deploy armed guards around Novgorod to manage the threat from the Dark Ones, though they are probably long gone. The military are remaining here, led by

Smitsky to assist. The survivors need to begin their plan to rebuild. I've spoken to them about the six surviving havens and provided the most commonly used radio frequencies.

We are planning to move on to the second bunker in the vicinity of Moscow now, our small force will be supplemented by the Russian soldiers. We have formed a task force with my men, plus the remaining 23 commissioned officers and grunts from the Russian Army. Colonel General Smitsky has avoided a discussion on who is in charge, which I am grateful for. We are just operating as comrades, as he put it. I wouldn't feel happy handing over my command to a goddamned Russian, and he knows it. However, the days of mutual enmity are long over, there are so few of us left. We need to start a new spirit of cooperation; I need to change my old ways; the Russians have. They are the friendliest people I have met, but I guess I would be friendly towards someone who saved me from certain suffocation and starvation. There are no races and cultures here, only people. We need to work together now. I am writing this as a record, an aide-mémoire to myself, to the bigoted old fool I had been.

17:55 We hit the outskirts of Moscow quite quickly, but we came across a troop of living Shroom. The trucks were heavy, we simply drove through them and were well past them before their spores erupted. We will need to avoid the route on the way home to avoid risk of infection. We had been complacent by not being equipped to protect ourselves from the infection properly, we'd seen so little activity lately. The Russians had opened fire as we smashed through the troop and managed to eliminate the remaining Shroom as we hoofed past them. I explained to Smitsky that dry sulphur powder also destroyed

Shroom, but we hadn't brought any with us. We agreed to stop at the large sulphuric acid plant in Moscow to stock up before returning. Several of the troops knew its location, I couldn't even begin to pronounce its name.

19:56 Our task force arrived at Moscow bunker a little later than we'd hoped, it was almost dark. No lights working other than from the vehicles and our LED lanterns. Its location was confirmed as National Park Zavidovo, it was nestled amongst the enormous forests. Both bunkers had been hidden in national parks. It seemed like a good place to locate them, hiding in plain sight. The bunker fences must have been accepted by the locals and tourists somehow, perhaps they could be pretending to house protected wildlife. Zavidovo is also a place of outstanding beauty. Apparently, my favourite composer, Tchaikovsky, was born here according to Smitsky. He seems to be a remarkably interesting man. His English is far superior to my non-existent Russian. He claimed to have visited England several times when he and his brother acquired properties in Liverpool by the waterside. Now it matters not, he says, 'All gone'. There seem to be a great many mouldy Shroom in the Moscow area; we needed to dodge them as we drove in. They'd turned green and looked gangrenous, so they appear to be quite safe. However, I advised caution; like rats, where there is one Shroom there may be many more.

Date: Day 00669

06:15 We made an early start on the Zavidovo bunker door. The attackers had used another articulated lorry tractor unit and a T-14 Armata heavily armoured tank this time. It was going to be problematic as the attackers had crippled the tank, its tracks and removed the wheels from the truck.

11:33 The tractor unit has been removed, it was driven out on its steel rims, once the guys had managed to get it running. The tank is still stuck fast, the caterpillar tracks were damaged beyond repair, and the drive wheels were smashed in the collision with the door on one side. Obviously, the engine had also been sabotaged, the tank wasn't going anywhere fast. Smitsky has established basic Morse comms with the team inside, much to their delight. Many inhabitants are dead, and their corpses have been locked in one of the vaults. Only 24 survivors, some of the toxin managed to penetrate the complex, the infected ran wild inside until they sealed off their section. An infected person had also entered the lobby, causing half of the bunker to be locked down. The inhabitants in the main area at the time died. Harsh but understandable, it was like cutting off a limb to stop the progress of gangrene. The survivors were living in an exceedingly small, enclosed space near to the main door. It must have been hell. They are starving to death.

14:55 Attempts to drag the tank have failed, it's too heavy. The team have resorted to shaped explosive charges; I know this won't even begin to dent the massive doors. They were built to withstand a nuclear warhead and will take anything thrown at them. I've pulled my men off that particular task; I feel it's a waste of time. I suggested we try to blow through the rock and excavate, rather than access via the front. Smitsky advised this may take longer than the door, there is steel behind the rock to reinforce it. The survivors have begged us to hurry, there was little oxygen left, the electricity for the air circulation system was shot and the system was failing.

17:15 So far, our attempts have been unsuccessful. Even a nuke won't break open this place, it's a tomb. Callaghan has been working on a hunch and took a team of Russians to disassemble a vent, to check for a way in. The Russians say access is impossible, due to the design but perhaps creating a route in has more chance working from both the inside and outside. Fingers crossed.

21:01 A section of vent header has been removed, the assembly had huge heavy rivets and welds. The team were making truly little progress so far. Breaking for the day.

Date: Day 00670

11:19 Breakthrough. Callaghan has penetrated and cut through the vent system with help from the team on the inside. He used a couple of shaped charges to blow the heavy cover plate, then both teams used oxyacetylene to cut from each of the sides, although it was burning through the last of their oxygen. We are now pulling the survivors out one by one using a rough and ready block and tackle winch system. It will take hours to fully evac, but it's looking promising.

21:00 During watch, Thompson spotted a man dressed in black watching us through binoculars. I am concerned the individual is one of the assassins. It reminded me of something Paul Collin mentioned to me about a Dark One observing Summer Haven, they took out the said individual and they said it burst into white hot flame, which sounds a little farfetched to me. We need to move quickly, there may be more. I've dispatched Howard to observe and follow. He has orders to take the target down if necessary.

A Doctrine of Fear - Paul JC Edge

Date: Day 00671

09:15 Howard MIA and is uncontactable. Dispatched Thompson and a small team of Russians to assist. Smitsky concerned and has been supportive in our actions. He has a deep hatred for these bastards, whoever they are.

11:01 Howard still missing, assumed dead. Thompson continues the search and rescue mission, no news so far.

14:07 24 survivors rescued from the building in total. Leaving the dead behind, there's no point in burying them. Smitsky assumed command, he's planning to move the survivors to Novgorod Kremlin, his home is nearby so the area is familiar to him and the survivors. We will be heading back to Novgorod when Thompson's team returns. Due to the limited vehicles, survivors will be evacuated in shifts, we will take five. We are planning to pass food and clean water to those remaining in the building.

17:15 Thompson returned with the team. They found Howard, thrown in a ditch like trash with his throat cut. His body was still warm, so he'd not long died. It looked as though someone had attempted to drain the blood from his body, there was extraordinarily little gore for such a deep cut to the main carotid artery. The team found the assassin's trail not far from the body. Although the trail had been well covered, one Russian was an expert tracker and woodsman. They cornered the assassin after a long chase through the woodland and treated him to a volley of parabellums. The man burst into flame. Paul wasn't bullshitting about the spontaneous combustion after all, it seems. The team were quite disconcerted by the reaction, several of the Russian team crossed themselves as though the figure was evil and might bring some kind of bad juju.

Thompson was clearly upset; he and Howard were bunk mates. Howard was given a makeshift burial with military honour and due respect. Howard was a good man and a competent soldier and will be sorely missed. Thompson handed me Howard's dog tags for my records, the formality seems pointless now, but I aim to continue with it out of respect for the fallen.

21:43 Our new friends hosted a dinner at the Kremlin building in our honour. They provided good wine and a very reasonable meal, made from fresh foods they'd foraged, supplemented with tinned and dried goods. The vodka was top end too. It was the best meal I have had since A Day, almost two years ago. We agreed to keep in touch via the long wave ham radio which was located in a nearby radio station building. The Russian comms team have already contacted the remaining havens and started to exchange intel. We made some friends here; god knows, we might need them yet.

Date: Day 00679

The team returned to the port in Leningrad. I was corrected for using the old name, it's been called St Petersburg since 1991. It shows my age! We received an honour guard all the way to the port with Russian armoured cars, a sincere and warm send off from our friends. We returned to HMS Astute to continue our onward journey. Caterham was happy to see us; we held a one-minute silence in Howard's honour.

A Doctrine of Fear - Paul JC Edge

Extract from the HMS Astute ship's log:
Commanding officer: Captain B. K. McCreedy
CLASSIFIED
Dates and coordinates redacted

Date: Day 00673
Coordinates: XXXXXXX   Course: WSW   Sea: Choppy   Wind: High   Temp: 3°C
Remarks: First Officer Caterham relieved of command. Heading out to sea, full speed to Reykjavik, via Denmark to drop off supplies package. Planning to surface at Helsinki for the night to break out our new vodka rations, the crew deserve some R&R.

12.   Finding the Uomo Bianco

Father Enzo was concerned we were leaving the Sanctuary on an infeasible search for God. "The uomo bianco, the figure you've encountered in your dreams, is clearly our Lord, the Holy Father said it himself, God rest his soul. Our lord is in everything, he is everywhere, it's central to our belief system. He can't be found, it's an impossible mission! It's a crazy world out there, it's foolhardy to go on this wild goose chase!" Enzo begged. I explained that we needed to check if the voices and feelings in the dreams were from a third party, rather than from God himself. It was a simple act of respect for our comrades from Summer Haven, he should show patience. "But if the uomo bianco is a person, a man, then how can he perform such acts. Feats such as entering dreams forewarning of the infection are simply impossible!" Enzo added passionately. "If it is somehow feasible, then the white figure saved us. We are living in very strange times, either way we've seen the hand of God in action either directly or through the uomo bianco. The outcome and the stimulus are the same".

The frigate was fully prepared, its crew made ready to depart. A small group of islanders congregated to wish us well, some appeared deeply concerned and were praying vociferously. I waved to them and prayed briefly. I kissed Bridget, promising I would return safely, James and I undertook not to take reckless chances. "Keep in touch on the radio", she demanded gently, "we need regular updates for our sanity's sake".

As I stepped on the ship's main deck, the gangplank was lifted. The ropes were untied from the cleats and were thrown to the crew. Our vessel left the quay, and we were underway. The ship got moving, we travelled in the general direction of the Italian mainland. "So where are we headed?" I questioned. It seemed crazy to board a ship, with no idea of our course.

Franc looked at me strangely, I asked, "What's wrong Franc?" He called the others to gather round. My arm's skin writings were changing. The words 'Vulcano Ristorante Vincenzino' were plainly visibly. A clear directive was the last thing I expected, I anticipated meandering around aimlessly until we found a lead, or not. I felt like some kind of human notepad. It was clear someone was watching our every move and was keen to meet us. My misgivings were proven unfounded, perhaps we had not been talking to the lord after all.

"Which volcano are we talking about? There are dozens around here", queried Spall. "No, it's Vulcano, another Aeolian Island. It's the next island, but one, in the chain. We don't have far to travel, I guess I expected a long sea voyage to the other side of the world", I explained.

The volcano on the island of Vulcano had always been more active than the five on Salina. I surmised the sulphur concentration in the air would be high, which should hopefully inhibit the spores. I excused myself and popped back to the comms room to update Bridget and Father Enzo, they would be less worried knowing we weren't travelling far. I re-joined my alleged brothers in the bridge.

Spall was concerned the ship hadn't been refuelled during the preparations. "This frigate runs on nuclear power, it's quite unique", explained James proudly, "It'll run for months, if not years without needing more fuel". "Ok", Spall responded "We don't know where we're heading for next, I just hope it doesn't give out in the middle of the Mediterranean". "Tyrrhenian Sea actually", added James enthusiastically. Spall wasn't the guy to become picky with, James would learn in time. James was given a jovial but rather rough slap on the back for his trouble.

In a little over an hour, we reached the harbour on Vulcano, having circled the island slowly looking for activity. There was none, in fact there appeared to be no one on the island whatsoever, the main quay of Vulcano was like a ghost town. It was usual for towns and cities to be empty these days, but this one had little evidence that life had ever existed. José dropped anchor out to sea, and we approached the small quayside in a RIB. The main guns and missile turrets on the frigate were directed towards the town in readiness. Phil's crew left nothing to chance.

We dressed in Kevlar armour without hazard suits and breathing apparatus, we were armed with H&K submachine guns. I holstered my pistol. Jane and James both wore a grenade belt with a mix of incendiaries, smokers, and explosives. I noticed Franc had strapped his katana to his back, it looked cumbersome over his Kevlar vest; he peered into my eyes, sensed my thoughts, and winked.

We disembarked at the small quayside. Spall helped me out of the boat, my footing was uncertain as it shifted with the ebb and flow of the waves. Jane and Spall instructed us to wait, whilst they performed a quick recce. They soon located the Vincenzino restaurant, some of the tables in the street had been overturned and were damaged. There was evidence of a struggle, but there was sign of casualties. It was odd, no one lowered their guard, which indicated we were all thinking the same. The restaurant reeked of spoiled food but also something more insidious. "It stinks in here", offered Franc stating the obvious. Swirling flies filled the air in a dance of death, like a pre orchestration warning us of events to come.

A community of just under a thousand people had lived on the island, across three main towns. Where were they? The island's main industry was mining sulphur, so surely the island would be well protected from spores. Even if the sulphur theory were wrong, there should be some evidence of life.

James and Spall found where the townsfolk had gone, the revelation came rather suddenly. A shout from James, sounding more like rage than an alert, forewarned us. At the building's rear, he'd found a warehouse full of stacked cadavers. He cautioned us to prepare ourselves, he said the place was hideous. I entered through the rotten wooden door, and I must admit my step faltered, I was shaken to the core of my being, as I saw the horrors before me. We now knew the location of the islanders; they were stacked in piles in the warehouse. The bodies had been arranged to impress, or more likely intimidate, anyone entering the building. Pyramids of rotting skulls were arranged almost decoratively. The walls were thick with flies, it soon became clear that they were daubed in the victim's blood.

Hundreds of fine threads hung from the ceiling, adorned with an array of bodily parts. Cords with ears, the soft cartilage from noses, eyeballs, eyelids, fingers, toes, toenails, nipples, torn pieces of flesh and genitalia from both men and women threaded together. "Holy shit!" exclaimed Jane. I spotted cadavers of children and small babies hanging by a noose in the corner of the warehouse. It was an evil mausoleum of persecution and death. I ran from the building, vomited in the gutter, sat and wept. The rest of the team gathered at the front of the restaurant, gaunt and horrified, even Spall's eyes glistened. Conversation was dead, like the poor souls on display. Life would never be the same after witnessing such horror, we had seen hell in its unadulterated and vilified state.

Spall speculated that the towns' folk had been interrogated in the warehouse, "It's likely they were forced to listen to the cries and see the body parts of other victims before they were tortured themselves. The captors were clearly seeking answers and didn't show restraint, mercy, or remorse". There was a high probability we would find a place like this in each of the island's three communities. The captors were cruel wicked monsters; it could only be the work of the Dark One. I vowed I would bring the perpetrators to justice for this mass extinction.

After an hour of contemplation and forlorn thoughts, we re-entered the building reluctantly. James commented, "I've checked twenty or so bodies, they've all been killed by a cut to the throat, a quick end to their ordeal. The blood seems to have been drained into large tanks at the rear of the warehouse. The tanks contain traces of blood but have been emptied".

"Every single body showed evidence of torture, even the children", Spall observed, "the captors went to a lot of trouble. They were clearly looking for something important and were prepared to sink to the lowest levels to find it, no matter how vile". I crossed myself and murmured a prayer for the poor folk en masse. We agreed to return one day to give the victims a decent burial. Jane estimated the deaths occurred at least ten days ago, from the level of decomposition and emergence of blowflies from their pupae state.

A clear understanding of why the Pope had insisted on taking my family into the protection of the Vatican hit me in one brutal flash. What if this was my family and friends? I could only vocalise an open question to the universe, I looked up to the skies and screamed aloud, "Why?"

A weak voice penetrated the silence. "Because they were looking for me and would stop at nothing". A partially obscured figure in the shadows at the rear of the warehouse walked towards us with visibly empty hands. "Many islanders knew of me, but no one was aware of my location. I thought by obscuring my home, they would remain safe. I appeared when and where I fancied without frequenting a specific area. These poor people had no chance, they were overwhelmed by a small but well-armed strike force. It was over before it came to my attention, there was nothing I could do to help these poor souls. I come here to remind myself that his evil must be stopped once and for all. It's too much for me to bear!"

The figure slowly followed us into the brightness of the street, we backed out to ensure we weren't being flanked. The man was bathed in the bright sunlight as he stepped out from the shadows of the building. His face seemed familiar, but I couldn't quite make sense of it. Despite his age, his appearance was remarkably similar to my brothers and me. It was as if he was an eighty-year-old version of us.

"You must have many questions for me, let's go somewhere more suitable and I will attempt to answer them". We sensed no threat from the man, but we remained on our guard as he may not have been alone. Paul nudged me to confirm that the man was the figure in his dreams, Franc nodded his agreement.

The figure was real, he was mortal, despite possessing unnatural abilities.

Shaken, we followed old man along the waterfront, then headed inland. The sea caressed the black volcanic sands, unaffected by the horror in its immediate proximity. The world carried on regardless. I wished the waves would rise up and wash the horrors of the warehouse from the face of the Earth. Reconsidering our agreement to conduct a decent burial, Spall later doused the building in kerosene and set it alight.

The old man led us to a small hotel, set well back from the waterfront. We sat down, Spall passed around bottled drinks from the bar, nothing could wash away the bad taste in my mouth. "So where do I start?" uttered the old man rhetorically. "At the very beginning of this nightmare", offered Paul.

"Please indulge me for a moment, let me provide you with some background, before you ask questions. There's a lot I need to explain to give you the context of the terrible events which have occurred on this planet", the old man asked. "You make it sound like this isn't the only planet you've visited", replied Spall with a wry smile. "That's the very heart of the truth", uttered the old man, "please, let me continue". We all looked at each other, wondering where his story was going. Was the old man in control of all his faculties? Our silence was absolute, we settled down to listen to his account. We owed him that much, at the very least.

The old man looked around the group, then started. "We, my cousin and I, are representatives from a race called the Pareth-ng. We travelled here from a planet hundreds of light years away, our home world is not even visible to your telescopes. I was dispatched here on a reconnaissance mission. Our planets were dying, and our race needed to undertake a huge initiative to discover new worlds on which to live. My name in your language is Melak 3-15-22, I am 186 Earth years old. The numbers in my name indicate my clone pattern, which I will explain in a moment". We all exchanged bemused looks; our brief interactions were not lost on our host.

"In our world we use technology to extend our lives, far beyond your lifespan. As a result, we must limit births, to avoid over population. We have long discouraged animalistic mating and courtship rituals as practiced on Earth. Our race was careful to manage the population of our worlds, so the rich biodiversity was not ruined by pollution, as such we avoided being forced into conflict for territory. We are born as clones of our family heads, as one clone dies a replacement grows, inheriting the person's memories. Of the seven families of my people, I originate from the third, as my name implies. There are forty-nine leaders in each Pareth-ng family, we are each identified by a clone sequence deriving from our leader's variant. Our culture has propagated in this way for millennia. Since living on Earth, I have come to believe my race has gone too far at the price of stagnating our gene pool. But that's another story for later.

"Our worlds were dying, but not through mistreatment. They were slowly being pulled into an exponentially expanding neutron star. The star's gravity increased subtly at first, but over the centuries it started to affect weather systems and tides. Eventually its affects magnified, it slowly altered the planets' orbits around our sun, changing seasons and climates profoundly. The planets were gradually getting colder, animal and plant species were becoming extinct. By the end of the millennium, just five generations, the planets would fold into its huge gravitational mass, and there would be no trace of our existence.

"Our leaders allocated a range of planets able to sustain life to each family. My family were allocated Earth, I was dispatched here on an exploratory mission. My cousin Barak was lucky, although his initial selection was unsuitable, he was able to travel a relatively short distance to join me here. In a risky manoeuvre, he used the extreme gravity field of a neutron star to slingshot his ship at high velocity across the Milky Way. His family are heading towards the other planets in their cluster, we don't know their location. We signed up to a one-way venture, for many of my family the discovery trip resulted in death.

"The rationale for considering our people expendable is that they could simply be re-cloned. Cloning has cheapened life in our worlds, we don't understand its true value as you do. Each time we re-clone, we shed experience and wisdom. The body is reborn with its memories, but the mind, the understanding and experience are lost. My trip here lasted hundreds of the most tedious years; I was re-cloned eleven times during the journey.

"Human knowledge of space travel is virtually non-existent, other than a small number of dangerous rocket rides into Earth's orbit. I have watched your movies and seen how you imagine space travel would be. Let me re-set your expectations right now as to what is feasible. No space warping drives or freeze chambers exist which will facilitate travel over great distances in a single lifetime, it's all a pipe dream. You cannot disassemble a soul and beam it to another place. Even though it is possible to replicate your body with your memories, the replicant wouldn't truly be 'you'.

"It's impossible to travel at the speed of light as your great scientist, Einstein, postulated. The extreme forces would cause a ship to disintegrate. Biological beings occupying the vessel would disintegrate long before the ship. Small particles in the vacuum of space would rip through a ship's hull, like a hot knife through butter. We needed long lasting, self-repairing vessels with sufficient food growing capability to allow us to live and die as we flew through space over the span of several lifetimes. It was a hardship beyond my ability to explain, living in such cramped and unpleasant spaces. It was like a prison life sentence repeated over and over. Many clones went insane and were reborn to continue, with their more recent memories suppressed.

"The communities that left our planet were honourable and decent, but those who arrive here will not have experienced a normal life. They will have compromised values and little concern for anyone but themselves. I suffered initially, as did my cousin. But for me, Earth and the kindness of its people healed me. I am whole again and have come to value life in a way none of my race could imagine. I cannot say the same for Barak.

"My ship was small and fast, whereas the main population occupy slow enormous mother ships, one per family. The mother ships are heading to different galaxies many light years apart. We sacrificed being together to ensure the survival of our species. I know our propagation appears to be catastrophic from a genetic variation point of view, but bear in mind, we do not mate in the same way as you. The clones continue relentlessly, with no genetic mutations. It's mindlessly dull, no new and refreshing personalities are introduced into the population. There is no creativity or innovation anymore, we have the same ideas, our brains work in the same way as our predecessors. We have experienced no significant advances in technology in a millennium and have become extremely poor at adapting to change. Therefore, we've struggled to adjust to life on spaceships. The unexpected suicides onboard were the first examples of creative ideas we had witnessed in many lifetimes, although the concept was less than constructive.

"We departed from our planets simultaneously. The family leaders carefully selected their team for the mother ship, each vessel containing seven landing craft accommodating 49 individuals. The mother ships were configured with full living environments, simulated gravity, artificial seasons, and daily cycles. They followed behind the faster discovery craft.

"Our discovery mission was to take samples to verify the suitability of each planet for colonisation and beam the data back. Our aim was to select a world where the mother ship would ultimately land and set up home. Interactive communication is not possible at such long distances, but a concentrated energy beam could send a simple semaphore across space. It took twenty Earth years for my message to confirm this planet as a suitable home to be colonised. The mother ship is heading here as we speak, expecting to occupy their new home.

"The next part of my story isn't pleasant; it will offend you to the core of your being. I need you to trust me and hear me out. I am not proud of my mission and my actions on arriving here, but I feel I have redeemed myself since". Melak hesitated for a long spell, taking a deep breath before continuing, "The second part of my mission was to exterminate all intelligent life from this planet". His admission triggered one hell of a rumble; we glanced at each other angrily. "Let's do as he says, let's at least hear him out before we say anything rash", I urged. Melak had played a part in the destruction of our people. His message was horrific, but I was aware he'd also helped us by sending warnings to Paul and the others in their dreams. The group calmed down a little and continued to listen when the adrenaline and sense of injustice had faded.

"The approach for extermination was to modify one of our standard arrays of pathogens and adapt it to kill a species with a specific genome. We needed to choose the correct pathogen for the gene sequence we sought to eliminate. My cousin, Barak, selected an unusual fungal pathogen. He mutated the infection to optimise its spread, enabling self-propagation until it successfully eliminated the species. We coded the pathogen to efficiently exterminate humans, whereas plant and animal life would be virtually untouched.

"After a few years, the planet would become a natural, unpolluted garden allowing us to settle in harmony. Earth is sufficiently large to remain unspoiled if we controlled our population. The parameters of the mission forbade us from becoming familiar with the intelligent lifeforms, we needed to remain independent for the mission to be successful.

"After thirty years of living on Earth, I failed to meet my mission parameters; I grew to value your way of life. I began to see the way you lived, the love you held for each other, the joy, the companionship. There has been much fighting and many horrific wars over the last century, but there was something precious here I couldn't ignore. My race had lost its passion and zest for life over the years of constant cloning and gene optimisation. Our race had gone astray, we were wrong and had become spoiled.

"I couldn't eradicate something so beautiful. My cousin and I engaged in long bitter arguments concerning my change of allegiance. He was a good man and loyal to his kin, but I fundamentally couldn't allow him to commit genocide. I tried to persuade him that we could live in harmony with your race and restore the planet to its natural state. Helping to remove your dependency on fossil fuels and eliminate pollution. We could also improve food supplies using protein replication technologies. It would be relatively easy to encourage and clone the rarer biodiverse lifeforms which were facing extinction.

"However, my cousin disagreed; he considered me a traitor and tried to kill me. I was younger then and a little hot headed. I fended him off and sabotaged his spaceship so he couldn't communicate with the mother ship or complete the assignment. At first, I opted to go into hiding, later I gained confidence but moved around to protect myself. I hid my ship close to here, in the crater of the active volcano. My cousin left defeated but threatened to return to punish my treason. It took him decades, but the horrors you have seen are evidence of his revenge. The killing was my fault, and I will never forgive myself. Many victims were my friends, I shouldn't have come back here.

"I have no means of diverting the mother ship to another location, the message has been sent and my opportunity to redirect has expended, there was only a narrow window of opportunity to transmit the message when the planets aligned sufficiently. I could only hope my family's plans changed if a more suitable planet were identified. It was the slimmest of hopes, a fool's dream. As the years passed, my sensors indicated they were still on course to arrive here on schedule.

"You must understand, war and large-scale conflict has long been avoided by our race. We perceive such behaviour as a risk to our continued survival, so coexistence with a competitive species was never an option. Our aim was to avoid worlds where technology and philosophy exceeded our own. We would be unwelcome and unable to retain our independence.

"As a race we face conflict, but we have long attempted to control it. In ancient times, we introduced measures to minimise bloodshed. At a last resort, bitter disputes were settled by mortal combat, one on one, to avoid large scale casualties. Formal contests were a fight with Kadyur blood daggers. You may have seen replicas used by those you call 'Dark Ones'. Although it may seem barbaric, our methods were vastly preferable to going to war. In the early days, a victor triumphed by taking first blood, but on many occasions the clash continued to the death. To avoid the contests falling into barbarism, we developed Maarn body suits, the loser incinerated when the first significant blow was struck. The losing clone was reborn and life continued. However, the blood feuds and politics often resurfaced between the families over time, which tested our civilisation to the core. In a rare a moment of inspiration, we decided it was best for the families to go their separate ways, so we could live in peace.

"Following my sabotage, Barak was untraceable for decades. My ship's sensors can't locate him, he may have hidden his vessel near to his centre of operations, bearing in mind his engines were compromised. I closed down all routes of communication between us, but I continued to monitor events that appeared to be linked to him. My knowledge of his activities was sufficient to sense he was gathering a sect of followers.

"Barak founded a cult of brainwashed fanatics who indulged in his every twisted whim. He demanded power, so he could exact revenge and take my ship to reactivate his plans of genocide. He intended to use it to manufacture and distribute the pathogen. I hid my ship here on Vulcano and obscured it in the magma of the inactive volcano, so my location could be kept secret. It allowed me to live in a community but return to my ship when I needed. I am getting older and weaker, so I extensively used the ship's physical regeneration capabilities.

"Barak controls his cult by manipulating them, using their darkest fears. He has adapted the mythology of Satan, as it's a common theme across many religions and causes trepidation across the world. Barak manipulated satanic mythology to build the legend of the Dark One which he used to gather followers. He has slowly and steadily twisted the minds of his sect so they would comply with his demands, then sent them into the world to build his network globally. Barak's reach is long and his grip on his follower's minds is virtually unbreakable. You see, my cousin and I have empathetic abilities, which he has used to terrible effect. Without the amplification capability of our technology, he is forced to coerce his followers in person. It has taken him a long time to build a dedicated faction, but he has achieved it over the decades. It's a testament to his evil determination.

A Doctrine of Fear - Paul JC Edge

"His sect was growing exponentially, and I needed to counter him. Alone, my actions would have little impact. I was forced to use my ship's technology to clone myself once again. I created six clone embryos of myself over a five-year period, establishing 'The Seven'. I needed to protect my clones until the time was right. When producing a clone, it's possible to implant the donor's memories, known as a rebirth. In my case, I didn't want the clones to be implanted with my memories, I wanted them to experience life; I chose to make them new-born. I distributed the embryos to fertility clinics across Europe. The embryos were successfully implanted in five loving mothers in various countries. I made the clones anonymous, to keep them safe, until the time when I needed to act.

"The next part of my story will become difficult again. Just to warn you, I have some shocking news. There is no easy way to say this, so I will just blurt it out. Paul, Franc and Joe, you are three of my clone sons". Melak paused, took a drink from his coke can and looked into our eyes one by one. He smiled warmly. We exchanged frantic looks.

"Paul and Franc are identical twins; they split from the same ovum and shared the same birth mother. Franc was adopted at an early age. I used my empathy to keep in touch with both of you from time to time. I utilized my race's technology and an inherited implant in your brains to supplement my natural abilities. The link is stronger over short distances, my communication with Paul was weak as he was further north. I could only make contact with him during his REM state sleep, due to the distance involved.

"Genetics introduces variation, occasionally a wildcard appears across the generations. In rare cases a clone can be born with special abilities; in Joe's case this manifested as an ability to heal. Our scientists understand the genetic combinations leading to the variation but can't explain the power itself. Those of us who pray to a greater intelligence in the universe believe it's a divine gift. I knew Joe wouldn't be receptive to my influence and would be completely cut off from my telepathic abilities.

"I had no means to protect and guide you, Joe. I couldn't leave a baby with anything physical, such as a device, or something that would make you appear different. Therefore, I adapted the sub dermal layers within your skin to show simple messages. I used the writings to communicate with you. An additional benefaction was the messages helped influence the church, they were a known phenomenon in some echelons.

"I knew that of all my children, you would you be seen as the greatest threat to the Dark One. So, I influenced the leader of the Catholic church to help you. I unscrupulously manipulated the Pope, by posing as his God in order to secure his undivided attention. My actions were dishonest, but I had no choice. I needed to protect you. The sub dermal messages proved useful, they complemented old legends and folklore around stigmata and skin writings. Clearly my efforts worked well, you are alive despite Barak's numerous attempts to eliminate you.

"Of the seven, you may be the only ones who have survived. I have lost contact with Sacha in France and also Lars in Denmark, I presume they are dead. The other remaining brother, Bartholomew, seems to fade in and out from time to time. I have no clue of his location. I have watched you all from birth using the satellite systems surrounding the planet and I have used my empathetic abilities to try to help you when needed. I'm sorry it must be a terrible shock; to suddenly find you don't originate from Earth, despite your wonderful upbringing by such kind human beings. It turns your life upside down, no? It will take time for my revelations sink in". We exchanged incredulous looks, Melak's story explained much but overall sounded like a complete fantasy, a nonsense.

Melak continued, "When I reviewed my ship's records, after a moment of paranoia, I discovered my cousin had taken a sample of the prototype pathogen. Many biohazard equipped laboratories on Earth are able to manufacture unlimited samples of a known biological pathogen, simply by growing cultures in a sterile environment. Productionising the fungus was easy for him to achieve once his followers had infiltrated the right organisations. They infected themselves and spread the pathogen in highly populated areas on A-Day, to coincide with the collision of the meteorites. Barak's followers considered their sacrifice as the greatest honour, they genuinely believed they would be rewarded in the afterlife.

"There are 195 countries in the world, so it was a challenging problem to synchronise the attack. Many countries are so large that Barak needed to select multiple infection sites, his main issue was penetrating the bunkers that had been constructed. Barak sacrificed thousands of his followers to commit his evil crimes against your species. He took many risks; the genocide could have easily gone wrong. Barak needed to cover his actions, to enable him to continue his work in the event of failure. He used the cover of the impending meteor storm to perform his heinous crime, so it couldn't be traced back to him. As you have witnessed, Barak's plan worked only too well.

A Doctrine of Fear - Paul JC Edge

"I only had a few years warning of Barak's final plan, I foolishly thought I'd managed to block his mission. His many followers were secretive, it was hard to keep track. No one would believe my warnings; providing me with no means to stop the infection once it was released. Identifying Barak's cult members involved in the dissipation of the pathogen proved impossible. Using my empathetic abilities, I influenced you and a number of others to build havens in order to survive the impending apocalypse.

"I simulated the infection pattern, based on the intel I had gathered, in order to identify the safest places to build havens. The analysis centred on the size of population, the flow of air carrying the spores and the natural minerals and gases in the regions. I knew Barak wouldn't have the resources to cover every island, he would need to rely on the infections innate ability to self-propagate. Seven havens were built, some were well considered, some less successful. We managed to save a small but significant population so we could start to rebuild a life for the human race. The Dark One's closest disciples went underground for a period of time, to avoid being infected. As you can see from their handywork, they are starting to surface once more. They present a greater danger, now there are fewer steadfast communities to stand against them.

"The issue facing us is the imminent arrival of the mother ship. The crews of the seven landing craft are expecting a world purged of the human race. When they realise there are pockets of survivors, they will hunt and exterminate to the last man. It's inevitable the pursuit will become a sport, assuming their poor mental state after such long interstellar travel. Your only chance is to surprise them with decisive and devastating force.

"You may have perceived unusual behaviour patterns during conflict with the Dark Ones. It manifests as a preference for combat with ceremonial daggers. They only escalate to more sophisticated weaponry when they are outmatched. My race will engage in similar fashion. Given your reduced numbers, you must attack their ships simultaneously. You need to eliminate my cousin before he can inform the mother ship that human life remains on Earth. I will place my ship and its AI at your disposal, you must take out Barak before the mother ship enters Earth's Solar system.

"I understand my story is difficult for you to believe. Naturally, you will experience the deepest doubts. Joe, it seems to undermine the faith you live by, but I promise it does not. True faith in God is more significant than life on your planet alone, God is the architect of the Universe. The Universe is enormous, trust me I've travelled across a ridiculously small corner of it. Don't let your faith fail you, it gives you strength. I must leave you now; I've said enough. Use the time to consider my words carefully. I need to rest; I will return an hour after sunrise with tangible evidence to help you understand my account. I will answer any questions, I'm certain you will have many. There is food in the kitchen and comfortable beds with clean linen for you to rest".

We were dumbstruck by Melak's story. We probably looked like drooling cretins, with lights on but no one at home. How could we start to believe such a tall story, it was ridiculous? How can I possibly accept I am an alien? "What can you physically show me to make this loony tunes story believable?" asked Spall pointedly. "It's really quite simple, my friend Spall. In the morning, I will begin by giving you a tour of my spaceship".

"Let me pose a final question before I leave", requested Melak. "I suspect the most difficult aspect for you to understand is your parentage. Joe, have you experienced difficulties in learning Latin and Italian? How many lessons did you have and how long did it take you? How about you Franc, how long did it take you to learn Spanish when you arrived in Spain as a young child? Finally, Paul, have you been exposed to the infection and survived? If so, how can you persist when no human is immune to the fungus?" Melak backed into a corner and disappeared into the shadows. No one elected to follow him, we sat back and reflected. His questions were like a ton of straw heaped upon the camel's broken back.

IV. Disciples of the Uno Oscuro

"Faithless is he that says farewell when the road darkens."

J.R.R. Tolkien, The Fellowship of the Ring

1. The Unbelievable Unfolds

We contemplated the insanity surrounding us long into the night. Dusk arrived, but no one really noticed. In our fatigue, we became a little careless, not thinking to place lookouts around the buildings. Finally giving in to our hunger, we grabbed some food and drink but imparted little conversation.

Our energy levels rose as we consumed the carbs and the discussion began in earnest, as darkness fell on Vulcano. "Why did he ask you about learning languages?" sought James. I consulted Franc for support. "I can't say I remember being taught Spanish, but memories of my early years are patchy to be honest". I thought aloud, "I guess for me languages were a more recent thing, it started only a few years ago when I was extracted from the UK to be ordained in Italy. I hadn't taken lessons in Italian or French, they came naturally. I struggled with pronunciations for a while, but I never had difficulty understanding the languages. It was the same with Latin, I just read it from the service books really, I hadn't given it a second thought".

Paul was introspective for a moment, then observed, "Don't you find it a little odd? Surely language students spend years developing from terrible pronunciation and basic phrases to fluent speech. Spall interjected, "It's more than odd, no one can pick up a language like that. I read once that an autistic boy went to Iceland and learned their language in a single week. The experts believed he had total memory recall; his brain was wired slightly differently allowing him to focus 100% on the task. Most people can only concentrate up to 10% of their mind at any point in time, no matter how keen they are.

A Doctrine of Fear - Paul JC Edge

Perhaps Melak is suggesting your brains are wired a little differently?" James pointed out, "You don't seem to have an issue understanding Italian, Paul. Many locals have spoken to you in their language whilst you have been on the island". Paul was thunderstruck, "So the folks on Salina aren't speaking English?" "I don't have a clue what they are talking about, most of the time", confirmed Spall. "Thinking about it, I picked it up quickly too", pointed out James whilst looking at me weirdly. "Well, you are my son, James. You must have inherited the ability from me", I added, not realising my statement carried a measure of acceptance of Melak's story.

Paul asked Franc about his exposures to the infection. Franc counted on his hands, "I've come into contact with the infection four or five times. The very first time…", he stopped and became quite emotional before gently resuming. "The first time, I was locked in a room with my family when the infection killed them, a fruit exploded in the room. I was exposed to the spores for at least three days. I was ill, but I soon recovered to full strength once I had eaten. My mental state worried me most at the time". "So, you were in a room breathing spores for three days and you survived?" queried Paul. "I believe Melak is right, I must have some kind of immunity to the spores", confirmed Franc. "As do you, Paul. Remember the quayside at Summer Haven after you thought I had died; I was covered in spores? We quarantined together in a hut for a week with that adorable dog, Rosie. We suffered mild fevers, but a couple of days later we were fine".

Paul considered his brother's comments carefully, "I thought I was just lucky, and hadn't been exposed to the spores, but I guess I must have". "Melak's story is quite incredible. All I know for fact is we have immunity, and he has been watching and communicating with us somehow. He has helped us to stay alive in a catastrophe, so we owe him time to explain himself", I suggested. "I have a lot of questions, as I'm sure you all do. I guess seeing his spaceship will go a long way to proving his identity. But it doesn't mean everything he says is true or his motives pure".

Spall still had significant doubts, "Melak is asking us to believe he is prepared to see his whole family destroyed, because he likes humans and has learned to appreciate our way of life. It seems a bit bloody thin to me. If we succeed, we will most certainly kill his family without negotiation. They have tried to exterminate us and damn near succeeded, there is no coming back from that. We come in peace; really sorry about the 7.8 billion we murdered before we got to know you! He is sacrificing his entire race, in order for us to survive. Why? It stinks to high heaven; I don't like it!"

Jane moved on to the end game, "Even if we stop the Dark One from warning the invasion force, how can we take down seven large landing ships? How can so few of us attack so many vessels simultaneously with 'decisive force', especially if they land on different continents. We will be lucky to deploy a task force of ten to face hundreds of dagger wielding aliens on each ship".

Jane continued, "The Dark Ones will upgrade to machine guns as soon as we open fire. Will they switch to laser rifles after the first missile hits the ship? Even the best-case scenario seems an impossible challenge; assuming Melak's story is true of course". "We need to find a way to take out the ships before they land", suggested Paul. "How the hell do we achieve that, with an anti-aircraft missile? Their vessels must be huge; it will take hundreds of warheads. Also, our missile engines may not be effective in space. We don't know our enemy's vulnerabilities", challenged Spall. Paul argued, "The main part of the alien vessel will remain in space; the habitats, the hydroponics, everything they need to survive. The could be hundreds of drop ships. We need to hit them in the mother ship somehow".

The group shared much suspicion of Melak and his motives, balanced by fear. We were in no position to start an interstellar war; we were struggling to survive. I desperately needed tangible intelligence concerning the enemy vessels. We retired early; it had been a long day. But none of us slept well.

In the morning, after breakfast, Melak appeared mysteriously, as if he had simply blended into the room. He seemed to understand why his reception was lukewarm, he anticipated our concerns. Our race was inexperienced in matters outside our own world, it was in the realms of fantasy and entertainment. He seemed to know that more words were not going to influence us, we needed something tangible.

Melak led us up the side of the volcano on a rough slaggy path, circling away from the town. Roughly halfway up, in a secluded spot, he directed us to a hidden cave, the doorway was cleverly disguised. The portal was crafted from a material that looked similar to basalt, but it was a fraction of the weight. The door pivoted easily, as if it was cantilevered from the inside, though I saw no evidence of a mechanism as we entered. The dark narrow walkway had been cut precisely in the rock, as if by some kind of industrial laser. We turned to the left and descended a flight of perfectly hewn stairs, the path opened up into a larger cavern.

A Doctrine of Fear - Paul JC Edge

At the far side of the space was a large metallic ovoid, it was smooth with no discernible markings, other than the broad legs on which it sat. The ovoid was the size of a 747-airliner cabin, but slightly shorter. Part of the ship was buried in the side of the cave.

"Oh, my dear god", breathed Spall, as his logical metaphysical world fell apart. He strode over to touch the surface of the egg shape. The metal seemed to mould around his hand like it was a liquid, similar in texture to mercury. Spall's shocked expression just about summed it up for us all. I was unsure of our expectations, but it wasn't actually finding real evidence we were alien. I guess our subconscious minds were looking for evidence to refute last night's story, rather than substantiate it. As Melak approached, the ship's side flexed like it was being poured, a ramp flowed from body of the vessel, forming into steps leading inside. The doorway went way beyond our understanding of a portal.

We entered cautiously, holding our breath. I had seen spaceships in movies, but it was nothing quite like being in a real one. The inside of the hull was silver and featureless, like the smooth inside of an eggshell. Melak placed a metal circlet over his head, a horizontal disk slid up from the centre of the floor. I noted his circlet was similar to the one we found on the head of the Dark One we killed at the volcano. Clearly Jane thought the same, from the sidelong look she gave me.

A full display of the solar system appeared before us in a three-dimensional projection. Melak showed us a recording of a cluster of three meteorites travelling from a point behind Saturn and approaching Earth. He then demonstrated how their course was slightly altered at a specific point, he froze the display. "The meteoroids' path changed here, probably by some type of seismic charge. The device could have been planted in space decades before". The meteoroids entered the atmosphere and hit Earth. He then showed how the larger group of meteorites' trajectories altered in a similar fashion. The second group systematically pummelled Earth's continents.

Melak had started with basic orientation; his purpose was to demonstrate the occurrence of the catastrophe. It helped to provide us with a frame of reference for things to come. The display zoomed out, allowing us to see far beyond the reaches of our solar system. The Milky Way became a small dot in the corner of the room. The view revealed the mother ship heading in our direction. Its form was complex; I'd seen nothing quite like it, seven rings wrapped around a central rod, like doughnuts on a spike. A huge, round edged cube at the rear overlooked the rings like the bridge of a ship. The rings contra-rotated slowly as the vessel moved forwards. It looked enormous. Paul wondered aloud; he speculated that each disk appeared to be the size of a small island such as Summer Haven. It was hard to acquire a frame of reference, there was nothing to give a sense of scale. Melak affirmed Paul's estimation, each was a square mile in area.

Spall was understandably cynical, "How do we know this huge alien ship is real, it could be an animation? Forgive me, I am impressed by your vessel, I've never seen anything like it. I'm confident you are genuine, to be fair". Melak spoke patiently, "I understand, but how can I prove the display is real? It is showing a live feed, but I can't provide you with alternative evidence to corroborate?" Paul asked if the display could zoom to the dark side of our moon, to demonstrate it was a living view. Melak obliged, the large image moved back into our solar system and zoomed in on the surface of the moon. The images of the stars around our heads moved quickly, which was really quite disorientating. The display rotated to expose the rear of the moon. Paul stepped closer to the image; he identified the sea of tranquillity. He then directed the AI to focus in at a specific point and illuminate it. We could clearly see the NASA landing module's base. The name on the side identified the craft as 'The Eagle'. "Wow, so Apollo 11 wasn't faked after all", exclaimed James in wonder.

"It could still be an animated image, can you show Vulcano harbour?" requested Jane pragmatically. The image moved to the large blue planet next to the moon, it expanded the island at the toe of the boot of Italy, panned to the southernmost of three small islands to the north. Then zoomed into the bay where we'd moored our ship, showing outlines rather than a full satellite image. We could identify Phil on the deck looking out towards the town. It all seemed pretty real to me. "Where is the Dark One?" I asked. "That's not how the system works", replied Melak, "you would need to look for him. It's why you'd be extremely unlucky for the mother ship to see human life on Earth, there are so few of you and it's such a large planet. It would be like searching for a needle in a haystack. The AI can watch specific locations, but it would need to know precisely what to look for".

"Can your ship fly?" James wondered aloud. "Not presently, the power source is low and as you can see it is burrowed into this hillside. The ship's hull and engines are undamaged, but it has no means to cut its way out of the magma cavern. The high energy proton beam projectors were a casualty of our rough landing, and we don't have the materials to make repairs. As Barak was pursuing me, the AI cut its way into the cave in a hurry, hence the bumpy landing. We experienced a small landslide after the impact, burying the rear of the ship in basalt and lava. I used the proton beams to carve a doorway and staircase into the rock before it failed, otherwise I may have been buried here forever. "How long have you lived here?" Franc questioned. "Roughly eighty-five years off and on, my son. I have waited an awfully long time for our meeting".

Melak gestured to the centre of the room. Metallic seats emerged from the sides of the vessel, and a table raised from the floor. We sat down and were provided with a selection of chilled but out of date Diet Coke and Fanta cans. Although they were ten years past their sell by date, they tasted fine. "Please take no notice of the date on the can, the ship precisely replicates the sample I gave it a few years back, with the exception of a few harmful additives", explained Melak. "Now, I expect you have questions for me, I will try my very best to answer them accurately".

My first priority was to establish my true origins. My memories were of a normal upbringing, and a typical human life. "Why do we remember a regular childhood with loving parents when you say we are actually, forgive my use of the term, 'alien' clones?" Melak explained our cloned embryos had been frozen in his spaceship. The five embryos were distributed to five mothers surreptitiously via fertility clinics around Europe, to avoid any suspicion.

"One egg split to become Paul and Franc, hence their especially strong bond. Their mother, Beatrice, was a lovely woman, I got to know her quite well. As part of our agreement,

A Doctrine of Fear - Paul JC Edge

Beatrice was obliged to arrange for Franc to be adopted by a young Spanish family. It was critical you were separated. Together your unusual abilities would become too apparent, making it easier for the Dark Ones to identify you. I arranged for the amendment of Franc's birth certificates and details in government databases, so his true origin could not be traced.

My only influence was to ensure you were all brought up by devoted and loving families". Franc looked down and smiled at his recollections before he looked up at Melak and agreed, he had obviously loved his family dearly, as did we all. "Luckily, Barak was unable to track you down, except for Joe. He was alerted to your presence as soon as you made a connection with the church. The Vatican had been infiltrated by Barak; Joe was betrayed almost immediately". "We know all about the treachery of Father Alfredo", I confirmed. In the back of my mind, I could almost hear Bridget hissing the word 'rattlesnake'.

"How were you able to manipulate our dreams, they seemed so real?" queried Paul. "As I said, I too have an ability. I'm known among my people as 'Gara-ka', which roughly translates to empath in your language. It's a form of telepathy, it helps me to influence the thoughts of others. I used my ability to reach out to you. The strength of my empathy is stronger over short distances. Technology can be used to amplify my abilities, but long distances are problematic. When Paul was in England, I could only reach him in his sleep, when he was the most susceptible. Franc was nearby in Spain, so I could assist him a little more.

"However, your location didn't matter Joe, your natural ability blocks mine. I can't pass thoughts or feelings to you at all, which forced me to make alternative arrangements. I always knew everyone's rough location, excluding Joe and also Bartholomew as he grew older. I vaguely connect with Bart from time to time, I suspect he's still alive. I can only hope it's the case. I've said all this before".

Melak handed a silver disk to each of the three brothers. They found it strange; almost weightless, the disk appeared to be a circular metal headband, slightly smaller than the circumference of my head. Two parts of the circle were missing at opposing sides, they seemed to be a single object; it was like the missing parts were invisible. In order to demonstrate, Melak placed his disk on his head, with the gaps at the front and back. It looked like the hoop emerged from his temple and re-joined his skull just behind his ear on both sides. The overall effect was a circular band, partly embedded into his skull; it was irrefutably the device we had seen worn by the Dark One on the volcano at Salina.

Melak encouraged us to try the device. The three of us were not keen, we were all hesitant. "What does the band actually do?" demanded Franc. Melak explained, "From the day you were born, you inherited a small biological interface into your brain and this tool connects to it. Think of it like a smartphone, but with a full connection to your mind. It's quite safe, I assure you. The Carocle, as we call it, enables your implants to link with each other and with the ship's AI. Try it, please don't be afraid, it won't harm you".

Melak continued, "The Carocle will prove you are members of my race". "Don't do it!", demanded Jane as I started to place the circlet onto my head. "You don't know what it does, or even who this man is". Spall nodded his agreement solemnly. I explained that I had to try it. My whole being, my faith, and all I understood about the world had been shaken up. I needed to know the circlet was real. I placed the device on my head before they could argue further. It adjusted to fit me perfectly; it gave me a cool soothing feeling as it connected to my skull... my brain.

I almost fell from my chair in surprise, the Carocle made me feel like my world suddenly inverted. The simple ring had a profound impact on my senses. My mind suddenly opened up, I could see my memories in complete clarity and could easily remember anything I had ever experienced or learned. It was as if my life was a set of recordings I could fast forward and rewind, like having the nth generation of Google implanted into my brain. I had access to languages I had never spoken, it was liberating, but also frightening. "You are seeing the ship's AI and 'database', as well as a clear window into your own mind", said Melak. I was amazed I didn't see his mouth move; he was communicating with me by thought. I replied in the same fashion, "Do any of you hear me?" "They won't until they fit their Carocle. Try to reach out to me", he suggested. I concentrated on Melak, I could see into his mind, his experiences, and his true identity. I was certain his words were true, although there was much I failed to comprehend.

"Melak is telling the truth", I spoke aloud, taking the device from my head. It made me a little nauseous when I removed it, my newfound information supply simply disappeared. I felt naked and off-balance without the Carocle. It would be easy to become addicted to the device. I recounted my experience to Paul and Franc; they reluctantly lifted them to their heads. "How does it stay on your head? asked Franc. Melak explained the implant formed a loose electrochemical bond with the device, akin to welding two pieces of metal together. "Yet you can remove it so easily", observed Franc. Melak further expanded, "Yes, it accesses to your thoughts and knows you wish to remove it and simply disengages".

My brothers placed the Carocle on their heads. "Whoa!" exclaimed Franc. Paul enthused, "Wow, I like this! It's like being online all the time, it's simply amazing". Paul chose to wear the circlet for the rest of his life. Franc and I were a little more cautious. The others, especially Jane and Spall remained cynical. They felt we may be being subtly manipulated. Despite our assurances, they kept their distance and remained objective. I wouldn't say they became wary of us, but they were distrustful of small changes in our behaviour, any indicators of us being controlled or overtly influenced. Over time they simply concluded the Carocle was akin to a new iPad, to put it crudely, and ignored it.

After the revelation of the Carocle, our confidence in the information Melak imparted increased. Our questions began to flow again. James questioned why the three of us were immune to the infection. Melak explained the infection specifically targeted human DNA, although we were similar, our DNA had significant differences, so the infection didn't affect us. For us, the worst symptoms were akin to common influenza.

Jane moved the discussion on, "So how do we find the Dark One, Barak, and how do we eliminate him?" Melak pondered for a second. He explained he wasn't able to locate Barak, but killing him was simple, he was just a man like any other. Barak would probably surround himself with the more dangerous of his followers. He aspired to model his personal guard on the

Immortals who protected Darius in Persian history. Barak loved Earth's folklore, that was certain.

The questions continued, in no particular order. I could sense Melak's patience, he gave equal importance to both the impactful questions and the trivia. I'm not sure I would be so tolerant.

Jane and James started a barrage of questions concerning the Dark Ones, they were particularly interested, due to their relentless pursuit. They needed to know how to counter the threat they presented. Melak repeated his previous answers, there were few new insights. "How will Barak communicate the presence of humans on Earth to the invasion force, if you've sabotaged his ship?" wondered Jane. "I have no idea, but he will find a way. When the invasion force hits our part of the solar system, they will assume your species is gone. Your race is trivial to them; therefore, they won't be looking for a human presence. Barak will find something novel to draw their attention to you. Like motorists, who don't see a car parked on a motorway's hard shoulder unless it's slanted. The brain's cognitive system sees the side of the car as an exception, which immediately alerts the forebrain. If Barak is unable to communicate using his ship, he will resort to something more basic. A simple visual message on the landing site will trigger a response from the crew. He could construct a warning symbol in our language using rocks or flares or use a radiation source; the possibilities are endless".

"How did the Dark Ones survive the infection, when the majority of them have human DNA?" queried James. "That is a simple one, those who weren't sacrificed in the pathogen's distribution hibernated when the infection was at its most virulent. Since then, they have inhabited safe locations and wear protective clothing. Though it's possible my cousin has provided an antidote".

Jane looked pensive for a moment, and then asked a further question, "Why do the Dark Ones' suits burst into flame with the slightest wound, when clearly it impairs them?" "My cousin's motive is to keep his plot secret. He could not risk his plan being exposed; the suits ensure no evidence is left behind if a follower is compromised. His disciples wear the suits because they are fanatics. They have been conditioned to do everything their leader mandates. Of course, his clone sons do not wear the suits, as your experience on Salina testifies.

Our race has worn the vests in ritual combat for millennia, to stop the contests becoming brutal and animalistic. The ship's AI easily replicates the vests when it's provided with the correct raw materials". "How does the ship's AI manufacture them? They are like a woven fabric of nuclear reactors", I queried. "The AI has sophisticated technologies; the ship can mould to form complex laboratory and manufacturing facilities when needed. It saves carrying all manner of equipment for long distances during interstellar travel".

"How are the ships powered?" I asked. "However, they can", Melak replied, "they accept solar power, heat from the air, kinetic energy; my ship is currently using a heat exchanger, the bore hole extends deep into the volcano. The default power source is similar to your nuclear fission, but it's the AI's last resort, we class it as dirty energy. When I sabotaged Barak's ship, I overrode the security, withdrawing his access to the AI, I also disabled the main drive. It's unlikely he could repair the engines, but he may have found a way back into the AI. He's had many years to figure it out, perhaps he got lucky".

"Why did Barak release the pathogen with the first three meteorites? Surely, he was in danger of giving the game away?" questioned Paul. "I believe it was a test of the pathogen's efficacy, and your race's ability to counter it. By operating under the cover of the meteorites, he removed any suspicion away from himself. The feds would pursue a perpetrator relentlessly. Barak could not defend himself against the CIA or the Russian secret police".

Paul progressed the discussion to the mechanism that had enabled him to raise money for Summer Haven. "The prediction of lottery numbers, race results and stock market movements would need visibility of future events. How is that possible?" "Well to be honest, it was a simple sleight of hand. Horse races were easy, I attended the races and used my empathetic ability to influence the outcome; some horses simply didn't feel the need to win. The stock market was also straightforward, I gave you the names of companies I'd provided with small evolutionary improvements in their technology, so their productivity increased. The lottery was more difficult, I needed to influence an unbiased machine from a distance. In the end, I used my empathy on the engineers, persuading them to swap out the numbered balls for self-aware versions I could control by AI. I gave all seven havens the same tips; it had the side effect of bankrupting several gambling institutions". "How very sad", I shared sarcastically. "They're not doing so well these days", added Spall with a wink.

Franc became troubled as he remembered when he was forced to defend the staff and patients in a hospital in Spain.

He had treated their injuries with medical skills he didn't possess. "Did your influence help me treat the patients in Spain?" "Yes, I did help you. I allowed your implant's AI to supply the necessary information to guide your hand. My empathy gave you comfort and confidence, the rest was down to you". "Ok, so how did you help me to kill the tiger?" asked Franc changing subject a little too quickly. Melak explained, "I didn't. You were lucky, but you also showed great skill. I was so proud of you; I thought you were going to die. I simply suggested you should 'be brave'. Something else happened on that day I wasn't expecting, a metaphysical connection". Franc clarified, "It was my brother, Paul. I felt him in the last moments of the attack. He was with me, we fought together, our strength was joined. It seemed as though I had borrowed his life force for a moment". "Yes, I felt that too. I was terrified, I sensed the attack, panicked and flailed my arm in self-defence. It was like an out of body experience", added Paul. Melak concluded, "Somehow your actions helped Franc. Your souls fought the tiger together".

Melak moved on to more profound thoughts, "Perhaps we have created a small evolution by merging Pareth-ng and human DNA. A wild card has been introduced which seems to accelerate unnatural abilities. Joe's healing skills are an order of magnitude beyond anything our race has ever experienced. Your minds have continued to rapidly evolve since my ship entered Earth's atmosphere. It could be because I was forced to introduce human DNA into your genetic sequence, to prevent your mother from rejecting your embryos".

Spall and James continued a deep conversation at the end of the table, whilst Melak answered the previous question. Spall ventured, "What kind of weaponry does the invasion force have available in its arsenal?" Melak gave a knowing look to James and Spall. "What are your worst fears? Deadly weapons from the books you have read. Planet killers, photon torpedoes, laser guns? Yes, I've seen the paranoia in human movies.

"As I said, we fight honourably with daggers. If the need arises, we will use whatever is at hand. The landing craft won't carry weaponry. They're expecting a clear planet with no sentient life, they will only carry blades. If the invasion force is attacked with rifles, they will gather or manufacture a similar weapon and fight back. They will have greater numbers, so you can't risk fighting hand to hand; nor can you risk an escalation of weaponry. You need to be decisive and hit them hard and fast".

"What with?" Spall whispered to Paul quietly. "Hell knows", he replied in kind. Melak gave Paul a knowing look, "My advice is to eat the elephant in bite sized pieces. You need to immediately focus on preventing Barak's warning to the invasion force".

Melak rose, he looked weary, our questions had exhausted him. "Please excuse me; I need to rest. I fear my time remaining in this world is limited". A pod slid out from the ship's side wall, Melak climbed in and lay down. A transparent lid closed over him. Paul asserted, "Melak has requested we leave in search of Barak post haste guys, we need to pick up the sword on his behalf".

I took one last look at the spaceship as we exited the cave. We walked down the hill to the hotel in silence. So much information had been imparted, I felt like my brain had swollen.

A Doctrine of Fear - Paul JC Edge

Paul encouraged Franc and I to wear our Carocles. Franc put my thoughts into words, "I don't want Melak looking into my thoughts, he might not like what he finds". I also felt that so much had happened to fundamentally shake my beliefs. I'm not sure I could forgive Melak for manipulating the church the way he had. Melak saw his exploitation as a means to save humanity, but my feelings ran deeper. However, we were alive and without him the human race would be gone. The only thing I could be sure of was that we'd heard the truth, the good and bad of it. Melak hadn't omitted the parts that cast him in a poor light, I respected him for that much, at the very least.

I went for a therapeutic walk to clear my mind. The others sat in the hotel restaurant discussing the afternoon's revelations. I had been agnostic until the Holy Father converted me with his thoughtful logic. For me, the main thrust was that I was suddenly exposed to demon-like creatures. I believed if Hell could exist, then so could Heaven. It gave me faith, but true faith shouldn't need corroboration. From my discussions with the Pope, my theology grew into a profound belief in our Lord. However, the understanding I had gained today had badly shaken me. The recent events had been shaped by man; they were not conceived in Heaven or Hell.

I felt I needed more time to contemplate, but time was something we didn't have. I could resolve the issues with my faith later, we had work to do. The threat of the alien invasion was real, we had to move fast. Jane discussed ways to attack the invasion force and mulled over options to eliminate the aliens. I guess it's actions that define a person, rather than origins or beliefs.

Paul used his Carocle to send our regards to Melak and explain our intentions. Melak had provided a spare Carocle in case we encountered Bart, our last remaining brother. The Carocle would be pivotal to demonstrate our story was genuine. It appeared unlikely Melak would re-clone, he was tired and had lost his appetite for life. He had achieved all he could, it was now down to the four of us.

2. Seeking Out Evil

We sailed to Salina; everyone was pleased to see us back so soon; Bridget ran up and wrapped her arms around me. She kept staring at Paul, I presumed her interest was because we looked alike. After a while she asked, "What's the headband Paul is wearing, it looks really strange? Is he a fashion diva?" I explained it was a Carocle. I decided not to broach the topic of my brothers and I being aliens at this point, I simply enjoyed her embrace. Paul quickly informed his and Spall's family that all was well. My next priority was to update the wider team, and then start building a plan with their help.

Later at the café, we tried to convey our new sense of purpose to Bridget, Gio and Father Enzo. It proved difficult, as they hadn't shared our recent experience. Eventually, they realised our stories were consistent, as crazy as they sounded, they felt obliged to accept them. Bridget couldn't believe I was an alien; she said that part was utter tosh. If she had seen Melak, she would have noted our resemblance was irrefutable.

Spall asked, "How we do we find the Dark One and eliminate him?" I personally couldn't agree with killing, but my thoughts weren't so clear when dealing with someone as evil as Barak. After all he was a man who had hunted me for years, and I had no trouble shooting his dreadful followers. We had all seen the cruelty they had inflicted on the townsfolk at Vulcano. I was careful not to paint the tragedy in its full colour, I'm not sure Enzo's heart could take it. Spall rearticulated the question, but this time to the sky, "Where's the son of a bitch hiding?"

Bridget suddenly became animated; her enthusiasm was infectious. "Well, we know the answer to that, I think. He's in

Gehenna just south of the walls of Jerusalem". She asked Father Enzo to share the parchment with us. Bridget mentioned the Hebrew verse, the translation, and Enzo's concerns about its authenticity. Father Enzo soon reappeared with his papers; he could move quite quickly when he needed to. He unfolded a vacuum sealed parchment and laid it on the table. He placed a pencil written translation next to it, which Bridget read aloud.

Long I have crafted, the beginning and the end
Apocalyptic plague, your souls to rend
Archetypal madness will lead to my forge
Discarded children, graveless, rotten and gorged
Seek me in Gehenna at the end of days
We'll meet in Gehenna where children blaze

I am Aleph and Tav, the beginning and the end
The oldest religion, your soul's fires tend
The Anti-Religion from which births the scourge
I am the Dark One, Moloch; I am Shaytan; The Purge

I asked, "Bridget, is this related to the article you read, concerning Dr Columbine and his expedition?" She affirmed. Enzo explained Columbine had found the parchment prior to his untimely death. Father Enzo reiterated his belief that the document was fake, modern Hebrew was used in an ancient document. He also covered Bridget's comments about the rhyme existing in the translated form, but not in Hebrew. "How could there be a rhyming inconsistency, when the parchment was carbon dated to 2000 years BC?" questioned Franc. Paul clarified, "It's because the parchment is original, but the ink has somehow been reconstituted at the molecular level to appear ancient". "How the hell could anyone possibly know that?" asked Bridget. Paul looked at her and gently tapped the Carocle encircling his head. "Gehenna is a trap", announced Spall solemnly without looking up, he knew this without the assistance of AI augmentation.

Father Enzo took my confession that evening, I acknowledged my crisis of faith. Melak's revelations had fundamentally shaken the basis of my beliefs. "My congregation love me because they think God heals through me, they think I am somehow close to our Lord". "No! Your flock love you because you're their priest, they trust you. No-one does more for them, you are not just their spiritual leader you are their civil leader too. I doubt any of us would be alive today if it weren't for your actions". Father Enzo settled back in his chair, challenging me, "Allow me to play Devil's advocate for a moment, if you'll excuse the term. Let's assume you're actually an alien. You have been brought up as a human being, and a good one for that matter. What's the difference? Let's say you heal people with your gift, and it's because you're an alien you have the ability. Who gave this to the aliens?" I couldn't really answer, I didn't see where he was leading me. "Could the answer be God himself? If there is only one true God, then surely he welcomes all life, not just the life on this very small planet? Regardless of whether you are an alien or not, God gave you your gift. Nothing has changed, my dear friend. Nothing at all".

Father Enzo was right, I felt it in my bones, I had been shaken; all the parts of me had been hurled into the air and hit the ground in a jumble. I needed to reassemble myself from the pieces, I worried I would never be precisely the person I was. Enzo continued, "If Melak has helped us to survive, then God must have given him the clarity of thought to realise we were worth saving. Melak is a man; you are a man. We are all the same, we all live under God's roof". "Amen", I whispered quietly.

Paul started to plan the trip to Israel. Spall insisted we prepared for the worst, we also needed to deal with the spores. Spall felt we needed to take a significant force, the army that attacked Vulcano were still out there, they were strong enough overpower a thousand islanders with daggers. We hoped that since the attack on Salina and the multitude of suicidal missions during the spread of the infection, their numbers would be depleted. Spall refused to call our enemy the Dark Ones, in his mind they'd simply become terrorists with whom we would negotiate using the barrel of a gun. Creating a significant force would leave the havens in a weakened state and a stealthy mission is impossible with a large number of soldiers. A sizeable force would need transport and would be too conspicuous. Therefore, Spall decided that we needed to keep the strike group small and tight.

On our final evening, I felt a little mischievous, probably due to imbibing too much wine. I asked James and Jane a question that had been playing on my mind. "I have noticed that you two are sitting much closer to each other lately. Is there something that you would like to tell us?" I dropped the bombshell and smiled cheekily at them both. After some awkward bum shuffling, the small gap between them expanded. "Do you honestly think you can pull the wool over my eyes so easily?" I followed with an exaggerated wink to Bridget. Father Enzo smiled broadly; he worked hard to suppress a laugh. James' only response was a flushed face and a fake quizzical look. "Really? You haven't even spoken to each other about it yet? Come on, the world needs all the happiness we can muster. James, why don't you tell Jane how you feel? You only get one life you know". James was deeply embarrassed; he looked at Jane who had precisely the same unreadable expression on her face. The courage left him; I could feel it. "Go on", I encouraged gently.

Jane thought for a while and then clarified her position a little more formally than I think she intended. "You must understand, we are Swiss Guard. We are your protectors. We can't consider personal relationships, Joe, it's unprofessional". "Ok, let me think about that for a moment", I mockingly responded. "So, who are the Swiss Guard these days? I would like to take this matter up with your commander in chief". James and Jane looked at each other once more and said nothing. It was blindingly obvious that their organisation no longer existed. The military unit whose sole purpose was to guard the Holy Father had no Pope to guard.

"The world has changed. Old allegiances mean nothing to any one anymore. The only loyalty we must encourage is to each other...and love". Finally, Jane softened, she grinned faintly and teased James, "Is this true then, James?" He went a darker shade of crimson and mumbled, "I guess it is, yes". That was all it took, there was no discussion, no contemplation, and no negotiation. Jane reached forward and grabbed him almost violently, kissing him full on the lips and refused to let go. Bridget light-heartedly scolded me, "You old reprobate".

Soon, it was time to leave on our quest. My brothers and I opted to wear our Carocles for the trip, to maintain close contact with Melak. The ship left port with the crew plus James, Jane, Spall, Phil and José. Despite the rejuvenation procedures being carried out by his pod, Melak was still able to converse with us. We headed out for Israel at an impressive 45 knots. Our journey of 1000 nautical miles was scheduled to take over 24 hours, even at the frigate's top speed.

The wake behind the relatively small ship was enormous, the water crashed against the prow. By wearing my Carocle, I could visualise our precise location. As we coasted past Crete, we saw dolphins swimming in the bays near Pelekanos. Appropriately, Pelicans fished in the bay; they swooped through the air with massive three metre wingspans. It amused me, they always emerged from the water facing the opposite direction to how had entered it. It was mid-morning the following day by the time we sailed within striking distance of Israel's coast.

We donned Kevlar suits and armour as we prepared to disembark the ship. The temperature was almost 35°C, we were baking alive. My brothers and I chose to forgo the additional hazmat suit on the advice of Melak, as did James. We carried M16 rifles and sidearms. Bridget had joked that I was the first gun toting priest since the wild west. Her levity failed to camouflage the pain on her face when I left.

Spall carried one of Steve's innovations, a specially modified flare gun. Rather than deploying an incendiary, the charge exploded, dispersing a cloud of sulphur. Although the tests were incomplete, it was the best weapon to counter virulent spores. The port appeared abandoned, as did everywhere. The blue star of David, the flag of Israel, flew from the highest point. We made port and docked, José and two crew members tied the ropes to the cleats and slid the ship's gangway to the wall in preparation for disembarkation.

Our hunting party walked purposefully through Ashkelon port, out of the gates to the roadside car parks. We took the first two large vehicles we found with keys in their ignition. They started after a little chugging, luckily their tanks were more than half full, we were ready to roll. We took route 3 into town.

It wasn't long before we approached the centre of Jerusalem. We followed Paul's lead to the south side of the old city and took the road down to the valley of Hinnom. Paul didn't need satellite navigation; he was wearing his headband. Those of us wearing a Carocle had a pretty clear view of our route, it felt like we already knew the city. Melak's data gathering was excellent, even down to road systems. We managed to avoid a number of abandoned cars on the highway. We observed no obvious Shroom activity, they were rotten and green tinged, having been long inactive.

We arrived at a tree lined park below the old city walls. We exited the car on the Gai Ben Hinom Road, leaving the doors open to make a quick escape. The area was abandoned, as we expected. Considering the biblical reputation of the accursed valley, it seemed really quite ordinary. A stony area between the buildings led uphill to the Mount of Olives in the east. The ancient city wall framed the north of the valley, the remainder was surrounded by asphalt roads and green trees. We couldn't lose our focus; this was, after all, the 'destination of the wicked'. If Herod had burned children here, there was certainly no evidence of it. We looked around for signs of life. It was a pleasant tree lined area; the walls of the city looked beautiful with the blue sky behind them. Man, it was hot!

There was no sign of the Dark One, it was just a small park with nothing of interest. We had started to relax a little when a deep discordant voice whispered in our ears. "Welcome to the abode of the dead, join us in Hell!" The voice was in our heads, coming from our Carocles. Spall, James, and Jane heard nothing.

Shrooms charged down the hill from the Mount of Olives Cemetery, screaming guttural curses and crying out for our blood. There were thousands of them, it looked like all the Shroom in the region had gathered with a single purpose. It surprised me how they'd survived so long without prey. Jane sensed my thought, "Are the Dark Ones using the blood they collect to feed these bastards?"

"Incoming", shouted Spall, he took the flare gun from his belt and loaded an oversized flare charge. He fired cartridge after cartridge above the heads of the Shrooms, creating a wall of yellow sulphurous dust between us and the infected. The wind gently blew the cloud of sulphur towards the Shrooms. Although there wasn't sufficient sulphur to fully douse the Shroom, it certainly slowed them.

The Shroom made gagging sounds as Spall took a grenade launcher from his large webbing bag. Jane spoke into her battlefield radio urgently; Spall quickly assembled the makeshift tripod and centre tube on the ground. James emptied dozens of finned grenades onto the floor next to the launcher. Within seconds, Spall was launching grenades as quickly as James could load them. Spall continually changed the pitch and vector of the launcher as each grenade was lobbed into the sky.

A cacophony of explosions rendered our assailants. From left to right huge detonations catapulted the Shrooms through the air. They died by their hundreds, but still more came, completely undeterred. The sulphur dust started to clear as Jane, Paul and Franc opened up with their M16 rifles. Spall fired the remaining sulphur flares directly into the hordes, so the detonations would concentrate the sulphur in smaller areas. The yellow cloud proved more effective, but soon his belt was empty. The grenade launcher resumed its bombardment, the Shrooms front line was upon us. Jane shouted, "Here comes the air cover, get down". "Funny", called Spall, but then he changed tune as a wing of thirty drones appeared overhead. "Get down!" Jane reiterated aggressively.

Mass produced drones, powered with four propellors, flew directly in grid formation over the heads of the Shroom, then dropped out of the sky. When they had fallen within a metre of the ground, below chest height of the Shroom, they detonated. High velocity ball bearings were emitted laterally in all directions, driven by the explosions. The shrapnel ripped through the Shroom as if they were paper, they fell in large groups, riven and torn to pieces. A few Shroom continued pushing forwards but stumbled over those who had died. Franc pulled out his katana, grinned and leapt into the fray. He slashed left and right as he took out the Shroom around him. He was a brutally effective killing machine; we focused our weapons on the Shroom that attempted to outflank him.

A Shroom broke from the group attacking Franc and charged directly at me. I was slow to respond, Jane pulled her Sig and shot it point blank in the head, fragments of the Shroom's matted skull were sent everywhere. Franc must have killed hundreds with his sword, he was relentless. We were starting to thin out the troop, when another legion came over the ridge screaming, there was no sulphur to slow them this time. Jane radioed the ship again; all I could hear was the sound of gurgling Shroom, bodies were strewn everywhere.

The explosions were deafening as the ordnance hit the hillside. Moving the frigate north along the coastline brought our location within range of its enhanced sea sparrow missiles. The massive explosions threw the Shroom across the hillside like rag dolls, the shrapnel took care of the remainder. They were wiped out within minutes. Franc and James finished the last of the Shroom as their fruit began to pop. "Get the hell out of here", shouted Spall. Another wave of drones was approaching as we jumped into the cars to retreat to a safe distance.

The crew of the frigate assessed the situation using their onboard cameras and piloted the drones in a holding position. When Spall gave the all clear, the drones headed back to the ship. Jane waved to the camera on the lead drone to express her thanks. I was a little concerned, there might be more infected, and the drones may be needed. However, the battery life on a drone was limited and it was a few clicks back to their drop pod on the ship's helicopter.

I turned my back on the cadaver littered hillside, it was a horrific sight. Spall and Jane watched for further attacks. The bodies were damaged to an extent that most were unable to grow fruit, yet many formed. The air was filled with spores, luckily the breeze pushed them towards the Mount of Olives. Franc assessed the situation, wiped his sword on the long yellow grass, then sheathed it. "We should be ok here for some time. The Shroom are dying, and they are in limited numbers. To experience such numbers, they must have been Shrooming for weeks in anticipation of our mission. Someone must have influenced them, and I think we know who. It's unusual for Shroom to be directed. When Shroom attack, they group together like a herd. They don't think strategically or hold back reserves, it is a free for all, a swarm. All the Shroom in the area will most likely be dead now". "Let's hope so, I hate those bloody things", spat Jane. "What next?" caroceled Franc to Paul and me privately. "I have no idea", I responded, Paul reluctantly concurred.

We sat in the cars for a while and grabbed water and energy bars. Franc ate almost a third of our total supply before realising he was being a glutton. None of us minded, he'd expelled so much energy in the battle. He mopped his sweaty brow with a towel. The valley of Hinnom was once again filled with death and flames of biblical proportions. A haunted feel to the valley made us keen to leave the place.

A discordant voice boomed in our minds via our Carocles, "Long ago, when Melak and I first came to this world, we shared a common purpose. Melak set his fate when he committed the highest sacrilege and turned his back on our fathers. As his cousin, I urged him to stop such foolishness, humans deserved no respect; they are merely animals. Look at the destruction they have wrought. The gardens of Babylon and Eden are no more, they've been polluted and ruined by human sacrilege. As his followers, it's too late to change your road now, you are traitors. Your only path is death, it will lead you to me".

His threats angered me, so I responded in kind. "Come here brave one", I urged, "I shall put an end to your suffering". Barak retorted, "You dare to threaten me, priest? What kind of a clergyman are you? A Father who threatens to bring death to his own uncle? One who wages war instead of sharing love. You're a sham, you have no faith, you're a wandering bitch in a dog collar". Franc retorted angrily, "Joe may be a gentle soul, but underneath it all he is my brother, this is why he refuses to bow to you. Come and face us you coward, or do you always get others to do your dirty work?" The dust had barely settled when an army of Dark Ones appeared on the walls of Jerusalem, they repeatedly shouted as one "We are the army of the Dark One; Moloch; Shaytan; The Bringer; The Purge".

Jane radioed our coordinates to Phil aboard the Phoenix, as the chanting began. The Phoenix launched Sea Sparrow missiles, but due to the ship's distance, she feared there may not have been sufficient deployment time. The shouting was building to a crescendo; like Genghis Khan's armies, the Dark Ones were most likely to attack at the high point when an enemy's trepidation was at its greatest. The chanting reached the point of climax as we finally heard the inbound missiles. The Dark Ones began their charge, the exploding ordnance took down the south section of the sacred wall of Palestine. The dust cloud from the detonations was illuminated by the intense white flames of the Dark Ones. "That's gotta hurt", whispered James.

3. The Broken Temple

The square became as quiet as a graveyard. No Dark Ones were visible, the remaining soldiers must have retreated. We drove to the city walls of Jerusalem to eliminate survivors and survey the devastated area. The ancient Zion Gate in the Armenian quarter had been devastated by our ordnance, a necessary but heinous act of destruction to a precious holy site. I must admit I valued my survival more.

I needed to find Barak and put an end to this madness, once and for all. Saving the human race was a priority, a wall can be rebuilt. We continued into the old city on foot, the sun was at its highest, it was sweltering. I cannot imagine how Jane and the others felt in their suits and visors; seeing this, Paul called a halt to locate somewhere cool.

Heading past the Zion Gate, we found a large square castellated building with a huge entrance. Dozens of market stalls smelt of rotten goods, the decaying goods and flesh had long since been taken away by armies of rats, mice, and beetles. We marched past line after line of old stone buildings, once studied for their antiquity, our weapons at the ready. Remains of corpses became increasingly prevalent as we moved into the city. It felt like the empty eye sockets of skulls stared at me accusingly, demanding to know how we were still alive, when they were left on the street like trash.

Spall headed into the citadel in the northwest side of the Armenian quarter. It was once a lovely area surrounded by arches built into the ancient stone buildings. As the human population had been eradicated, animals had moved into the city in greater numbers. Pigeons and vermin thrived in roof voids and wall cavities of unoccupied buildings. Larger animals such as wild dogs and mountain lions prowled, looking for easy prey. We remained on our guard for all manner of predators, human and animal. The cool shady arches were ideal, I stripped off my body armour and sat down, hot and exhausted and grateful for the respite.

Spall was concerned we were milling around without a clear objective. His military training didn't lend itself to such vague missions. Spall ensured we took turns watching the main ingress points, but we didn't have sufficient numbers to provide full cover. The city waited quietly; we had no idea how many Dark Ones remained. We rested for a while in the cool.

As the hot afternoon sun eased, we headed out into the streets once more. Many stalls had been closed for the night at the time of the apocalypse, however, perished wares were displayed on small trestle tables and hung from walls. James picked up a faded 'I Love Jerusalem' cap and dropped it on his head mischievously, with the visor facing backward, it fitted ok with a small adjustment. Jane smirked at the irony but declined to pass comment. The food stalls were horrible, with infestations of rats and cockroaches; they no longer seemed to view us as an apex predator. The vermin looked at us from the shadows, like we were their next meal.

Jane took point as we headed east into the Muslim quarter towards Temple Mount and the Dome of the Rock. It was commonly believed Mohammed ascended to heaven there, the black satire of Barak using a holy place for his evil made me feel uneasy. As we walked north along the outer side of the wailing wall, I stopped; something felt wrong. Franc and Paul felt it too. Franc spoke cautiously, "Ignore it, Barak is projecting bad feelings. He's trying to intimidate us, hoping we will make mistakes".

We entered the Temple Mount area from the northwest corner, it was a huge, paved space with a golden domed shrine in the centre. The square was partly filled with rotting Shroom and the remains of human clothing and paraphernalia. It felt like it had been the place where the people in the city had made a last stand. Thousands of lives must have been taken here, it was hideous. I felt sick, a surge of bile rose into my throat, Paul looked pale too.

Both the shrine and Al-Aqsa Mosque had been horribly desecrated. The square was covered with graffiti, toppled works of art and beautiful architecture was smashed on the rock floor. The symbol of Baphomet was inscribed on the gilded dome. The icon was a combination of the serpent Leviathan, the goat, and an inverted pentacle. Classic satanism clichés, which Barak seemed to promote ruthlessly to his advantage. We must be getting close.

The square was surrounded by retaining walls, built during Herod the Great's reign, as an expansion of the temple. It was dominated by three significant structures: the al-Aqsa Mosque, the Dome of the Rock, and the Dome of the Chain. In addition, there were four impressive minarets pointing accusingly up at the heavens. Herodian walls and gates encircled the mount and were ruined beyond repair. The pointless vandalism sickened me.

A small Arabian leopard looked up at us, it scattered as we moved further into the square. From the front of the Dome of the Rock building emerged three dark figures, two clone sons, with Barak at the rear, he was dressed in a black hooded robe; they looked near identical. Two more figures emerged behind Barak clinging to the shadows. Dark Ones entered the square from all directions, there were too many to count. Spall and Jane tensed; we were completely surrounded by the warriors. "Welcome to my temple", projected Barak. He looked incredibly old. "Let me introduce you to my sons, Supay, T'an-mo, Tchort and Thamuz. They nodded solemnly when their name was uttered. My Carocle told me their names were demonic or satanic figures from ancient religions. Barak's sons' names represented darkness in many tongues and cultures: Inca, Chinese, Russian, Sumerian, Egyptian and Greek. I recognised some of the names from Bridget's magazines.

Barak gloated, "My son, Thoth, was sadly lost at Salina, you were lucky on that occasion". "The more we learn, the luckier we get", interjected Jane sarcastically. Barak looked at her darkly, but continued undeterred, "Typhon will return from his fishing trip to Russia soon, he has unfinished business in Denmark. I might ask him to pay a passing visit to your precious Summer Haven, Paul", he smiled menacingly.

Barak turned his gaze to Franc, "Also, let me introduce my Immortals; they are more than a match for you, Franc. You're not quite the predator your friends think you are, I admit I feel quite disappointed". He addressed the group again, "Put down your weapons, my Immortals are fully armed and hoping for resistance. You have killed enough of my children with your pathetic projectile weapons". Spall, Jane, and James lowered their rifles resignedly, we were hopelessly outnumbered. There was no point in antagonising Barak or his followers at this point.

A Doctrine of Fear - Paul JC Edge

Melak's familiar white figure appeared at my side. Franc and Paul looked towards him; the others were unaware of his presence. "It's a shame you couldn't come in person, old one. You could watch as your children burn; too bad, only three remain and you are unable to face me as a seven, you must be disappointed. Let me think, Sacha was stabbed through the heart by Supay at Mont St Michel recently. How terribly sad, please accept my deepest condolences. Another of your seven, Lars-Åke, died on Samsø only last night at the hands of my son Typhon, his throat was cut from ear to ear. His blood was syphoned into a KamKassa jar to feed our foot soldiers. Again, accept my heartfelt condolences. This leaves only Bart; tell me Melak, where is your son Bartholomew? Is he afraid to face us? I've been unable to silence him, his cowardice is exacerbated by his preference for hiding". "Honestly, I have no idea, he is lost to me, I am unable to contact him. Rest assured, he'll fight you to his last breath", responded Melak's image. "Your remaining breaths are limited, soon Bart will join you in Gehenna", retorted Barak coldly.

"You betrayed yourself and your kin when you formed your band of rag tag heroes. When you're dead, we will burn you and your children's bodies at Gehenna. You're no longer a threat to our plans; Earth is ours. The Pareth-ng will assume their rightful place over a lesser species", continued Barak mercilessly. "You don't understand", argued Melak, "humans are not a lesser species. Genocide of the human race is cowardly murder. Our race is no more advanced as sentient beings than humans, we simply have more progressive technology. In our endless cloning, we're missing the joy of life, the pleasures of the joining between male and female, the delights of good company and loyalty to each other. We've lost our spark, a spark fundamental to life itself. We cannot simply exterminate the human race; they are unique and wonderful". "It's time to stand before the Dark One", breathed Barak. "Each of your sons will face ceremonial combat, using only the Kadyur". The Kadyur was an ancient blade the Parethng used for duelling. Spall moved closer and whispered to me, "You can't do this, they'll kill you". I couldn't disagree, "Yes, probably. I'm not sure we have a lot of choice. We're heavily outnumbered".

I spoke up for the group. "If we engage in one-on-one combat as you suggest, I request we keep the conflict to my brothers and I and let the others go. They are of no interest to you; they should be with their kin". Jane shouted, "Over my dead fucking body". "If necessary", replied Barak with an evil smile. It was a simple decision, ceremonial combat, or we all die. Jane lifted her radio to call for assistance; a Dark One shot it from her hand with a single well-placed round. She yelped and cradled her hand protectively. "No more help from your pathetic battleship, not this time. It's dishonourable and discredits you, Melak". "As my friends from Earth would eloquently articulate. Fuck you!" he responded defiantly. Barak smiled, "Humans think of nothing but fornication, why would you choose to emulate them?"

First to enter battle was Franc, he stood against T'an-mo, he was handed a Kadyur dagger. Franc turned the dagger over in his hand cautiously. Franc stimulated his rage by thinking about his family, "He is one of the bastards who infected and murdered my beautiful Colletta and Lucy". As Franc wore his Carocle, I could feel his rage building. There was a darkness in

Franc, which he worked hard to control, now he was deliberately feeding it, his visage was darkening. I could sense the monster surging forward and baring its teeth. I reached for his arm gently, "Be calm my brother, rage won't help you in battle. It'll cloud your senses and force you to make rash decisions". It was to no avail; I couldn't help Franc; he seethed with the surge of adrenaline rushing through his arteries.

I conversed with Melak via my Carocle, "What can I do? Is there a weakness I can exploit to stop us getting killed? Melak responded carefully, "Barak genuinely believes he is Satan, he is insane. He has superior numbers, there's nothing you can do other than use your wits". I queried, "Can you use your empathy to persuade Barak to stop, or turn his followers against him?" Melak shook his head, "It doesn't work like that. My empathy is subtle, I can use it to encourage and support, but it cannot function against such hate". Paul contributed, "The only weakness Barak has is his followers. They are brainwashed; they've been twisted to his purpose over many years. They don't know what's happening, he has corrupted them. They don't realise they'll be wiped out when the invasion force lands, they're just pawns in a great game".

I assumed Barak's sons wouldn't wear an incendiary vest, due to the fight with Thoth at Salina (by process of elimination). Barak called, "Gumna hox kabara", his soldiers raised the palms of their hands to their temples. Franc's opponent smiled and immediately thrusted straight for Franc's heart. A simple move, either T'an-mo greatly underestimated Franc, or perhaps he was testing his rival. Franc blocked his opponent's blade and hit him with a left-handed uraken strike, a backhanded whiplash punch to the bridge of the nose. T'an-mo hadn't expected a punch, I suspect he was focussing on the blade. Franc used his whole body to engage T'an-mo, he used the blade as an extension of his arm. The Dark One slid back smiling, he looked more menacing with blood running onto his teeth. The sight of T'an-mo's blood made his enemy look vulnerable, Franc smiled coldly; he attacked with a slice aiming for his opponent's head. T'an-mo dodged, but he failed to see Franc's feint, he spun, kicking T'an-mo's legs from beneath him. T'an-mo rolled nimbly, regaining his feet in a fraction of a second. T'an-mo was no ordinary opponent; he was extremely well trained. Spall breathed, "Jeeze, this isn't going to be easy".

Paul carocled me as the fight progressed, desperately seeking an answer. "If Barak's followers are so screwed up, how has he brainwashed them? Can we use the same conditioning against him?" Melak interjected, "No, they are mentally deranged. Barak has driven them insane. They have been coerced to believe he is Satan; the penalty of disobedience is to spend eternity in the fires of hell. We can't combat brainwashing by persuasion". "I can hear you", uttered Barak menacingly, "Stop wasting your time and use it to prepare yourselves for your inevitable death".

In the continuing melee, Franc took a nasty laceration to his left arm, it was bleeding profusely. He knew that if he continued to bleed at this rate, his strength would be diminished, all T'an-mo needed was time. The fight intensified as T'an-mo pushed his advantage, leading with his dagger as a ruse, only to deliver a savage roundhouse kick to Franc's ribs. Franc saw it coming, blocked the blow and smashed T'an-mo's kneecap with the heel of his open palm. T'an-mo howled in agony and launched himself at Franc with his good leg, his knife arm sweeping down in a desperate disembowelling arc.

Barak had bent his followers' minds, moulding them to believe his warped doctrine. As I watched the combat in horror, I noticed all eyes were on the compelling fight. Not a single Dark One was looking in our direction, Paul's assessment of their paranoia cycled through my head. My reflections led to a desperate idea, paranoia is a mental illness, and an illness could be cured.

Franc diverted the arcing blade using the hilt of his dagger, on the backhand swing he cut T'an-mo's throat. Blood gushed as the Dark One fell lifeless to the ground. Barak was thunderstruck, the Dark Ones looked on in shock and revulsion, it wasn't the outcome they'd anticipated. T'an-mo was a master, he was invulnerable in their minds.

I seized the moment and quietly eased to the side of the square, standing next to one of Barak's disciples. The group noticed my presence, but obviously didn't see me as a threat, I had already dropped my weapon. Their attention was focussed on the shocking scene of T'an-mo in death throes on the floor of the plaza, gurgling as life left him. I touched the arm of the man next to me, he looked at me suddenly as he felt my gentle hand. I prayed to the Lord to heal his mind; I extended my prayer to all Barak's followers. Bright light filled the arena as Barak screamed, "Nooo! Kill him! Kill him now!"

Barak's disciple was rocked as he saw the man he had become. I explained, "See the truth about the Dark One. Observe how you are forced to wear a suicide vest, but his sons are not. See how he has twisted and hurt you". Barak's disciples froze to the spot, observing and then healing. They reached to each other to pass on my gift. It was like chain lightning travelling between them one by one. The light became intense.

James shielded his eyes but continued to watch the scene as it unfolded before him. I heard Spall whisper, "Look at the whites of Joe's eyes, they're on fire". The follower nearest me shook in anger, "The Dark One's doctrine is a lie". I spoke aloud, so Barak's followers could hear me clearly. "Your leader is not Satan; he's an alien from another world. He's here with one purpose, to destroy mankind and he will kill you too. Barak is preparing to take over our world. He's poisoned your minds, twisting them for his purposes. He uses you like a tool; one he will sacrifice on a whim. He has no love for you, please let me help you. Join me, together we can fight Barak's evil".

Barak's followers were bewildered for a moment, but their resolve began to strengthen. Barak became aware of the threat instantly and sent his remaining sons forward to eliminate me and my companions. Unusually, they chose automatic pistols. Spall and Jane quickly retrieved their M16's from the ground and shot Barak's sons as they levelled their weapons. They fell in the blinding light of the square, dying in a pool of crimson.

The crowd began to understand how they'd been poisoned and manipulated. They were individuals who had interests in satanism and dark magic, but in reality, it was merely a passionate hobby. They weren't killers by nature. A feeling of outrage built until they started to shriek.

The mob found its blood lust and charged Barak. They were a hysterical gang with revenge at the forefront of their minds. I had healed the majority of Barak's followers, but a few were genuinely evil. In the chaos, those who could not be healed seized their moment and launched an assault on my brothers. Spall spotted our attackers immediately; he opened fire, exacerbating the disruption. We grabbed our weapons and engaged them.

Two figures flamed as another screamed and ran towards me. Jane intercepted, she took my attacker down with a vicious kick to the abdomen and shot him in the back of his neck, stepping back from the heat as he flamed. Franc attempted to defend himself but was clearly impaired. Paul lifted his Glock to shoot Franc's assailant as another attacked Paul from the flank. The pandemonium spread as the fighting persisted, the healed were confused but their anger and hatred drove them towards Barak at the temple. Paul dodged a parried blade by a narrow margin, as Spall shot the attacker in the chest. It was chaos.

Barak fled into the temple as the angry mob pressed forward, reappearing momentarily holding an object. He activated the trigger device, the dissenting disciples stopped, in a state of shock. The flame was intense, the image burned into our retinas as many of Barak's followers combusted instantly. Hundreds of bright white flames filled the square, Barak had decided his disciples were expendable and punished them for their disloyalty. He was evil. After a few minutes, our eyesight returned to normal, by then Barak had gone, he had vanished into the Dome of the Rock.

Twilight fell as a welcome backdrop to the myriads of hot ashes that filled the sky. I felt overwhelmed by the evil that had been unleashed. Barak was happy to murder his followers, simply because they stopped worshipping his doctrine. He was too old to run from them, so instead he terminated them like snuffing out cockroaches.

The AI informed us that the Dome of the Rock is located on a stony outcrop known as Mount Moriah. Where, according to Jewish belief, Abraham offered his son, Isaac, as a sacrifice. Beneath the dome, the rock forms the centre of the temple. Beneath is a small cavern called the 'Well of Souls'. As I researched the temple, Jane gently assisted Franc to sit down and opened her medical kit. She cleaned his wound, sutured it, and applied a field dressing to his arm. Franc looked at her gratefully though he was clearly in discomfort, she smiled back faintly.

I read aloud the data provided by my Carocle, "The Well of Souls is a part natural, part man-made cave located inside the Foundation Stone. The name 'Well of Souls' derives from a medieval Islamic legend; there the spirits of the dead can be heard awaiting Judgment Day. The name relates to a depression in the floor of the cave and also a hypothetical chamber beneath it. The AI quotes from the Christian Bible, Genesis 22:2: 'And he said, take thy son, the beloved one, whom thou hast loved - Isaac, and go into the high land and offer him there for a whole-burnt-offering on one of the mountains which I will tell thee of'. I'm not sure if it helps, but it is a potential hiding place at the very least".

4. Black Heart Hunting

Franc was weakened by his injury; he had lost a significant amount of blood. I ran over to him, removed his newly applied dressing, and placed my hand on his brutally slashed arm. I prayed once again for God to heal. Franc hadn't been outmatched like Barak wanted us to believe with his pathetic mind games. As the colour slowly returned to his face, he gave me a warm smile; I felt an overwhelming gratitude to God once again. Franc looked at me, "You have a remarkable gift, Joe. Thanks, brother".

The light from the healing illuminated the building beneath the dome for a moment, allowing Spall and Jane to look for the chamber where Barak had secreted himself. Melak spoke to those of us wearing Carocles before his image disappeared from view, "I thought all was lost, but I shouldn't give in to despair. You did well my sons. Barak's a coward, he will run. No-one is safe until you find him". I felt physically impaired by the sheer volume of healings, but I couldn't let it weaken my resolve.

Barak was nowhere to be seen in the shrine; he'd vanished. Paul couldn't understand, "He can't disappear. He's either found a way out or he's still here. We must find him, or we are all dead". We knew Barak couldn't leave from the rear, all of the doors were chained shut, but he had used the front door previously. There were no stairs up, the only available path was down, it was simple logic.

The dome's interior was breathtakingly beautiful, even at twilight. Above the arches supporting the main dome were many curved windows with stunning aniconic Islamic patterns.

A Doctrine of Fear - Paul JC Edge

The rock rose in the centre beneath the great dome. The doorways in the middle of each face of the building were chained; usually, non-Muslims were not permitted to enter the temple despite being sacred to both Muslims and Jews. It was no wonder it had been controversial, but there was no-one left to argue anymore.

The steps led to the Well of Souls, where 'the voices of the dead are said to be heard falling into the river of paradise and on to eternity'. Conspiracy theories indicate the Ark of the Covenant was hidden in a warren of passages before the Babylonians destroyed Herod's First Temple in 586 B.C. The Dome of the Rock was later constructed on the site of the First Temple. The wealth of knowledge provided by the AI never failed to amaze me.

"Barak must have gone to the Well of Souls", I excitedly shouted to Spall. "It's down the steps on the southeast side, below the Foundation Stone". We continued down the small staircase into the cold cramped cavern beneath. "Welcome to the Holy of Holies", I whispered quietly to myself. The cave was filled with plastic chairs, it extended upwards to an intricate stained-glass window mounted in carved plaster. The window penetrated the rock itself, allowing shards of dim light to break through the gloom. "Where could he be? The walls are stone, there's no way out", observed Jane. "The floor sounds hollow", pointed out James. I wondered if the myths of a large cave beneath the Well of Souls chamber were true.

The Carocle enabled me to find a diary entry of a young British surveyor, Captain Charles Warren, who conducted scientific exploration of the Temple Mount under the guise of pollution control. He had tipped coloured water into the drain to determine its outflow. "The Well of Souls has a drain into the Kidron Valley", I read aloud. "Where's the Kidron Valley?" asked Spall. "Behind the Mount of Olives Cemetery", I replied. "It's where the horde of Shroom came from when we were in Gehenna. It's where we started with this mess!" The problem was we couldn't understand how Barak could fit down a drain. "Find the grid", asserted Spall.

The drain had been widened, though we were unsure if the work was carried out recently or centuries ago. The widening work looked in keeping with the rough-hewn stone around it, so could be either recent or ancient. "No wait", why don't we head to the valley and cut him off, he can't crawl that quickly", suggested Paul. We left the Muslim quarter at speed through the Golden Gate in the square and east towards the valley.

Giving the dead Shroom a wide berth, we headed up through the Mount of Olives Cemetery. Spall and Jane were forced to wear their protective gear again. The cemetery looked like a huge array of large stone shoeboxes. In the darkness, we wove our way through hundreds, possibly thousands, of tombs and out the other side. We figured the top of the ridge would be a good viewpoint into the valley. "So, how are The Dome of the Rock, Hinnom Valley and Kidron Valley connected?" Paul queried aloud. We mulled it over for a while. The drain and the tombs were the most obvious connections. "The Mount of Olives sits between all three", answered James. "The gardens of Gethsemane, where Jesus was arrested prior to the crucifixion, sits central to all", I added. "Was the Virgin Mary also buried there?" offered Paul. I looked at him curiously but realised he was wearing a Carocle too. Jane called us from the rear of the cemetery. "I've found half a dozen insulated tanks. They've been used to store human blood; each tank holds about fifty litres. Your suspicions were correct, Paul; they've been damn well feeding them, the blood has kept the Shroom active". James gasped, "Is there no end to the filth, we need to catch this fucking animal".

"We know the drain comes out in the valley somewhere, but we won't see anything until morning", added Franc. Paul considered a search pattern, but I wasn't keen to split up. We didn't know if there were more disciples around. We certainly knew Typhon had been sent to attack the haven in Denmark and was on his way back, he was bound to have an assault team with him.

Spall whispered urgently, "I have him". He stood on the top of the highest tomb with his night vision binoculars. "Barak's in the gardens near the Seven Arches hotel. He's heading to the parklands". We headed down the hill at speed, arriving at the hotel in minutes, but couldn't locate him. Spall and Jane's night vision goggles found no trace of Barak. "What now?" remarked James impatiently. "We wait", replied Paul. After fifteen minutes, a car engine started, it could only be Barak, there was no one else in the city. We ran to our vehicles; but it was too late. "Where would he be going?" wondered Paul. I could only think he would head for the safety of his crippled ship. I consulted the extensive knowledge base using the Carocle, but it only recorded the last location of Barak's vessel before he hid it. Melak's scanners couldn't locate the vessel until it powered up, it wasn't emitting an energy signature sufficient to lock onto.

A Doctrine of Fear - Paul JC Edge

The parchment provided by Enzo had highlighted the trap that Barak had long prepared for us. I had researched the area around Jerusalem in advance. I consulted Melak's AI to investigate if it was feasible to patch into the long wave transmitters used by the haven. I felt it may be possible to tap into the extensive knowledge that Father Enzo had acquired on the subject over the years. The AI was aware of the long wave transmissions, Melak often listened to the havens' broadcasts. The AI hadn't transmitted messages, but the mechanism was simple enough. The AI patched me through to Brother Phillippe, the Benedictine Monk living at the Sanctuary. It was good to hear his voice again, "You are still alive Joe, praise be. I'll get Bridget, she is worried about you". "Could I speak to Father Enzo as well please, I need his help", I requested urgently.

Bridget was overjoyed to hear we were alive. I attempted to calm her inquisitiveness to focus on the urgent matter at hand. "Father Enzo, I wonder if you could help us with a small matter. Barak has escaped, we believe he may have returned to his ship. We have no idea of its location; it could be anywhere within a day's drive of Jerusalem. I last we saw Barak near the Mount of Olives Cemetery; he jumped in a car and drove off". "That's most odd, an alien using a humble automobile for transport", observed Father Enzo whimsically. He'd clearly not lost his cynicism.

Enzo enquired, "Roughly which direction did Barak go?" I replied, "He took the road north of the Mount of Olives cemetery going east". Paul interjected, applying his logical mind to the problem, "Barak's unlikely to be going to a location in Jerusalem, we would hear his car from miles away in this mausoleum. Therefore, he must be heading east on the main artery". Bridget built on Paul's thoughts using a detailed world atlas from the sanctuary library. "Highway 1 heads for Amman in Jordan, from there he could follow the road to Saudi, the Red Sea or Iraq". Nothing rang a bell for us, there were too many options, it became an impasse. He could also be leading a false trail.

Father Enzo continued, "From the sound, could you estimate how far the car travelled in an easterly direction?" I replied, "It was probably a couple of miles, until he passed the Mount of Olives itself. Jerusalem is as quiet as a crypt, so it was easy to hear". Bridget reacted suddenly when I inflected the word crypt, making a leap of intuition. "The tomb!" she exclaimed. "Where was the tomb of the Dark One, where they found the parchment? It was somewhere in Iraq, right?" Father Enzo had no idea, he had been handed the vacuum sealed envelope, he wasn't interested in archaeology.

The Carocle allowed me to gain full access to my memories. "An Najaf", I replied ecstatically. "How in the name of God did you remember that", asked Bridget, "Oh sorry Enzo, I forgot again, I keep doing that". She knew I wasn't worried about blasphemy; I'd been doing it all my life; but she was embarrassed in case it offended Enzo. I quickly explained to Bridget how the Carocle improved my memory. We gave Bridget and Enzo our thanks and a brief goodbye before we set off on Highway 1 to Iraq. "Be careful", added Bridget anxiously.

James shouted, "Yes!" when he realised the satellite navigation system was still operational in one of the cars. He plotted a route to the An Najaf waypoint and headed off. I didn't have the heart to explain that the AI could direct us anyway. James found a filling station on the main road, we didn't have enough fuel for the 655-mile trip, obviously there was no electricity for the pumps. Spall broke into the hut, emerging triumphantly with the keys for the metal tank covers. He inserted them into the grid and pulled up the heavy steel cover. "Nice one", smiled James. James used buckets and rope to pull diesel from the tanks directly. Luckily, it had better chemical stability than unleaded fuel. Spall filled several 5-gallon containers lifted from the shop, to be on the safe side. "It's going to take 12.5 hours if the traffic is light", joked James. "Yes, it's evening so let's hope the Shrooms are at the mosque", added Spall. "Enough of that please", I chided with a giggle.

The vehicles headed out of town; it was going to be a long uncomfortable journey in extreme heat. The car's air conditioning had failed, the refrigerant had evaporated, but at 100mph with the windows down, we managed to keep cool. To avoid the abandoned cars littering the main road, we used the shoulder of hard sandy ground.

The border crossing was easy enough, Spall broke the barrier with a jemmy to get through. "Don't forget your passport, visa and driving license", remarked Spall. "My driving license has expired, should I send it to the DVLC for renewal?" asked Paul with a wide grin. There'll be a backlog". "Yeah, join the queue behind the 17-year-old Shrooms". Spall and Paul laughed, but nobody really understood their banter. Jane pointed out the infected couldn't drive cars, therefore the conversation was pointless, knowing Jane it might have been sarcasm.

At Amman we faced a long jaunt on the sand covered roads of the Syrian Desert. It was a large city backdrop with many high mirrored skyscrapers. We bypassed the centre to avoid active Shroom. In a failed attempt to break the monotony, Paul commented, "During the Iron Age, this city was the home of the Ammonites, they called it the Islamic period. It was called Philadelphia in the Greek and Roman periods". "Take off the bloody Carocle, or I'll choke you with it", laughed Spall. "Wow, Philadelphia! Did they invent cheese steak?" exclaimed James, "Are they the same ammonites we found in the rocks on Whitby beach, Dad?" The bad humour was rubbing off in the extreme boredom. "What the hell?" I remarked. James was in the other car; how did he hear us? James excitedly explained, "I snagged T'an-mo's Carocle when he was killed. It really works Dad! I must have inherited the brain implant from you". "You took an unnecessary risk; it could have hurt you", I pointed out grumpily.

James stopped halfway to fill the fuel tanks from our large fuel drums. The endless roads were rough and bumpy. It was a tedious drive with little but sand for miles. Even the distant mountains started to look like heaps of sand. From time to time, we passed small villages of six or seven dilapidated houses. James slowed to check if Barak had stopped or hidden his car. I wondered if we had made a mistake, our assumption of Barak's direction may have been incorrect. Spall examined the dust on the road, the compressions showed a car passed by recently, it gave us a measure of optimism, it could only be Barak.

After ten long hours, we arrived at the small town of An Najaf dangerously low on fuel. James stopped at a rickety old petrol station to refill the cars and our drums. Spall managed to lever the fuel tank covers using a pair of hunting knives. We used buckets to extract the fuel again, the diesel didn't look too clean, there were particles in the fluid. It would have to do; we had no choice. Spall's idea to strain the fuel with a sock seemed to take the worst of the particles from the fuel. Hopefully, Spall's efforts would be enough to prevent fuel line filters blocking up. When Spall wrung out his sock and put it back on, I found it disconcerting. He advised us to ditch the cars soon, the diesel filters could soon become shot. James found edible candy date bars in the hut, the sugar would help sustain us for a while; they weren't good, but they were food of a kind.

We headed into the centre of the town and saw no obvious signs of life. On Spall's advice we killed the engines and listened. In the quiet of the morning, we could hear Barak's car engine nearby. Fortune was on our side; Bridget's insight had proved accurate. We'd travelled at high speed, so had managed to gain on Barak during the night. By pursuing him on foot, we would avoid Barak hearing the car engine, apart from Barak's car, the only sound was the bazaar awnings flapping in the hot breeze.

We followed Barak's car on foot, past several blocks of houses. Spall headed left, past a small white mosque with a blue dome, moving further into the outskirts of the city. He stopped every few minutes to listen and obtain a fix on Barak's location. When Barak's engine shut down, it became guesswork from then on in. Spall found car tracks on the sandy parts of the street, which verified we were heading in the right direction. The years of inactivity in the town made it easy for Spall and Jane to track him.

We continued down the streets until we found a brown saloon car, it was similar to the one Spall had seen from the Mount of Olives Cemetery. He checked the engine, it was warm; we knew we were in the right place. "Be careful, Barak will be defensive, we don't know if he's set traps or if there are disciples here", pointed out Franc. Spall and Jane climbed onto the roof of a nearby building to give them a better view with their binoculars. Barak would be slow on foot, after all he was an old man.

After a few minutes patiently scanning the streets, Spall spotted Barak. He was roughly 200 metres away, heading into to the town centre. It was dusty, the wind whipped up the sand, making it abrasive. We were forced to cover our mouths and noses with fabric. Luckily, we managed to find smelly old scarves from a nearby broken-down stall. Spall and Jane moved stealthily upwind, whilst we lagged behind out of sight. Barak would easily hear us or detect our overripe body odour.

Barak had ambled his way into a large building, its stone facade hid a corrugated iron barn behind. I assumed Barak had used the building for decades, since his ship was grounded. We entered the barn, Jane stood in the doorway, keeping watch. Inside Spall immediately acquired Barak and roughly grabbed him by his jacket collar, Barak was held fast and going nowhere. He was lucky to be still standing after the heinous acts he'd committed.

Barak's ship was part buried in the ground, at the bottom of a large hole in the centre. A door in the side of the ship was clearly visible. Sand covered the remainder of the dusty metallic egg-shaped structure. Clearly, Barak was going to ground until we departed. Barak's ship wasn't operational, according to Melak, his progress on repairs was unclear. I asked Paul to check the ship's status.

Barak spat, "We meet again. The murderer priest and his doomed pack of vermin". It was a clear he was exhibiting a show of bravado, Barak was less confident without his foot soldiers. He was a sad old man, who had played his last move. I replied, "We can't allow you to murder any more of our people Barak. You've caused enough damage to our world. How can you speak of murderers? You are the worst genocidal maniac our planet has ever witnessed. Don't start pretending to be high and mighty, you are human detritus". "It won't matter, you are too late; our mother ship is scheduled to enter your solar system in a few weeks. You have no chance; you are too few and too feeble. Enjoy your last few days as masters of your world. I've already warned the fleet you are here, they are preparing for your final eradication", he replied defiantly. "You are lying, your ship is inoperable", I retorted.

"Look Barak, cooperate with us and we'll let you live out your life in peace", I said. Barak glanced at his ship and looked at me, doubt was written all over his face. "You lie, you will take my ship and my life". "Don't judge me by your standards Barak, I'm telling the truth. All I need you to do is to send a message to your fleet informing them the planet is inhospitable; your initial findings were wrong". He looked weak; a broken man hunched over in pain. Barak stooped, placing his hand over his mouth as if to cough, but instead he swiftly drew his Kadyur dagger.

Barak moved surprisingly fast with unbelievable agility for his age. He twisted out of Spalls grip, turned his dagger, and lashed out; Barak thrusted his knife into my chest. As I fell forward, the tip of Franc's blade emerged from Barak's throat, and he gasped. My memory faded as I collapsed to my knees and fell into unconsciousness.

I awoke a few moments later with Jane kneeling beside me on the floor. Spall shook his head as he spoke gently, holding up my cruciform, "The damnedest thing, his knife cut through your Kevlar vest and shirt like butter; but this cross saved your life". The old cross was the one I'd been given by a Greek orthodox priest, when we were on vacation in Crete. For certain my survival was a sign, the aged priest had told me the cruciform would save me from the 'Dark One'.

I had sustained a large but superficial laceration across my chest, where the dagger had deflected, luckily it wasn't too deep. My chest felt tight and sore, but I could move around with care. Jane had sutured and dressed the wound whilst I was unconscious. Melak made contact; he was pleased by our success, but I sensed a hint of sadness too. He advised us to enter the ship, the close proximity of our Carocles would allow him to gain access to the AI. Melak repaired the AI's microcode and verified the ship was fully operational. The AI then confirmed it was unable to send s sufficiently rapid message to the alien vessel heading our way.

Spall suggested destroying Barak's spaceship, but we agreed it was no longer a threat and could possibly be of use. "Barak indicated the invasion force was nearby, is that true?" I asked. Melak confirmed the ship would enter orbit in roughly five months. We needed to act quickly to protect ourselves from the invasion force; we now needed a plan.

James found canned foods in a small bazaar nearby, many proved perfectly edible and helped satisfy our hunger. We returned to the cars and headed back to Jerusalem. It was a long drive in the fierce heat, dusk approached as we neared the city. James drove directly to the port at Ashkelon, and we boarded the ship. Phil was waiting, he cast off immediately. We were out to sea in minutes, overjoyed to be rid of our sweaty Kevlar suits.

In the morning, over breakfast, we entered into a heated discussion. Jane stated the obvious, "As if we haven't faced enough trouble, we have seven spaceships heading our way, with hundreds of aliens aboard". Paul replied, "What the hell are we going to do? We don't have any spaceships, weaponry, or missiles that can travel through space. We have no means to defend ourselves". "As Melak stated, the invading ships are merely transports, they don't carry special weaponry. His race will be armed with their ceremonial daggers and whatever they can manufacture or take from us", clarified Spall. I added, "But we're outnumbered. The ships could land in different continents, we have no way to mobilise a strike force in seven places at once, it's impossible". "Melak advised we hit the landing shops simultaneously or they would use our weapons against us!" added James. "We'll find a way; we haven't failed so far!" I urged. "You only fail once when playing for high stakes", pointed out Spall unhelpfully.

We sailed back to Salina; on arrival we were welcomed home by a full reception committee. Even Melak joined the islanders to greet us. Bridget spotted I was standing awkwardly and became worried. I explained I had been injured, but Jane had taken good care of me, it hurt but it wasn't bad. Spall overheard and cut in, "Joe used his healing ability to unravel the twisted minds of the Dark Ones, they turned against their leaders. We'd all be dead if it wasn't for Joe!"

Franc reminded us that Typhon, one of Barak's sons, was out there with a strike force large enough to take down a haven.

A Doctrine of Fear - Paul JC Edge

We radioed the communities to pass on the warning concerning the Dark Ones and the invasion ship. Their response was quiet, they were justifiably fearful. An unknown force was coming our way, we would need to work together or perish.

The team and I worked hard planning our defence against the incoming threat. The only approach we considered sensible, was to attack the mother ship before the landing crafts separated. Melak agreed with our strategy but stressed we would need to be smart. We had no means of creating interstellar missiles and no armed spaceships. Paul agreed the Pareth-ng spaceships were the only option for encounters in space. I needed to liberate Barak's craft and find a way to exhume Melak's ship from its basalt tomb. Paul's plan was to take Melak to An Najaf to fully repair the spaceship's engines.

Bridget exclaimed, "It's Summer Haven, they're under attack, you need to come quickly". Spall and Paul jumped to their feet, running to the radio room, Franc and I followed at speed. One of their team, Rusty, spoke fervently, "A strike force of Dark Ones arrived last night in motor torpedo boats. We sank one of the boats with a black shark torpedo, the surviving invaders swam to the mainland. The remaining boat is harboured nearby, the hull was damaged when we engaged it with the gatling gun. We tracked the vessel using radar, it headed for Ullapool, we think it's preparing for another attack. A gathering of Dark Ones on the shore at Polbain are taking pot shots at us with sniper rifles, so we're forced to stay low. We can't get out to tend the farms, it's only a matter of time before they send rockets or RPGs over. We need help quickly".

Paul replied calmly, though I'm sure he didn't feel too calm; after all, his family were resident at the haven. "First of all, they're not demons, they're just men. They wear incendiary shirts that trigger when they are hurt. Dark Ones are skilled, but they're no better trained than you are". Rusty replied, "Sure". Spall interjected, "You have the firepower to hold them at bay but take care, they might attack via the water, they did that here at Salina. You need to guard every defence post on the island 24x7".

Gio confirmed it would take three days non-stop to sail to Summer Haven in the frigate. It could all be over by then, Summer Haven needed urgent support. Spall suggested contacting Captain McCreedy on the HMS Astute for assistance, his ship would be a faster option. They were closer and had a full crew of 98 sailors.

5. The Siege of Summer Haven (HMS Astute Log)

Extract from the ships log of HMS Astute: Captain B. K. McCreedy

CLASSIFIED: Dates and coordinates redacted

Date: Day 00681
Coordinates: XXXXXXX   Course: W   Sea: Choppy   Wind: Light   Temp: 6°C
19:00 Received radio contact from Salina warning of attack on Summer Haven. Confirmed able to assist. Full ahead to the Summer Islands. Estimated travel time 13 hours with a fair current.
It would be good to inflict karma on the Dark Ones after the horrific attacks on the Russian bunkers, I know a few volunteers who would join us, if time wasn't so critical. First Officer will radio Novgorod to explain our status.

Date: Day 60082
Coordinates: XXXXXXX   Course: W   Sea: Choppy   Wind: Light   Temp: 6°C
07:23 Arrived Summer Islands. Observations via the scope indicate damage at Summer Haven, the quayside has been compromised by explosive ordnance. Housing near the quay has also been damaged. Sonar indicates an enemy anti-submarine vessel has been sunk near the rocks at Achiltibuie. It has a clear radar signature. The first order of the day is crippling their transportation and main means of ingress. Full ahead to Ullapool.

08:57 Russian Project 1124M anti-submarine vessel spotted in the harbour at Ullapool. Caution required, it's not one of the older HKs, it's an ultra-modern submarine hunter killer. Not sure if the enemy understand its full capabilities but can't afford to take the risk. The sub hunter will be equipped with forward looking infra-red and depth charges as a minimum. We will engage the vessel from a safe distance.

09:23 Tubes A and B vented. Two Spearfish torpedoes launched.

400m and closing – No action from the vessel. Spearfish not observed by the target. Clearly, they are not utilising sonar or exhibiting appropriate vigilance.

200m – Torpedoes observed by the ship's watch, the Dark Ones are raising the alarm. It's too late to take evasive measures. Evac has been ordered; simultaneously the pilot is trying to reverse out of port.

Direct hit on both counts. Not clear re casualties aboard, observed 6 flaming figures on impact. The flames were brighter than the explosives from the torpedo, they were intense. Chaos on the shoreline; the unit is disorganised. Intend to bubble and engage with main cannon and the Vickers machine gun.

09:44 Engagement complete, observed a further 5 flamers.

10:13 Moving to a defensive position 1k from the coast at Polbain. Too risky to approach, enemy ordnance could damage the hull.

11:00 Moved to engagement distance near Polbain. Strafing and bombarding the enemy with conventional weaponry: QF 4-inch naval gun and Oerlikon 20 mm cannon. Engaged the main mass of the enemy, 300m inland. The British Vickers machine gun took out the enemy in proximity of the shoreline.

12:58 Remainder of the enemy pulled back after a significant pounding. A further 30 casualties estimated. A successful engagement overall. Setting course for Summer Haven goods quay.

14:01 Taking a small landing party ashore. First Officer Caterham remaining in command.

A Doctrine of Fear - Paul JC Edge

From the personal journal of Captain B. K. McCreedy

CLASSIFIED: Dates and coordinates redacted

Date: Day 00682

Received quite a welcoming party with cheering at the quayside once the RIB had been hoisted onto the cliffs by the crane. It was the first time I had set foot on the island; the infection was rife on our last visit. Rusty, a red-haired man with a large beard, rushed up to introduce himself and shook my hand in gratitude. As Rusty approached, he looked at my face attentively, he froze stopping mid stride with his jaw wide open. "Captain Bartholomew McCreedy at your service. Permission to come ashore?" I made the request in a more informal tone with a wink.

Rusty smiled and apologised, "I'm so sorry for my shocked expression Captain, you look just like our leader, Paul Collin, and his brother Franc. We've got used to them being identical twins, but you look exactly the same, although you may be a decade younger". I thought it was odd, perhaps his eyesight was poor, I don't have siblings. "I'm so sorry, follow me, let's grab a beer and something to eat". "You have fresh beer?" I asked uncertainly. I hadn't had a beer for years, our beer cans had long since perished. "Yes, Phil brews beer in the old Post Office. He also distils a reasonable whisky, though it's nothing like a proper Highlands single malt. We still have a few bottles of Jura lying around, I think. I'll have a look; this is a special occasion. Paul says we should rejoice good events vigorously now the world has gone to shit". It was weird, it seemed that Paul routinely used one of my favourite sayings.

A Doctrine of Fear - Paul JC Edge

Our landing party mingled with several islanders over a decent meal. I'd heard of several of the community before; it was good to put faces to names. I met Simon and Kim plus a rather handy looking guy called Wrench. However, the star of the show was the lovely Sheena, Rusty's wife. She was a fine woman, clearly military trained from the way she stood, but with a certain warmth. Sheena stood with a small babe in her arms. "Thanks for the assist Captain", she greeted me with a smile. "No problem, I was in need of a little target practice, my crew were getting rusty, no pun intended", I replied. "Sorry, for staring but you're the dead spit of Paul and his brother, the tiger guy", she clarified. I smiled and had to ask. "Who on earth is the tiger guy?" "Oh, it's Sheena's nickname for Franc, she likes to bring him down a peg or two, though he doesn't really need it, he's pretty grounded", chipped in Rusty jovially.

"But why the tiger guy?" I asked quizzically. "Oh, you know, because of the El Tigre thing". "Sorry, you mean Franc is El Tigre?" I reaffirmed, I thought I'd mis-heard. I'd encountered reports of El Tigre; they called him the Shroom slayer in the ranks in Valletta before it fell. Before the apocalypse, he'd allegedly killed a tiger with his bare hands. My Second Officer, Stenham, had shown me a video a few years back on Instagram. The guys often spoke of the story, there was so little to talk about on the boat. They often joked that I looked a little like him, without the blood.

Wrench resumed his vigilance at the crow's nest. I opted to stay over at Summer Haven for a couple of days, I allowed the crew to join us on land. They were thrilled to be off the ship, despite the cold. The team at Summer Haven were most welcoming, it was good to spend time with folks from England

and Scotland. The Icelanders and Russians were decent enough, but communication was tricky. We had a good laugh with our fellow Brits, and took some welcome R&R. There were a couple of occasions where my crew became a little rowdy, but a few sharp words and they settled down. They were a good bunch.

Date: Day 00685

I received an early call from the ship's watch, the submarine's radar had detected a military frigate moving into the Minch, the main waterway between the island and Lewis. It was heading for the head of loch Broom where the island was located. First Officer Caterham advised us to put out to sea PDQ to avoid getting trapped in the goods quay. The vessel didn't exhibit a standard radar signature, so Caterham couldn't identify it using the ship's software. I appraised Rusty of the situation; he reassured me the ship was sailing from Isola Salina and was friendly, Paul, Franc and Joe were aboard. It was my chance to see for myself if they shared my appearance, or if someone was having a laugh.

All quiet on the mainland. Wrench updated me that the island's CCTV system had been sabotaged. The only view of events on the mainland was from a sophisticated telescope in the crow's nest. The intruders had gone to ground for the time being, we patiently awaited the arrival of the frigate.

Many had gathered in preparation for the return of their leader. Paul's sister-in-law, Fiona, waited with a distraught look on her face, "Where is Kate?" she called to the gathering. Ciara, Paul's daughter, was hanging around her looking confused. "She'll be along in a moment", replied Simes, a little too patronisingly. "Where is she? I haven't seen her for at least an hour", Fiona continued. "Kate won't miss Paul's return", comforted Phil.

The ultra-modern frigate pulled into the waters by the quay. The crew weighed anchor just outside the salmon farm. The anchor held steady as a small motorboat appeared from the aft section of the ship. The boat was piloted directly into the makeshift quay, the sailor in the front of the boat clearly surveyed the damage as he passed the wreckage and docked. As it neared, they could see it was Paul. "Hello everyone, how are you all doing?" he called out excitedly. He managed to climb onto the damaged quayside unassisted and beamed at everyone. "Where's Kate?" he asked. When Paul saw me, his face clouded, as I'm sure did mine. The guy was my absolute double, if a little older.

6. Fourth of the Seven (Paul)

From the journal of Paul Collin

Joe, Spall, and I arrived at the quay on the motorboat, I heard the faint sound of water splashing behind me. I didn't really pay attention; I was so desperate to see Kate and the kids. The quayside was severely damaged, but had been temporarily repaired with sandbags, to keep it stable. It had been hit with some kind of missile and had burned aggressively, it was obvious from the charred wood and damage. It was nothing Drake couldn't fix, given a little time.

Wrench had radioed to report that HMS Astute had destroyed the enemy ship and shelled their impromptu base, the enemy had retreated; at least for the time being. Many of the enemy were killed, the remainder probably chose to withdraw. The Dark Ones were possibly unaware that Barak was dead. Typhon, the assault group's leader, must have informed them. The Dark Ones believed Barak was Satan, surely the death of their leader would sow seeds of doubt in their ranks.

As the boat gently touched the sandbags, Barry took the rope and tied it off. "Hey Bro, how's it going?" I asked. "Better for seeing you alive", he replied. I addressed the group, "Hello everyone, how are you all doing? Where's Kate?"

Barry caught sight of Joe for the first time and did a double take. "What the hell's going on?" Barry asked. I explained Joe was yet another brother I didn't realise existed. Then it was my turn to double take as I caught sight of Bart on the waterside. Bart had seen both Joe and me and was shocked. The situation was getting weirder by the moment.

The quayside bubbled with excitement, but there were lots of questions. Ciara jumped into my arms and whispered, "Daddy, why do so many men look like you? Are you catching?" "I'll explain later sweetheart, they're the brothers I didn't know I had. They're your uncles". She accepted the family additions easily. Ciara was far too excited; Daddy was home, and everyone was making a fuss.

It shocked the crowd when the dogs started to grow fiercely, my attention was immediately drawn to the crow's nest. Three dark figures approached the lookout post from the flank, using the scrub of the hillside as cover. The crowd's interest was drawn to the quay when Franc suddenly yelled a warning.

Sheena launched herself from the sandbags around the crow's nest. She flew through the air, throwing spinning disks at two of the invaders, who burst into bright flames. The third attacked Sheena with a long dagger, she spun on her heel and launched an aggressive flying reverse roundhouse kick to his head. It was a difficult manoeuvre to pull off on the steep hillside. The Dark One ducked the blow but stumbled backwards. Sheena drew her claymore in mid-air. She landed heavily on the incline and slid a metre or so down the hillside.

Sheena and the Dark One launched themselves at each other, their blades clashed. She thrust the blade at the assassin's stomach, which he parried as her kick landed on the side of his head. The Dark One fell back but managed to compose himself quickly as she screamed and charged again. The Dark One evaded her charge as the blades clashed over their heads, but Sheena overran a few metres, due to the incline. She controlled her speed and turned as the Dark One attacked again. The report of an unexpected gunshot rang out from the crow's nest. The third assassin flamed, Rusty lifted his head from the sandbags and smiled, "Sloch that, you bastard".

A slow hand clap sounded from the rough beach, he lifted Kate up from the ground by her hair and held a wicked dagger to her throat. "Welcome home Paul, I thought I would arrange a little coming home party for you". Another Dark One appeared behind Kate, holding a Kadyur dagger to my son's neck. "Allow me to introduce myself. I'm Typhon, son of Barak, I'm here to avenge my father with your blood". I thrust Ciara into the safety of Barry's arms, he took her away quickly. I didn't want her to witness the spectacle unfolding before us. I tried to use the Carocle to contact Typhon, but surprisingly it was unsuccessful. I shouted him as I walked to the beach, "Your captives have done you no harm, they're innocent. Let them go and take me instead". Sheena arrived at the edge of the beach and aimed both her automatic pistols at the Dark One holding Matt. I asked her with a gentle wave of my hand to stand down, she refused.

Joe warned me not to surrender, the assassin would take great joy in killing my family before killing me, he was not to be trusted. Typhon wasn't wearing a Carocle, immediately raising my suspicions. "What is your clone name?" I asked. When I received no answer, I pressed the point, "Your clone name, is it Barak 7-12-12?" Typhon's face clouded, but he pressed on without reference to my mention of Barak. "Give yourself to me, or we will kill your wife and son, you have five seconds to comply". He began to count down from five slowly. Joe caught my drift quickly and interrogated Typhon as I slowly edged forward. "You're not Typhon; you're just a foot soldier. Typhon is a clone of Barak, who is an alien from another galaxy, he came here to destroy humanity. There's an alien spaceship heading to Earth to begin occupation of our planet". Joe's words had no effect, the assassin was indoctrinated. Too twisted with the hypnotic suggestions and the deep psychotic programming of his master.

I stood before the assassins holding my family to ransom; I admit I've not felt such consuming fear as Typhon's count slowly reached two. The Dark Ones stood before me with sharp knives ready to end their lives. "Prostrate yourself before your enemy". I started to kneel; looking into the darkness before me, I felt hopeless. Wrench and Rusty's rifles were sighted, but they couldn't take a shot without putting Kate and Matt at risk.

Joe tried to bargain with the Dark One for a second time. "Your mission is suicidal, if you harm anyone, you will be killed in seconds. Put down your weapons, let's talk this through. Every day of your life is a day of second chances. I give you my word you won't be harmed". The Dark One laughed, as he tightened his grip on Kate. She stared at me with resignation in her eyes. Her fear was for herself but also for me and Matt". She shook her head and mouthed the words, "Don't do it", but I had no choice. I put my hands on the floor before me and slowly lowered my body. I looked up; the dark figures were overshadowed by a greater and more malevolent darkness rising from the floor behind them. The shape grew into the fearsome figure of a man.

The Dark One slowly became aware of the presence behind him. He inclined his blade to stab Kate in the throat, however his arm slid from his shoulder and fell to the floor as he erupted into white flame. I leapt forward and pulled Kate from the incineration. The second assassin holding Matt burst into flame a fraction of a second later. Franc withdrew his blade from the back of the burning man. Matt dropped to the ground as the assassin's burning arms released him, the dagger embedded deep in his throat. Matt lay lifeless, blood pooling. Kate screamed; Joe ran towards us and picked up Matt, pulling the dagger from his neck. Arterial blood sprayed over them both. Joe placed his hands on Matt's neck to stem the flow and prayed. A sudden hope filled me. I grabbed Kate to stop her from getting involved, "It'll be ok. Joe's a healer, he'll save him". This time the healing seemed to take too long, there was no light shining from Joe's eyes, there were only tears. Joe looked up at Kate and me with sorrow and horror, "It's too late Paul. The knife has penetrated his brain stem, there's nothing I can do". We surged forward, grabbing Matt, and pulling him to us, sobbing uncontrollably. I now better understood the deep-seated anger that lay within my brother, Franc.

Over the days that followed I buried myself in grief. Kate dealt with Matt's death in a different way, she spent most of her time with Ciara who was too young to understand the full impact of our loss. In Ciara's company, Kate appeared fine; but when Ciara slept, she became distraught and wept in my arms. Franc visited us with Joe, both were distressed, they felt they had let us down in the worst way possible. I made it absolutely clear to Joe there was nothing he could do. I spoke to Franc at length about Matt's death. It was clear to me the assassins planned to kill my wife and child in front of me, then kill me; just as Joe had predicted. It was the twisted way in which the Dark Ones worked, aiming to drive their enemies to despair. The reality was Franc had saved Kate and me, it was the vile assassin who took Matt's life.

A Doctrine of Fear - Paul JC Edge

Although my thought process was glass half full, it did little to help Franc, over time I knew he would see it my way. The big problem was Kate couldn't reconcile Matt's death the way I did. She felt Franc's actions had caused it. No amount of explaining would make her realise the Dark One was completely evil and intended to murder us all. There was no reasoning with her. Kate's friendship with Franc became lukewarm. Though she was polite, she blamed Franc and there was a coldness in her interactions with him, it was heart breaking to experience.

In the evening, the bodies of Kimball and his partner, Bryan, were found at the defence point in the north, near the wind farm. Dark Ones had entered the island over the rocks and killed them. Kimball and Bryan hadn't even been given a chance to discharge their weapons. The attack had been a complete surprise, they died quickly and painlessly. Luckily for our friends, the Dark Ones had been in a hurry, so they didn't have time to torture them. Bryan's death washed over Kate due to the loss of her son. He had worked in the kitchens with her, they were good friends. The whole community was rocked by their loss.

Our community had fought mindless Shroom for more than two years, though it was vastly different from being attacked by men with evil in their hearts. As the hours rolled by, we needed to communicate to the islanders. Morale was low and there was much confusion. they needed answers.

Franc kindly addressed the group with Joe, as I didn't feel strong enough. It would be months before I was myself again in the truest sense. Franc and Joe explained about the imminent invasion and that the infection was a part of the alien's assault plan. They detailed how we had stopped Barak from warning the invasion force of our survival. Franc and Joe stressed the need for us to work together to counter the invasion, which was imminent. Although a harsh message, everyone needed to put aside their grief and fight, there would be time to mourn later. It was a wakeup call for us all. Our next action was to construct a plan, and quickly.

Kate didn't believe a single word my brothers said, she thought it was an attempt to deflect the tragic events away from Franc. Joe and Franc went on to explain that the four of us were clones of Melak, who was part of an expedition from another world. At that point, Kate walked out, disgusted.

Bart saved his questions for a private discussion after the meeting. "What the fuck is all this nonsense? You're saying I'm some kind of alien clone, are you out of your fucking minds? It's hard enough to believe I have three brothers I didn't know existed", he demanded aggressively. Bart looked like he might explode, his face was red and fuelled by rage. Joe tried to calm him with his gentle logic, he explained that when Melak briefed us, we didn't believe it either. But when he showed us his spaceship, it was hard to ignore his story. "What kind of drugs did he give you, to addle you minds?" Bart demanded, slightly less harshly than before, but full of anger.

Joe pulled the Carocle from his bag and handed it to Bart. Bart was shocked by the appearance of the device; he found it lent a small amount of credence to our story, it was hard to believe it could be created on Earth by humankind. The Carocle defused the situation, Bart's aggression was replaced by curiosity. "I'd noticed the metal headbands you were wearing, but I didn't get a chance to ask", he offered. Joe explained that when the band was placed on the owner's head, it permitted direct contact with the AI on Melak's ship. In addition, the Carocles allowed us to communicate mind to mind and provided total recall of the wearer's thoughts and memories. Bart looked at the Carocle turning it in his hands. "And it won't hurt me?" he queried. "No, but it will feel a little odd at first". "And I have an implant in my brain to link to it, you say?" He looked dubious, in the same way we had before we wore it. But he had to try it, as the old proverb says, 'curiosity killed the cat'.

Bart placed the Carocle on his head, but instantly took it off, it made him disorientated. "It stuck to my head, but then it came off easily", he observed. "Yes, the Carocle connects to your implant, but disconnects when you want to remove it", Joe explained. Bart placed the Carocle back on his head, he looked blank for a second, but suddenly became alert. Bart was exploring with the device. From experience, the first encounter was the ability to access life memories clearly. It brought the past back in a very real way. After a few minutes Bart would probably probe the network, the knowledge in the data bank and the minds of his brothers. Bart was overwhelmed, he looked sad, tears filled his eyes. It was strange to see a tough military guy showing his vulnerable side, it was a life changing experience.

"Are you ok Bart?" asked Joe gently. Bart looked at Franc and then me, "How do you live with the pain and responsibility? The Carocle makes memories feel real, raw like they've just happened. It refreshes the deaths of your family in your mind, like an open wound. Time heals, it deemphasises bad memories as a kindness, the Carocle reverses the healing process cruelly".

A Doctrine of Fear - Paul JC Edge

Joe and I considered Bart's thoughts, memories weren't such an issue for me, my deepest wounds were recent. I let Franc answer, it was too soon for me to comfortably talk about death. "I guess your memories make you who you are. My terrible memories burn inside me every day, the blessing of the Carocle is I can clearly recall the happy and wonderful times too. I relive times with my wife and daughter. I can feel, smell, and touch them again. I remember my first kiss, the birth of my daughter, the sunshine on the day of my wedding. If I focus on the good, it makes the bad easier to bear. I have learned to avoid looking into the darker doorways too much; but it takes time to master, and it hurts".

Bart observed, "I can see key events from your life, the shock, the feelings of revulsion, the gradual acceptance. The fear that no one would understand you. I now realise the story is true, but I can also see the subject that currently occupies your mind. The huge spaceship nearing our solar system. We must find a way to destroy it, and quickly", added Bart. I explained that the Carocles and the AI would help us to plan our counterattack. Using the Carocle we could share thoughts and experiences quickly; communicate wherever we were. We could access a rich set of data from the ship, giving us a significant tactical advantage when coupled with surprise.

Bart accepted us; however, others in the haven found the story alarming, they worried for our state of mind. Kate stopped listening at the clone part of our update, she clearly couldn't accept the idea and walled it off. She was in denial and simply wouldn't discuss the matter. It seemed to be driving a wedge between us, I was forced to ignore our problems for the time being, survival was our first priority, though I knew a delayed resolution could cause a rift in the long term.

My main worry was that Typhon was still out there somewhere. I suspected he would head for one of three locations: Barak's spaceship, the isle of Vulcano or Jerusalem. I directed the AI to monitor all three places, we needed to identify and track anyone who visited them. I also asked the AI to watch the coastline around each of the remaining havens. The AI would notify us if it detected unusual activity, which I guess these days was any activity at all. We needed to strike back at the aliens, they had severely damaged us. We had to stop them from wiping our race from the face of the planet and give them a taste of retribution.

7. Planning the Impossible (Paul)

From the journal of Paul Collin

It was imperative we focus our minds on defending ourselves against the incoming fleet, so we felt obliged to hold a makeshift funeral for Matt, Kimball, and Bryan. We, the four brothers, met in the island café, our impromptu meeting space for confidential discussions. The café was the other side of the water processing plant, allowing a little distance from the community. James, Spall, Jane and Rusty joined us.

Spall kicked off the session, "So we have a month to figure out how to destroy the invasion force that's heading our way across space". Spall's intent hadn't changed, it was to engage the attackers' ships before they separated. To him, the thought of a battle across multiple continents was infeasible. I built on his thought, "We can't fight the invasion force in space, so we need to engage them before they split to enter Earth's atmosphere. We must hit all seven spaceships simultaneously and hit them hard". "We've been through this countless times! Hit them with what? Your big gatling gun won't help you", pointed out Jane.

Melak advised, "We also need to prevent the ships from growing clones to supplement their army, once they see the threat we represent. They grow clones in weeks, rather than the years it takes for a human to develop". If they were permitted to land, our only option was combat with rifles, machine guns and RPGs, it would be impossible to wipe out a large ship quickly and decisively.

A Doctrine of Fear - Paul JC Edge

Spall clarified, "If they survive our initial strike, then we need to hit them with missiles or bombs, but we're not trained to operate military aircraft. Another option is to use ground to ground or ground to air missiles. We could scour our military bases for missiles and then train ourselves to operate them. We can reach out to Formentera or Mont St Michel (MSM), who may have skills in this field, but I have my doubts. MSM are mainly scientists and farmers who carry small arms. Formentera is a mixed bag, but they do have some naval officers".

Bart pointed out the submarine was equipped with tomahawk missiles, with a 1000-mile range, but if the seven ships landed in different locations, it could only engage one or possibly two landing craft. A Tomahawk's payload was a nuclear warhead and there would be fallout from the attack, so we needed to be careful where we deployed them. Bart's team included weapons specialists with missile and warhead expertise, but they didn't have much knowledge of general explosives and bombs.

Bart explained that many of our Russian allies were soldiers who would be happy to assist. Using our Carocles, we reviewed how Bart had rescued the Russians from bunkers. It also itemised a rough breakdown of Russian military personnel. We engaged Melak to check how the ships would land. He was now resting again in his ship; he wasn't getting any stronger and I knew we wouldn't have him for many more days.

Melak displayed a virtual makeshift holomap in front of us. He explained, "Essentially, Barak and I looked for large land masses in an optimal crop tolerant climate, encouraging livestock to thrive. Nothing too hilly or remote, with good access to the ocean. Hot countries between the Tropic of Cancer and the

A Doctrine of Fear - Paul JC Edge

Tropic of Capricorn or colder countries nearing the poles were excluded. Barak and I chose five highly populated areas near Europe as possible landing sites: Southern Russia, Germany, France, Spain, and Italy. The areas were easily accessible for trade, the conditions were good, and they were not too mountainous. We also selected two sites in the USA: North Carolina and Massachusetts. I'll share the exact coordinates of the landing sites we transmitted to the mother ship".

The biggest issue we faced was the topography of the seven landing sites, our force was small, it was impossible to hit all the ships simultaneously. Even if they travelled together, they would separate too early to engage them as a group with the weaponry we had. If we failed to hit them simultaneously, they would adapt, we would be overwhelmed. When we ruled out the possible, only the impossible remained. Spall's initial thoughts were confirmed yet again, we must hit the mother ship before the landing craft ejected, when they were in one place.

Spall came straight to the point, "Are there missiles in the bunkers around the world with space capability?" I searched the AI's data base. "No", I replied with disappointment. Steve was our best engineer, he took over the discussion, "Specific engines are used for space travel, we could try adding space capable drives to a missile, it would take over propulsion once out of Earth's atmosphere. We could even rig up a guidance system, but the modifications would take serious engineering. We could attach bombs to a space shuttle, but we don't have skills to launch and fly it, assuming the changes were successful".

It would have taken NASA several years of R&D to carry out the work, plus a crazy budget. Our team comprised of a few farmers, a couple of mechanics and an extremely limited time span". "What about Melak's ship?" suggested Spall, resurrecting the topic. "It's buried in tons of basalt, it would take serious drilling and controlled explosions to free it", pointed out Franc. "Drake could help us there, he built Summer Haven under a mountain of rock", I suggested. "Drake's hill was soft sandstone; basalt is dense, it could take months", added Steve.

James often thought out of the box and on this occasion, he didn't disappoint. "What about using Barak's ship, when Melak reprograms the engines and makes it operational again? Although we would need to take him to the ship. It is only covered with sand; we could dig it out quite easily. In fact, the AI indicates the ship could pull itself out of the hole with no effort". "We could load up Barak's spaceship with nuclear warheads and ram the mother ship. With enough explosives, we would annihilate it", suggested Spall. We hoped the nuclear warhead experts aboard the HMS Astute would be able to help.

Bart's imperative was to avoid the use of tomahawk warheads unless we had no choice. The tomahawk was our only defence if the ships landed. My thoughts progressed to the warheads in HMS Ambush which resided at the bottom of the sea near Summer Haven, we had been forced to destroy it. Bart sensed my recollections, damn the Carocle. I needed to avoid Bart accessing my memories to find we had sunk his sister ship without giving him a full explanation. Luckily, he also accepted my justification as well as the facts, he fully understood our actions.

There were ticking time bombs everywhere; nuclear weapons at the bottom of the sea and in bunkers throughout the world, all slowly corroding and potentially becoming unstable. What would happen if the devices became dangerous? Then there were the nuclear reactors powering numerous cities all over the planet. The AI confirmed a warhead wouldn't detonate without an explosion, but it could emit dangerous radiation, harming the environment. The nuclear power plants needed to be safely decommissioned to avoid serious damage, but it was a problem for later, we had no time to waste. The guys on the submarine were experienced in maintaining nuclear reactors safely, as were the crew of the Phoenix.

Bart contacted the Russian team on the radio, to update them on the situation and assess if they could assist with our complex undertaking. Meanwhile Rusty and Wrench sailed to the mainland to gather scuba gear from the diving school in Dundonnell, to survey and salvage the remains of HMS Ambush. Our main priority was to transport Melak to Barak's ship in Iraq, to release it from the sand. Drake and Jake agreed to travel to Vulcano to start the long and painstaking excavations of Melak's ship from the volcano.

Drake prepared explosives and excavation tools, plus a small JCB digger with drilling attachments. I guess we wouldn't need it at Summer Haven, at least for the time being. Joe and Franc immediately set sail for Salina with our excavation team on the frigate, our fastest means of travel. Joe's guard of honour, James and Jane, travelled with him. Bart, Spall, and I focussed on locating suitable weaponry.

I updated Melak regarding our plans to use Barak's ship to attack the invasion fleet. Melak had grave concerns that the mother ship would see Barak's vessel approaching and act aggressively when the appropriate protocols failed. Melak re-iterated that the mother ship didn't have a battery of offensive weapons, but it possessed engineering lasers strong enough to cut through the ship at close range. It also had limited projectile weapons that were used to break up or redirect asteroid fields, they could inflict critical damage in close combat. Melak agreed to give the matter some thought. He consented to the trip to Iraq, though he would require our assistance. Barak's constant need for regeneration meant we must act quickly.

Bart's Russian contacts responded to his message within the hour. Bart didn't need a translator and was able to converse in Russian, his newly acquired fluency in the language astounded not only General Smitsky's team, but also Bart himself. The General confirmed there were two nuclear missile silos in the vicinity of St Petersburg, and two of his team were specialised in missile tech, one with a specific expertise in nuclear warheads. The availability of these skills was a significant breakthrough. Smitsky agreed his team would gather as many warheads as they could and rig the bombs to be detonated by hand, rather than on proximity or impact. The Russians had access to military facilities via Colonel Raspirov, who had full clearance. Smitsky offered to update us on his progress in a couple of days.

Rusty and Wrench didn't have so much luck with HMS Ambush, the sea was deep, and the boat rolled around in the strong currents, making boarding the submerged vessel an extremely dangerous venture. They gained access to the torpedo room in the forward section of the vessel, but it was air locked. Bart recommended that they extract nukes from the submarines weapon store, but he realised it needed a specific electronic key which wouldn't work in water. Specialist equipment was needed to cut the hull, so Rusty and Wrench weren't able to make progress.

In a quiet moment my thoughts turned to Matt and his tragic demise. I spent a little time with Kate before things got manic again. Kate was disengaged, our conversations only consisted of simple small talk. Phil and his wife Robyn, offered to spend more time with Kate. I knew if anyone could help her, it was Phil. Kate spent much of her days working in the kitchen, she was a team of one since Bryan's demise. Others had been assigned to help, but they could only manage the basic kitchen porter jobs and would need training over time. I worried Kate would become exhausted without significant down time. The galley team from the Astute were more than happy to lend a hand, which relieved stress on the work front for a little.

The quietness of next few days was abruptly broken by a flurry of activity. Joe and Franc reached Salina, and Gio helped Drake and Jake with orientation and building an excavation team. The following day, Drake began the dig on Melak's ship on the neighbouring island of Vulcano. Melak assured us the necessary digging, drilling and small detonations required to remove his ship wouldn't harm it materially. The AI could keep watch on the seismic activity of the volcano, just in case. Drake called upon Umberto's scientific expertise to help him judge the feasibility of the excavation approach.

The Russian team confirmed the contents of both nearby silos had been compromised, they removed critical parts as spares. The remaining cold war silos in the vicinity had previously been emptied; their weapons decommissioned under NATO supervision. Smitsky knew the official disarmament story reported to the world was not the whole truth, he was confident they could find suitable weaponry, but it proved not to be the case locally.

Their backup plan was to locate other mobile missile launchers from army bases and possibly submarines in dry dock. Smitsky had liberated three warheads from a military compound near Moscow. A nuclear submarine had also been located in the large shipyard at St. Petersburg. The submarine 'Dmitriy Donskoy' was the last of the Akula (Shark) class submarines and was armed with numerous warheads. My Carocle revealed 'The Akula class submarines were the largest cold war leviathans ever built; they had capability to destroy up to two hundred targets. Their warheads were six times more powerful than those used at Hiroshima'. The ship was the last of its kind. The submarine held twenty R-39 missiles, classified by NATO as the SS-NX-20 "Sturgeon". Each R-39 packed ten one-hundred-kiloton warheads. The Russian team managed to liberate 200 warheads from the submarine. They were currently being modified by the team to allow them to be detonated by a dead man's switch. I dearly hoped the name of the switch didn't become a reality.

We found several possible locations for military bases at each of the intended landing sites. We hoped to liberate large scale mobile missile launchers or weaponry we could use to attack the alien landing craft. Leveraging Spall, Rusty and Bart's knowledge we identified the most suitable locations, they had worked in several of the bases in the past. Bart could cover the USA using HMS Astute, he could hit both potential sites from one central location using Tomahawks equipped with nuclear warheads. The other five landing sites would be a problem and needed significant planning. Germany could be covered by the Russian team. Summer Haven would cover France. There were no military staff at MSM or Salina, so we were forced to impose on a rather busy Generale Enrico at Formentera to defend Spain and Italy. Enrico understood the importance of the mission, and he allocated his best men to the task, but there were not enough.

Melak advised we use Barak's ship to transport the warheads to Summer Haven, once we had made it operational. The spaceships hull was able to change form and could hold the devices safely in custom-built enclosures to prevent vibration or jarring of the delicate mechanisms. We would use the ship to transport the bombs to the point of detonation, with luck it would be classed as a friendly vessel by the alien mother ship.

8. Preparing a Stellar Welcome

First and foremost, I am a priest who believes in peace and love. Building a missile to end the lives of thousands wasn't something I expected to be involved in, and I certainly don't want it included on my epitaph. Despite the aliens' plan to bring about genocide of the human race, I found it hard to condone murder, let alone one on such a scale. I focussed my mind on the fact the aliens would kill us if they were allowed to land. We had witnessed their ruthlessness first-hand; It was imperative I protected the people in my care, I had a duty to my family and to the communities of Earth. Like the pacifistic Jewish community moving to Israel after WWII, experiencing genocide changes you, one quickly learns to defend oneself.

We arrived at Salina to make our final preparations. I quickly departed to mobilise the excavation team on Vulcano island. Melak still looked unwell, we managed to help him to the ship where he could rest in his cabin.

When we showed Drake the location of the spaceship, his first reaction was shock and awe. "It's true then, you are from another world?" Jake commented with a little sarcasm. "No, I'm from Wolverhampton", I replied with a smile, "My cells were cloned from someone who came from another world. I was born here, my roots are a mile deep", I winked. Drake, however, was lost in the moment; it wasn't an everyday occurrence to see an alien spaceship in the flesh. I ran over the brief with him one last time, "It's essential we excavate the ship intact, we need it fully operational. Its hull is flexible and can squeeze through a relatively small hole. The AI will monitor the volcano for activity". "The rock is very hard which makes it difficult, we'll try our best", promised Drake.

Drake started by clearing the scree and slag using the JCB, so they could assess the situation. "There's food and drink in a few restaurants in town, you'll just need to trawl through the freezers and the cupboards for canned goods. Restaurant Vincenzino has a solar panelled freezer, stocked with Melak's synthesised food", I added. "One other thing Drake. The burned-out warehouse a block behind the restaurant, may be toxic, so keep well clear of it". I didn't want him poking around in the ashes of the horrific mausoleum containing the tortured cadavers of the locals. The guard had organised the removal of the bodies ready for proper burial, but it was impossible to dispel the evil surrounding the building.

When Jane, James and I re-joined the frigate; Franc hummed a tune while he dangled his legs in the water on the quayside steps. I recognised the melody but couldn't remember the title of the old blues song; the name would come to me eventually.

Phil set sail for Iraq at full speed. He felt we should be able to cover another seven or eight trips of a similar length, but we would then need to refuel the ship. The remaining fuel should be more than enough for our immediate needs. It took twenty-six hours to get to Israel, but it was no fun, the sea was choppy. James and I struggled with sea sickness, but Melak was the worst. He looked almost green as he stood in the centre of the ship looking at the horizon. The boat rocked to and fro, we couldn't see land in any direction. We'd made the crossing before, and most likely we would do it again. As a race, we needed to find our sea legs and handle the sickness a little better, sailing boats would soon be our only mode of transport.

A Doctrine of Fear - Paul JC Edge

Metal ships would soon be reduced to rust, whereas wood and sails could be repaired as we reacquired the skills. The name of the song that Franc had been humming clicked eventually, 'Hey Joe' by Hendrix, very amusing.

We arrived in Israel the following lunchtime, disembarking after food. As Spall always said, sleep and food are weapons, use them wisely. We chose not to take the vehicles we'd used previously; the dirty fuel could lead to engine problems. Bad fuel was like a ticking time bomb, it was too risky. Jane located a comfortable rental Mercedes SUV. Jane found the key on the wheel arch and started the engine first time; we were blessed with air conditioning and music this time. She found a memory stick in the glove box; she plugged it into the console and turned the music up. It held a wide selection of English and American rock, ranging from The Wildhearts to Aerosmith. It was a joy to listen to decent music again. Why a RAM disk would have been left in a rental car was anybody's guess, but I wasn't complaining. James moaned, he claimed it was old folks' music, but he was soon singing along. Melak simply looked at us in complete disbelief, he'd never quite understood the concept of dancing and singing. I suspect humans were the only species in the universe who liked music, but I admit I never really enjoyed dancing myself.

James took the fuel bucket and tubes from the vehicle we had previously used. I liberated the service station fuel tank cover keys; we would certainly them need to re-fill the tank. We hit the road to Amman and drove on to An Najaf. I napped in the back, Jane and James took turns driving in the hot afternoon sun. There was no let-up in the heat as we drove on through the night. It was morning when we arrived at the petrol station. At lunchtime we tucked into our dry ration packs, I washed the food down with warm bottled water. I couldn't quite face the warm coke that James guzzled, yuk!

Jane remembered the route around the outskirts of town, taking us to Barak's old warehouse. She approached the dusty façade to find a large part of the building's side had been removed. We left Melak sleeping in the back of the SUV while we checked the place out. It was clear there was no activity, everywhere was still. As James entered the warehouse he shouted. We headed into the building to find Barak's spaceship had gone, there was nothing but an almighty great hole in the ground. I surmised the Dark Ones had managed to repair the ship and fly it to another location. We were royally screwed now. I sat down, I needed time to think. I had no idea where they would take the vessel, it could be anywhere on the planet. Franc remained optimistic; he was sure we would find a way. He also said that there was no one left who could operate a Carocle and hence the ship, as Barak's sons were dead. I curtly reminded him that Typhon was still on the loose, to his embarrassment. His positivity niggled me; he had no ideas which would get us out of this mess. James and Jane stared into the hole like council roadworks supervisors, they looked resigned as if they had given up, but it proved not to be the case.

"Barak's ship isn't operational!" exclaimed James. "What do you mean?" I wondered where he was going with the remark. "The ship has been pulled out of the hole using a pair of backhoes and probably a tractor, you can see the caterpillar track marks. Indentations showed that a crane had also been used to lift it out of the ground, it explained the demolished rear wall of the warehouse. The Dark Ones have removed the crane and plant equipment to cover up their actions". "So, they just lifted the ship up and loaded it onto a truck?" I asked incredulously. "Yep, it was heavy though, it looks like it nearly tipped the crane a couple of times. Operating a crane on this sandy ground must be treacherous".

James showed me the indentations in the hard, dusty ground and the markings in the sand. Although the winds had eroded the tracks, imprints could clearly be seen in the hard compressed sand. Brushing the dust away from the surface revealed the truth beneath. I could use the concept as an analogy for one of my sermons if I survived to tell the tale. "Can we follow the tracks?" I asked optimistically. "Only to the road, obviously it left in a different direction to the way we came, who knows where it was taken". Franc interjected, "We would notice a lorry driving past with a spaceship on it presumably. But then perhaps we didn't, I was half asleep". Jane had enough of Franc's flippant remarks, "Hopefully, I was awake, I was driving. Let's stop pissing into the wind, we need to find the ship, or we're all dead".

We sat, looking at the map and the endless possibilities, from Baghdad to Oman. Franc wisely consulted Paul to check if he could add any insight. Franc looked up with a wide grin. "Paul instructed the AI to keep watch on Barak's warehouse", he exclaimed excitedly. We consulted the AI; it had observed the spaceship's removal. "Why didn't it warn us?" queried Franc. "Because nobody asked it to, the AI was instructed to monitor movements, which is exactly what it did. It's a computer, remember. It may be an amazing one, but it follows instructions", clarified Paul, "It was my bad". "Nobody's fault.

I'm just pleased you asked it keep watch; it was a great thought!" I added. Franc was confused, "I thought the ship's voice represented an Artificial Intelligence. It should emulate the human brain and think for itself. Why didn't it realise the significance of the spaceship to us?" "Perhaps it's because we didn't think to explain why the spaceship was so important. We gave the AI a menial task, rather than a full explanation. It's all about accountability, we didn't give it any. Maybe we should treat the AI more like a real person", suggested Paul. "Perhaps it emulates a human brain too well, we forgot and so did it?" laughed James. Either way we'd learned something important, we needed to treat the AI as one of us and involve it more closely in our planning.

The AI replayed the spaceship's removal so we could see the excavation in more detail. In tracing Barak's spaceship, we followed the articulated lorry as it headed towards Damascus, then down towards Beirut. The port was clearly its destination, but we had no time to intercept it. Jane spoke to José on the Phoenix using her comms link and explained the situation. Five minutes later Phil replied, the Phoenix was already on course towards Beirut. Jane clearly warned Phil of the dangers of the Dark Ones, he should engage them with care. His orders were to stop the spaceship leaving the port. I found it funny how Jane had simply assumed command of the ship; Phil had no intention of contesting her. He probably found her manner too scary to argue with; I know I did.

The AI continued to trace the progress of Barak's ship. I asked for updates if their route deviated materially. I took the time to explain our plans and rationale in more detail, to avoid past mistakes. We jumped in the car and headed to the petrol station to load up with dirty fuel. We'd brought a funnel from the ship with a filter built into it. We were learning, albeit slowly.

Jane headed back towards Jerusalem but took the Damascus Road after we crossed the Syrian Desert. She drove like a maniac. Sadly, I believe Franc and James enjoyed the ride. The journey was certainly more comfortable in a luxury SUV. Melak slept, he looked so very tired. He slouched in the centre seat at the rear, propped up between Franc and me. I worried about him. A tiring day later, we arrived in Damascus. José called Jane to explain they had seen the lorry nearing the port. There were seven men dressed in black accompanying the vehicles, two in the lorry and five in a Jeep following in close convoy.

As the Dark Ones purposefully headed into the ferry port, one of their associates appeared to be preparing the Cyprus ferry for departure. The ferry had been disused for quite some time prior to A-Day due to unrest in Israel. The ship's crew seemed confident they could make the ship operational. They eventually started the engines and lowered the tail onto the port side, the ship's capacity was more than sufficient to take the lorry with its oversized load. Transporting the vehicle up the ramps onto the ship would be a slow process. The spaceship protruded either side of the trailer by quite a margin, creating a stability issue. The care needed in the transportation explained the lorry's slow progress. We needed to be vigilant; they would replan their route if they spotted the Phoenix, but we couldn't allow them to board the ferry. We needed to retrieve the spaceship intact.

Decisively, Jane ordered José to pilot a couple of blast drones into the port. They were quiet but could take down countless enemy when detonated near their target. Moving Barak's ship would be problematic with less people. We received a full blow by blow report from José via our Carocles, using long wave radio.

José piloted the drones quietly over the water, staying low to avoid alerting the enemy. As the Dark Ones engaged the ferry ramp, they moved towards the lorry. The drones neared the vehicle, but kept a sufficient distance, their fans would be audible as soon as the ramp motors stopped. Five made their way to the trailer, to move their precious cargo.

Phil sailed the Phoenix further into the port, José flew the drones in quickly and detonated them on either side of the enemy. Four Dark Ones flamed immediately, as the high velocity ball bearings tore through their bodies. Synchronised with the explosion, a gunner on the Phoenix opened fire with the main cannon, targeting the port entry point. The aim was to block attempts to hastily exit using their vehicles. Phil's ship launched three sea sparrow missiles, which blew a huge hole dead centre on the waterline of the ferry's hull. The ferry began to sink; the water was shallow, and it partially submerged.

The ferry blocked the mouth of the port, preventing ingress of other vessels. On the trailer, several tyres were torn apart, causing the lorry to list to one side precariously. The trailer was in serious danger of tipping onto its side, it was going nowhere, plus the road out of the port was non-existent. A black figure ran quickly down the ramp from the ferry and leapt across the water. The ramp had been torn from the wall and had dropped into the sea, the Dark One collided with the harbour wall and grabbed handholds in the stone. He lithely ascended and joined his comrades hiding in the cover of the cab.

A Doctrine of Fear - Paul JC Edge

A Dark One pulled out a large green cylinder from the tailgate of their Jeep and shouldered it. Phil spotted the weapon with his binoculars; he realised it was a portable rocket launcher. Phil ordered José to take the ship out of range pronto, whilst the main cannon opened fire on the Jeep. José fired up the ship's engines and moved away at speed, causing loose items on the ship's deck to tumble. The ship wasn't moving fast enough to avoid the enemy missile which was heading in its direction at significant velocity. It was impossible to identify the missile from a distance, however, Phil presumed it wasn't being guided manually, the three figures were clearly visible via optics and weren't operating a device. Their ship was not being marked by a laser, inferring it was heat seeking. The missile arced through the air in the ship's direction until its guidance system's seeker acquired the ship as a target, it then took a straight line towards the keel of the frigate.

José initiated the ship's Sea Gnat counter measures system as the missile neared. An array of small rounds was launched into the sky, each opened into a small parachute carrying a device emitting intense bursts of infra-red to foil the missile's guidance system. The missile would be programmed to aim for the centre point of our ship's heat signature. Due to our Sea Gnat's infra-red sources disguising the centre of heat, the missile struck the sea on the port side and exploded.

The missile detonated with a colossal sound; water crashed over the deck. Before the Dark One could launch another missile, the ship's main gun fired. The BAE Systems / Bofors 57 mm Mk 110 gun was devastating at such short range, a single shell completely wiped out the Jeep. The explosion launched the vehicle into the air, taking out three of the enemy. They flared brightly as the remaining figure dropped the missile launcher and ran for the port exit.

As our vehicle neared the port we heard the explosions; so far, we had monitored events using our Carocles. The noise finally woke Melak who looked out of the SUV bleary eyed. Our path was blocked by rubble, Jane stopped the car. It was the remains of the ferry port gates, blown to pieces by the cannon fire. She deliberately positioned the vehicle to block the enemy's exit. Jane and James drew their weapons as they exited the car. I heard the Dark One's Jeep explode, luckily, we were distant enough to avoid shrapnel.

Franc jumped out the car a moment later, disappearing behind the remnants of the port gate. I left Melak lying on the back seat. The remaining Dark One spotted me as he leapt, clearing the mounds of rubble in a single bound, he opened fire in mid-air. Jane saw the danger immediately and launched herself in front of me, taking three shots to her body. The Dark One hit the ground running but was impaled by Franc's blade as my brother rose from the rubble. The figure burst into white light, burning furiously.

The shots had been blocked by Jane's heavy Kevlar vest, she was clearly bruised and winded. She turned to deliver her trademark wink, as her head moved, I saw the side of her skull was missing, her hair matted with blood. There was a delayed reaction before blood started to pour from her. James screamed, "No!" as I scooped her into my arms and prayed. There was no blinding light, no healing, Jane's soul had departed her lifeless body. "Fix her, Dad, go on pray again", pleaded James. "I can't James, she's gone, it's too late. I'm so sorry Son", I whispered through my tears. James grabbed Jane and wept uncontrollably. His screams of pain filled the dusk evening with his agony. Franc looked on understandingly, he knew such desperate pain all too well. There was nothing Franc could do to help, other than check for remaining threats, not wanting Jane's sacrifice to be in vain. It's said the greatest honour for a bodyguard is to take a bullet for the person they are protecting, but it seemed pretty shit to me. In the morning, we would pray and carried Jane's body to the ship together to bury her with the dignity she deserved when we returned to Salina.

The ferry was submerged to its top deck, the two funnels and mast emerged from the water, its bridge barely visible. Melak was nowhere to be seen. The spaceship sat on the flatbed of the severely damaged articulated lorry on the quayside. It tilted to one side on the trailer's shredded tyres, the cab had been smashed to small pieces by the ball bearings. James removed the securing straps from the spaceship, staying busy was his strategy to keep grief at bay. Ropes were attached to the high side of the vehicle and secured to a cleat on the harbour wall to stabilise it and prevent the trailer from tipping further.

Franc and I clambered into the spacecraft to find Melak already inside. Regardless of the exterior angle of the ship, the interior was completely level. Barak's ship was larger in the hole at An Najaf, it had since contracted to enable easier transportation. The AI confirmed Barak's ship was made from organic titanium and was able to change size and form, but not its overall mass. It made no sense to me, but there was no time for questions, we had other more pressing matters to deal with.

Along came the moment of truth, it was time to see if Melak's attempt to restore Barak's sabotaged engine had worked. He needed to determine if it was fully operational. Melak's advanced years had caught up with him all at once, there wasn't a fix for old age; we weren't in California. His pod in the spaceship clearly helped him, but it only provided a bolstering effect. I placed my arm under Melak's shoulder and lifted him to his feet, Franc took his other shoulder. We half carried him to a pod which appeared on the hull wall. Melak's control panel used to access the ship re-formed inside his pod as he continued to work on the software. It took him a couple of hours to reverse the remaining hacks he had made to the AI. "Both ships are configured to accept instructions from the Carocles, I will rest in my pod whilst I finish setting up the engine array. The ship is solar charging using its photovoltaic skin and will also deploy a heat exchanger in the ground. It will have sufficient charge to fly in a couple of days. Please accept my apologies, I must rest. Melak looked more comfortable in his pod but was extremely frail.

I noticed that Barak's ship was drilling a probe into the ground at the side of the trailer with little effort or sound, it must have been the heat exchanger mechanism. Franc, James, and I gathered our thoughts; we had a couple of days to kill. We re-joined Phil and the crew on the Phoenix for dinner. We were desperate for real food; we'd survived on basic supplies for a few days. I radioed Bridget to give her our terrible news and explain our situation. Bridget was heartbroken for James. I promised to be home soon, but I wanted to stay with Franc until the ship was fully operational.

It was a long, boring wait; we spent much of our time playing poker for dry biscuits. When the ship was finally charged, Franc and I re-boarded, "So how do we fly this thing?" he pondered, "I had assumed Melak would pilot it". We asked the AI for guidance, the method proved rather simple, the AI facilitated all the hard work. There were no controls, complex levers, or dials to operate, we simply needed to provide the AI with the required destination, it was like having our own invisible pilot.

Allowing a machine to fly the ship filled me with more than a little trepidation. I guess I preferred a skilled pilot to be in control, but the training needed to become proficient with such technology didn't bear thinking about. I shouldn't have worried, the ship launched, and the test flight was smooth and very straight forward. The AI assured us the ship was now fully functional, and ready for our next mission. Apparently the ship's power levels were still quite low, it had an operational range of 0.0478 light years without a recharge. I suspected a light millisecond was all we would need. Franc and I shook hands, I left him on board with Melak. Franc gave James a hug and looked into his eyes wishing he could help.

James and I carefully climbed down the ramp to re-join Phil. The frigate couldn't enter the ferry port itself, due to the crippled ferry, so it was loitering as close to the harbour wall as was feasible. We strolled back to the frigate and crossed the makeshift gang plank between the port and the ships deck. James was dragging his feet a little, he was a long way from his normal self. Phil sailed out of Beirut carefully, avoiding the waterlogged ferry, setting sail for Salina once more.

A Doctrine of Fear - Paul JC Edge

As we left Israel's continental shelf, we noticed a silver shimmer from the port. The silver egg shaped craft lifted into the sky and started to hum gently. There was a brief metamorphosis as the hull reshaped to provide a matching pair of large fans, the ship now looked more like a huge drone. It elevated into the sky and transformed into a longer, more aerodynamic, dart shape. The alien ship soared low across the sea, as it quickly picked up speed. I heard Franc yell, "Whee", from the ship via the Carocle. It moved at one hell of a pace, leaving ripples in the water beneath it. "Fare well brother", I transmitted into the Carocle. "See you soon Amigo!" responded Franc eagerly.

Across the waterside, I spotted a large pagoda style building, a Chinese restaurant. We hadn't seen it whilst we were exploring. The last Chinese zodiac sign was the year of the Tiger. It was certainly appropriate, given the adventures of my brother, El Tigre. The AI couldn't understand my thoughts and logically insisted it was the year of the 'water rabbit', whatever one of those was. In my mind the Carocle showed an image of a water rabbit fully submerged in a river, with just its nose breaking the surface.

James and I returned home to Bridget and Enzo, thankfully the crossing was much easier than the choppy trip out to Israel. The four of us sat on the front steps of the sanctuary with our tails between our legs, drinking coffee. We planned a hero's funeral for Jane on the following day, we were choked. I was just grateful to have had her in our lives.

9. The Year of the Water Rabbit (Paul)

From the journal of Paul Collin

Kate and I sat on the newly bolstered quay wall, watching the world go by. I had worked on its repairs with Phil, as Drake and his son Jake had travelled to Vulcano to excavate Melak's spaceship. It wasn't a professional job, but it would do until Drake returned. The physical work helped me to think; to come to terms with recent events and those yet to come.

I worried if we had sufficient time to blow the mother ship before it separated into landing craft. I still hadn't worked out how to gain sufficient proximity to destroy the target. Obviously, they would recognise Barak's vessel as their own, but the AI would identify as unmanned, and the radioactive uranium would register on their scanners. Their suspicions could lead them to take the ship out before it was close enough to be effective.

Kate struggled to engage me in conversation anymore, whenever I spoke, I dug myself a deeper hole. I really didn't know what to say any more, it was becoming complicated. We were broken by the death of Matt, both individually but also our relationship seemed terminally damaged. She regarded me as a compulsive liar who used incredulous stories to justify extended absences. Kate felt the community humoured me because I was their leader and had saved their lives. Phil and Robyn supported her, whilst gently explaining that dark times meant Franc and I must prioritise our community's survival over personal relationships.

Wrench sounded the intermittent alert, signifying an impending threat. The team quickly emerged, gathering weapons, and moving to their posts. I could see nothing threatening from my vantage point. Spall waved from the crow's nest to attract my attention, he anticipated my confusion and pointed up to the sky. My eyes followed a silver ellipse with two huge drone fans floating through the white clouds in our direction. Spall advised Wrench to stand down the alert, the vessel was piloted by Melak and Franc. The kids became excited, 'look a flying saucer' they shouted. Their use of the old-fashioned term for a UFO was probably a playful dig at me, it was the term I often used.

Kate's reaction to the spectacle was nothing short of remarkable, she stared at the silver ellipse fiercely in utter disbelief. An image a child could accept easily, an adult struggled to assimilate. "What the hell is it?" she asked frantically. "It's Melak and Franc in Barak's spaceship. They recovered it in Israel; don't you remember we talked about it?" She repeated as if I hadn't answered, "Don't be stupid. What the hell is it?" and she started to weep gently as she repeated the phrase over and over. I wrapped her in my arms and told her everything was going to be ok. "You always say that, but things invariably get worse", she replied. However, the spaceship was enough of a disruptor to make her rethink. She looked into my eyes for the first time in an exceptionally long time. "Is all this shit you've been talking actually true?" she questioned sincerely. Kate continued hesitantly, "You are a clone of an alien, and more aliens are coming across space to destroy us?" I responded with empathy, "Yes, it is, sadly. I dearly wish it weren't true. But I am me, I am not some alien from outer space. Mum was human, she was implanted with my embryo in a fertility clinic. It doesn't make me a different person. The Dark Ones have done a rather good job of destroying us already, there are so few of us left. I hope we can send this ship to destroy their landing craft before they arrive". Kate pressed further, "So meteoroids didn't really bring the infection, it was these aliens? The Dark Ones killed everybody. Was the man who held the knife to my throat one of the Dark Ones? Was it a Dark One who killed Matt?" "Yes, they were, and it was", I'd explained this a hundred times, but she hadn't heard me until now. Her face changed to anger. I hadn't seen her quite so strong and determined before. "Then I'm glad Franc skewered those evil bastards", she spat vehemently.

The ship landed on the training field, as Spall announced its arrival and gave assurances over the tannoy. It hovered as silver legs and a door flowed out from the hull. The adults coerced the children back to safety. When Franc emerged from the egg shape, relief filled the adults' faces and the kids were allowed to indulge their curiosity, they jostled to get a glimpse inside.

I walked down the quay with Kate and paced over to the landing site. "Nice one!" I shouted over. Franc ran over and hugged me, then glanced at Kate uncomfortably. Kate stared at Franc with a measure of aggression, making us both uneasy, then she relented and grabbed him in a strong embrace.

Kate spoke to Franc, her voice faltered with emotion. "I'm sorry Franc. I've not thanked you for saving my life or for trying to save Matt's. I didn't understand the situation you were handling. I didn't believe the stories; they were too tall to be true, especially anything involving those evil creatures. I just wouldn't listen; I was so broken up. I'm so sorry". "I'm sorry too, if only I had been a little faster", replied Franc. "Let me stop you right there", Kate stated firmly. "It was an impossible situation; you could only save one of us. I personally wish you'd saved Matt rather than me, but you didn't have time to reason. It was all down to which of the Dark Ones moved first, I can see it now. It wasn't a choice of who should live and who should die, it was merely unfortunate timing. A millisecond later and we'd both be dead. It wasn't your fault; it was those evil monsters who hunger to kill everyone". She then hugged me and whispered, "I'm sorry Paul". "There is nothing to be sorry about, we've lost our son. You should be angry, I am too. But let's be angry at those who caused all this", I replied with more than a measure of relief.

Barak's ship was identical to Melak's in every way, the AI even sounded the same in my head. Franc had instructed the AI to answer to 'Beryl', which was amusing at first, before it started to grate on my nerves. We decided to fly the ship to Russia with Bart the following day, in order to weaponize the spacecraft. We needed to plan our attack with Melak, I was unsure he was up to solutioning anything, but he always showed great resilience when needs must. Bart and a handful of his crew members were keen to look over the ship as well. It was perfectly natural, everyone wanted to see the alien vessel.

The ship provided four comfortable captain style chairs, plus a pod for Melak. The crew consisted of myself, Franc and Bart plus Spall, he simply came along without a discussion. I was glad he was with me; we needed both his tactical analysis and practical expertise. Franc spoke quietly to the AI using the Carocle and his voice simultaneously, "Beryl, take us to

Novgorod, Russia, Rápida!" He smirked to himself as the ship gently hummed, floating into the air. It then headed northeast and accelerated smoothly to high velocity. It was like riding a roller coaster but without the bumps. Within twenty minutes we were hovering over the city of Novgorod. "Where would you like to land?" asked Beryl. "Next to the Kremlin building please, in the great square", Bart replied. The ship gently hummed and dropped down into the plaza in front of a rather impressive looking county hall. The square suddenly filled with soldiers; rifles pointed in our direction. The troops looked frightened, as you would expect when seeing a spacecraft for the first time. Clearly Commander Smitsky, hadn't shared our plans with the guards. "Haven't they ever seen a bloody UFO before, what's up with them?" mocked Spall, "how do we handle this, gentlemen?" Bart said he was on it.

The entry ramp lowered slowly, Bart made a point of going first, unarmed with his empty hands out in the open. When the soldiers recognised his face they smiled, lowered their weapons, and ran over to shake hands and hug him. Since Bart had saved the soldiers from the bunker, they treated him like their best friend. When Franc and I finally exited the ship, we caused a stir. They weren't expecting to see replicas of Bart. They noted Franc's scars, they recognised him from the news, the reports really must have gone viral. Franc was suddenly their new best friend too. Spall and I felt like we were the tag alongs, but at least everyone was friendly.

The main man, Colonel General Smitsky, ushered us into a meeting room in the Kremlin building. I was grateful to be inside, it was so cold in this country, it felt like my bones were already frozen. Smitsky was keen to learn more about our spaceship. We spent a little time bringing him up to speed with our plans. Bart had explained our ideas over the radio, but it was still a surprise when the craft landed. The spaceship brought sudden focus and importance to our mission; it became more tangible.

Smitsky provided an itemised list of the warheads collected from numerous sources, many of them sourced from the gargantuan submarine they had located. The devices had been checked by his experts and were fully operational. We simply needed to trigger a small explosion in each warhead to begin the nuclear chain reaction. Each trigger could be easily wired to a single dead man's switch. Beryl assured me she could mould the ordnance into the hull itself to secure them during flight. No racks or strappings were required, we could simply lift and shift the devices into the walls of the vessel from the outside.

After a couple of glasses of vodka with Smitsky and his First Officer, Starshy Leytenant (Senior Lieutenant) Gravdov, six camouflaged lorries arrived with the warheads. They moved very slowly avoiding bumps in the road, for obvious reasons. Beryl automatically scanned the payload and flexed the size of the hull to accommodate the cargo. The onlookers were amazed when the ship metamorphosised. It became more like a long rounded submarine shape, rather than a winged egg shape.

From the yard, we helped however we could. Beryl instructed the men to simply touch the ship's hull with each device in turn, she softened the hull membrane to allow its insertion. The men wore radioactivity shielded suits and carefully moved the devices. We stood with main group of spectators at a safe distance. Beryl affirmed we would be protected from the radiation, once they were in the vessel. After an excruciating couple of hours, the payload was secured in the ship and the detonators were passed over for connection. I continually hunched my shoulders and ground my teeth, terrified of a single bump or slip. Beryl took care of connecting the triggers. We were captivated by such advanced technology.

Gravdov didn't speak much English, but the Carocle translated and guided me to physically form the phonemes in the Russian language. It was like the signals from my brain were intercepted, they were translated by the Carocle into Russian before I spoke. Spall was bewildered, "I don't have a clue what you are saying". We translated a summary for him from time to time to keep him up to date.

Gravdov articulated a concern about the AI on the ship transferring loyalty to its alien makers, "Could it simply refuse to detonate the warheads?" It was a good question, we consulted Melak. He confirmed the AI was an extension of his mind, and he had delegated authority to his sons. The mother ship could communicate with its crew but could not interrogate the AI itself. Historically, Pareth-ng families had pilfered ships from each other, so the additional security had been installed. It was a relief. Smitsky then asked a killer question, "but do you trust Melak? He's from the race we seek to destroy. Why would he want to help us eliminate them?" I explained Melak had helped us so much already, we trusted him; we had no other choice. We had come so far; we had to finish it.

The ship was fully loaded with warheads and ready to depart. We agreed to prepare for the worst and deploy forces to meet invading ships in the pre-agreed four defensive quadrants, in case our plan failed. Spall had raided military bases in the south of England and gathered rockets, missiles, and other large impact weaponry. Three of the larger weapons were positioned in France and three in Spain. They surrounded the valleys where the landing ships planned to arrive, according to Melak's data.

Formentera had managed to secure a pair of Italian mobile ballistic missiles and were moving them into position in Italy and Spain. It was risky because we weren't able to test the missiles before the event. The teams continued their ongoing search for additional weaponry. Formentera encountered a number of Shroom during the scavenging in Italy, but their losses were minimal. Our Russian friends had a whole arsenal ready to greet spaceships in their quadrant. Bart dispatched HMS Astute to Washington, where it could engage the two landing craft targeting the USA. We were as ready as we could be, but the plan was fraught with risk

As we were about to depart, one of the Russian engineers hurried across the square. He hobbled, dragging his left leg slightly, he was clearly in a rush to catch us. We signalled to show him we would wait. Bart and I agreed if he was causing himself so much discomfort to talk to us before we left, we should give him the time to explain himself. As he approached, he babbled in Russian. Smitsky gave him a stern look, the man immediately fell silent. Smitsky introduced him, "This is our chief nuclear scientist Comrade Bustok, I think he has a small concern".

Bustok began to articulate slowly and systematically, so we could understand, essentially the warheads wouldn't trigger in space. Nuclear fission was the source of energy for the main explosion, the chain reaction started using a small, controlled detonation of conventional explosives. In space, the lack of oxygen would stop the initial detonation. The bomb would therefore fail when we needed it the most. He explained it was critical the ship's hull had a rich supply of oxygen permeating the devices to enable the explosion. I instructed Beryl to make this part of the detonation procedure. Smitsky realised the importance of Bustok's input, he arranged for someone to drive him back to his lab in comfort.

Our extensive goodbyes took quite some time, eventually we climbed the ramp and entered the long, thin vessel. The ship deployed four propeller fans for propulsion. "Will someone explain to me what just happened with the lame guy?" requested Spall tactlessly. Beryl displayed a holo-transcript allowing him to catch up. We arrived back at Summer Haven very quickly, Beryl carefully landed the ship close to the mainland facility, rather than on the island. It felt more sensible; but in reality, we were carrying enough explosives to take out most of the Highlands. I guess my main worry was radiation, regardless of Beryl's assurances. After a quick call to the haven, Rusty collected us in the RIB.

It had now become a waiting game; we needed to address how we would pilot the ship. I had reconsidered, in order to convince the mothership we were genuine, one of the brothers needed to be on board, as we were clones and could legitimately claim to be a member of their race.

Beryl tracked the mother ship as it entered our solar system; Franc, Paul, and I constantly monitored the invading ship, with trepidation building. We connected with Melak and Joe using our Carocles to decide who would pilot the ship. Bart joined the meeting from the USA, he and the crew of HMS Astute had recently arrived and were ready for action. "It's time", announced Melak solemnly, "I will pilot the ship on its last mission". "No, you can't", responded Bart, "you will be destroyed along with everything else". "It's the only way, I will not rouse their suspicions. I know them, and you do not. I am dying, I only have a few weeks remaining. I will perform this one last service. I caused this mess, I will finish it, once and for all", Melak replied calmly. He was clearly at peace with himself and his decision.

Joe joined Spall, Franc, and I for a final meeting in the Phoenix in port at Salina, a mobile meeting room was another useful feature of the vessel's emporium of technology. It was a sombre farewell, Melak assured us he would live on through us, in his race's time-honoured fashion. When Joe assured Melak we would all meet again in the next life, he strangely accepted it as fact. We helped Melak into his life support pod where he planned to complete his mission and shook his hand. We'd only met Melak recently, but we felt we'd known him all our lives. It was a sad parting, but we were grateful for Melak's sacrifice. We disembarked Barak's vessel, Kate and Bridget joined us. It was wonderful Kate came to support us; she had started to engage again.

"We love you Melak", Joe spoke for us all. The ship gently rose and accelerated into the clouds. Melak's AI gave us a continuous view of the state of play via our Carocles. We watched nervously as the mother ship slowly crept towards Earth, and Melak's ship gradually closed on them. Our six defence forces were ready for action, as a contingency.

A Doctrine of Fear - Paul JC Edge

As a result of Drake's excavations, Melak's ship eventually became operational. Over time, we established quicker links and trade picked up between the havens. The spaceship became a useful transport vessel, it was able to expand its hull to carry a wide range of cargo. The communities exchanged vegetables, meats and grain, there was also the whisky, vodka, and wines too! This provided the benefits of greater access to fresh food all year round. We even managed to travel to China and India for spices and rice, although we did locate paddy fields in Spain (who would have thought). Our rice stocks in Salina were perishing, so the additional supplies were most welcome. I can't imagine an Italian island without rice for risotto. Many children were born in the following year, life was becoming relatively normal again.

10. A New Sun

Comms transcript as provided by Melak's Discovery Ship AI
(Earth UK English)

Status: Distance to target – 0.021 parsecs

Melak – Communication to Earth:

I'm closing on the mother ship. My ship is roughly 0.07 light years from target. It will take 2.5 weeks to arrive, assuming similar velocities. I will retire to my pod for another week. I feel extremely tired.

Franc – Take care Melak, we all send our love my friend.

Status: Distance to target – 0.012 parsecs

Melak – Communication to Earth:

I am roughly 0.04 light years from the mother ship, ETA 9 days. Everything looks ok. We will come into comms range at 0.002 parsecs with a considerable delay between transmissions until we close further. Transmissions will take several days to arrive. I will try to stay awake from now on. The AI is programmed to take over if I fail to wake. I hope all is ok on Earth, and your contingency plans are going well.

Bart – Hi Melak. We wish you well. Our preparations are in place, we just hope they will suffice. Please advise us re the actual landing times of the fleet, we need to coordinate our attacks. (DELAYED RECEIPT – 3.0 HOURS)

A Doctrine of Fear - Paul JC Edge

Melak – Communication to Earth:

The ships will land precisely 16.25 days from the outbound timestamp of this message. My AI will use this to create a countdown clock for you. My initial communications with the mother ship will have a large time lag which will play to my advantage, this will reduce when the ships move closer to each other. The comms can only travel at the speed of light unfortunately. Thank you for your well wishes, I love you all my sons. Look after yourselves, and good luck!

Status: Distance to target – 0.002 parsecs

Melak – Communication to Earth:

I am roughly 0.007 light years from the mother ship, ETA 1.5 days. I am initiating communication with the mother ship now.

Franc – Good luck (DELAYED RECEIPT – 7.0 HOURS)

Melak – I will do my absolute best, thank you. I have rehearsed my script, but not too much as I don't want it to seem canned. The mother ship will detect nervousness or awkwardness. They will be paranoid after such a long journey through space.

Melak – Communication to Mother Ship 4 from Discovery Ship 4/4/1.

Message from Melak-eq 3-15-22. Message target: Sjilak-en-1-124 or successor. I am seeking to postpone your landing mission on planet Earth due to significant issues. There is proving to be long term viral activity. I am weak, I have an aggressive fast evolving virus known ironically on Earth as the 'common cold'. The planet itself is clear of intelligent life and primed for your occupation as per my protocol. I request a full debrief with your governance council prior to your initiation of the landing sequence. You need to fully understand the risks to our people before landing. I will prepare a full report and deliver it when I join your ship in 36 hours (approximate) for quarantine. For your information, your sensors will identify movement of another vessel on the planet surface, designation 3/4/2, Barak is finalising the checks and preparations for your arrival. It has been too long, my uncle. I look forward to our meeting, please give my kind regards to the council of elders.

Status: Distance to target – 0.001 parsecs

Melak – Communication to Earth:

I am roughly 0.003 light years from the Mother Ship, ETA 0.7 days. Receiving communications now.

Sjilak – Message from Mother Ship 4 to Discovery Ship 4/4/1: Sjilak-en-1-129.

Message received. Note - your suggested delay departs from your protocol, please desist and return to the planet surface. We do not have sufficient fuel to amend heading or velocity at such a late stage in our journey. Send a detailed report for analysis. We have no option but to land on Earth, we are fully committed, it is too late to change course. It's good to hear from you my nephew, I understand you are unwell, I hope our medical capability will facilitate a swift recovery.

A Doctrine of Fear - Paul JC Edge

Melak – Understand your message but I am unable to transmit the data as you have requested. I will need to bring it in person when I dock with you. My ship is damaged, it's unable to perform re-entry into Earth's atmosphere. I am requesting to join a landing ship, to return to the planet's surface. I await further instructions. I look forward to meeting you again very soon. I hope you have some Parenthian <Ethyl alcohol form> in your reserves so we can drink to your health once again.

Status: Distance to target – 0.0007 parsecs

Melak – Communication to Earth:

I am roughly 0.002 light years from the mother ship, ETA 12 hours. Receiving communication from the Mother Ship; moving to real time duplex.

Sjilak – Message from Mother Ship 4 to Discovery Ship 4/4/1: Barak-en-1-129.

Message received, joining a landing craft is forbidden until we understand your condition and the issue with Earth. Present yourself for quarantine and debrief in docking bay 3/6. Our supplies of the Parenthian <Ethyl alcohol form> is low, but I'm sure we can find a little so we can <SLANG: wet the beak?> on our reunion.

Melak – Understood, your approach is incredibly wise, I would not want to risk contaminating the family. The full biological data package is ready for your analysis. I am really looking forward to meeting you once again, it has been lonely out here.

Sjilak – Understood, we are suffering the effects of isolation too. The journey has been too long my nephew. I dearly hope it has been worth it.

Melak – Yes, but your journey is nearly over. It has been worth it; Earth is a wondrous planet. I will tell you all about it when I arrive. We need to get over a few initial <SLANG: tooth/teething?> issues, that is all my friend.

Status: Distance to target – 0.001 parsecs

Melak – Communication to Earth:

We are roughly 0.003 light years from the mother ship, ETA 2 hours.

Borkn – To Discovery vessel 4/4/1:

Prepare for docking procedure. Slow to 0.05 light speed.

Melak – Confirmed. Decelerating.

Status: Distance to target – 0.0002 parsecs (transcript)

Melak – Communication to Earth:

I am roughly 0.0006 light years from the mother ship, ETA 30 minutes.

A Doctrine of Fear - Paul JC Edge

Borkn – To Discovery vessel 4/4/1:

Prepare for docking procedure stage 2. Slow to docking speed as requested in previous message, your ship is coming in too hot.

Melak – Confirmed. Decelerating now.

Sjilak – We are receiving unusual radiation readings from your craft. What is the status of your main fusion drive? We need to assess the risk to our craft. It looks like the nuclear shielding is defective.

Melak – All readings are normal.

Sjilak – They are not normal. Run a diagnostic array immediately.

Melak – Confirmed, running diagnostic now.

Melak (closed channel) – Communication to Earth:

I plan to detonate on the mother ship's side pointing away from your sun, Sol. My aim is to blow what is left of the Mother Ship towards the sun, then the suns gravity will pull in any fragments. I don't want to leave evidence up here, just in case.

I have a small gift for you. I have lived your life alongside you in so many ways. I have felt the intensity of your pain, it was beautiful because it was born out of love. Love is something my species do not understand, and it's their weakness, I know this now. Joe, please take your brothers to Vulcano, I will send you the location and more details. Goodbye my sons, I love you all. The World is yours, if our plan works as we intend. Live long lives and be at peace.

A Doctrine of Fear - Paul JC Edge

My long-range sensors are picking up something odd in the wider star fields of the milky way, please keep an eye on it, your AI has the details. Melak out. (DELAYED RECEIPT OF REPLY – 17.7 HOURS)

Sjilak – – To Discovery vessel 4/4/1: Do you have a diagnostic Melak?

Melak – Yes, my engine is running fusion heavy, I was damaged by a micro-asteroid. The heat should reduce as I decelerate. The levels of radiation are manageable, but do not enter the ship without protection.

Sjilak – We will continue to monitor. Send through the data <packet> urgently.

Status: Distance to target – 0.0000 parsecs (transcript)

Melak – communication to Earth:

I am roughly 0.0001 light years from the mother ship, ETA 5 minutes.

Borkn – Discovery vessel 4/4/1: Postponing docking. Please hold your position. We need your full diagnostic analysis before you can connect, Melak.

Melak – Understood. Transmitting now.

Borkn – I have not received it Melak.

A Doctrine of Fear - Paul JC Edge

Sjilak – Send us the data immediately, or we will be forced to leave you behind. We are not happy with your status. It sounds like you are being evasive, why would you do this? We cannot halt our vessel. Get us the data and stop <messing> around!

Melak – Understood. Transmitting now. I'm having a few issues, bear with me.

Borkn – You are closing too quickly. Hold your position or we will be forced to destroy your vessel.

Sjilak – Melak, what are you doing? Halt the vessel immediately!

Melak – I'm having issues with my guidance systems.

Sjilak – We are running out of options nephew. You need to resolve your issues immediately.

Melak – I have spent a lifetime on this beautiful planet. I have come to know its seasons, its wildlife, its foods, and its oceans and so much more. It's a uniquely beautiful place you are approaching. The pollution is so much less now, and nature is flourishing once again.

Sjilak – Melak? What are you doing? You are accelerating, are you insane? Preparing protocols for disintegration!

Melak – Most of all I have come to love the people here. Yes, they have petty squabbles, but the wars have stopped recently. The ability that selected me for my mission was to influence humans, so I could continue my work without interference. It was a two-way street, my skill allowed me to see their true nature. By intermingling with good people, I learned to love their culture. Barak surrounded himself with evil people,

A Doctrine of Fear - Paul JC Edge

they influenced him in terrible ways. Barak killed many survivors of the infection, but a few remain; enough to start again.

I am part of a rebellion, a mutiny of one. I can't see you destroy the human species. They have so much, and we are so alike. We have ruined our race through endless cloning. We have lost our souls, Sjilak. We have forgotten the pleasure of love and mating and rearing children. We don't know how to live any more. I am afraid I will have to destroy you, in order to protect these wonderful people. It's justice and reciprocity for the ruin we have inflicted upon them. We have no right to march across the universe and wipe out a sentient lifeform, it is an act of evil. I will see you in the next life when I will stand before you and accept penance. Goodbye Sjilak. As my friend Spall would say, 'We are going to rip you a new asshole!'

Sjilak – Melak? What are you talking about? It makes no sense, have you lost your mind? {BACKGROUND CHATTER} Destroy the ship now!

<Transmission from mother ship 4 corrupted>

Melak – Beryl, flood the cabin with oxygen and expose the devices.

AI – Complete Melak.

Melak -- Ok Beryl, detonate the devices. Let's see what these dirty bombs can do. We'll give the Milky Way a new sun, it will briefly illuminate the planets to celebrate the survival of the human race.

AI – Trigger complete – transcript transmitted.

V. Afterimage – Epilogue

Battle ready, Paul, Franc and Bart watched the AI's tactical display via their Carocles, the two ships juxtaposed and vanished in a blaze of fission. Bridget, Enzo, Gio, James and I sat close to Melak's spacecraft on Vulcano. Drake had worked around the clock to excavate and expose Melak's ship to the regenerative power of the sun. We watched a holo-projection the AI had set up for us.

Had Melak's attack worked, or did we face an invasion? Our soldiers were on standby all over Europe and the USA. We looked to the sky hoping, it would take roughly eight or nine minutes before there was visible evidence of the explosion, due to the significant distance the light had to travel. The detonation was confirmed by a bright light close to the horizon, like a smaller second sun in the sky for three or four minutes. Despite the group cheering, I needed confirmation the mother ship had been destroyed. We had seen evidence of an explosion, but I wasn't certain the landing craft were destroyed. Melak's ship's scanners indicated that both ships were annihilated. The debris from the explosion was being pulled towards the gravitational mass of the sun. We would experience a number of small solar flares when the spaceship burned up.

I updated our anxious team and instructed them to stand down. Phil transmitted the good news to Salina and Formentera; Bart informed the Russian team. That night we celebrated with gusto; I have never drank so much.

We didn't notice the transcript of Melak's last words had been received by the AI. I retired to the hotel on the island as the sun rose. Apparently, the guys went completely bananas in Novgorod, I'm not sure there was enough Russian vodka left to fuel that party, they probably progressed to methylated spirits.

A few days later, in a spell of boredom, Franc reconfigured the AI of Melak's vessel to respond to the name 'Cindy'. Cindy's transcript of Melak's parting soliloquy was particularly touching, but also hard to bear. Melak enjoyed an exceedingly long and rewarding life on our planet. I cannot condone the killing of so many, but I celebrate we are alive.

Cindy detected a disturbing detail, another presence several light years away. Could it be another Pareth-ng mother ship on a voyage to a different planet in the Milky Way? We'd promised Melak we would monitor the potential contact on our sensors. The vessel was far from Sol and would be unlikely to detect the disappearance of its sister ship, reducing the chances of it becoming hostile. At the time, we didn't notice the ship numbering discrepancies in Melak's communications with the mother ship.

Melak's 'gift' to Franc and Paul brought a tear to my eye when I became aware of the details. Although, the more I thought about it, the more I started to worry. It took a few days for me to broach the subject with them, we mutually agreed a day to meet and honour Melak's last request. As the time approached, my concerns intensified.

Bridget and I had discussed my reservations concerning Melak's gift, we travelled to Vulcano to assess the situation and reconcile my trepidation, but it did nothing to help me. She thought it was not my place to withhold the 'gift'. Bridget agreed to proactively work with Kate to anticipate the dilemma she would face, so I could focus on helping my brothers. We returned to Salina to prepare for their visit and all it may bring.

Franc, Paul, Kate, Ciara, and me met on the Melak's spaceship, they had flown into Salina from Summer Haven. Bridget took the girls for a tour of Salina, whilst my brothers and I flew to Vulcano. We touched down in the tiny community of Lentia on the northwest of the island, after flying low over the large caldera. Cindy kept the ship's doors closed on my request, Paul and Franc peered at me strangely. A handful of small, whitewashed houses were visible through the large viewing port at the front of the ship. Before us was 'Case Vacanza a Lentia', formerly a holiday guest house.

I attempted to explain my mixed feelings about Melak's gift and the dilemma it had created for me. "I have to warn you both, what you are about to see may be deeply upsetting. Melak left you a gift, but from a theological point of view, I cannot work out if it's a blessing or a curse. We must discuss this before I let you go any further, it's an emotionally complex situation. No words can explain the wonderful abomination you are about to witness. Cindy, show the other side of the house please".

Cindy's display panned around, my brothers were aghast, tears streamed down their faces. Their next sentiment on their emotional rollercoaster was anger. "What the fuck is this? What has he done? Is this some kind of sick fucking joke?"

The holo-display showed Franc's late wife, Lucy playing catch in the swimming pool with their deceased child, Colletta. They were smiling broadly and chattering excitedly. Paul gasped as

Matthew came out of the house and dived in and swam to meet them to join in the game. "What the fuck?" reiterated Franc angrily. I asked Cindy to play the recording Melak had left, he appeared on the screen.

"Hello, my dear sons. If you are watching this recording then...", he paused and started again. "You understand I have learned to be human by living and interacting with Earth's amazing people. I have felt your pain, my sons, but also your overwhelming love. I couldn't leave this world without trying to resolve something I feel I was a part of. Joe will have shown you my gift, but I would like the chance to explain it properly. The figures you see are not your loved ones, but they are their clones. They are identical in many ways.

You were created from my DNA but were left to live a normal life without the memory of how you were brought into being. The four of you remain as the last of my sons. You were grown in my ship and implanted into your mothers as fertilised eggs. The clones you see before you are quite different. As our challenge to save the human race was great, I anticipated casualties. I took DNA samples from my sons and their immediate families. I obtained the DNA of your loved ones in secret using a third party; someone whose wider role you will understand in time. It was easy enough to obtain the biological samples. To capture memories, I used the Carocle and the inherited augmentation by trickery. It was easy enough to slip a Carocle inside a hat. I grew the clones of Lucy, Colletta and Matthew in my ship and accelerated their growth, so they were 'born' close to the age you last saw them. Obviously, they have no memories of their own, other than those they've created here in their little home.

Lucy posed an interesting challenge. She has been given the basic knowledge of an adult female of her age, supplemented with the memories you have of her. The recollections have been inverted so they feel like they are hers. She will know who you are and feel an affinity for you, but do not mistake this for love, she hasn't actually met you so she will need to build feelings once again. Colletta, is the same but she's young and adaptable; she will accept you as her father very quickly I suspect.

As for you, Paul, the situation is not quite the same. I gained full access to Matthew's memories and have recreated them in the mind of his clone, he knows nothing of his life's ending. He currently, and quite correctly, accepts Lucy as his aunt and is waiting for you to collect him following his vacation. With care and gentle understanding, you should be able to build his life once again from where he left off.

I know it's a shock, but I hope you take it as a positive opportunity. Joe, you may think my medalling has created a monstrosity, but you must understand the healing it will bring to these fractured families. My only question is, can you accept my gift? If you choose not to accept it, Joe will ensure the clones live a full and happy life. Their memories of you can be wiped without causing them any harm. Live long happy lives my sons. I hope my gift will begin to repair the suffering you've endured. Goodbye, and thank you. It has been an honour to be a part of your special lives".

I looked at my brothers, I felt their deep wounds had been savagely ripped open. I tried to convey my thoughts, "You must understand the clones you see are not your loved ones. They have memories and look the same, but they do not have the same souls. Please be careful, perhaps you need time to think this through before you act? The gift is quite unnatural, we are not meant to play God in this way". Part of me hoped Melak's gift would help to heal their wounds. Paul and Franc opened the door, the exit ramp appeared, and they walked cautiously down it. They paused to look at each other and proceeded towards the rear of the house. I followed cautiously. Matt had gone back into the kitchen. I gently asked Paul to wait until he returned, rather than following him, to avoid giving him a sudden shock.

Franc expelled a shuddering breath before walking into the open. Colletta glanced at him with a troubled look, "Daddy?" Franc opened his arms, and she ran into them. Lucy was completely confused by the sight. She muttered, "I don't understand, why would Colletta call you Daddy? I remember your face, but my recollections are strange. It feels like I'm watching a movie".

I stepped forward; she instantly saw my resemblance. "I'm Joe, Francisco's brother. You suffered a terrible trauma which caused loss of your memory. You've been recuperating here with Colletta for some time. You may not remember, but this is Franc, your husband. He's missed you more than you could ever imagine". Franc's deep emotion was hard to read. Lucy cautiously walked over to him; she reached out to touch the scars on his cheek. "Oh my god, the tiger. The little children". She lifted his shirt to look at Franc's other scars, "The shark. Those horrible men in the hospital". She pondered for a second, looking deeply into Franc's eyes, wiping the tears from his cheek.

Lucy gently took Franc's hand. "Come on, we need a cup of tea. Let's sit down under the pergola and talk". Franc walked over to the small patio with Colletta in his arms. I don't think I ever saw him so happy. It didn't matter that Lucy and Colletta were copies of his loved ones, they were the same even if their souls were different, only their memories of events without Franc were missing. They had a lifetime to make new ones.

Matt emerged from the house. Paul was sat on a wall, but rose as he saw his son, but then froze. He had no idea how to behave. "Why are you crying Dad? Has someone stolen your wallet?" Matt laughed; Paul joined in through the tears. "It's been too long son", he replied in a choked voice. He walked over and embraced Matt. "Shall we return to Salina? your Mum has missed you terribly".

Paul, Matt, and I left Franc with his family, they played and laughed in the sunshine. He hardly noticed we'd gone. We lifted off gently. "Cindy, do you understand the concept of a promise?" I asked. "Yes Joe. If I promise something, then I must never break it". "That is quite right. Will you promise me something?" "Of course". "Promise me that no matter who asks, you will not create more clones". Cindy thought for a while and responded, "No problem, Joe".

We were soon back in Salina. Bridget and Kate sat with Ciara under a lemon tree sipping coffee. I asked Paul and Matt to wait until I had pre-warned Kate of Matt's arrival. I needn't have bothered; Bridget had fully explained the situation to Kate. I wasn't sure if Kate would be convinced, or ethically horrified by the cloning. Matt's re-appearance might deeply upset her.

Ciara spotted Matt first, she ran full tilt into his arms screaming his name and laughing. Kate stared in complete disbelief, as she watched her son with Ciara. Kate wailed as she ran across to embrace him, tears streaming from her eyes. Luckily, I'd warned Matt she might be a little emotional, he just shrugged, "What's new?" She reverted to type quickly, "Oh my goodness Matt, you look so well, so strong, so tall". "Leave it out Mum", he replied with a twinkle in his eye. Kate shuddered and spoke gently, "I'm so sorry. I thought you were dead". Paul caught up and embraced them both and whispered, "It was all a dream. A really, really bad dream".

I prayed for them all. Cloning a human being defied the laws of nature and was an affront to God himself. I struggled to come to terms with family members reappearing from the dead, it was a horrible, twisted version of reality. I felt a bad omen, no good would come of this. I suspected would pay for Melak's interference. I just hoped my brothers would be able to deal with the complexities of their newly created loved ones reappearing in their lives. How would their friends react to the re-emergence of the family units? Would the community demand that we resurrect those they had lost? Would they resent my brothers and their families? Would they treat them like monsters? Come what may, I would help them however I could. Whether it proved a blessing, or a curse, their future was yet to be played out in the great theatre of life.

This story continues in Summer Haven III: A Moonlit Armageddon

Printed in Dunstable, United Kingdom